T0193353

THE
QUESTOR'S ADVENTURES

THE ROUND HOUSE
and
THE MOANING WALLS

Louis Paul DeGrado

iUniverse, Inc.
Bloomington

THE QUESTOR'S ADVENTURES
The Round House and The Moaning Walls

iUniverse books may be ordered through booksellers or by contacting:

iUniverse
1663 Liberty Drive
Bloomington, IN 47403
www.iuniverse.com
1-800-Authors (1-800-288-4677)

ISBN: 978-1-4759-4470-9 (sc)
ISBN: 978-1-4759-4469-3 (hc)
ISBN: 978-1-4759-4471-6 (e)

Library of Congress Control Number: 2012916491

Printed in the United States of America

iUniverse rev. date: 8/28/2012

Also Available from Author
Louis Paul DeGrado

SAVIOR
Finalist: Foreword Magazine book of the year contest.

Glimpse the future in this exciting thriller about where cloning and stem cell research can lead us. How far will we go to save ourselves? Faced with our own demise, mankind turns to science for answers and governments approve drastic measures including the use of human test subjects.

Battle lines are drawn when a religious crusader and the medical director of the world's largest research firm clash over the fate of the Twenties; thousands of people frozen in cryogenic stasis. The question of mortality and morality lies in the balance when humans play creator. How far will we go to save ourselves?

THE PEOPLE ACROSS THE SEA

Within the towering walls of the city by the sea, a dark secret is kept. Its history was wiped out by foreign invasion and even now, the city stands poised to repel another attack from the dreaded people across the sea.

A culture based on fear, and the threat of invasion, has spawned a leader, a council, and the Law of Survivors. Aldran Alfer is now the Keeper of the law, and the council leader. He knows the hidden terror that threatens to rip the city apart.

Sons of Aldran, Brit and Caln, find themselves caught in a web of danger, and mystery. Brit finds himself on the run from the Black Guard, veiled men who prowl the streets and crush any who oppose the council's will.

While Caln remains in the city, struggling to hold his family's position on the council, Brit heads to the forbidden desert to seek out the Wizard; a man with strange powers who was banished from the city.

In the company of the Wizard, and a mythical desert wanderer, Brit will find his destiny. He must cross the land of the Sand Demons, fierce predators who stalk the desert, where he searches for a way to carry out his father's plan to lead their people to safety and end the threat from the *People Across the Sea*.

THE
ROUND HOUSE

This book is dedicated to the Questors:
Shane, Chad, my brother Mike, and to all youngsters
who dare to seek out the mysteries of the unknown

If you love adventure and are not faint of heart, read on.
If you are easily scared, go no further.

To the Quest!

Contents

Chapter One

How it all Started:
Doug's Dare

Doug had the flashlight. It was his turn to tell a story. I would be next. In our room of the double-wide trailer on Twenty-Fifth lane, lights off, were my two brothers, Mike, ten years old, Eric, sixteen, and our friends Doug, also sixteen, Chad, ten, and Shane, same age as me as I had just turned thirteen. We gathered for our Friday night ritual of story-telling.

"The story I'm going to tell you is true," Doug stated.

The air in the room thickened. True stories were always hard to top and drew more attention. I knew I would have to come up with something good if I went next. I started thinking about my opening line, it would have to be thrilling, and then Doug said, "It's about a haunted house by where I live."

"You only live two miles away," Chad blurted out. "That means we have a haunted house in our neighborhood." Chad's observation trumped my thoughts; Doug's story would be hard to top, if it were true.

"Quiet!" Doug scolded. "I have the flashlight. Only I can talk. Maybe this is too scary to tell."

"No, tell it," we pleaded.

"Quiet then," Doug said and looked at each of us before starting. "Louie," he spoke to me, "make sure the door is closed. I don't want to get in trouble for telling you this story."

I stood up and made sure the door was shut tight and returned to my position sitting with my legs crisscross by Shane.

"The shrill sound pierced my dream, rousing me from my sleep," Doug said. The light came up under his chin and lit a face framed with a brown crew-cut that held no trace of a smile. "Glancing at the clock I saw it was midnight, too late for my parents to be up watching television. The screams came again, moving past the cracks in the shutters and through the glass panes, laying an icicle on my spine. Goosebumps dancing on my arms and legs, I eased from by bed and snuck down the stairs to see what had caused such a horrible sound.

"I spotted my mom and dad peering through the living room window. My dad turned away from the window, his eyes revealing a concerned look like he got whenever he and my mother talked about the bills. He spotted me there on the stairs still fidgeting from the cold. I braced myself for a scolding for being up so late, but instead he said, 'Get your shoes on and grab your shotgun.'

"My mother, her face as pale as her white cotton nightgown, did not protest so I ran upstairs and did as I'd been told. I returned to find my father at the front door with his camouflage-hunting jacket pulled over his red flannel pajamas, his shotgun at his side. His large, black and green boots clashed with the red-checkered pattern of his pants."

"'Call the sheriff,' he instructed my mom as he looked at me and nodded. "Let's go." We headed out the door."

"'AHHHH!' A scream came from a house two blocks down and across the road. 'It looks like there's someone in every room turning the lights off and on,' my dad said, switching on his flashlight. "Those people moved out of that house a month ago. No word, just up and left. Something strange is going on here." We headed toward the house.

"'Power going out?' I asked.

"'No.' my dad said, 'Look, the rooms are all lighting up at different times. If the power was going out the lights would go on and off at the same time.' We stood there in the road watching the house. Shivers ran across my arms as the cold continued to sink its teeth into me. The only thing keeping my hair from standing on end was the old hunting cap I had pulled over my head.

"My dad stood stiller than I'd ever seen him stand when the scream came again. 'AHHHHHH!'"

"Dad turned to me and said, 'Maybe just some kids goofing around, but let's be careful. Whatever happens, stick close to me and make sure you don't let that thing go off in my direction.'"

"Wait?" Shane interrupted Doug's story. "Your dad really let you carry your shotgun?"

"Of course, moron," Doug said. "We live clear out here in the county, who knows what could be going on. Might have been a wild dog or animal. He lets me carry it all the time when we're hunting."

"It's bad enough mom won't let us use the car tonight and we got stuck with you guys," Eric said. "Now shut up and let him tell the story."

"Okay," Doug looked around the room. No one said a word. "My dad's the type of person that wants to know what's going on, and help out if he can. He led us down the driveway to the house. It was pitch black except for the flashlight he held and the lights in the house flickering on and off. I heard what sounded like furniture moving from within as we approached.

"Soon as my dad stepped onto the porch, the sounds stopped and the lights went out. He stood and listened. The silence was so loud I could hear my own breathing. My dad moved slowly, quietly, like he does when we go hunting and we're getting ready to make a kill. He loaded shells into his shotgun, passing two back to me. I wasn't scared anymore. I've seen what a shotgun could do. My dad reached forward and knocked on the door.

"'What's going on in there!' he called loudly. The door flew open, but there was nothing there. My dad jumped back, dropping the flashlight to the ground. We were standing side-by-side when a gust of wind blew past us. It was the coldest wind I've ever felt. Colder than any winter wind. I gripped my shotgun sure that something was coming at us. There was an odor, furniture polish and smoke. Not the smoke of a fireplace, but of something rotten burning. The beam of the flashlight rocked back and forth and then came to a rest. My hands were shaking.

"Suddenly, there were flashing lights behind us. I whirled around.

"'Put that gun down!' a loud, deep voice said. It was Sheriff Mike Johnson, with ten, maybe twenty deputies. 'What's going on?' He asked my dad.

Dad didn't say nothing but just stood there. Then he pointed to the house. "'You should've brought more men. Something strange is going on in there.'"

"'Bill,' Sheriff Johnson said removing his black, ten gallon hat with the star in the middle, 'you should know better than to be out here with your boy like this.'

"A stream of tobacco left his mouth in a clean, directed spit. 'Those people living here moved out under some strange circumstances. Right after someone tried to rob their house. Looked mighty scared if you asked me. I don't mind if you tag along, but send your boy home; we'll take care of this.' Two of the deputies went around to the back of the house as the sheriff spoke.

"Dad bent over and picked up the flashlight, looked down at me and back to the sheriff. 'You're on your own, boys.' He put his hand on my shoulder. 'Time to go home Doug. No guns are going to do you any good with what's going on in there, that place is haunted' he called back over his shoulder. Then we went home.

"My mom and I watched through the window until the sheriff left. My dad sat in the front room on the couch staring into space. His look, much worse than the one he has when he's worrying about money. Later he came to my room, I was still awake, and he told me that there was something bad in that house. He told me I was never to go near it again because it was too dangerous. We hadn't been to church for six months or longer, and only went on holidays. Now, we're regulars."

"You could've died?" Chad gasped. "Why did your dad say the guns were not good?"

"You can't shoot what you can't see," Doug replied. "That house has spirits living there."

The room remained quiet as the story sank in. Doug's tale was fine in form and had all the suspense needed to keep us interested. The fact that he stated it was true made it hard to follow. It was my turn next. I didn't worry about going next. I wanted to find out more from Doug.

"Wow, was your gun really loaded?" Chad asked. The runt of the group, he often got more than his fair share when it came time to pick on someone.

"Wouldn't do me no good if it wasn't," Doug crossed his arms and nodded.

"Did the sheriff find anything?" Eric asked.

"I can't believe that happened to you," Shane said.

"You bet it did. The sheriff didn't find nothing. That house is haunted! And anyone who goes inside…" Doug's eyes shifted around the room.

"What?"

"Well, I just dare anyone to go."

For a brief moment I looked at Shane and put my finger to my lips. I knew he was thinking the same thing: *finally, a real adventure!*

"If it's really haunted," Mike said, "how come we haven't heard about it. You know all about that stuff." He looked at me. I shrugged my shoulders. "Where is this house?"

"It's that house at the end of County High Road by the old Miller farm," Doug stated.

"The Roundhouse?" I said.

"What?"

"The kids at school nicknamed it 'The Roundhouse' because of the arched doorway and round windows. We pass by it when we go to church."

"I guess the name fits. I'm sure the sheriff don't want a bunch of kids going there so they keep it secret" Doug said. "Besides, I'm telling you now, so you did hear about it."

"I heard the owner died there," Eric said.

"I didn't know anything about that," Doug replied. "My dad told me the guy who built the house only lived there two years, and that he was strange. He never talked to anyone and was always in a hurry."

"Was he psycho?" Eric asked.

"My father didn't think so. Just weird. He was from California." We all nodded our heads wisely, as if that alone was sufficient to explain being weird. "No one lives there now."

"That's the same place where that old brick house used to be, the one that burned down," I offered, hoping to gain standing in the conversation.

Eric nodded. "Only a few walls and the fireplace were left standing. We used to ride by it on our bikes and dare each other to go there."

"We did go in," I stated.

"But only in broad daylight."

"Do you think someone died in the fire?" Shane asked.

"Maybe that's why the house is haunted now," Doug said. "Who knows?"

I caught Eric nodding at Doug and suspected a prank was in the works.

"Now the house is empty," Doug said, "but there's no For Sale sign on it." The room was silent.

"It's against the law to sell a haunted house, isn't it?" Eric asked.

"I don't know, but my mom and dad said we are probably going to move soon. Probably because of that house."

I looked at the faces around the room. Mike, closest to the door, had the wary look of someone who'd fallen victim one too many times. His eyes were fixed on Doug and he looked ready to run at a second's notice. Chad sat with his legs crossed and looked to be without a care. Shane's face had that surprised look that it did whenever he was called on during class and didn't know the answer.

Doug spoke up. "No one lives there now, but I stay up sometimes and look out my window. I can see the lights flashing on and off."

"Then the house is haunted," Eric stated. "And it's right down the street from us."

"Let's just say if I'm walking down the street, I'd walk on the opposite side of that house. I dare any of you to go there."

"No way."

"I'm too young to die."

"Can I borrow your shotgun?"

"I'll be right behind you, pushing you ahead, but behind you." Everyone joked except Mike.

"What if there is a ghost in that house and it follows you back to your house?" Mike asked wide-eyed.

"Louie's next," Shane said. "I bet he can top Doug's story."

"No way," Eric said tugging on Shane's blond hair. "You need a haircut boy. You're starting to look a little girlish."

"Stop it. That's what my dad's always saying."

"Okay, knock it off," I said. "I have the flashlight, no one else can talk."

With all eyes on me I took the flashlight from Doug as we changed places. His story would be hard to beat. As I started my story, I couldn't help but think about the possibility that a haunted house lie so close to us. One that we could actually visit!

"Remember at the end of the year when we went camping, and the campground was closed due to construction?" Several heads nodded. "The signs were fake. I know someone who told me the real truth about why the area was closed." I did my best to compete with Doug, all the while my mind raced with the possibilities ahead of me: to actually visit a real haunted house.

"Hey, you going to tell us the rest?" Eric asked shaking me out of my daze.

"You remember Kyle Halm?" Two heads nodded. "You didn't see him or his brother Andy return for school right?" More heads nodded. "Strange that no one knows anything about them. If they moved, you think they would have told someone. UNLESS," I raised my voice, "the police needed to keep the whole thing a secret.

"Talk to any forest ranger and they'll tell you something's going on in the mountains, the animals are changing. They are getting fed up with the people taking up all the land, and hunting them. The spirit of a deer, fast and evasive, a lion, predator and hunter, and a bear, strong and mighty, have all been unleashed and formed into a new beast. No one who has seen it has lived to tell about it. They only know from the evidence left behind."

"What evidence?" Eric asked.

"SHH! Footprints of all kinds of different animals' side-by-side. Animals that would normally be enemies were seen together," I said.

"Oh."

"Sure enough," I said. "Kyle and his family were at that campground along with a dozen other people. The rangers never found them.

"The signs, well, they were just put up to keep others out. They sent in a tracker, but he never came back. The creature is still loose and some believe it's only a matter of time before it comes out of the mountains looking for revenge. No one knows where it is, or when it will strike again. They called it, Preydator, because it's both prey and predator. OH NO! There it is!" I turned off the flashlight and panic and laughter ensued. Someone opened the door and left the room but I couldn't tell who.

"Good story," Doug said turning on the light. "Was it true? I mean, there were construction signs there just like you said."

"They were just repaving the road. And I think Kyle just goes to a new school. Your story was better, if it's true. Is it?"

Doug, pale as snow turned to me as the others walked out of the room. "My dad told me I was never to go back to that house. Now, we're moving and I don't know why, but I'm sure it's because of that house. I'm not even supposed to talk about it. Something's really wrong. I wouldn't go there. I'd stay far away."

I headed to the hall where Mike and Chad were standing, still not sure if Doug was acting or telling the truth.

"Do you think it's true?" Shane asked.

"Jury's still out," I said. "I'm still catching my breath from the story I told." I proceeded down the hall away from Doug and Eric's ears. "The house does look strange and the look on his face when he talked about it…we need to investigate."

My mom poked her head around the corner. "You boys keep it down," she muttered before disappearing back into the living room.

"Oh no," Shane said.

"What?"

"You've got that look."

"What look?"

"It's a warning sign. Your freckles get darker because your skin turns lighter. I think it's because all the blood is rushing to your brain. Next thing I know you're talking me into something that can get me into trouble. Don't smile, it's not funny."

I couldn't help myself. "We haven't been caught doing anything yet, my short friend."

"Hey, I'm taller than Chad."

"And two years older. Besides, one of these days, I'm going to write a story about our adventures and you'll be glad I was around to make your life interesting."

"Sure. But this is a lot different than sneaking out in the summer to light fireworks or walk around on top of the school building. What if this house is really haunted?"

"I can only hope. Look," I stated, "We live miles away from anything remotely exciting. What else do we have to do?"

"Right!" Shane's eyes lit up as the hamster spun faster. "The bragging rights alone would make it popular. Maybe no one else has heard about the house yet." Shane but his hands on my shoulders and looked me in the eyes, "We've got to get there first."

"That's not what I mean," I took a step back. "I just don't want to regret not doing something exciting with my life."

"I see," Shane said. "We've almost made it through the first year of this decade, why would we want to make it to 1981?"

"Oh, we'll make it. The Eighties are going to be the best times of our lives."

We knew we had to visit the Round House. The hammering calls of adventure and curiosity pounded out any semblance of reason.

"Someone's going to hear us," I said as my sister walked down the hallway to her room. "We need a safe place to talk."

"We'll talk about it tomorrow."

"I want to go," Chad said nudging his way into our conversation.

"You guys have to keep this a secret," Shane said. "If my mom find out she'll kill me."

Mike stood in the hallway listening but didn't look at me.

"First we need a plan," I said. "A secret plan and a safe place to meet. We don't want someone else to get there first, and if our parents find out they'll say we can't go."

Eric and Doug came out of my room laughing and went down the hall to the living room.

"Where can we meet?"

"The tree house?" Shane said. "Your house doesn't have an upstairs or downstairs."

"That's because it's a trailer," Mike said.

"It's pretty big inside though," Shane said. "But sound does carry."

"Then it's the tree house," I confirmed. "Now let's go see what's on Shock Theatre tonight. And Chad, we're going to need a can of paint first thing in the morning."

Innocently enough, that's how it started. With Doug's story and a dare. It was a chance we couldn't refuse.

🦅　🦅

I woke the next morning to find myself alone. The light filtering in between the rose-colored curtains reflected off the television screen into my eyes. I blinked twice to clear my vision and looked around the front room. The others were gone. Of the sleeping bags, blankets, and other toys we'd left scattered about, a single pillow and some empty candy wrappers were all that remained to show that my brother and our friends had been there during the night. I unzipped my sleeping bag rolled out of it and stood keeping my guard.

"Where is everybody?" I asked.

More than once my active imagination and vivid dreams had fooled me; a quick pinch to my arm I assured me I was awake.

Silently, I made my way down the hall. No one else stirred at this early hour and the house remained silent. All the bedroom doors were closed including the door to my room.

"Hmm," I said turning the handle. It didn't budge. I leaned into the door and slowly shoved until I could see what blocked the path. "Why is the bed pushed against the door?" I stepped into the room.

Six sleepy eyes looked up at me.

"You guys are who I'm taking to the haunted house with me? I said shaking my head. We didn't even watch a scary movie last night."

"I know," Shane replied clearing the long bangs of hair from his eyes so he could see. "But that story you told, and Doug told, and then I heard steps in the kitchen."

"Probably just my dad. He always gets up for a late night snack."

Mike looked up, "What, it can't be morning already." He rolled over and buried his head back in his pillow pulling a blanket over it. "Go away, and turn off that flashlight."

"It's called the SUN, and it is morning." I looked at Shane. "You guys left me out there by myself?"

"We thought you'd get mad," Chad said.

"You were supposed to have an alarm so we could wake up before him," Shane shook his head and glared at Chad.

"I guess I don't know how to work it right." Chad shook a huge, black watch that sat on his arm. "It has a compass in case we get lost we can find our way."

"Too bad it can't help you find courage," I chuckled. "Come on; let's eat so we can get out to the tree house. You too Michelle."

"Don't call me that," Mike said and with a growl rolled out of bed.

We chewed with purpose that morning and headed outside into the cool, crisp, October air.

Shane shivered and pulled his jacket tighter. "When my parents said we were moving to Colorado for the clean air, I didn't know it'd be so cold."

"Hey, with the clean air, you'll live longer," I said.

"If I don't freeze to death. I can't believe it's so cold in the mornings and it's now even snowing yet."

"Won't snow till all the leaves have fallen," Mike said. "They don't have snow in South Carolina?"

"Not like here. It sure is brown everywhere. And cold."

"The tree house will be warmer," I said.

Towering over our world in all its' majesty, the oak tree stood at the head of the driveway leading to the green doublewide trailer where we lived. It had always been there, strong, silent and enduring over the years. The old man spread out his branches making a perfect space for us to build our fortress. The nails we placed upon his skin were a small price to pay to be young again living through our adventures.

With four sturdy walls, a patio roof, and a floor with an entrance hatch the tree house was a place to think, to plan, to get away from reality. Here we discussed the important things that happened in our lives without having to worry about being embarrassed by peer or parental pressures.

In order to get into the tree house, one needed special climbing skills. We went as far as putting a roof on it and installing a sturdy floor, but we never did put a good ladder in place to make it easy to get up. The formidable entrance kept out the smaller kids, and the ants, spiders, and other bugs kept out the faint-hearted as well as the enemies of any boys on important missions: girls.

Shane, Chad, Mike, and I headed for the tree house. Chad, who lived in the house immediately behind ours, detoured to his house and came back with a can of red paint.

"Here you go. What's it for?"

"Our new sign," I said. "Mike, get the board."

Mike climbed up, reached his hand inside the entrance, and pulled out a board that was about two feet long and handed it to me. Then he handed me an old hammer and two rusty nails. Chad opened the paint can and we used, for lack of anything better, a stick to write out our message:

"KEEP OUT!"

"There," I said, nailing the sign to the base of the tree. "That should do it."

"Yep, looks good," Chad said. "Let's go."

"Didn't you break your wrist just last month?" Shane asked, helping Chad reach the first handhold.

"That got better. This cast is for my arm. It doesn't hurt as much; it's just a minor break."

"Just a minor break?"

"That means it didn't break all the way through the bone," Chad said.

"We can pick you out in a crowd," I joked.

"I don't understand." Shane said. "You play football with us, wrestle, bike ride, and climb up to the tree house. You never get hurt."

"I know," Chad said.

"Maybe you should hang out with us more."

"My mom already says I'm over here so much I might as well move in. These shoes should help. They have extra tread for traction. You know for climbing and running."

"You're always changing shoes to try to find a way to be stronger or faster," Shane said.

"Can you blame him? He's the runt of our group," I said causing Chad to turn red. "Maybe you should find some shoes that keep you from falling."

"Ha, ha. Very funny," Chad stuck his tongue out.

"Be careful," Mike stated. "No telling what crawled up here to keep warm."

"What? You didn't put bugs up here too?" I asked.

"No," Mike said.

"I can't believe you're the only one out of our group who is actually on the football team and you like insects."

"Some teams have insects as their mascots," Mike said.

"He has a point," Shane said. "Our high school mascot is a Hornet."

"Right, but most people who have insect collections put pins through them and put them in shadow boxes."

"Gross," Mike said. "That's no fun; you don't get to see what they do."

"I hate bugs," Chad said.

"It's probably too cold for bugs up here," Mike said looking around the tree house. "I'm not sure. I'd be more worried about some animal or cat."

"We have to go to the house," Shane boldly stated. "If it's haunted we have to."

"No doubt," I said entering the tree house. I closed the hatch behind me.

"What about Eric, and Doug?" Mike asked.

"What about them?"

"Shouldn't we include them?"

"They're too old to be trusted," Chad stated. "I know, I have two older brothers. They're always telling on me if I do something wrong."

"Is that why you come over so much?" Mike asked. Chad nodded.

"They could've made up the story just to scare us," I said. "Still, the house is so close we have to check it out for ourselves. There's no reason not too."

"How about death. If we could die would that be a reason to not go?" Chad grinned.

I sat down on the plywood floor. "We need to get some chairs up here or something."

"And some heat," Chad said. "Other than these few old blankets, there's no way to stay warm." He pulled an old green blanket over his shoulders.

"We'll never get another chance like this," Shane said.

Mike scanned the walls and floors. I couldn't tell if he was listening or looking for bugs.

"C'mon, we can't pass this up," Shane said.

Chad nodded. "It's perfect timing with Halloween coming up and all."

I knew I could count on Shane and Chad to go along. Mike was another matter. He didn't like the scary movies we stayed up to watch or the haunted houses we created in the back of the house every Halloween.

"We can't tell anyone else," Shane said. "And we can't go tonight. My parents won't let me stay over two nights in a row, and you guys can't go without me."

"You always have so many chores," I said.

"My dad said almost no one can make it as a farmer anymore, not unless you have all kinds of land. He says it's a sign of the times. But he still wants the pigs and chickens and stuff."

"But you get to take care of them because he has to work."

Shane shrugged his shoulders.

"I didn't plan going so soon anyway," I said. "We need a plan before we go."

"A plan, why?" Chad asked.

"Well, we can't just break into the house," I said. "We need to make sure no one is living there."

"Right. Good idea. My dad would shoot anyone breaking in," Chad said.

"Didn't Eric say you couldn't sell a haunted house?" Shane asked.

"I don't know if that's true."

"Is it OK to go if the house is for sale?"

"If no one lives there I don't see why not," Chad said.

"As long as we don't steal anything, I don't see the harm," I said.

"What if we get caught?" Mike said.

"You're no fun," Chad shot back.

"If I thought we'd get caught, we wouldn't go. That's why we need a plan," I said. "Besides, we're too young for them to do anything. We'll just get in trouble at home."

"Great, I'll be grounded for the rest of my life," Shane said.

"And do what? More chores?"

"Ok, but promise me you'll visit me in the dungeon," Shane said causing the rest of us laugh. "There's that look again. You guys don't notice it?" Shane pointed at me.

I laughed and looked around at the others as I formed a plan. "Tomorrow, we'll ride our bikes to the house. If anyone lives there, they should be home on the weekend because all of the banks and stores are closed."

"What if they work at a gas station?" Chad asked. "Gas stations are open on Sunday."

"They could just be on vacation or something," Shane said.

"Then we should see some mail or a car in the garage. Something like that," I said. "We should find out if anyone at school knows anything. For all we know someone lives there that's in one of our classes. Ask around, but not too much, we don't want anyone to get wise, and stay away from the Falter brothers. If they find out the whole school will know."

"We should send them there," Shane said, "especially if it's haunted. Maybe something bad would happen to them."

"No one would miss those bullies," Chad said.

"I heard they both been held back a grade or two," Shane said. "That's why no one really knows how old they are."

"Just be careful who you talk too," I said. "Chad, your Uncle Johnny, he drives a trash truck, right? If that's his rout, he might know if anyone lives there."

"Okay, I'll ask."

"What about me?" Shane said. "What can I do?"

I wanted to give Shane something to do but I knew he had more chores then the rest of us.

"You just get ready to tie your shoes tight," I remarked. Shane had a habit of wearing his shoelaces loose unless he was getting ready to run or play football.

"And practice your running because we're going to need to move fast." He smiled.

"What are you going to do?" Shane asked.

"I'll try to find a book about ghosts so that we know what to do if we run into one."

"That's right," Shane said in a cocky voice, "you read about it, bookworm, and just let me handle the action." In a quick motion he jerked his head and shoulders left then right, hand straight out in the air making karate like cuts causing us all to laugh.

"What do we do if we get there and there is a ghost or something?" Mike asked, letting a small spider crawl on his hand.

In a moment of panic, my body shook as though the spider were on me. "I thought you said we wouldn't see any bugs."

"Sometimes the weather gets hot enough," Mike stated, "and I think they get confused and think it's summer again. He set the spider on the floor and I immediately flicked it through a crack in the wall ignoring the dirty look Mike gave me.

"Don't ask any grownups or teachers," Shane said. "We need to keep this quiet."

"When do we go?"

"We'll go next Friday." Everyone nodded in agreement.

Shane stood. "One more thing. This is our adventure! This is a chance for us to do something grownups would do."

I looked around at the others. Shane was right. So much of our lives were ruled by what we had to do: go to school, study, go to bed on time, and eat the right foods. This decision would be ours to make.

"We need to swear on it," Chad broke the silence. He stood causing Mike and I to stand.

"Right. We need a code," Shane replied. The three of us looked at him, not sure what he meant.

"You know, like in the movies when the knights go out on quests, they follow a code. We need a code that says we are brothers and that we will defend each other and not tell our secrets to anyone else. You know, stuff like that."

"Good idea. Until we have a code we will agree to all the stuff Shane just said. Put out your hand." We gathered close and put out a hand, one on top of the other. "Shane, it was your idea."

Shane moved forward and was the last to put his hand on the pile. "We do here promise to keep our quest a secret and to defend our secret to the end, even if it means to the death."

"We promise," the rest of us added. Shane got up and left.

"Where's he going?" Mike asked.

"To call his parents and see if he can stay over another night."

"I bet he can't," Chad commented. "He never can, I can, but he never can. Not two nights in a row."

"It's wasn't poisonous," Mike said, looking through the cracks in the wall to see where the spider went.

"Doesn't matter," I said. "Spiders creep me out. What would the football team say if they knew one of their linebackers liked bugs?"

"Insects," Mike said. "There are more of them then us. They'd probably think it's cool."

"My brother has a tarantula," Chad said. "I think it's gonna die because he never feeds it."

"Your mom let him have a tarantula?"

"She doesn't know."

"See if he'll give it to me," Mike said.

"I'd rather be a running back then a linebacker," Chad said.

"No!" I cut in. "No spiders! Not in the house, not in the tree house."

"You really don't like spiders, huh. Linebackers get to hit people and sack the quarterback," Mike said. "That's the fun part of playing."

"I like outside spiders that stay outside," I said.

Mike smiled. It was the first smile I'd seen from him since we started talking about our plan.

"But line backers never get to score," Chad said.

"If you hit the guy with the ball hard enough," Mike said, "it pops out; you pick it up and score."

"I guess I'm too small to think about hitting anyone," Chad said. "Mostly I hope they don't hit me."

"What?" Stunned, Mike and I looked at each other and then at Chad who, though we constantly kidded, never admitted that he was small.

"Sorry guys," Shane's head peeped through the hatch, "My parent's want me home tonight."

"No matter," I said. "It gives us time to prepare."

The idea of an adventure sparked something in all of us. I could hear the anticipation in Chad's voice, see the excitement in Shane's eyes, and tell by his lack of protest that Mike was intrigued.

"Nothing like a good adventure in winter to awaken our spirits."

"Let's just hope we don't wake any other, spirits I mean," Chad said. "I can't wait until summer. Or at least Spring Break. Winter's so boring."

"No way," Mike argued, "football season's the best."

"But after that it gets too cold to do anything."

"I like winter because I have less chores," Shane said.

"Now can we play some football?"

"Shall we play in the field or the yard?"

"Your yard is perfect," Shane said. "It has grass and is about half as big as a real football field."

"Right. But my dad will probably tell us to get off the grass when he wakes up and we'll have to go play in the field."

"So, let's play."

I smiled back and, looking around the tree house, could tell that he'd get no argument from the rest of us. Clambering down the tree, we made our way from several different directions to the yard, where we did the only thing young boys on an early October day without snow knew to do: we played football.

Chad and I huddled up. "I don't understand your brother," Chad said. "He's tall, strong, stout, yet he's always holding back. I mean, other than the fact that you guys both have red hair and blue eyes, no one could tell you were brothers."

"I don't know," I said getting ready to kickoff. "He's kept me out of trouble more than once."

"Throw it to Shane."

"He's harder to catch."

"That's okay," I said. "He doesn't hit as hard."

"Can you catch with that cast on?" I asked Chad, pointing to his arm.

"I won't know until you throw it."

I flung the ball down the field and we charged. Shane was the type of kid that my dad would say needed a haircut. He had blond hair and blue eyes, and was quick, wiry, and agile and good at practically anything he did but had a small build. Mike was the biggest next to me so we played on opposite teams to make them equal.

After a few runs back and forth where no one attempted any real tackling, Chad finally downed the ball so that he could play.

"Enough of this running around," Chad said. "Let's do some passing."

I took my usual position as quarterback for the simple reason that Chad was too short to throw over anyone's head.

"Hut, hut!"

At his age, Chad was the smallest kid in his grade. With brown hair and a freckled face, he made an excellent football teammate. What he lacked in size, he made up in his ability to jump and catch. We often kidded that he came equipped with springs in his legs and glue on his fingertips.

Shane's hand went for the ball but it was too late and Chad came away with it scoring a touchdown. "That's right! You know it," Chad said and spiked the ball.

Shane bent down and tied his shoelaces tight. "Oh, you want to get rough." He and Mike went to the other end of the yard.

"That was a good play," Chad said handing me the ball."

I smiled. "Anyone thirsty?"

"Water break," Shane protested. "I was just getting started."

We walked around the corner of our trailer to where the garden hose lay. "I can almost feel my hands again. Won't the water freeze in the ground?" Shane took the hose in his hands. "My dad never lets us run the hose in the winter."

"I don't know," I said, turning on the box that activated the pump. "This water comes from a well deep underground. I guess if it's frozen down there it won't come up."

"What if we get caught going to this house?" Mike asked, handing the garden hose to me.

I took a drink and wiped my mouth on my sleeve then passed it to Shane. "You're still worried about that?"

He nodded.

"We've gone sneaking around the neighborhood before. Even late at night."

"Yeah, but it's usually in the summer," Mike said. "It will be cold, dark, and it might even snow."

"That's all the better because no one will be outside to see us."

"We've never gone into a house that someone might live in."

"We'll go there and make sure no one lives there first. This is perfect with Halloween coming. Are you scared?"

"No. Just don't want to get in trouble."

"That's why we need to make sure the place is empty before we go. Then we can plan a late-night visit."

"It will be something to talk about," Shane said. "Think about how brave all the girls will think you were for going into a haunted house."

"Is that why you got those shoes? To impress the girls," I asked.

"No. They're the latest fashion, high-tops. You better get some or you won't fit in."

"Do you think I fit in now?"

"No. But, you don't get picked on because you're tall."

"Hmm. I guess I'd rather be original than have to copy someone else or do something so outrageous it seems I'm shouting out 'LOOK I'm Different.'"

"Geez, I thought we were just going to the house to do something exciting," Mike said.

"It'll make a good story," I said.

"If we live to tell about it," Chad said.

"You keep bringing that up."

Chad shrugged his shoulders. "In all those scary movies you watch that you say some are based on true stories, how do they always start? With a group of curious people just wanting to explore an old house, or campground, or building. They're out partying and having a good time, and in the end, somebody is always dead." He nodded his head and looked at me.

"Obviously, that's the movies," I shot back. "Besides, those people in the movie are careless. Which is why we need to be ready."

"Ready for what? We don't know what we're going to find." Shane said.

"Exactly!"

Chapter Two

BUILDING THE MYTH

"THEY WERE ALL MURDERED! All six of them living in the house. No bodies were found. Just the heads."

"No," I decided after listening to the story I created. "This is too easy for them to find out it's not true." Worried that Mike would not go to the Round House, I toyed with the idea of making up a reason for it to be haunted hoping it would convince him to go.

The Round House hadn't been there for long. Any major event would still be talked about. I needed an event that was more subtle and distant.

"The house isn't old and I don't know the history behind it. I need to find out if someone died there," I whispered to myself.

Early Sunday morning I sat down at my small desk and outlined what I knew.

I'd seen enough scary movies and read enough ghost stories to know that any haunted house worth its weight had a history behind it. The Round House did not fall into this category.

"The house is too modern to qualify as an authentic haunted house. It needs to be old."

I couldn't risk asking my parents or teachers about Doug's story or else they might find out what I was up to. At the same time, without their help it would be difficult to find out the truth.

"Why would the house be haunted?" I wrote it down. After all, even ghosts have their reasons. Nothing bad had occurred at the Round House that I knew of.

"Wait," I said to myself. "It's right by that burned out house." I heard noise in the hallway. The sound of heavy footsteps… My dad. I shot out of my room and stood in front of him.

"Did anyone die in that fire on County High Road?" I blurted out. Immediately I realized my carelessness and qualified my question. "I'm doing a school project on fire safety. Do we have enough alarms in the house?"

My dad stood there with a blank face, his eyes aimed down the hallway toward the kitchen. It was then I realized I'd caught him before he'd had his coffee and like most adults, the wheel in his head didn't spin so well before he had his morning oil.

"No. No one died there," my dad said. "The house was torn down. I think some kids messing around in the house playing with matches started the fire. Stay away from abandoned houses and don't play with matches. There's a tip for your project."

Disappointed, I frowned and moved aside to let my dad pass. Doug's story had no basis in truth. So be it. It was then I decided that our reasons for visiting the house needed to match the risk we would take. If the house wasn't truly haunted, it would be by the time I got done with it.

Just as science had yet to find the tenth planet in our solar system, it also had yet to explain why young boys are compelled to explore abandoned mine tunnels, dive off cliffs into water, ride motorbikes and go-carts recklessly, and explore old, abandoned buildings. The mostly rural neighborhood of Pueblo County provided little opportunity in these categories. None of these compared with the excitement of a brush with the unknown.

The minute chance there was a haunted house less than two miles away was too valuable an opportunity to pass up. *"Odd looking,"* I wrote down. Then I added, *"House haunted, but new.*

Land haunted." I underlined. "*Anything built on that land haunted!*" It was from these humble beginnings that I began creating my own story just in case we needed something to fall back on. I told Shane that Monday at school.

"That stretch of road in front of the Round House is haunted," I said in the most convincing voice I could muster. We walked down the hall towards the lunchroom. I veered into the computer lab. "Come on, nobody comes in here during lunch."

I looked around to make sure there was no one in the room and turned back to Shane. "Some lady got hit by a car and died right there in front. Hit and run. Never solved."

"No way!" Shane replied eyes bulging. "That's probably who's haunting the house now."

I kept a straight face, but inside I was grinning from ear to ear. My story worked. Shane needed no proof, no word of honor or promise from me. We were best friends, and if I told him something were true, he believed it to be so.

"Okay, I was just kidding about that."

"What?" Shane shook his head.

"I was just thinking about making up a story so it'd be more believable than just Doug's story. I want to make sure Mike's convinced."

"So the house isn't haunted?" Shane asked.

"I don't know about that. But what happens if we go there and nothing happens?"

"I was kind of hoping nothing would."

"Then we couldn't tell anyone about it."

"I thought you didn't want to tell anyone about it."

"Not until after we've been there. But we can sure create a story about why the house is haunted."

Shane nodded. "I get what you mean. In case nothing happens, we all tell the same story about the house and make everyone believe it's haunted, and that we went there."

"Good idea! I'll work out the details. "Now let's get out of here before someone thinks we touched one of these computers and caused it to freeze-up."

"I know," I said. "These things are always crashing."

⚜ ⚜

After school on Wednesday, I relayed the story to Mike and Chad in the tree house. I could tell by the looks on their faces the story was sinking in.

"So, we create a ghost if there isn't one there," Chad said. "No one at school knows who lives in the house. But some think the house is haunted. My Uncle Johnny said that, too."

"You didn't tell him we were planning on going there," I said.

"No."

"It's getting dark outside," Mike commented.

"Maybe Doug heard the story from someone else," I said.

An aura of mystery began to surround the Round House. Was it the simple fact that it was an odd looking house that had been abandoned that attracted the label "haunted"? Or was it because no one knew much about the owners, including their reasons for leaving the house empty. The mystery compelled me forward.

"Just think," Chad said. "If the story gets out we can say, 'Oh, that old house? I've been there at night. Didn't scare me.'"

"Hey, you guys up there?" Shane's voice rang out.

"Come on up," I hollered down.

Shane made his way up the tree and plopped down on one of the blankets. "I can't stay long. Chad? You're always here."

"I live right next door. Hey, my uncle Johnny said that house is haunted."

"Can you believe that?" I said. "We don't need our back up story; the house may have a real ghost. What's up?" I noticed Shane's lips curled together like they did in class when he was struggling with a hard math problem.

"You and your brother go to church. That probably gives you some protection against ghosts and spirits and stuff like that. But Chad and I don't," Shane said.

"I wouldn't worry about that, you'll be with us."

"Aren't you worried that someone upstairs might get upset, you know, us poking around with something like this?"

| 26 |

"My parents watch the news at dinner sometimes. It's pretty bad. I figure God has his hands busy with all that's going on. It's not like were the Falters, picking on kids and animals and destroying stuff."

"My mom said that it doesn't matter what you do if you go to confection," Chad stated.

"It's called confession," I laughed. "We still need to go by and make sure no one lives there. Just to be safe."

"I have football practice," Mike said, "and a game Friday. Maybe we should wait and go Saturday. That way we can ride by it during the day."

"We could wait until Saturday night to go, but I need time to make a plan."

"Plan?"

I nodded my head. "How are we going to get there? How are we going to get in? What supplies will we need to take?"

"Crosses and Bibles," Chad said. "And maybe garlic."

"Bring me some," Shane said.

"Right and we need to plan our escape. In case something happens."

"Like what?" Shane asked.

"Obviously, if something went wrong like someone came home or something like that."

"I'll go tomorrow night after school," Chad said. "Nothing better to do."

"It will have to be right after we get home. It's starting to get dark earlier."

"Speaking of that," Shane said, "I better get going."

With an oath of silence fresh on our breath, we heeded our mom's call to dinner and headed indoors as Shane jumped on his bike and sped home.

CHAPTER THREE

THIS OLD MAN, HE SCARED ME

"ANYONE STUPID ENOUGH TO visit a suspected haunted house at night without first staking it out during the day is just looking for trouble," I said. Standing outside by our small shed, I took my bike; it was a yellow bike with an orange flame pattern down the sides. Across the front handlebars was a sign, a racing-bike sign. In black, bold letters the words "BMX" and the number "38" gave the bike its spicy flavor. I pushed on the tires to make sure they weren't flat.

From under an oversized, brown furry hat, Chad frowned at me.

"What?"

Chad looked at me and shook his head. "You said stupid. That's a bad word. So why are we riding all the way to see the house now?"

"We need to decide the best way to approach the place without being noticed. Where we would exit and escape if things go bad and a meeting point in case we get separated. Not to mention the need to check for hazards, such as large dogs with big teeth, nosy neighbors, and barbed wire fences. Where did you get that ugly hat?"

"It's my dads and it's warm. I thought we were just going to make sure no one lives there."

"That too."

I turned and closed the door on the shed and we slowly walked around the circular driveway to the road. The top of our driveway angled down thirty five degrees from the main road and made a great starting point for a bike race.

"Do we need any gear?" Chad asked as we made it to the top of the driveway.

"Not for this trip. At least I don't think we need anything, but we need to discuss equipment needs at the next meeting. I don't have the slightest idea what sort of stuff we might need in a haunted house."

"Whatever it is, I can get it," Chad said.

"I have no doubt."

"Shane going to meet us?"

I shook my head. "I don't think he can. He has too many chores."

"Too bad."

I heard a jingling sound from Chad.

"You got a bunch of change in your pockets?"

Chad pulled out a handful of small metallic medallions. "These are the Catholic Saints."

I shook my head.

"There's one for traveling and school and one for girls and all kinds of them."

"Which ones do you have?"

"I wasn't sure which would be best, so I got all of them. Just to be safe."

"Your mom didn't ask why you wanted them?"

"Nope. She thinks I got scared staying up late and watching movies with you guys."

"Make sure your chain is oiled for this weekend."

The air was cool, and overhead the sky was filling with clouds. "I hope we don't have an early snow before we go."

"That would be hard to pedal in," Chad said. "I told my mom that we were going to watch your brother practice."

"Good. If we don't spend much time at the house, we might run into him on the way back. We better go before it gets too late." We jumped on our bikes and headed out.

The elementary school where my brother was practicing football was less than a mile away from our house, and on the same road as the Round House. My allergy problems and Chad's brittle bones kept us both out of school sports, although, we did plenty of rough play on our own to compensate.

I glanced at my watch and mentally planned our pace to give us enough time to meet my brother after his practice. We approached the intersection that led down County High road. With widely spaced houses along it, the smooth, paved road itself was wide enough to be three lanes which gave us plenty of room to ride on either side. One turn and we headed swiftly to the Round House.

"Hey," I called out. "Are those new tires?"

"Yep. They make the bike faster."

I eyed Chad's bike. It was only a month old as he had wrecked his previous bike on a ramp in our yard.

"Watch this." He sped up and then slid to a halt.

"Neat. You've got a hand brake," I said circling around him.

"It's just on the back tire so you can do cool slides."

I pulled up beside him and stopped. Chrome on Chad's bike caught the light from the sun hanging low in the western sky and sparked an idea. "We'll have to do something about our reflectors. If we get caught we need to be able to cut across a field or something without anyone being able to see us."

"We can put tape over them."

"Good idea. See, that's why we need to plan."

Chad pointed forward. "Do you have a plan for that?"

We looked down the two-lane road ahead of us. "Did your new bike come with a rocket?"

We came to a stop for a reason. In our neighborhood, there was never a shortage of unchained dogs, most were harmless, but we could never tell. We tended to ride our bikes often because of this. Only one dog did we truly dread. His name was "Mutt."

"The black terror. The horror of County High Road. The dark death. The supremo meano," Chad said.

"That's enough, I get the point."

Looking west down County High Road, on the left side of the street adjacent to the next intersection there was a house; Mutt's house. We called him "Mutt" because that's what he looked like—his breeding background was anyone's guess. The best we could come up with was that he was a crossbreed between, well, two mean dogs that weren't that smart.

"Mutt's lived on that corner clear back when Eric went to Elementary school," I said.

"My brothers used to talk about him," Chad said. "He must be really old."

"But still runs fast."

"See, he's abnormal. He doesn't age. Even his bark is unnatural. Sounds like a tuba that's been dropped too many times."

"What?" I laughed. "Well, his view is blocked on both sides by that wooden fence. It should give us the advantage of surprise."

Chad shook his head.

Our usual strategy was to start picking up speed about three houses in advance and then race by the yard. By the time Mutt knew we were passing by, he didn't stand a chance of picking up enough speed to catch us, which didn't keep him from running out in the street and barking just to let us know he was there.

"We better make sure all of our bikes are in tip-top shape," I said. "At night, there won't be any noise to distract him or cars to hide behind."

We usually rode on the opposite side of the road from Mutt's house and waited for an oncoming car to cross hoping Mutt would not run out in front of it.

"Dang, where's a car when you need one. We could go around," Chad said.

"That will take twenty minutes. We need to come up with something better. We can't have any delays tomorrow night." We kept our eyes pointed down the road.

"Oh great," Chad slapped his hand against his leg and looked back.

I thought Mutt had appeared but looking behind us I spotted something equally bad. "The Falter brothers. Don't worry, you're with me."

Jay and Jim Falter were red-headed brothers we believed were about two-years apart in age and attracted mayhem like butter attracts flies. Jay, the older of the two, went to middle-school and Jim went to elementary school. When they got together, there was trouble brewing. Alone, Chad wouldn't stand a chance as the Falter brother's had a habit of picking on kids smaller than themselves. Due to my height they tended not to bother me.

"I don't know. They look like they're ready for trouble," Chad said.

"Guess it's a good thing you're with me."

Chad laughed and we looked back toward our goal.

"Ready," I said, looking over to Chad.

He glanced back the way we came. "So long, family." He smiled and looked at me. "Time to try out my new tires," he boldly stated, keeping his bike pointed in the direction of surefire peril.

"We're about to visit a haunted house," I muttered, more to myself than to Chad. "We can't let a dog get in our way." I looked back to make sure no cars were coming and then I looked over at Chad and nodded. He nodded back and we both stood up on our pedals to push down on them with all our weight.

"Let's give him a run," Chad called out.

As though executing a synchronized cycling routine, Chad and I picked up speed in tandem. We came within view and I spotted Mutt at the corner of the house sleeping on the lawn. My heart raced, and I prayed that my chain would stay on. With adrenaline pouring through our veins, we cruised silently past Mutt without incident and resumed a normal pace. With a despondent look on their face, Jay and Jim stopped short of Mutt's house and looked on.

"Ha. We lost em," I stated. "Looks like they didn't want to tangle with Mutt. Guess they're not so brave when they are facing real danger."

Chad was still trying to catch his breath as he pulled up beside me. "At least Mutt wasn't up for a chase today."

"It's after school. He's probably all chased out. Or maybe one of your saints protected us." I grinned.

"We got lucky. He'll be rested when we come back. What are we going to do Friday night when it's dark and we can't see where he is? And it will be quiet out, with nothing else for him to do but watch the road?"

"I got a bat."

We both knew it was a matter for further discussion. We would have enough problems sneaking out of our house. We didn't need the added distraction of Mutt chasing us up and down the street, and it would be hard to explain if anyone got hurt.

After passing the elementary school and three more intersections, none that contained a stop light, we approached our destination. The Round House sat across the road from a new housing development where Doug lived.

"Look," I said. "There's Doug's house." I pointed to a neat row of five houses. "His house seems farther away than I expected."

We approached the Round House from the opposite side of the road, finding no apparent activity in the yard or house I came to a halt on the shoulder.

"There it is," Chad said. "Right where we expected it."

The Round House sat back from the main road and this concerned me. It would be hard ground to cover without being noticed from the road of from the single house that stood to the east of it. Facing north toward the main road we were on, it was the last house on its side of the road, which intersected with another road about a half-mile up. For the first time, I took a good, long look at the house.

"We're at a crossroads." I said.

The house appeared modern, unlike the venerable garage set to one side and the small tin shed behind it. "It doesn't look like a haunted house," Chad said. "It's too modern looking. Maybe it's the garage that's haunted."

"What do we really know about haunted houses? Just what we've seen on TV and movies?"

"Yep. And it doesn't look like any of those."

We knew from passing by the place that the garage had once served as a barn for the house that had been there before. The new doors on the front of it didn't go with the rest of the structure, and apart from the paint, white with light-brown trim; the garage didn't match the house.

"Who'd paint a house light blue out here?" Chad said. "Doesn't look like anyone's taking care of the yard."

The grass, brown and dry, and judging by its height hadn't been mowed since the end of summer, was covered with leaves fallen from a single maple tree in the front yard. A row of fur trees lined the east side of the house, and a chain-link fence ran along the front and sides of the yard.

"Look at that," I said to Chad, pointing at the fence.

"We could jump it if needed."

"No, look at the edges," I pointed.

"Right, ouch!"

"The wire ends stick up above the top bar in sharp jutting edges. I've cut my hand too many times crossing fences like that," I said.

"I've snagged a few pants," Chad said.

"That wall and row of trees running there between it and the neighbor's house will come in handy. It blocks the neighbors view once we're off the main road."

Chad pointed to the houses. "That's something I never understood. People build their houses so close together but then put fences, walls, trees, anything to make a barrier. Why not just build farther apart?"

"Well, at least there's only one neighbor to worry about." To the west of the house lay a vacant tilled field that half a mile down ended at a junction of roads. A barbed-wire fence ran along the border of the field.

"Act like you're checking your tire when this car comes by."

Chad dismounted and played decoy, pretending to check out a problem with his bike as the car drove by. I continued to survey the surroundings.

"The gate's wide open," I said. "If anyone lives here they must not have a dog in the yard."

"They haven't raked their leaves yet."

"Maybe they're waiting for the stragglers to fall."

"I hate it when you just rake and then more fall off."

"The grass is high, and it doesn't look like anyone's walked on it. There's no mail or newspapers in this box here. No name on the box either. Of course, they might not get any."

"It's not for sale. But didn't Eric say it was illegal to sell a haunted house?"

"I don't know about that. It appears no one is home. But are they just gone for the moment, or did they leave in a hurry like Doug suggested." I thought out loud confusing Chad.

"What?"

"Never mind." Even as my feet rested against the pedals and were poised to ride away, something drew me to the house; it's odd, arched windows and door. "Okay," I addressed the house, "what's your story that's got everyone so worked up about you?"

I started riding down the driveway and immediately my wheels sank into the thick gravel. I got off my bike and guided it up the driveway. "We won't be able to ride down the driveway with this thick gravel."

"Let's see if anyone's home," Chad said and came to where I stood in the driveway.

"Let's get a closer look. Followed me."

The house stood two stories tall and was a faded blue with red trim. There was a window on either side of the door, the one closest to the garage being the smaller of the two, and both were arched on top in a half-circle. The front door, likewise arch-shaped, is why we had nicknamed it the Roundhouse. Other than the odd design, there was nothing in its appearance suggesting a haunted house like those I had read about or seen in movies. It was too modern looking, with its gutters and shiny glass windows.

"Why don't you go up to the door and knock?" Chad said.

"And say what?"

"Ask if they want someone to rake the leaves."

"Good idea."

Chad smiled with pride.

"But if they take me up on it, you and Mike are helping." His smile disappeared.

While Chad remained in the driveway, I stepped through the open gate of the chain-link fence and mounted the two cement steps leading to the small porch. I approached the large, red door, with its strange arched top. There was no window on the door itself, but stepping closer I noticed the windows to the right and left of it were dusty, as though they hadn't been cleaned in months. I peered into the one on the left.

I looked through the window into the living room. I could see a brown, leather couch, a round, dark wood coffee table, and two cushioned high-back chairs. While the furniture looked expensive, there were no decorations around it from what I could see. There were no plants, fake or real, and no ornaments on any of the small tables. There were no magazines or papers on the coffee table and no blankets or pillows on the couch.

I pushed the doorbell but no sound came forth. The house stood quiet, still. I tried the doorbell again. Nothing. I looked back at Chad and shrugged my shoulders. Another car approached and we both watched anxiously hoping it wouldn't turn in the driveway. It kept going. I turned back to the door and decided to try knocking. My hand fell against the wooden door and a loud echo of emptiness returned from within.

A chill ran from the base of my neck down my back, and along my arms, goose bumps sprang wild when I heard a strange whispering sound come from within the house. It was as though the stale air itself, disturbed by my knocking, responded with a sigh, but we could not possibly speak the same language. I hesitated, my hand poised mid-knock, not knowing if I should try again or turn and run. I was about to knock one last time when a voice rang out that separated my shoes from my feet.

"Whatchya doing over there!"

The deep, male voice came from the house next door. I turned and spotted an old man leaning over the adobe wall looking at me.

"What is it you want?" he asked as I took a couple of steps toward the wall. I looked over to Chad but he was out of sight.

"I'm trying to see if anyone is home."

The old man, whose gray hair stuck out from under his faded, brown hat, did not respond. The words on his hat were illegible, as were the words he spoke as he chewed on a fat cigar. His weathered face reminded me of the many farmers' faces I'd seen, and the calloused dry hands let me know that was exactly how he made his living.

"Do you know when they'll be back?" I asked.

His eyes narrowed, the cigar went from one side of mouth to the other, no smoke coming from it. His eyebrows came together over his long forehead; his mouth quivered a little as he looked beyond me to the house. I followed his gaze to the second floor.

"What fer?"

I turned back to him. "Excuse me?"

"Why do you want to know?"

"I wondered if they needed someone to rake their leaves," I said, using Chad's idea. "You know, make a little money." I glanced over and spotted Chad trying to peek in the garage. He didn't seem to notice I was talking with the neighbor.

I looked at the yard of the house next door, which is where I imagined this old fellow had come from. The yard wasn't in much better condition. I had no desire to rake leaves and hoped the old man was too proud to offer us a job.

"They been gone for weeks. Maybe longer. Why don't you try back next month," he stated.

I nodded and glanced around the yard. The man didn't appear to be going anywhere and continued leaning over the fence. I sensed he intended to stay there until I left. I looked at the door again and in the window, hoping for some closure.

"I said try back next month," the man repeated.

Reluctant to disagree or continue scouting the house under the watchful eye of the nosy neighbor, I concluded that no one was home and stepped off the porch and headed toward the gate. The old man's hesitation to provide any information and his suggestion that I come back in a month left me suspicious, but helped to convince me the house was probably vacant.

"Thanks," I called back as I stepped through the gate but the old man was gone. I looked across to the yard but there was no sign of him at the wall or in his yard. I shook my head.

I headed over to the driveway and picked up my bike. I studied the Roundhouse, trying to take in as much detail as I could. I noticed Chad back on his bike waited at the end of the driveway.

"There's no dog in the back," he said as I approached.

"Good. I'd call this a successful mission. We've scouted the possible routes for our approach and escape. Plus we've discovered there are no dogs to give away our presence."

"Did you look inside?"

"Yep. There's at least a dozen dead people in the living room," I joked.

"It doesn't look like a haunted house." We both began to ride down the road.

Looking back at the house, I noticed a broken window on the second floor that was covered by a piece of plastic. I wondered if this is where the old man had looked when we were talking. At the time I didn't know how we would reach it, but it would serve as a perfect entrance when we went back to the house.

"Did you get a look in the garage?" I asked.

"The windows were too high and I kept hearing sounds."

"What kind of sounds?"

"I don't know. Like leaves blowing or someone sweeping. I couldn't tell exactly."

We pedaled forward, our eyes on the road, which was unusually quiet and devoid of traffic.

"Let's take the long way back," I told Chad. "I'm not in the mood to tangle with Mutt or worry about running into the Falter brothers."

"I have time," Chad said, looking at his watch.

"Besides, Mike probably started home and I know he'll be taking the long way back."

"You think the place is haunted? Are we coming back this weekend?"

"Sure. If only to bury the dead bodies I saw." I winked. "What else we got to do?"

Chad shrugged his shoulders. "We could go bowling."

"Bowling?"

"That's the only thing I can think of until the drive-in opens up."

"There's something strange about the house," I said. "I felt something while peering into the window. I can't explain it. I would have gotten a better look inside if it wasn't for that nosy old man."

"What old man?"

"The one standing at the fence," I said. At the time, I didn't give Chad's comment a second thought.

Chapter Four

DELAY

"WE'RE RUNNING OUT OF time," I panicked. Immediately regretting the words I spoke to Shane over the phone. It was Friday night and I called Shane to see if our plans to have him spend the night was still on. Chad had just come over and we stood in the back bedroom where using the phone offered more privacy.

"He can't come over tonight." I knew Shane had little control over the situation, but the weather was getting colder as we approached mid-October. It would be hard for us to travel if it snowed.

"Maybe you guys should go without me," he said. "My mom and dad want to go see my grandma this weekend and I'm not going to change their minds."

Chad listened to our conversation but seemed unconcerned. "Just go next week," he whispered to me, as if such an easy solution would so readily present itself.

"You still want to go, right?" I asked Shane.

"If you can wait."

"There's a window on the side of the house. If all else fails, that's where we'll enter. I don't think anyone could get there but you," I said, trying to play down my disappointment. "Besides, it gives us a chance to go by the house one more time, just to make sure no one lives there."

"Right," Chad nodded. "We still gotta figure out what to do about Mutt."

"This time we'll go on the weekend or late at night. If anyone lives there, they should be home."

The logic of young boys is, to them, black and white, even if it isn't sound. Our reasoning stated that as long as the house was abandoned, it wouldn't hurt if we visited the place. After all, we didn't intend to steal or vandalize anything. We were just looking for some adventure. It would be like going to a museum.

"How about next Friday? Can you stay over then?" I asked Shane.

"I don't know. It's too early to ask my folks," he replied, clearly disappointed. "I'll try to act up a little bit this week. You know, so they'll want a break from me."

"Don't get in trouble," I said.

"Hey, you're talking to an expert. Noo problemo. So, the neighbor guy didn't tell you if there were anyone living there?"

"Nope. Said they'd been gone. He wasn't what you'd call friendly."

"Make sure no one lives there, man, we can't get caught. I can't afford to get into trouble. Most of the time what we're doing would be considered minor infractions." Shane's kid logic kicked in. "But this is going into someone else's house."

"But not if it's vacant."

"Right."

"How could we be sure no one lives there?" I asked.

"You got any firecrackers?" Shane said. "Just light one and shoot it into the front yard. Then sit back and see if anyone comes out to see what's going on."

"Right!" I smiled and nodded to Chad. "The firework test is a sure way to wake them up."

"And the whole neighborhood," Chad said.

"I don't think we have to worry about that," I said. "Other than the old man next to them, there's no other houses close by." I spoke back into the receiver. "I don't have any firecrackers, but I'm sure Chad does." Chad nodded. "I just don't know about riding all the way over there to do it. I hate to try to sneak out there at night twice. If we get caught, there won't be a next time."

"If someone lives there," Shane said, "the lights will probably be on at night. At least an outside light or hallway light. Maybe you can get your mom or Eric to drive down the road."

"Good idea. Eric sometimes will take us places if we buy him a pop. If we can't go by at night, maybe we can ride by Sunday after church. I'll let you know."

"I'll call you when we get back from grandma's house."

Chad and I went to find Mike and brief him on the plan. I opened the door to our bedroom to find him sitting on the corner of his bed.

"What is on your finger? Yuck!"

"Close the door," Mike said, his eyes wide and face panicked.

Chad and I closed the door behind us.

"I don't want mom to find out, she might make me kill it."

"It's a bug," I said.

"Cool," Chad said, reaching out to touch it. The bug hissed and Chad jerked his arm away. I laughed.

Perched on my brother's left index finger was a large cockroach.

"It's a Madagascar hissing cockroach.

"What?"

"Did it make that sound?"

"Some people keep them as pets."

"What if it has babies? Then we'll have 'em all over the place," I said, panicked.

"Don't worry," Mike said, pointing with his right finger. "See these little horns?" I nodded but kept my distance. "It's a male. It can't have babies."

"It sure is tame," Chad said, stroking the brown and black shell causing it to hiss more. The antennae probed around. The bug moved, I jumped, and Mike laughed.

"It won't hurt you. And they're very clean."

"That must be why people like them in their house." I said. "No wait, they don't like them. They trap, poison, kill, and use them for pet food."

"Very funny."

"Where did you get it?" I asked.

"I bought it at school."

"I guess we won't have to worry about you having a girlfriend, ever."

"I need to get a box made up so I can put Reggie in the shed."

"Reggie?"

"That's what I named him."

"See if you can get one of Dad's cigar boxes," I said.

Our dad was an avid cigar smoker and bought his cigars in a six by twelve inch cigar box made of strong cardboard. It was perfect for holding match box cars, dominoes, and other assorted toys.

"What do they eat?" Chad asked.

"He needs to go outside. He can't stay in our room," I stated.

"Okay. Just for tonight?" Mike said.

"Well, I guess we're sleeping in the front room anyway. Just make sure he can't get out. I don't want him crawling all over the house."

With Chad staying over for the night, the three of us talked in our room telling stories until my dad went to bed. It was then we ran to the front room and set up the pillows and sleeping bags and took over.

In the living room, the largest room in our house and on the opposite side from our parent's bedroom, our Friday night domain was in front of the television. It was all ours after the ten-o-clock news and usually remained in our control until late Saturday morning.

"Mmm," Chad said. "Smells like your mom is made us some brownies. Where's Eric?

"He went to stay over a friend's house. Didn't say who."

"I can't wait to see what's on tonight," I said.

"Why," Mike said. He brought in a plate full of warm brownies from the kitchen. "The cast of characters is always the same: monsters, ghosts, witches, vampires, werewolves, and psychos."

"Exactly," I said. "It plays right into my fascination with the paranormal. The show is creepy, scary, unrealistic, but gets under your skin all at the same time."

"Wait. This is the same one we watched in the summer," Chad said.

"Consider it research," I said. "And training. You have to be brave enough to make it through an entire episode. Here, have a brownie."

"They don't have many shows about ghosts. Mostly monsters," Mike said.

"And the dead coming back to life and stuff," Chad said. "Or haunted houses. Are we going to make a haunted house this year? I mean, Halloween's in two weeks."

"Too bad it's on a school night. That would be cool visiting a haunted house on Halloween," I said.

"And miss out on all the candy? Are you crazy?"

"Someone always dies in these movies," Mike said.

"That's because they get careless or they don't believe in what's happening," I instructed. "You have to be on the alert and pay attention."

"I hate when that happens," Chad said turning his attention back to the movie. "Someone is trying to warn the others and they think they're crazy and won't listen. If they'd just listen."

"This is a good point," I said.

"About what?" Mike asked.

"About how ready we are, or aren't for that matter."

"Ready or not, I'm going to sleep," he said and pulled his sleeping bag over his head.

"I should see if you guys can come over to my house," Chad said. "We've got the satellite dish and can get lots of scary movies."

I turned the TV down. "I wish we had a satellite dish."

"They cost thousands of dollars," Chad said. "It's not like everyone can have one."

"We need to think about this whole thing. When we play football, we practice. These movies aren't real, but at least they don't scare us. That's got to mean something. Right? Chad?"

Chad's eyes were closed.

"Well, TV, it's you and me again. I guess if they don't get scared and leave early, they fall asleep because the movie's on too late or it's too boring. Why are there so few good scary movies?" I talked out loud.

The flickering light of the television hypnotized me into watching the rest of the flick, which ended with a group of monsters waving weapons boarding a boat and heading into town.

"Cool. There'll be a party in the big town tonight." I chuckled and went to dreamland.

The following morning, I called a meeting in the tree house right after breakfast. The three of us moved slowly through the hatch and immediately slid under the blankets.

"These blankets are too cold," Chad said. "You need a heater up here."

"Let's go back and watch cartoons," Mike said.

"Wait," I said. "I have something important to say. If Shane can't go next weekend, I don't think we can wait. It'll be snowing soon and too cold to make the trip late at night."

"Besides that, Halloween is coming and I don't want to miss out on the haunted houses or getting candy," Chad added.

"I guess we have some thinking to do anyway," Mike said. "We need to do something about Mutt. It's because of him I've been taking the long way from football practice. He's never chained. I wish someone would call the dog pound."

"He probably ate the chain," Chad said, causing us to laugh.

"Right. When we went by the other day he was loose. Lucky for us he was asleep. Going the long way takes time we don't have, and we need figure out what to take with us."

"Like what?"

"A camera?"

"Ghosts are invisible, aren't they?"

"I'm not taking the picture anyhow. I'll be too busy running away."

"I guess some are, but not all of them. Who's got a camera?"

"I can get three flashlights, two sets of shoulder pads. You could probably fit into my brother's," Chad said. "I can get two football helmets."

"Make sure the batteries work."

"What about candles?"

"No, we don't want to get wax on anything, or start a fire, but we will need matches."

"For what?"

"Firecrackers. Do you still have some? We may need to create a diversion."

"Just don't light them around here. Our dogs hate them," Mike said.

A light went on in my brain after Mike's comment. "Dogs hate them."

Chad smiled at me, a gleam in his eyes, and I knew we had both hit on the same idea.

"We don't have to be quiet all the way there, right?" Chad asked.

"It would be preferable," I said.

"Dogs hate firecrackers," Chad said.

"If we set off a couple and ride fast we can clear out of there before anyone sees us. Bet we won't have a problem getting back either. He'll probably hide in that doghouse all night."

Mike looked up from the Reggie. "But you can't hurt him."

"Where did he come from?" I pointed to Reggie.

"I've been keeping him in my pocket. It zips up so he can't get out."

"Do you have a soft spot for Mutt?"

"He's just reacting and protecting his territory," Mike said.

"Don't worry, we won't hurt him," I said watching in fascination how he kept Reggie still on his finger. "We just wanted to give him a good scare. Are you going?" He hadn't made it clear if he would. He nodded. "Good. Now, how to make sure no one lives there. I suppose we could go by tomorrow after church, or maybe sometime next week to check things out."

"I can go with you this time," Mike offered. "We lost our last game Friday. Football season's over."

"Last time we went during the day," Chad said. "Won't do us any good to go there at the same time."

"Right," I said. "If someone lives there, they could just be at work. We need to go right before dinner or after dark. The only problem is how to get there after dark before next Friday. We only go that way when we're going to church Sunday morning."

"It sure would be nice if we could figure that out. That's our biggest problem," Chad said hanging his head as though an answer would emerge from the wood.

"We need a clear sign that no one lives there."

As luck would have it, we didn't have to resort to any of our tests. The following morning on our way to church my dad took the back way and we passed the Round House. There on the hibernating lawn in front of the house we spotted a "For Sale" sign. Now we wouldn't be breaking into someone's home, we would simply be having our own open house…late at night, of course.

That morning as we passed by the house I sat on the side closest to it. Strangely, it seemed as if the car slowed as we passed. The arches and dark interior beyond hid a mystery that I was determined to solve. No, it wasn't the car that slowed down, but times itself, as if some unseen power were giving me a chance to think twice about my plans to visit the house.

In the early morning light, the Round House looked like it had aged years since my last visit. The paint faded and the windows streaked and filthy. Haunted or not, it was still standing there, inviting as ever, and my need for adventure had the best of me.

Chapter Five

❧ ❦

SAVING HERMAN

"UH OH!" MY BROTHER'S voice carried across the dark room from his bed to mine. It was late at night and we were both supposed to be asleep.

"What?" I asked.

"Nothing." He got up, and I spotted his flashlight beam zoom up and down his bed then frantically zip around the floor and under his bed.

"Man, don't tell me you have one of your bugs in here."

"Help me find him," he pleaded.

I had to choose between helping or being victimized if the creature found its way to me. The thought of a bug crawling on me, well, made my skin crawl! "You need a new hobby." I reluctantly joined in the search.

"One day you're going to appreciate what insects do for the world."

"Outside. I appreciate them outside. Where'd you have him?"

"On my dresser. I bumped the box and it fell down."

"Where did you gooo, little roachy," I sang out in a hushed voice.

Mike's flashlight stopped panning. "It's not Reggie that's lost, it's Herman."

"How am I supposed to keep them straight?" I asked in frustration. "Who's Herman?"

"Reggie's the cockroach; Herman's the tarantula I got from Chad's brother."

"WHAT!" I jumped back on my bed. "Have you lost your mind!"

"Don't worry. They don't normally bite, but if you find him you should let me pick him up."

"It's not poisonous like a Black Widow is it?" Mike didn't respond right away. "New rule, no bugs kept inside the bedroom. Wait, that was the old rule. New rule is I'M GOING TO KILL YOU!" I raised my fist and pretended to attack.

Suddenly, the door swung open, and Mike and I were confronted with the less-than-happy look on my mother's face.

"What are you two doing in here?" she asked. "You are supposed to be asleep."

I wanted to scream, "CLOSE THE DOOR!" but instead I did the best I could to explain our situation. "Did you know that if you have a head injury and you close your eyes in the dark, you can't stand up straight?"

I knew by the look my mom returned that I was the "stupid" kid in the family at that moment.

"No more science experiments tonight. Get to bed."

The door closed. *It worked, we didn't get into trouble!*

We kept quiet for a few minutes until we were certain mom was back in bed.

"Good thinking," Mike said and resumed his search with his flashlight. "They don't normally bite unless they feel threatened, are you going to help me?"

"Only if you keep your promise."

"I did. You said Reggie had to go outside and he is."

"All bugs. All bugs stay outside until you get your own HOUSE!"

"He's not here," Mike whispered.

"Oh, and by the way, I won't be visiting much," I said.

"What are you talking about?"

"Your house. I won't be visiting much. Not you and your bugs. Did he get out when mom opened the door?"

Mike headed for the door, opened it and quickly looked down the hallway. He started to step out but I pulled him back in the room.

"You're going to get us in trouble, and then we won't be able to do anything. We'll have to wait until morning to search out there. Now, help me look around my bed because if he crawls on me during the night I'll kill him, and then you."

"He's not that small," Mike said. "I don't know where he could be?"

"Hopefully, he's hiding. I need some sleep."

I didn't get any. The thought of Herman crawling up my bed and snuggling up beside me kept me up all night. I left my flashlight on, positioning it on the carpet between my half of the room and my brother's hoping Herman would not cross the beam and that, if he did, I might glimpse him before he crossed to my side of the room. I watched the light slowly fade as did I in and out of sleep. In the brief moments before the batteries surrendered their last energy and the room went dark, I scanned the floor once more. No sign of Herman.

The lack of sleep overtook me during the night and I jarred myself awake in the early morning light, quickly looking around my bed to make sure I was alone. My stomach growled and I slowly opened the door and carefully tiptoed down the hallway checking where I stepped. I headed to the kitchen to eat some cereal.

"First one up," I said proudly. I enjoyed the silence along with the fact that I found an unopened box of cereal. The sunlight peeked in through the front room windows and for a minute I enjoyed the peace and quiet as its warm light brushed my face. I finished eating and went back to wake Mike so we could finish our search for Herman.

Passing by my sister's room, adjacent to ours, I noticed her door open. *Could Herman have crawled in there?* I took a step back and looked through the door. I was standing there when Dee Dee saw me.

"What do you want?" her usual older-sister tone scraped at me.

I wanted to tell her a tarantula was on the loose just to see the look on her face. Another part of me wanted her to go back to sleep so I could find Herman and put him on her head. What fun that would be.

She rolled her eyes at me when I didn't answer, stepped forward, and closed the door. Before the wood met the frame, I caught sight of something out of the corner of my eye and ran into my room.

"Mike! Wake up!" I shook the bundle of tangled covers on his bed. "Herman's in Dee Dee's room on the ceiling!"

Tired eyes tried to open. A voice came from deep down. "They can walk upside down like that. Little hairs on their feet…"

"No time for a lesson! Get his box," I said. "We've got to get him out of there or we're both in trouble and Herman's dead!"

Mike's eyes opened wide and a spark of wit materialized. He grabbed the cigar box he'd kept Herman in. "What?"

"I think that's the first time I've seen you get out of bed so fast. Except maybe for Christmas morning."

"Ha. Very funny. Can we get on with this."

"I'll distract Dee Dee; you go in and get him." I went down the hall to the kitchen and took the phone off the hook. Then I approached my sister's door and knocked. "Phone."

She opened the door and went down the hall. I motioned Mike with a quick wave of my hand.

"There you are," Mike said. Pulling my sister's chair into position, he stood up and grabbed Herman.

"Here she comes!" We were too late. I stood in the hall, but Mike didn't get out in time.

"The phone was dead," my sister said. "Who was it?"

"I don't know, some girl. Why would I care?" I tried to stand in the way hoping she would go to the kitchen or bathroom or anywhere but back in her own room.

Dee Dee squeezed by me and into her room, immediately noticing her desk chair had been moved. She shot me an accusing look. "Stay out of my room!" And with that, the door slammed shut.

The lack of a scream led me to believe Mike had hidden safely, but I knew his time was short. I ran to the phone and dialed.

"Hello?"

"Shane, I need you to do me a favor."

"My dad doesn't like it when you call this early."

"Kind of an emergency. Call me back right away and let the phone ring. Wait for my sister to answer and then hang up. I'll explain later." I ran back down the hall to my sister's door. "C'mon, Shane," I said under my breath. "Hurry up and call."

"Rrriiing…"

"Phone again, Dee Dee, probably that girl calling back. You want me to get it?"

The door opened, "I'll get it so you don't hang up on her," my sister said and headed down the hall.

"Coast is clear," I called into the room.

Mike emerged from my sister's closet, Herman in hand, and together we darted into our room. "From now on you've got to keep these things outside."

"I guess he's safer out there. If Dee Dee would have seen him, she would have killed him. And me."

"We have a chance to visit an actual haunted house," I said to my brother. "Something we'll probably talk about for years and years. I know you don't really want to go, but don't mess up and get us in trouble. Brother," I handed Mike his shoes, "you've got to do something with that thing," I pointed to the tarantula. "If mom finds out you have something like that in the house, well, no telling what she'd do."

"I'm afraid if I put him outside he'll get too cold and die," Mike pleaded.

"It's a spider. They live outside. Besides, he's gonna die anyway. Insects don't live that long."

"I'll have you know," Mike raised his voice.

"Shh," I put my finger across my lips.

"I'll have you know," he stated in a quieter voice, "that Tarantulas have been known to live up to thirty years." He walked out of the room with his shoes untied; the laces flopped along as he held the cigar box with Herman in it close to his side.

My quick wit failed as my brother's revelation stupefied me. My mouth hung open to help breath in air. "If he gets on my side of the room he won't live long." I walked out into the hallway.

"Humph!" my sister said, passing me in the hallway. "If anyone calls for me tell them I'm busy."

🦋   🦋

The week crept by, and outside the days were getting shorter and colder. The leaves completed their annual migration to the ground and remained scattered, blanketing the land. The lull of winter was setting in, and after seven weeks of school the urge to do something exciting intensified.

We charged into the week headstrong and committed to our mission of confronting the mystery of the Round House. Without football practice, Mike came home early, and we played football in the back yard. Our games were unusually quiet as we closed in on Friday. I knew I was preoccupied with the task before us; Sometimes, obsessing about the smallest items.

"That's enough for tonight," I called out as Mike tackled Chad. "We need to check our bikes."

"Again?" Mike asked as we all headed to the shed to collect our bikes.

"You don't want to get stuck if a ghost follows you back, do you?" I teased. "Bring your bike over here when you're done and I'll check it for you."

Mike rode around the yard while Chad and I did practice runs to prepare ourselves for the plan we had come up with to deal with Mutt. Mike dropped his bike by me. "I'm going to feed my insects."

"Thanks for the batteries," I said. "I wore mine out the other night."

"My dad buys them by the gross," Chad said.

"I think we're ready," I said to Chad as he came off his last run. "Just make sure we stay together in case Mutt gets close. One of us will have to cut him off."

"Here," I said, handing Chad some electrical tape. "Put this over your reflectors.

"Good idea. Let's do Mike's too."

We covered our reflectors with the black tape, and did the same to Mike's plain, red bike.

"You really think our plan is going to work? How do we get Mutt in front of us?" Chad asked.

I looked around as though I had top-secret information to disclose, and then turned to him. "We send Mike and Shane ahead of us as a decoy and draw him out. We'll come up behind him and let him have it. Just don't tell them they're bait."

"Why do you think he's so mean?"

"I don't know," I said. "Too many people get dogs and stick them in their back yards. Don't play with them or take them for walks. Maybe he's mad because he never gets attention. Or maybe a kid or someone hurt him so he chases after everything."

"Like the Falter brothers," Chad said. "Maybe no one pays attention to them or let's them do stuff. So they treat everyone else bad."

"Good point. But I don't think that's an excuse. If we are smarter than the animals, we shouldn't treat them bad just because we can."

"You mean like the Falter brothers bullying everyone?" Mike said coming up behind us.

"Yes, using their strength to take advantage instead of protecting," I said. "If they're bullying because someone made them feel bad, then they're just doing the same thing to others."

"And making it bad for everyone."

"BURRRRPPP!" Chad laughed. "You guys are sounding too much like my parents."

"I just think if you are stronger than something else, you should protect and not hurt," I said.

"Maybe that's why your brother likes taking care of bugs, because everyone else picks on them. Well, see you later." Chad rode off toward his house.

I looked at my brother who picked up his bike and began heading to the shed. "Sorry."

He stopped and turned around. "For what?"

"I just don't like bugs. They gross me out. Guess we pick on them a lot. Poison them, step on them, and trap them. I can see why you protect them." For a moment I knew I had said something important to my brother and felt good about supporting him.

"I don't know what Chad was talking about. I just think they're cool. You going in?"

"No," I said not knowing how to respond. "I need a moment to think."

"About what?"

"Obviously, about what we are getting ready to do."

"It's a new challenge, right?"

I nodded.

"And a chance for adventure?"

I nodded again.

"So, don't worry. We're all fast runners, and good riders."

"You sure you left all your bugs outside?"

Mike winked at me and left.

I spent what time I could before the sunset in the tree house, drawing up a map of our plans on the back of a paper sack. Mike's words came back to me: "We're all fast runners."

"Yes, we are," I replied to the air. "But can we outrun something that's not of this world?"

CHAPTER SIX

VISITING A HAUNTED HOUSE

SHADES OF GRAY AND black surrounded me. The air was damp and hazy, but I couldn't explain why the inside of the house was foggy. The last thing I remembered was going to bed. All of the sudden, we were in the Round House. I shook my head.

"I must have blacked out."

"What?" Shane stood beside me. Chad and Mike beside him. Shane's flashlight went out. Mike dropped his and it broke.

"Careful," I said to Chad, but his light faded.

"I forgot to replace the batteries," Chad said.

I shook my head. There we stood, inside a haunted house, and I had the only working light. The fog surrounded us. "Something's wrong, we need to get out. One light won't do."

I couldn't remember how we got here, but the plan wasn't working. I didn't know where we came in or where we'd left our bikes. "C'mon, there's nothing here."

Suddenly a loud crash sounded behind us!

"Ahh! What was that?"

"Look out!"

"It's coming right for us!"

Thoughts of glory and triumph faded as I focused on my very survival. There was only one thing to do: GET OUT!

I whirled around, but my light couldn't pierce the fog. Then I heard a sound of scraping on the walls from the other side! I whirled again.

"It's behind us!"

"I can't see!" Mike's voice yelled out.

"This way," Shane said.

"NO!" I yelled at Shane as he moved forward into the fog without me. "Stay together," I said, hoping Mike and Chad would follow, but I turned the light around and found no one there. "Shane, Mike, Chad!" No answer.

At that moment, something hit the floor in front of me with a thud. I stepped back, holding the beam of my flashlight forward. "Where's my bat? I thought I brought my bat!"

"THUD!"

This time it was closer. The beam of my flashlight started fading! I knocked it against my leg and it went out, leaving only the sound of heavy breathing.

"Thump thump, thump thump."

My ears rang with the sound getting closer. *DO SOMETHING BESIDES STAND HERE!* A voice cried out in my head. Darkness overtook me.

I awoke with a start, my bedclothes drenched in sweat. "A dream. It was just a dream."

I sat up, immediately wondering what caused such a dream. I reasoned that it must be a sense carried over from a time when human life was threatened daily and instinct, not technology, was our only defense. This sense existed as an inner voice inside me warning of impending danger.

My inner voice activated and told me not to go to the house. But there was another voice present. It was the same voice I heard whenever my mom specifically told me not to do something and the voice in turn said, "Oh, go ahead, mom won't find out." This voice was hypnotic.

The dream was a warning. We were not prepared. I turned my flashlight on and grabbed a notebook putting my pencil to work:

Equipment: flashlights, batteries... new batteries... baseball bat... candles, no, might start a fire.

What if we run into trouble? Shane... fast, Chad... fast, me... fast, Mike... medium but fast enough. Rendezvous point?

No one is sick. Need a test of courage. Scary movies, stay the night at the cemetery—no, too cold, do later. I continued writing until I nodded off.

The next day we rode over to Shane's house after school.

"If you guys help me with my chores, then we can have some time to play," Shane said.

I nodded and Chad and Mike headed to the chicken pen to check for eggs and spread feed while Shane and I headed out to feed the pony and clean the stall.

"Why do you have two stalls?" I asked Shane.

"The one by those old barns is too small," Shane said. "That's what my dad said."

"Oh. How come we never come back here to play?"

"We aren't supposed to go pass the coral and those old barns are creep," Shane said pointing to a row of dilapidated buildings that ran east to west behind his house.

"Man, I hate all these chores," Shane kicked the ground. "I don't get to play football or baseball. In the summer it just gets worse because I have to mow the lawn."

"I guess that makes two of us," I said. "At least you don't have to get allergy shots all the time. We can always play sports together." We finished cleaning up the stall and headed back to the house where we met Mike and Chad.

"Wow! You guys found six eggs," Shane said surprised as Mike and Chad showed him the eggs. "My mom is sure to let us play now."

His mom gave us permission to play until dinner so we went up to his room on the second story of his house.

"You're lucky to have your own room," Mike said.

"I have my own room," Chad said. "But it's not as clean as this."

"My mom makes me keep it cleaned up," Shane said.

"Cool rock posters," Chad said looking at some of the posters Shane had on his walls. Along with two matching dressers and desk, Shane's twin bed sat to one corner of his room which overlooked the main road that ran in front of his house.

"As soon as my dad is done with the addition downstairs, I get to move into my parent's room at the end of the hall. It's a little bigger than mine. He plans to finish over Christmas break."

"Close the door," I said and recounted my dream for the others.

"Wow, tough dream," Shane said.

"I know. Now you understand why we need to have a plan."

"We're going to end up on the side of a milk carton," Chad said hanging his head. "Goodbye, cruel world."

While the three of us sat on Shane's bed, Mike sat across the room on a small chair at Shane's desk and said nothing.

"If you don't think we're ready, then, don't go," Shane said.

"No," I said. "Now we have to go more than ever. Something must be there."

Shane squinted and looked at the ceiling. "Okay, other than good flashlights and batteries, what else do we need, Professor?"

"Professor?"

"You're always studying and planning," Shane said. "I decided that name fits you."

I pulled out some notes.

"See," Shane said pointing to my notes.

"Hmm. I guess I can live with that nickname."

"What about a camera?" Chad said.

"Ghosts don't show up on film, do they?"

"I won't be sticking around long enough to take a picture if one shows up," Chad said.

"Shouldn't we tell someone we are going," Mike said, finally joining in the conversation. "In case something happens."

"At least they'll know where to find our bodies," Chad joked. No one laughed.

"Do you know anyone at school who's been to a haunted house?" Shane asked.

"I don't suppose many have," I replied. "Not here. But in a big city I bet there are lots."

"What about Doug or Eric? Should we let them go?" Chad asked.

"They're too old," Shane said. "Once you turn sixteen, it's all about cars and girls. And then you can't trust your own friends because girls cloud your judgment."

"How do you know?" I asked, but Shane nodded like he knew it was true.

"It's true," Chad said. "I have two older brothers."

"Just no one go alone. Not to the house or when we're in the house. Nothing's going to happen, and we'll make sure we can get out fast. So we need to plan our escape ahead of time and where we'll meet."

"Good idea. What else?" Shane asked.

"We need to wear dark clothes so no one can see us. Shane, you need to tie your shoes. And get to our house early so we can cover your reflectors with tape." Shane looked confused. "So cars can't see you."

"Oh. Don't worry, I'll be ready," Shane said.

"No joking around when we get inside the house. No scaring one another."

"Yeah, in the movies someone always gets killed when they mess around," Mike said. We all nodded.

"If you hear a noise, don't panic. Make sure you know where everyone else is at all times. Don't shine your flashlight into anyone's eyes. Our eyes will need to adjust to the dark."

"What about candles?"

"Fire hazard. No matches in the house. My dad said that's how the house that used to be there burned down. One more thing," I looked around the room. "Everyone needs to be ready to go. If you think you're going to be too afraid, stay behind."

In the minutes that followed, we each retreated into our own little corner of the room.

"If something grabs me," Shane started, "you guys better help and not run away. I mean, you ever see where a guy is with a girl or with a friend, and like the killer, a monster or a man grabs him and he's putting up a fight but no one helps?"

I laughed before replying. "Or they stand there to afraid to help."

"Screaming most of the time like that's going to help," Shane said.

"If they'd help maybe they'd beat the monster, because they're the next in line. Of course then the movie would have to end," I said.

"Good thing most of those movies aren't real," Shane said.

"That's what you think. But who knows?"

"Shane, time for your friends to go," Shane's mom's voice rang out.

"See you tomorrow at school." With Mike and Chad following we left on our bikes riding down the same road that the Round House was on, but on the opposite side of where our lane intersected.

"Man, Shane's house is kind of creepy," Chad said on the ride back.

"I know," Mike said. "It looks more like a big old house that would be haunted then the one we are going too."

I looked back at the house as we rode away. "Maybe that's why he's not afraid to go to the Round House."

CHAPTER SEVEN

FINDING OUR DESTINY

"SURRENDER!"

"Never!" the captain rang out. "We win or we die!" He took up position for the final battle.

The looks exchanged among the men revealed some of them knew they would not live through the day. The smell of sweat and dirt thick in the air, we'd come too far to give up.

"Louie, phone!" my mom called out.

"Gentlemen, the battle will have to wait." The plastic army men sprawled out on my desk breathed a sigh of relief as they survived another day. I headed toward the back room.

There were two phones in the house, one by the kitchen and one in my parents' bedroom at the back of the house. The bedroom offered more privacy.

"I've got it," I called out and waited for the other phone to be hung up.

"We still going?" Shane asked.

"We go or we die!" I stated then laughed. "Did you ask permission yet?"

"My mom said I had to wait until tomorrow night to find out."

"I guess it's only Wednesday. Is something wrong?" I asked.

"No, I just don't think she likes to say *yes* too early in case something comes up. But she didn't say no so that means if nothing comes up, I'll probably get to come over."

"Glad we're clear on that," I shook my head knowing Shane couldn't see me. "I think we're ready."

"Hey, I was thinking about what we were talking about in the treehouse. You know, that you and Mike go to church. I mean, if there is a ghost or something in that house, I don't even go to church or anything. You don't think I could go to, you know, the bad place that if I say the name I'll get grounded."

Shane's question surprised me. I did go to church but I didn't know the answer. "I suppose if God is protecting me, then he'd probably protect you because you were with me," I said.

"Then you better make sure we don't split up once we're inside the house. And Mike better stay with Chad because he don't go to church either."

"I don't plan on any of us being in the house alone. If we get that far," I said.

"I know what you mean. This week is really dragging."

Shane's words matched how I felt. It was as though time were taunting us, every minute dragged and every second made sure it was counted. The house was there, vacant, waiting for us. Chad was ready, Mike had accepted going, and I was eager despite the little warnings from my inner voice.

"All we need is for you to get permission and we're on," I said.

"I'll call you tomorrow night."

I went back to my room to find Mike standing over my desk. "Looks like they weren't doing so good." He pointed to my army men.

"They're brave. I'm sure some of them would've made it. Shane called. He doesn't know yet about Friday."

"We going anyway?"

I smiled, encouraged by brother's implied participation. "We wait no more."

Thursday evening I called Shane. While we were on the phone he asked his parents if he could spend the night at my house Friday night, and they approved. Chad and I met after school to finalize our plans of how we were going to deal with Mutt. Everything fell into place, and that night I hardly slept a wink. When I heard a noise across the room I realized my brother was having the same problem sleeping.

"Mike," I whispered, "what's that noise?"

"I was trying to get my flashlight to work so I can check on this cricket I caught by the tree house.

"I thought we had an agreement that all bugs stay outside."

"This one's harmless. I need to keep him until tomorrow. Herman needs to eat you know."

"Uggh. New subject. Make sure when you see Chad tomorrow, you tell him we need to meet right after school. As soon as he gets home he needs to come over."

Mike got his flashlight to work and pointed the beam to a small glass jar he held above his head that contained the cricket.

"I already told him."

"Make sure to remind him to bring the extra flashlights."

"Do you think the house is haunted?" Mike asked, shining the light in my face.

"Hey!" I cried out covering my eyes. He turned off the light and we waited to see if we woke our parents. "If not, we have our back-up story in place."

After seeing the Round House close up I felt I didn't need to exaggerate things. The house was mysterious enough all on its own.

"I couldn't tell the difference. You're always making stuff up like that. I'm just worried."

"Me too," I said.

"About what?"

"Getting caught. Being away from home that late at night."

"We've taken midnight excursions before," Mike said. "If we get in trouble, we deal with it. Just keep your grades up and they won't go so harsh."

"I guess what I'm really worried about is that we might actually find something"

"If that's the case," Mike said, "then I guess after tomorrow night you'll have a real story to tell. Goodnight."

In a few moments, the slow rhythm of breathing from the other side of the room let me know my brother was fast asleep.

"Goodnight," I whispered. Anticipation kept me up the rest of the night, and judging by the sounds coming from across the room, Mike didn't sleep well either. I didn't know what was on his mind, but an array of scenarios raced through mine. My doubts, outweighed by the need for adventure, slowly drifted into the darkness around me. Only one issue remained on my mind.

I turned on my flashlight and pointed it down at the floor as I got out of bed. "Let's just make sure you stay in that jar." I removed the jar from my brother's bed and sat it on the dresser. "This should do the trick." I placed a large book on top of the jar.

Satisfied that I had secured the cricket and put my gramar book to good use, I went back to bed.

🐦 🐦

The week went slow, but Friday zipped by, as if the master of time himself were eager to see four fools fall fast into their folly.

"I got the gear and the flashlights ready," Chad said with a backpack in his hands.

"You got the special stuff?" I asked.

"Yep! Pyromania, here we come."

"We might as well get some practice in while we're waiting for the others. Shane's riding over as soon as he finishes his chores."

We stood in the dirt field behind our house playing catch. I tossed the football to Chad. He dropped the backpack and caught the ball then raised his arms indicating a score.

"Why don't you bring the rest of the stuff over," I called out. "We'll put it in the tree house."

Chad threw the ball back and turned to go home.

"You might as well bring your bike over and make sure the tires are aired up," I yelled after him. He frowned at me. "Oh, that's right, they don't need air."

As Chad disappeared through the wood gate, Shane cruised down the driveway and slid to a halt in front of me.

"I hope you're ready to do that kind of driving tonight," I said.

"It's just too bad we're going at night," Shane said. "No one's going to notice how cool I look in the dark."

I laughed. "Come on. Let's tape those reflectors so no one can see you."

Shane and I went to the shed and taped the reflectors on his bike.

Chad brought the gear in a duffle bag that he handed to Shane and then went back for his bike.

"Bikes our good, let's go see what's in this bag," I said. Shane and I climbed up to the tree house before Chad came back. I poured the contents of the bag out on the floor: Two shoulder pads, two football helmets, and three flashlights toppled out. I immediately checked that both flashlights worked as Chad's head appeared at the hatch.

"Hey, your cast is gone," Shane noted as Chad entered the tree house.

"They took it off this morning," Chad said. "I parked my bike at the base of the tree. Did you try the pads out?" he asked, looking at me as he took a seat on the floor.

"We should put some carpet in here."

"Or get some lawn chairs."

"A heater would be nice."

As we tried on the pads Shane looked at me, and it occurred to me that we hadn't made any provision for equipment for him.

"I have an extra baseball bat you can carry," I said as I tried on the shoulder pads and adjusted the straps. "They'll fit."

"I'm not worried," Shane said. "If anything happens, I'll be quick as lightning." He moved his head and shoulders, dodging an invisible tackler. Chad and I laughed, but we knew his ability was real and many times he'd managed to dodge both of us in a game of football.

"The shoulder pads fit, but the helmet's too big," I said. "And I think it will block my view."

"Right," Shane said, eyeing the helmet. "And you're the leader so we wouldn't want anything to happen to that big head, would we?"

"You should wear your helmet and any other pads you have," I suggested to Chad.

"Hey, it's not funny; my mom said she's taking me to get some tests because I break my bones so easy."

"Do we have a suit of armor for him?" Shane said laughing.

I turned to Shane and winked. "You're going to be the first one in. That way we'll know if it's safe."

"I just hope we're still kidding around like this and having fun by the end of the night," Shane said. "So this is it. We're going tonight."

I looked at him and then at Chad. Everyone sat down. The air was still outside. Were we prepared? Could we be facing the end of our young lives? Minutes ticked by while the three of us remained in deep thought.

"Wham!" The hatch slammed open.

"Ahh!"

"What the!"

Mike's entrance caught us off guard. "Did I scare you?"

"No, we were just practicing, uh, for tonight," Shane said.

"Sorry I'm late. Our football meeting went longer than expected. They had to pass out all the awards and stuff." He held up several certificates.

"Hey, good job!"

"Right, good job."

"You guys helped me practice," Mike said. "Letting me hit you and all."

"Very funny," I said.

"Not that any of you were a real challenge, moving so slow and all."

"Now that we're all here, let's discuss the plan." I pulled out the paper bag on which I had sketched a map of the Round House and its surroundings.

"I just hope it isn't for nothing. I'd like to be able to see a ghost," Shane said.

"Cool shoulder pads," Mike said, looking at Chad and me. "I'll get mine and we can play football in these tomorrow."

"If there is a tomorrow," Chad said, though no one laughed at his wisecrack this time.

The more we talked about it, the more I realized there was no turning back. The quest was real. So was the danger.

"Okay," I said, "Shane, you and Mike will carry two flashlights, one for yourselves and one for each of us."

"Why? What are you going to carry?" Shane asked.

On cue, Chad produced a string of fireworks and some sparklers, handing some to me with a smile.

"Chad and I have another task." I grinned and raised an eyebrow. "When we get near the house where Mutt is, we'll stop long enough to light the sparklers. Then you and Mike will go in front to lure him out. When Mutt comes out to chase you, we'll sneak up on him and surprise him with these."

"I'm not sure I'm happy with being the bait at the end of the hook but all right!" Shane said, giving me a high five from his sitting position.

"When we get to the house," I continued, "we're going to take one last look to make sure no one is there. I figure we can hide across the street here," I pointed.

Mike and Chad moved closer and examined the map.

"I think we can leave our bikes on the other side of the street. There's a field on this side." I pointed to the map where I had drawn some brown wavy lines. "And we can go across it to the back of the house."

"How are we going to get in?" Mike asked.

"I think we need to look in a few windows first. After that, on this side…" I pointed to a rather poor sketch I had made of the house. "There's a busted window on the second floor covered with plastic."

Chad nodded, "I remember that window."

"You want me to climb up to that window," Shane said, "and go through?" I nodded. "Are there any trees near the house? That would make things a lot easier."

"No," I said. "There is one in the front yard, but it's too far from the house. There's a bunch of gutters and stuff. You can climb up one of those or get on my shoulders. Either way, you go through the window, and then you can open the back door and let us in."

It was an unspoken consensus to let Shane, with his wiry frame, be the one who would get us into the house.

"The back door?" Shane asked.

"Yes. Let's stay away from the front of the house just in case any cars come by. Unless you can't get the back door open. It might be late but we can't take a chance that a car goes by and sees us."

"I'm the smallest," Chad said. "I bet I can get through that window."

"NO!" three voices said in unison. Wide-eyed, Chad put his head down.

"Hey, we can't afford you getting hurt. How would you explain that one. Besides, you're still going. You're just as brave as the rest of us."

"I'm just tired of always worrying about getting hurt," Chad said.

"Don't worry, you've never broken a bone around us," Shane said.

"I guess you're right," Chad said. "But don't expect me to wait around for you if something goes wrong. I'm like," Chad flashed his fist across his body thumb out, "out of there."

Shane smiled. "If the window is on that side, why don't we go down this row of trees between the houses? That way we can jump over that small fence, and we won't have to worry about the barbed-wire fence in the field."

"Good idea. And all of this time I thought you weren't so bright."

Shane shook his head and rolled his eyes. "Besides, last time we ran through a field I tripped in the loose dirt. We can hide in the trees if a car passes."

"You're probably right. We can see better when we get there," I said. The fact that we wouldn't have to worry about crossing a barbed-wire fence appealed to me. I rubbed my chest where I had a scar from a barbed wire fence. "I don't remember how much room there is between the trees and the next house. I don't want to wake up the old man, he was kind of grouchy."

"What if he's up or someone is at the house?" Mike asked.

"If someone is at the house we have to come back. If the neighbor is up or we get noticed before we are in the house we will keep going to the next intersection and take the back road, wait a while, and then come back."

"I hope no one is there, I'm ready to do this," Chad said.

"That's right!" Shane said. "Only the brave are invited to the quest," he added, balling his hand into a fist he held his arm across his chest in a secretive salute.

"It's getting dark," Mike said, peering out one of the cracks in the wall.

"Right," I said. "If anything goes wrong, get out of the house and go as fast as you can to the first road crossing on the way back."

"Why there?" Shane asked.

"It's the first intersection. We can change our way back or split up if we need to. Before we go inside tonight, park your bikes by the base of the tree. Lay them down so no one will notice."

"What time do we go?"

"Right after Shock Theatre."

"What about your brother and sister?"

"I don't know how we got so lucky, but they're both staying with friends tonight. One last thing," I looked at Chad. "You think you can part with one of your tokens for Shane?"

Chad pulled out a handful of medallions that had stamped pictures on the front and names and sayings on the back and handed one to Shane.

"What's this?"

"Saint Christopher. He's the saint of travelers," Chad said.

"Thanks."

Swearing an oath to tell no one else of our plans and realizing that we still needed to work out our code, we climbed down and placed our bikes at the front of the driveway by the tree house. Shane and I went to get the bats.

"Wait a minute," I called out. "No, that's my bat."

"What? Aren't they the same," Shane said holding both in the air.

"Oh no. Look," I took the one from his right hand and turned it showing him the notches I'd carved. "This is my home run tally."

"Looks kinda weak."

"We don't exactly play baseball a lot around here. Come on; let's clamp these to our bikes."

It was too cold for us to ask if we could sleep outside, so we decided to sneak out later.

Being the last one in the house as we headed in for dinner I stepped inside the green doublewide trailer. Holding the door open, I stopped and looked back at the sunset.

All but a small edge of the sun disappeared below the mountains that lined the western sky. A dull glow bounced off the fluffy white clouds that moved in, and the evening seemed calm and pleasant. The sun in cool shades of orange and yellow dipped behind the clouds and a light breeze caressed my face, the fingers causing me to shiver. The last remnants of light faded and gave into the darkness whispering a warning that my inner voice could hear; "You're on your own now."

Chapter Eight

ADVENTURE

"This is it," my hands trembled and my voice cracked. "Don't blow it now. We need to keep it down to make sure my parents are sleeping but not get so settled we fall asleep."

Friday night was upon us. The one night a week we could stay up late without consequence. We had no reason to get up early Saturday whereas Sunday we often went to church, early, to avoid the crowd of the latter mass.

My mom and dad headed to bed leaving us a bowl of freshly popped pop corn and gave us the one soda we were allowed per week.

"I'll get the sleeping bags, you get the pillows," I said to Mike. He headed down the hall returning with every available pillow not in use and spread them across the floor. I took the sleeping bags and spread them out.

"You know," Shane said, "this trailer is so big inside it seems like just a normal house."

"Of course it's normal," I said.

"No, that's not what I mean. How many people have doublewide trailers that they live in? Not many that I know. And most trailers are in a trailer park, not out here among the rest of the houses."

"I guess I never paid attention," I said and went about the business of setting up the room.

We turned the lights off so only the television remained as a source of light. The living room became a different world in the flickering magic that took us beyond the corporeal realm. Beyond that light lie the unknown, subject to our imagination and exaggeration. Reality became a distant echo, barely audible.

"Don't worry about us," Shane said from his wrestling position on the floor. He and Chad were locked in combat and I could tell, like me, they were too anxious to think about sleeping. Thud! They rolled around.

"Hey, I said keep it down. Mike, check the hall."

Mike peeked around the corner and jumped back. "Dad's coming!"

"What do we do?"

"Act normal." We sat in front of the television watching the movie as my dad entered the kitchen.

"Why do we do this every Friday night?" Mike asked.

The refrigerator door opened and then closed. I listened to hear if my dad had left the kitchen. "It's our one chance to have an excuse to stay up really late and because there's no school tomorrow."

"I mean, why do we always watch this show?"

No footsteps exited the kitchen. I heard a few other drawers open and then came my dad's voice. "I know I had some electrical tape around here." His footsteps went across the kitchen floor and back down the hall.

"Science Fiction will make you creative," I said. "All week we do same routine and boring things. Watch comedies and dramas about surreal life. This show is about stuff that's weird and unusual. I'm telling you, it's good for your mental growth."

Mike's left eye squinted as he looked left. Then his right eyes squinted as he looked right. "The show's boring, they need better writers. And you can tell it's not real."

I nodded and shrugged my shoulders.

"I'll get up and see if dad's gone. We're clear," he said, looking around the corner.

"This movie isn't that good," Shane said.

I looked at the clock. It was half past midnight. "Mike. Check if Mom and Dad's door is closed."

I opened the hall closet and pulled out some old coats, "here, stuff the sleeping bags with these," and handed them to Chad and Shane.

"Should we leave the TV on?" Chad asked.

"Uh, I don't know. Let's turn it off in case dad sneaks down the hall. If he doesn't hear it, he'll think we're asleep. Otherwise, he might try to scare us or something," I replied.

"Door's closed," Mike said, standing at the entrance to the living room.

I heard three sighs join mine at the sound of his words. No one moved. We looked down at the stuffed sleeping bags.

"What if they wake up in the morning and all that's left of us is these stuffed dummies?" Chad said. "They'll never know what happened to us."

"Okay, we leave a note," I said. I grabbed a pen and paper from my dad's study that was adjacent to the living room. "If we're not here when you wake up, tell Eric we went to the Round House. He'll know where to look," I muttered as I wrote.

"This is what we've been waiting for, right?" Shane asked.

"Let's go," I said, turning off the television. "And be quiet until we get on the road, the bedroom window is right by the driveway."

"Milk carton, here we come," Chad said as the four of us made our way silently out the door and down the driveway to the tree house.

"Brrr," Shane whispered. "I wish it was warmer."

"The cold's in our favor," I whispered. "The bedroom window is closed and we probably won't see anybody outside at this hour."

On a partly cloudy October night, the moon and stars granted us enough light to see our way. Shane climbed to the tree house and tossed down the equipment. Mike brought his football pads, and the three of us, minus Shane, took off our jackets and put on shoulder pads. Chad wore a quarterbacks' helmet that had a single face guard, minus the chinstrap, for extra protection.

"You're sure we don't have to worry about Mutt?" Shane asked.

"These will keep Mutt in check," I replied, flashing the fireworks Chad gave me. "Just make sure you pick up enough speed to get by him. When he comes after you, we'll surprise him alright." I winked, but the effect was lost in the darkness of the night. Despite being armed for battle, if we encountered trouble our strategy was extremely solid; we'd run, ride, or hide.

Chad and I carefully picked up our bikes and walked them to the top of the driveway. I checked the road for cars. "At least there's no traffic."

"That's because everyone's in bed," Mike said.

"The smart ones are," Chad commented.

"Come on guys," Shane said as he knelt down and tied his shoelaces. "This is our adventure. Something we'll always remember."

Serious looks crossed serious faces. Chad strapped on his helmet. Mike and I tightened our shoulder pads. Four young boys mounted metal, two-wheeled steeds and prepared for adventure. Uniting at the middle of the road, our shadows, cast to the east of us by the widely spaced streetlights, looked unnatural as we began our ride.

With but a few street lamps around the intersections, a dark road lie before us. I noticed the breeze had a chill to it, but my body heat began to rise. We had picked a fine night for our adventure

We took a determined right at the first intersection and headed down County High Road to the Round House and our quest for glory. Unlike the main road, this one had no streetlights and only a few outside lights from the houses, sporadically placed along the road, helped guide us. For the most part, we were riding by the light of the moon.

I sped up, took the lead, and slowly came to a stop. The others pulled up beside me.

"Time for plan A," I said and nodded. Like a crack squad of espionage soldiers, Chad and I pulled our packs out and removed the fireworks while Mike and Shane moved into position in front of us.

"I hope you guys pull this off," Shane said. "Maybe you'll scare him so good he'll leave you alone for the rest of his life."

"I just hope no one calls the cops," I said. "You ready?"

"No, but let's go anyway."

"No matter what, keep going to the next lane. I don't want to be around long enough to find out if we wake anyone up."

"Okay."

Although dark, Chad's smile flickered to life in the flame of his lighter. He lit a sparkler and handed it to me before lighting one for himself. The light illuminated our faces with a splotchy glow and livened the mood.

"You're in the lead now. Don't slow down for nothing," I said, holding the row of Black Cats in one hand and the sparkler pinned against the handlebar in the other. Shane and Mike took off down the road.

"Let's go," I said to Chad as we watched Shane and Mike disappear. They were going much faster than us and were already a ways down the road.

Laden with fireworks, Chad and I struggled to pick up speed, and by the time Shane and Mike crossed Mutt's path, they were a good ten yards ahead of us making it by Mutt without incident.

"He's sleeping or chained up," Chad called out. "We prepared for nothing."

Feeling the heat against my skin, I looked down to check the progress of the sparkler, worried that it might singe my hand or go out. I considered dropping it. Then in the dancing light a dark shadow appeared by me and I heard GROWLING!

"Oh, crap!" Chad said, getting my attention.

Hurtling toward us at top speed the black terror was on a direct collision course. *THIS IS NOT PART OF THE PLAN!*

Mutt ignored the bait. Shane and Mike went by him too fast, and instead of following them he was zeroing in on us.

"Throw something!" I yelled. Everything seemed to happen in fast-forward. Being that I was on the left side of Chad, Mutt encountered me first and was at full run right beside me before I had time to light the fireworks. I tried to gain speed by standing up to bring my full weight down on the pedals and dropped my sparkler.

With no way to light the firecrackers, I pulled hard on my handlebars and pushed my feet down on the pedals. I felt Mutt nip at the back of my heel, his teeth seeking out my foot each time it rounded the sprocket. Thoughts of failure rushed through my head. We wouldn't make it to the house and I might get bitten.

PEDAL FASTER!

I felt Mutt brush up against my leg again and pushed harder, giving everything I had.

"BAM! BAM! BAM!" Suddenly flashes of smoke and lights littered the street. The explosions went off right under my bike. Chad succeeded in lighting his fireworks and threw them down near my pedals. Stunned by the noise and smoke, Mutt broke off his attack and Chad dropped his sparkler, joining me as we rode like the wind down the street.

"Go!"

"Don't stop!"

I glanced back to see Mutt's dark form, highlighted in the flashes, heading home faster than I'd ever seen him move. Inside I laughed. The time for payback was at hand: for all the times that dog had chased me, making my heart pound to the point it felt like it might leap right out of my chest. For all the smug looks he had given us while sitting in the road, his tail wagging up in the air as we raced away in terror. Tonight it was his turn to run scared, and run he did. With the fireworks still igniting, erupting and flashing in the still of the night, Mutt ran home with his tail between his legs.

"It worked!" Shane hollered as Chad and I approached the intersection. We stopped to catch our breath.

"That was close," I replied, checking that my shoes were intact. "That was a lot of firecrackers."

"I accidentally lit the whole pack," Chad said.

"Not exactly to plan."

"I'll say," Chad said, holding his hand with an expression of mixed glee and pain. He had burned it with the sparkler. "It's not bad, just stings a little. I can't believe I made that throw. You were going so fast."

"Maybe you should be the quarterback from now on."

Chad smiled.

"It worked, Professor," Shane said. "That's all that matters. It didn't have to be perfect."

"Let's get going before anyone comes out to see what all the noise is about," I said and started pedaling. "It's lucky for us the house where Mutt lives is right by the school. Anyone that heard our noise might think it was kids goofing off at the school playground."

"Let's keep riding fast, just in case," Shane said.

I glanced back a few times.

"No lights," Shane said. "We didn't even wake anyone."

"So far so good."

"No stopping us now. Haunted or not, here we come."

The next mile we covered without talking, our bike tires humming along the asphalt in a hypnotic cadence, eyes forward, ears out, listening to the silence of the night. My imagination worked overtime. The risk I was taking made easier by the fact that I was in good company.

The roads were usually quiet at this time of night with the exception of the occasional reveler coming home late. We usually rode apart in two's or single file, but this late at night we rode packed tight, as one singular form. Faces forward, nothing existed but the path ahead, there was no past, no going back. Every minute away from home, a minute closer to glory. Each stroke of the pedal carried us closer to our destiny, and danger.

"To the QUEST!" I couldn't help myself, the excitement poured out and I broke the silence.

"Ever notice how everything seems faster at night." Shane said. "I mean, is it me or are we riding faster than we would in the daytime?"

"I'm not even tired," Mike said. "And I've been up since six. I just hope it doesn't get any colder."

"I'm not tired either," Chad said. "I bet it will be colder on the way back."

"Not tired," I said, picking up the pace. "If you're feeling up to it, let's really move."

That youthful sense of invulnerability had overtaken any semblance of reason, and we headed to our destination without incident taking turns pulling out in front and falling back into formation. Mike led when we arrived at the house. He pulled off the road onto the shoulder opposite the Round House. The others stopped with him.

I kept going until I passed the house and turned around surveying the surroundings. In addition to the shards of moonlight that scraped down through the clouds, there was a single outside light on the front porch of the house next door, spilling illumination across both yards. The Round House itself stood void of light and lacked any sign of inhabitance. I pulled up to the others and stopped.

All eyes focused on the house. "I had lots of energy just a few minutes ago," Mike said. "I could have ridden across the whole city tonight. A warm bed sounds good about now."

"Two stories of sheer terror," I said. My feeling of invulnerability was tamed by the daunting task before us.

"We came, we saw," Shane said in a nervous voice. "It was dark outside, the house looks dark inside. Everyone remembers the story we made up right?"

"Yep," Chad said. "I say we go home and make something up. I mean, I'm too young to die."

"Ha-ha. Keep your voices down," I whispered. "Everything is just as planned. No one lives there and there's no traffic."

I looked at the house and couldn't help but notice the rounded windows gave the appearance of eyes staring out at us. For a brief moment, I wondered if the others were right in thinking we should leave. The house looked different in the night. In the daylight it appeared modern, but under a dark sky it looked like an ancient castle built of stone with its rounded arches and doorways.

"It's not lighting up like in Doug's story," Chad whispered. His voice echoed oddly from under the football helmet he wore.

"I read that some hauntings only happen on the same day or at the same time of the event that set them off," I said.

Everyone looked at me as if to say, "We followed you this far, now it's you first."

I pointed to the trees that separated the two houses, and we walked our bikes to the first one. Shane walked his bike in and stopped. I nodded to him noting that it was no longer visible from the road. He laid his bike down on the ground and the rest of us followed his lead. He took out the flashlights from his coat pocket and handed one to me and headed down the row of trees.

"It looks deserted," Chad whispered.

We fell flat against the ground startled by the sound of something close by. "Did you hear that?"

"SHH!" A strange sound of crunching came from the direction of the house. I looked at the house and then at the road. Chad shrugged his shoulders and shook his head when I looked at him. Again, the sound came from the direction Shane had gone.

"It's Shane!" The crushing sound of leaves penetrated the silence as he made his way down the row of trees. I looked at Chad and Mike and we stood

"I guess we don't have to worry about our reaction time," I said brushing myself off.

"No one panicked," Mike said. "Or screamed."

"I'm not so sure that's a good thing," I said, undoing the straps holding the baseball bat to my bike frame. We followed Shane, walking between the adobe wall and the row of trees. I turned back to see Mike was not with us. I went back to where he stood.

"Someone should guard the bikes," I said, assuming he didn't want to enter the house. "We might need a quick escape. Might be better if you stay here." I knew I didn't sound convincing. So,

I added a twist to make the request sound genuine. "Plus you can stand watch and warn us if anyone is coming. Just throw a rock at the roof. When we hear it, we'll know to get out." Mike nodded to me and stayed behind.

"I wouldn't stay out here by myself," Chad whispered as we met up with Shane.

"At least inside we'll be together," I replied.

Shane, Chad, and I were ready to cross over the small adobe wall when Mike came up behind us, giving us a start. "I guess he agreed," I said.

"Wouldn't want you to get in trouble without me," Mike stated.

"As long as we remain crouching, we're hidden from view of both houses," I said. "The trees behind us should keep us hidden form the neighbor."

I made my way up to the small, beige, adobe wall in front of us where I surveyed the scene. Shane came up beside me.

"Crossing the yard we're in plain sight," I whispered. "That is, if there is somebody inside to see us."

"Looks pretty quiet to me," Shane replied. "And dark. But I already said that, right?"

"Where's your bat?" I asked. He looked down at his hands as if expecting it to materialize.

"I guess I left it on the bike. I'll go get it."

"Oh, no. You're not getting away that easy. I don't think you'll need it, and besides, I have mine," I said, holding up the wooden bat for him to see. "If something comes after you just duck and I'll aim high." We turned our attention to the Round House. "Let's get to that tree."

"Right. Then I'll go around the side to the back. Maybe I can see in one of the back windows. We should look if there are any cars in the garage," Shane said. "Just to be safe."

"Good thinking. If it's deserted, there won't be any cars in the garage. Mike, you and Chad stay here until we get back. One of you watches the house in case any lights come on and keep an eye on the windows for movement. The other one can keep an eye on the neighbor's house. Stay behind the trees. We don't need that old man calling the police."

"What should we do if we spot something?" Chad asked.

"Whistle. You know, like they do in the movies. And keep your flashlights off unless it's an emergency."

Shane and I crawled over the adobe wall to take a look around while Mike and Chad watched both houses. Shane was ideally suited for quickness and stealth. He had a flexible frame and excellent balance. I was about to take another step when I heard someone whistle behind me. Shane and I immediately climbed back over the wall, looking around for signs of trouble.

"What is it?" I asked in a hushed voice, leaning back to where Chad and Mike were crouching.

"Sorry. I was just practicing," Chad replied.

"Geez," Shane said with a sigh. "You nearly gave me a heart attack."

"No more practicing," I said, shaking my head.

Shane and I went over the wall again, crossed over to the Maple tree in the front yard, and then sidled over to the side of the house. We were fast, but not as quiet as we wanted to be. The leaves in the yard gave away our every step. Suddenly, Shane stopped and I froze, looking back at him.

"What is it?" I whispered.

"SHH!" I waited.

"I thought I heard something."

I stood still and listened, but heard nothing. He started to walk and I followed him. Then, he stopped abruptly and turned to me.

"There it is again."

I listened but heard nothing more than the wind. "What did it sound like?"

"I'm not sure how to describe it. It could have come from behind us but I'm not sure."

I took a couple of steps forward until I was next to him. He looked down at the bottom of my coat and then up at my face, hanging and shaking his head. It was then I realized what he'd been hearing. Looking down, I took a couple of steps forward. "That the sound?"

"That's it?" He nodded.

Our coats betrayed our every move as the lower parts brushed against our jeans whistling forth into the air, "swish, swish."

"Between this and the leaves we're sure to get caught if anyone is home," Shane whispered, barely containing his laughter. "Unless they're old and have hearing aids or something."

"Crunch, crunch, swish, swish." As quietly as possible, we began moving again, but the ridiculous amount of noise we made in our effort to be quiet continued to hinder our progress.

At the side of the house we crouched in a corner between the front and side. "This room is attached to the living room," I whispered to Shane. "Maybe a study or something like that. The bedrooms are probably on the second floor."

"A little like my house," Shane said.

"Except yours isn't haunted."

Shane didn't respond.

"I'll meet you in the back yard in a couple of minutes," I whispered, pointing to the back of the house. "If something goes wrong, get back to the others." Shane nodded and began working his way down the side. I could see him peeking in the windows as he went.

I headed across the front to the garage to check for cars. So far, everything was going as planned. I crossed the driveway and moved quickly up to the garage, plastering myself against the wall like a SWAT team member; my bat held as though it were a rifle. I looked back at the house. On this side there were two windows on each floor. The second floor had a small window that looked like a bathroom window and a larger one toward the front.

A large, second-story window overlooked the back yard. "I hope no one's watching," I said to myself. No lights were on and no movement came from inside the house. I felt my pulse in my neck and blood rushed to my head causing me to feel dizzy. I brushed off the spell and turned to the garage.

I peered in through the garage window. It was dark, but I could see enough to tell that there were no cars parked inside. Switching the bat to my left hand, I took out the small flashlight in my coat pocket and pressed the side button that made it turn on and off quickly. An old refrigerator sat against one wall and a ladder hung down in the back that went through an opening in the roof. There was no indication that anyone had recently been in the garage and no cars were inside it.

I moved back to the side of the garage and faced the house. I spotted Shane darting from the tin shed to the back of the house. I made my way across the driveway to the side of the house toward the back. Convinced no one lived in the house, I grew less cautious. On this side lie the fields so I didn't worry about being spotted by neighbors, only passing cars and there were none at this hour.

Peering through a window, I could see into the kitchen. I looked across the sink to a table that sat on the far side of the room. I froze! Someone was in the kitchen!

My legs locked and refused to carry me anywhere. At any moment, I would be spotted looking in the window by whoever lurked in the kitchen. *MOVE! RUN!* My brain cried out. I finally regained control and immediately ducked. I didn't get a good look at the person, it was too dark, but suddenly our whole plan was in jeopardy. Someone lived in the house and we would have to leave!

I hurried around to the back of the house, where I stopped and looked for Shane. I couldn't see him in the backyard so I quickly retraced my steps and moved across to the front. I wasn't going to chance crossing the backyard, where whoever stood in the kitchen would have a clear view of me.

"The sheriff may already be on the way!" I muttered. I needed to get back and organize an emergency evac. I crossed the front of the house to the corner where Shane and I agreed to meet.

I looked over to the adobe wall, where I spotted Mike and Chad peering back at me. *Where is SHANE?*

Suddenly, the familiar crunching sound of leaves came from the side of house. Shane emerged from around the corner, stepping without care and making tons of noise. I waved him over ready to bolt at the first sign of trouble, sure that the person I'd seen inside had spotted him.

"What are you doing?" Shane asked.

"SHH! I pulled him to the ground."

"Hey?"

"Keep your voice down. Did you see anyone in the house?"

"No. The back door is open," Shane whispered. "It leads into a kitchen. There's a dining room to the side, and I could see some furniture."

I suddenly realized it was Shane I had seen moving in the kitchen.

"No sign of anyone."

"The garage is empty." I tried to regain my composure sitting up I brushed the leaves off my coat.

"There's a few tools left in the shed, but it looks like it's been cleaned out. If anyone lived here I don't think the door would be unlocked." A few silent minutes passed between us.

"There's one way to make sure," I said, leading the way. We both crossed the yard and went over the wall, taking up positions by Mike and Chad.

"What did you see?" Mike asked.

"It looks empty," I quietly stated to the two faces barely visible in the dark, "but we're going to make sure. Get ready to run. Okay Shane."

Shane grabbed a rock and let it fly at the Round House. It smacked against the roof. "Thud! Clap, clap, clap." The sound echoed off the low hanging clouds as the rock rolled down the opposite side of the house and landed on the gravel driveway. It made more noise than I expected and we remained crouched behind the wall, peeking enough to see any signs of life.

"Watch the neighbor's house," I whispered to Mike as I peeked over the wall to get a better look. For several minutes we waited. The sound of nervous breathing filled the air. No sounds came from within, no lights, and no movement. We had knocked one last time and the house had answered us with a silent, *"Come in."*

"I say it's clear," Shane whispered. "And with the back door open, I don't have to go through that window," he pointed to the broken window on the second floor.

"Nice shot, by the way."

"Thanks."

"All right then," I stood, "to the back of the house. Keep quiet and no flashlights until we're inside."

"Don't shine them around the windows or into anyone's eyes," Shane added.

"If something happens, meet back here and get the bikes ready."

With as much stealth as the leaves and our coats would allow, the four of us made our way over the wall, down the side of the house, and to the back door. With the door unlocked we would easily find our way inside. Shane and Chad led the way with Mike and I following.

We edged around to the back and crouched below the window that ran across an enclosed porch. We moved in through a screen door. To my surprise, Shane hesitated. Seeing that I was waiting he whispered, "You're the leader."

I shook my head. "You're taking this leader thing too far." I entered with the others in tow.

We found ourselves faced with another wall that had two doors. I didn't know where the door to our extreme right led, but I knew from peeking in the side window earlier that the one on front of us led into the kitchen, where I'd seen Shane. As I peered through another set of windows into a dining room, I placed my hand on some boxes only to find them covered in a thick coat of dust.

Shane tried the kitchen door carefully. I saw his hand reaching for the knob. I crept over and could see him turning the knob and pushing but the door didn't move.

"It's jammed," Shane whispered. I flashed my light over and immediately noticed the back door opened outward; another oddity of the house. My puzzling glance wasted in the darkness between us, I gestured my hand outward in the direction Shane should have pulled.

If Shane was in the house earlier, he should have remembered how the door opened. Jumping out of the way as he opened the door, I didn't have time to ponder.

Shane and I crammed our way into the doorway, attempting to squeeze through at the same time. Neither of us backed off and I nudged through with my shoulder pads crowding Shane, causing him to turn sideways to make it through.

"Oomph!"

"Oww! Thanks."

What happened next still makes me shudder to think about. Spider webs can be works of art, engineering masterpieces, and a wonder of nature…unless you walk through one and don't know where the spider is. Making our way through the door, Shane and I felt that sticky, clinging sensation across our faces. A shiver ran down my spine, through my toes, and to the floor and I shuddered like a stiff board that suddenly was upended.

SPIDER WEB! My inner voice screamed!

With lightning-quick reflexes my hands shot up and swiped the web from my face as both the bat and the flashlight I carried fell to the floor.

"Phftt! Yuck! Uck!"

I stood there picking the strands from my face while Shane spit several times.

"I guess it's safe to say the house is deserted," he said, turning on his flashlight and pointing it downward.

"Thanks," I said using his light to regain my bat, flashlight, and confidence.

I didn't feel the need to whisper any more. The spider web across the doorway served as the final assurance no one had been through the doorway in a long time and that the house, despite the dusty furniture left behind, lie empty.

"No spider," Shane said and turned his flashlight off. "Maybe he got scared out of here too."

"I'm just glad my mouth wasn't open."

Shane laughed and moved away from the door to let Mike and Chad enter. "They go first if there are any more doors to go through."

"Good idea," I agreed and turned on my flashlight, pointing it to the white, stone-tiled floor.

Against the wall to the right stood a small wooden table with three high-back chairs, one at each end and one on the side away from the wall. To the left were cabinets, a sink, and a refrigerator. In front of us there were more cabinets around a stove that completed the kitchen and to the right of this; a dark opening... the beam of my flashlight went forward to reveal a hall that led to the rest of the house.

Shane moved forward and I followed. "Look," Shane said, "all the furniture is still here, but there's nothing on the counters. No coffee maker, toaster, cookbook, or spices."

"And no dishes in the sink. Not even a salt and pepper shaker on the table." I walked over to the refrigerator, grabbed the cold, metal handle and pulled. "SMOCK!" The sealed strip made an eerie sound as it came undone, breaking through the silence and echoing down the hall.

I shrugged my shoulders. "I didn't expect it to be so loud." No light or cold air came from within the refrigerator. "Empty," I said, turning back to the others. Our confidence grew, as did our carelessness.

"It's deserted, all right," Mike spoke up. "Even that spider web you walked through is old and the spider wouldn't have built it across a doorway that's disturbed often. They'd be in corners or windows, not in frequently used doorways."

"Any other bug issues we should know about?" I asked.

"In a deserted house insects are all over the place unless somebody sprayed. Especially with all the trees behind the house and that field next door, there'll be bugs under the carpets, in the walls, cabinets, and basement.

"This house looks clean."

"Doesn't matter," Mike replied. "They're here. In dark corners, damp places. That spider in the doorway wasn't the only spider in the house. They could be anywhere."

"Thanks," I said. "I feel a lot better. Let's hope they stay hidden."

"Kind of like the ghosts if there's any here," Chad said. "Let's hope it stays hidden too."

"Whoever left did so in a hurry," Mike said. "Wonder what happened?"

"Or what went wrong," Shane added.

Mike and Shane's comments took the edge off my confidence and rounded it off with renewed caution. The wheels of suspicion were spinning their web of intrigue and I felt elated and sick at the same time.

"Doug's story might be true," Shane said. "The trip was worth it. We made it inside. We're in a haunted house."

"We gonna stand in the kitchen all night?" Chad said. He decided to move on and headed to the end of the kitchen. Stopping at the edge, he peered down the hall.

With Mike and me following, Shane went to the end of the kitchen and stood next to Chad. We peered down the hallway. To the right an opening led into the dining room adjacent to the kitchen and to the front living room that, more than a week ago, I had peered into from the window. To the left an open door went to a bathroom and through this, another door that was closed. The hallway extended to the front door.

"See anything," I whispered.

"Ouch!" Chad said, as I got too close and stepped on his foot.

"Sorry."

With the smallest in our group leading, I gripped my bat tightly in one hand and held my flashlight in the other. Chad used the click button on the side of his flashlight to briefly scan each area. He lifted his football helmet slightly and scratched his head.

"Why would someone leave all this furniture behind?" Chad said.

"I don't know," I said. "Like Doug said, they left in a hurry."

The dining and living rooms were sparsely furnished with antique-style wooden furniture complete with a grandfather clock stalled at three. The old furniture made the inside seem old in contrast to the modern exterior of the house.

"There's furniture," Shane said. "But other than the dust covering it there's nothing else. No magazines, books, decorations adorning the walls or doilies on the dining room table. Definitely strange."

"You two go that way," I said to Mike and Chad, pointing to the dining room. "We'll go this way."

"What are we looking for?"

"Look for anything suspicious."

"Like what?"

"I don't know. Anything that's out of place. Chalk marks on the floor in the outline of a body, red stains on the carpet or a note in the trash can. Anything that would give us a clue why someone left out of here in such a hurry."

"You mean someone could have died here?" Mike asked.

"You heard Doug's story."

"If you find a basement, don't go down there by yourselves."

Mike and Chad went to explore the dining and living room while Shane and I headed down the hall.

"The first floor is probably the safest for them," I said. Shane nodded.

"You think we should see where that door goes?" He pointed to the bathroom and the door on the other side.

"We can come back to it. Let's find out what's upstairs." I headed down the hallway. "I want to see the room with the broken window. If there's a mystery here, it's why has that window been left broken?"

At the end of the hall we found a stairway on the left that led up one flight before rounding a corner. We stood in silence at the base of the stairs, listening for any unusual sounds. All remained quiet; the floors and walls indifferent to the four creeping trespassers.

"Does it seem colder in here than outside?" Shane asked in a hushed voice. His nervous tone had its affect.

Goosebumps tickled the back of my neck as I nodded. My hands gripped the bat like I was in the ninth inning of the World Series and the winning run was up to me. I stood for a moment trying to catch my breath. I hadn't done any hard labor, but judging by my breathing I felt like I'd just run a marathon.

"Calm, take it easy," I said.

"What?"

"Nothing, just talking to myself."

"Do you smell that?"

I sniffed the air. The place had the odor of furniture oil, not spray from a can, but the expensive stuff that came in a bottle. There was another smell; that of smoke, a hint of tobacco. A sweet, fine tobacco used in a pipe. The image of an elderly man, not rich but well-to-do, roaming the hall smoking his pipe came to mind; A man that preferred to sit and read a good book instead of watching television.

The image solidified when the beam of my flashlight illuminated a small bookcase in what looked like a waiting area between the staircase and the front door. Several books remained on the shelves; worn, hard-covered books. The print on the spines was too small for me to make out the titles. To the right of the front door was the entrance to the living room. I heard an occasional creak emerge from this area and assumed it was Chad and Mike making their way around the first floor.

"The furniture looks old," Shane whispered. For some reason he lowered his voice to a whisper. "I mean, like the stuff in one of those antique shops my grandma goes to."

"Right. It looks expensive too."

"Doesn't make sense to pay more for old stuff, I mean when you could get new stuff."

"Adults go for that kind of thing," I said.

"Yep. Then they get mad at us when we want to actually sit on the furniture. It's always; wipe your hands, no eating on the couch." We shared a laugh.

"Too expensive looking for someone to just leave it here," I whispered.

"Somebody sure was in a hurry to get out of here to leave all this behind."

I took the flashlight and shined the beam in front of us. The light provided us a good view of the hallway and lit up the foot of the stairwell.

At the base of the stairway, Shane and I stood and listened for what seemed to be hours. Nothing. No sounds from the top of the stairs. I hesitated. My inner voice told me not to go up the stairs but was pushed aside by another one saying, "Cool, let's go!"

"We've come this far," Shane whispered.

I took his cue to begin going up the stairs. "I guess I got us into this. If I'm wrong..." I let the statement hang. True to what Shane had been saying, he let me lead the way. As I took my first step my flashlight went out.

"Crap," I said, hitting it against the side of the baseball bat and shaking it.

"Here," Shane said, handing me his light.

I handed Shane my flashlight before I took his. As soon as we switched, my flashlight began working again.

"Let me see that thing," I said, exchanging them back. I shook my flashlight but the beam streamed forth steadily, as if there were nothing wrong with it.

"That's strange."

"Stay close," I told Shane, "just in case my flashlight goes out again." We started up the stairs moving at a snail's pace crossing thin ice.

The carpeted stairway continued straight for seven steps before turning ninety degrees to the left. When we made it to the first bend we saw that it went up another five steps and then made another ninety-degree angle to the left. Instinctively, I reached for a railing, but the railing ended at the wall and didn't continue up the second flight. I brushed along side the wall as I continued up.

Shane stood beside me as we paused. High on the right side of the second flight, moonlight filtered through a window and lit the stairway just enough for us to safely switch off the flashlights.

"Stealth mode," I whispered to Shane, putting the flashlight in my jacket pocket. I gripped my bat with both hands and wielded it like a shield.

Nodding to each other, we began our ascent up the stairs, each step a step up the ladder of tension, climbing higher until we reached the pinnacle of glory. It didn't matter anymore if nothing happened from this moment on. We had dared to visit a haunted house.

"Creak!"

"It's not a staircase unless it has one creaky step in it," Shane whispered.

"Creak, creak, creak," the staircase responded.

Unfortunately, the staircase had several creaky steps and it became nerve-racking.

"Stealth mode failure," Shane whispered barely containing his laughter. "At least we don't have leaves in here."

"Shh! No kidding until we find out what's up there," I pleaded debating whether I really wanted to make it to the top of the stairs or turn around and run. The carpet helped muffle our steps, though our nervous breathing was enough to disturb the silence.

I took my left hand off the bat and checked my pocket to make sure the flashlight was close. I put my arm out in front of Shane and stopped short of the last step.

"Just in case something comes at us, I plan on throwing the bat at it to slow it down."

"Then what?" Shane asked.

"Run."

"Good plan. We made it past Mutt; we can make it out of here."

Without pausing again, I continued up the third flight of steps.

No longer parallel with him, I turned to see Shane following close behind. But he wasn't looking at me. He was looking past me to the top of the stairs, his eyes wide, his breathing rapid. I turned and walked up a few steps, worried that the slightest sound could send us fleeing.

As I approached the top I felt like I was outside in the cold without my jacket. The air cut through my clothes like a storm of icicles pricking my skin. I shuddered and stopped. I looked back as the feeling passed through me. Shane stood still in the moonlit stairway. His breath took physical form as it eased from his mouth like a fog. The air inside the house became inexplicably colder than outside. I took one last step and stood at the top of the stairs on the second floor.

Clouds covered the moon! All went dark. I wanted to scream! My best defense was to stand still and listen. I tried to calm my last steady nerve. *Don't get scared over nothing,* I said to myself, buoyed by the confidence that came from having watched many scary movies alone when the others had chickened out and gone to bed. I tried to put the night in perspective.

Nothing to be afraid of.

Standing at the top of the stairs, I couldn't shake the feeling something watched us from the cold darkness; a presence beyond that of four curious boys. Maybe it was something left over from the previous occupants, or maybe it was my imagination gone wild. Remembering my dream from earlier in the week, I bit down on my lip enough to let me know I was awake.

An answer to my silent prayer, the moonlight returned as did a small sense of security. Shane climbed the last few steps and stood beside me. Again we lost the light coming in the window as the moon went behind a cloud. When it returned I spotted a closed door to our immediate right. To our left it was too dark to see. Taking one step forward, we stood facing down the hallway and listened. We heard nothing apart from the sound of our labored breathing.

I flicked on my flashlight for a brief moment, long enough to see the doorway to a bathroom at our left. I reached out and pushed the door open to let in the moonlight that streamed through a small, circular window high on the bathroom wall. I could see the hallway before us and another bedroom at the end with its door ajar. Down the hall to our right lie another closed door that I assumed led to the room with the broken window we'd viewed from the east side of the house.

The bathroom itself was small and I could see inside to a single shower stall, empty with no shower curtain. The room in front had no curtains on the window, but I could make out a chair and the side of a bed frame.

"More clouds must be moving in," I whispered to Shane, challenging the silence more confident now that I had seen both floors. "So far so good."

"Better check behind us." Shane stepped forward to the door and came right back. "The door's locked."

"The room up there looks empty."

"Well, we did it."

"Yep, bragging rights that we visited a haunted house."

"If you want to call it that. It's just an empty house. Cold and kind of eerie, but empty."

"CREAK!"

We jumped in unison from the sound of footsteps on the stairway! In my fright I tried to turn on the bat and held the flashlight up to defend myself.

"Tell me that's just Mike and Chad," Shane said.

I confirmed which hand held which instrument, and with valiant hesitation I stepped past Shane, who froze in place, and looked down the stairs. Two forms rounded the corner, a small frame with large shoulders, an over-sized head, and wide eyes, and a taller one with broad shoulders behind him.

"That looks odd," Shane commented as Mike with his shoulder pads, and Chad, with his football helmet on, looked like alien beings coming up the stairs.

"I guess if there were ghosts in the house, we might do just as good a job scaring them as they would of scaring us," Shane said, stepping to the top of the staircase.

We must have given them a start standing at the top of the stairs because Chad dropped his flashlight and Mike started backing up.

"You guys see anything?" Shane asked as he shined the flashlight on them and then on the steps to light the rest of the way.

"Nope," Mike replied. "No basement either. Why is it so cold up here?"

"I don't know, maybe a window's open or something."

"There's a door at the end of the bathroom downstairs. It might go to the basement," Shane said. "There's nothing up here. That door is locked, and that one probably is, too." He pointed to the door down the hall. "Looks like an empty bedroom down there."

"Nothing downstairs either," Mike said. "Just and old couch, a fireplace that hasn't been cleaned and a fancy dining room table."

"You wanted to see if we could find the room with that broken window right?" Shane asked. I nodded. "Let's check the other rooms," he said, making his way down the hall to the bedroom that overlooked the main road. He disappeared into the room and then came back down to the door across from the bathroom. Mike and I made our way to the middle of the hall.

"It's locked," Shane said somberly as he tried the handle.

"I don't think we should break in. We haven't damaged anything," Mike said.

"We should head back. Get going while the going is good," Chad said. "It's a long ride back."

"I don't think anyone lives here, just like Doug said," I said to the others.

Chad stepped forward. He raised his helmet and peeked out. I loosened the death grip I had on my bat while Shane's shoulders sagged. We stood in the middle of the second floor in front of the door that I believed led to the bedroom with the broken window.

"I guess this is better than getting in trouble," Mike said, "even if there isn't much here to talk about."

"See," I said, "I told you it wouldn't be so bad."

"I guess not. And what you guys did to Mutt, I guess he had it coming."

"We can still say we came here. That's worth something, ain't it?" Chad asked.

"Not unless everyone else believes the house is haunted," I replied. "All we've done is visited a deserted house."

"We should thank Doug, and tell him to tell his story to more people."

"He might have told the story, but you convinced us to come," Shane said patting my shoulder. "And it's been an adventure. I mean, I've never been this scared over what might happen."

"Maybe we should make something up, you know, more than your story. To make it seem more real." Shane grinned at me as Chad said this. "There were bloodstains on the floor, coffins in the bedroom, something like that."

"We don't have to make anything up," I said. "We came here. No one else did. We don't have to say anything more than that. Let their imaginations run wild."

"Guess we better get back before we get in trouble," Mike sounded concerned.

"Nothing to see here, boys," Shane said, feigning an adult voice as the mood became jovial.

"Just us ghosts," Chad said, putting his flashlight up under his chin and turning it on for a split second.

Everyone chuckled with relief. There was no use staying in the house any longer.

"Let's," I cut my statement short when I noticed something that caused my heart to skip a beat. In the following second I aged a full year.

The bedroom door behind Mike and Chad, the one at the head of the stairs that had been closed and locked just moments ago, was now wide open.

"The, the door," Shane stammered, slowly raising his arm and pointing.

I felt a chill come over me, and suddenly I felt sick to my stomach, dizzy, excited, and scared, all at the same time. No one stood in the doorway; the door was simply open. A trembling whisper came from my mouth.

"Who...who...opened that door?"

Chad and Mike turned around in slow motion and Chad pulled his helmet back in place.

Suddenly, the house shook as what sounded like a door slammed shut with tremendous force downstairs. The four of us jumped and then froze where we stood. *Someone was downstairs and we were trapped!*

"OH POOP!" Except I didn't say "poop." I had no idea what to do next. I, the one who was always quick with his wits, was at a total loss for what to do. I looked around, but everyone else was looking to me! I pictured my inner voice inside of me sitting with its arms crossed, frowning, shaking its head unwilling to give me any advice.

"Turn the flashlights off!" I said.

"Quick, we need to hide, someone's downstairs," Shane sputtered.

"The window," I said, "we can climb out." I stepped over and tried the door to the room with the broken window. I shoved on it and twisted the knob harder, left, then right. It didn't appear to be locked but the door was stuck. I knew if we could get into the room we could get out through the window. Panic began to build in me. I expected to hear footsteps coming up the stairs any minute. The other three stood watching and waiting.

I felt something push against me from the direction of the door and moved backward. I looked at the others, thinking one of them might have pulled me back and I hadn't noticed, but they were all standing too far away to have touched me.

Baffled, I had no time to dwell on this as the sound of shattering glass came from inside the room; the glass striking the other side of the door in front of me caused me to back away.

"It's got to be the Falter brothers or someone playing a joke," Mike stepped forward and yelled, "HEY! Knock it off!"

In response to his request, the bedroom doors at each end of the hallway slammed shut, opened again, and slammed shut. Two flashlights went on, but I didn't know whose. The door slammer remained a phantom and then a cold breeze penetrated my clothes and a chill overtook me. It was the same feeling I had on the stairs earlier. I panicked!

"MOVE! MOVE! MOVE! Down the stairs!" I hollered out as Mike, who was closest to the stairs, turned and ran down the hallway.

We bolted down the stairs as fast as we could, but they seemed to be flooded with quicksand and the walls closed in so that we didn't have room to make it down side-by-side and had to struggle through single file. I figured if there was someone downstairs we would surprise him and, in the confusion, make it to the door.

"Oomph."

"Ouch!"

"Watch it!"

"Don't stop!"

"Keep going."

I stumbled and tripped countless times. The others faired no better as we ended up tangled together at the bottom of the second flight jammed against the side railing. A shooting pain went up my arm as it bounced off Chad's helmet and the bat I held tumbled off the side of the stairs, landing somewhere by the small hutch.

Chad ended up at the bottom of the pile with his head crashing into the wall. "I'm OK. My helmet saved me," Chad said.

"Keep going. We've got to get outside."

We struggled down the last flight as if caught in molasses. All of us wanted to get out as fast as we could, and all of us were fast runners, but the house had turned on us and everything in it became an obstacle.

Two flashlights beams were going haywire in the darkness flashing around the house. I managed to get ahead of the others and led the way to the bottom. I stepped off the last stair only to trip over a bench that had been placed directly in front of the steps. I knew it hadn't been there before, and I suspected Chad and Mike had nothing to do with it.

The lights flashed on as the whole house lit up, and I found my face parallel with the floor. "The Ghost of Windy Hill?" I read the title of the book that rested within an inch of my nose. The lights went off again. With no desire to find out the mystery of the bench or the books, I abandoned my bat and struggled to get up.

"Grab my hand," Mike said.

Shane and Mike helped me, and we bolted down the hallway to the back door. A light flashed in front of us as the kitchen lit up and then went dark. To the right the lights in the living room came on and went off. I heard footsteps across the floor from above us. No, it was more like someone jumping up and down on the second floor. A door slammed. The noise and flashing lights worked against us, causing us to falter and lose our vision.

"To the back door," I yelled, trying to shake off the spell cast upon me.

As I made it to the kitchen I considered using Chad, with his football helmet, as a battering ram if needed to get out of the house.

"Where's the table?" Shane called out. "Look at the chairs!"

The kitchen table had gone missing. The chairs were against the wall, stacked one on top of the other in an impossible formation with only two legs making contact and the other two suspended in midair.

Crossing the tile floor, Shane and I both tripped.

"LOOK OUT," Shane called and reached out a hand. I grabbed it and we braced each other as we slid forward across the floor.

"Thanks," I said, grateful for Shane's agility.

"Go! Go!" Shane yelled as Mike and Chad went through the kitchen. In the next flash of light I looked down and could see that we had slid on books that were strewn about the floor. They looked like the ones that had been on the hutch by the front door. I made my way to the back where Chad and Mike were stopped.

"It's stuck," Mike said pushing against the door.

"Oomph!" Shane and I crashed into the door. It was stuck! *We're all going to die!* My inner voice screamed out.

Without stopping, Mike and Chad piled into our backs. In a frenzy of panic, I turned the knob and the door gave way. Stumbling through the porch and out the screen door, we made it to the safety of the back yard.

"To the bikes!"

Stealth and secrecy abandoned, we had no plans to be around long enough to care if we were discovered. Four sets of sneakers tore around the house, carrying their owners to new nighttime speed records as they headed for the bikes.

I wasn't looking at the house but still heard doors slamming and what sounded like someone pounding on the walls. The lights continued to flicker on and off. I slowed to account for everyone. *Mike, Chad, Where's SHANE?*

I stopped and turned around. Shane fell to the ground holding his knee. He had tripped over a metal cover that might have been an entrance to the storm cellar. I raced back to help him.

"Can you get up?"

He made it to his knees and spit. He had landed face first, getting a face full of grass and leaves. "I'm all right."

With his back to the house, I helped Shane stand up. He didn't move. The lights had stopped flashing, but a light from the second story, from the room with the broken window, remained on. I could make out a silhouette cast onto the lawn, as though someone or something was looking down at us. I couldn't tell if it was a man or woman because it didn't quite take shape so I looked up at the window.

There, with a flickering light behind him, stood the old man I had seen before in the yard next to the house. My heart raced and I stood still as I noticed a man in the room who had a gun. Suddenly, the old man leapt across the room tackling the man with the gun and the two crashed through the window. I flinched as they fell toward me but looked up when nothing hit the ground.

"A vision?" I asked the air as the light on the second-story bedroom went out.

"What is it," Shane asked.

"Don't look up, just run," I said and put my hand on Shane's shoulder, turned him around, and urged him onward. He regained his stride and we jumped across the adobe wall.

By the time we made it over the adobe wall we had awakened a primitive survival instinct and our actions became automatic. We ran to the road, where Mike and Chad had our bikes. It didn't take long to find the pedals, and eight tires left rubber on the road.

"Go! Go! Go!" I yelled out.

I cast a brief glance over at the neighbor's house to see if we'd roused him in the commotion. Unconcerned about attracting attention, we intended to make ourselves scarce. Riding madly, the pace we set was too fast for the dark night, and I knew if we tried to maintain it we'd all run out of steam. Still, I rode steady until we made it to the first intersection away from the house before I even considered stopping. I looked around, making sure everyone kept up.

I stood up on my pedals and weaved in front of the others before I pulled over to the side of the road. "Stop," I called out, barely able to catch my breath long enough to get the words out.

Everyone came to a halt. By the sounds of it, we were all out of breath. Quick, wide-eyed looks darted about checking for signs of danger. Curiously, the clouds had all but vanished and the night was clear.

I rubbed my shin.

"You okay?" Mike asked.

"I hit my shin on a little bench at the bottom of the stairs," I said. "You guys didn't..."

Mike shook his head.

"Man, I've never felt like this before. I think I could lift a house or something," Shane said breaking the silence.

"It's adrenaline."

"Maybe that's why my knee doesn't hurt so bad."

"What the heck just happened?"

"I don't know, but we need to get out of here."

"Yeah, we're still too close. Let's talk about this later."

"Wait a minute," I said, looking back the way we'd come.

"I'm not going back."

"Me neither."

"You're on your own."

"I didn't say we were going back," I said. "We need to make sure no one's following us in case we need to change our route or split up or something."

"There are no headlights from a car, and they'll never catch us by foot if we keep going," Shane said.

"Let's just go," Mike said, his eyes looking back and forth as he wheeled over to me. "We can talk later about what happened."

"Or we can never talk about it," Chad said. "That's my vote."

"Okay. Calm down. There are no sirens or cars. I guess we made a good escape."

"And very brave the way we ran out of there," Shane said but no one laughed.

"Let's start back. The short way, but be careful, and save some energy just in case Mutt has recovered."

"I'm so wound up that dog would need a turbo charger to keep up with me," Shane said. We set out at a breakneck pace back home.

Mutt was nowhere too be seen as we rode by his house. Other than the low hum of our bike tires against the asphalt and rapid breathing, nothing around us stirred. The night remained quiet, dead silent, giving us plenty of quiet time to reflect on our escapade.

My thoughts drifted back to everything that had just transpired. Letting Mike and Chad take the lead, I hung back making sure we weren't followed. My eyes strained against the darkness, shadows played games, but I made nothing out of them. Shane pulled up beside me.

"What's wrong?"

"I don't know," I said. "We made too many mistakes. We should have left someone outside so that we could make sure no one snuck up on us. And we should've guarded the bikes. We're lucky no one took them."

"You're taking it too serious. You really think someone was out to get us?"

"What else could have happened?"

"You were right. Doug was right. That house is haunted, and when it woke up and found us inside, it viciously rejected us."

Shane's words sparked the memory of the cold, icy feeling that touched my skin while we were in the house. I felt a remnant of that touch on the exposed skin of my neck and turned to look behind.

"I feel it, too," Shane said.

"What?" I replied.

"Something's following us. I can't see it, but it's there."

I said nothing and kept up with the others until we made it to our lane. At the final intersection, we passed under the street lamps, their light a beacon of safety. I looked back many times too see if anything else came into the light, but nothing came around the corner. At the house before ours we stopped and began walking our bikes the rest of the way.

"We were sure brave getting out of that place," Shane said.

I laughed this time at his comment thinking how ridiculous we must have looked running out of the house stumbling over everything.

"There's no way one person could have done all that. Not even two," Mike said.

"It couldn't have been the Falter brothers. Not slamming doors at both ends of the hall and making noise and turning lights on and off all over."

"That doesn't even count for who was making noise in the room with the broken window."

"Doug and Eric?" Mike asked.

"I don't know," I said. "I'm too tired to think about it." My head ached.

"Are you hurt?" I asked Shane.

"I think I bruised my knee."

"Once we reach the driveway we have to be totally quiet," I said. "No talking when we get inside. We'll talk in the morning."

"Good idea," Shane said. "No point in getting in trouble when we made it this far."

Everyone remained quiet, and I wondered if they were having the same indigestion trying to make sense of the night's happenings. With barely a sound we rested our bikes on the ground by the tree house and packed our gear just inside the entrance.

It had been a long day full of excitement. We had been up for almost twenty-four hours. With the day's events weighing heavy on my eyelids, I led the troop to the door. Being the last one to sneak in the house, I took one final look into the night, finding the darkness more unsettling than when we first started our adventure. I closed and locked the door. "Hurry up, sun."

When I entered the living room Shane, Mike, and Chad were all standing, sleeping bags in hand.

"We can't talk now," I whispered.

"That's not it," Shane replied.

"Out here, we're surrounded by more windows than anywhere else in the house." Mike said.

"And we're right between the front and back door," Chad added.

"Good point." I bent down, grabbed my sleeping bag, and led the way down the hall to my bedroom. Once there the four of us barricaded ourselves inside and went to sleep.

CHAPTER NINE

AFTERMATH

"NO!" I SAID WAKING up just in time to keep Shane from opening the cigar box. "There's no telling what he's got in there." I searched around for my grammer book and secured the box shut.

Shane, eyebrows raised, looked on as he sat at my small desk. The light coming in from the window let me know it was morning.

"How long you been up?" I asked, sitting at the edge of my bed.

"I don't know if I ever slept."

"Me either."

Chad and Mike remained sleeping under a pile of covers in the middle of the floor. Mikes bed was still propped against the door.

"Did last night really happen?"

"Afraid so. Worst part is, I left my bat there. I dropped it off the side of the stairs when we were all tumbling down."

"We're lucky no one got hurt too bad."

"Shh. I think I hear my sister. When it's quiet like this, she can hear us through the walls. We'll have to wait and talk later."

"I can't wait to get to the tree house."

"I gotta eat first," my stomach rumbled. Get up you guys," I pulled on the sleeping bag covering Mike and Chad.

Groggy eyes appeared from under the pillows. "Did we make it to morning?" Chad said.

Shane and I pulled the bed back away from the door along with the pile of clothes and shoes. I opened the door. We headed to the kitchen and our morning ritual of milk and cereal. Surprisingly, no one turned on the television to watch Saturday morning cartoons.

"Mom's up," Mike said although I couldn't tell how he knew since his eyes were still closed.

"Shh," I put my fingers to my lips, "no talking about last night until we're outside."

I opened the cupboard and handed out cereal boxes.

"You boys want pancakes?" mom asked as she came into the kitchen. On any other day the answer would be a clear and resounding "Yes," but we didn't have time. Mike continued to the table with the cereal and I got the milk.

"No thanks. Just cereal today," I said.

Staring at us for a moment in disbelief, my mom headed back down the hall turning around at the last minute. "You boys stay close to home today. Your father said there were reports of gunshots last night just down the road by the school."

Mike dropped a box of cereal and little colored circles flew across the kitchen floor.

"We're just going out to the tree house," I told her as I helped Mike clean up the mess. I looked back and Shane and Chad smiled.

I shoveled in the sugar frosted flakes to fuel the furnace and threw my dish in the sink.

Throwing on our coats, we marched single file to the tree house and labored up. It was the earliest meeting we'd ever called.

"Quick, close the hatch, it's cold."

"It's cold up here. We need a heater," Mike said.

"You say that every time," I said.

"Since we started this adventure, we've been out here a lot more."

"I don't think I can play football today, I'm too tired," Mike said.

Chad was the last one to make it up. "I didn't sleep at all." He closed the hatch. We huddled close together wrapping the blankets over our shoulders.

"Me neither," Shane said. "What happened last night?" They looked at me.

"I'm sorry, I don't think we should have gone," I said. "I put you all in danger."

"Who cares about that?" Shane blurted. "That house is haunted! And we went there!"

I nodded in agreement as did Chad.

"Not just there, we went inside," Mike said. Proudly we recounted the events of the previous night.

"Man, your eyes were so wide you didn't need a flashlight!" Chad said.

"Me? I thought we'd have to stop at the bathroom so you wouldn't pee your pants."

"I'm just glad the chain didn't fall off my bike for once," I said.

"Or get a flat tire," Shane said. "Good thing Chad wore a helmet."

"Not just any helmet, a Denver Bronco helmet. That way I looked real cool falling down the steps," Chad said.

In the daylight the events of the previous night seemed distant. No matter how many times we tried to rationalize what happened, we couldn't

"There's no way it was a prank. How would anyone know we would be coming last night," Shane said. "And the doors, lights, and sounds. It would have taken lot of people but there were no cars there."

"No one saw anybody?" I asked.

"No," three heads shook.

"I did," I said to the group.

"What?"

"Something I can't explain. I think it was a replay of a past event we witnessed. It happened when we were outside and you fell. I looked up and saw something, but nothing was there."

"You don't need to make stuff up, we believe the house was haunted," Shane said.

"I'm not. I think something happened in the room on the second floor. That's why it was broken."

"I think what the Professor is trying to tell us is that we met a ghost," Shane said.

"What now?" I challenged.

"We won't know if we don't go back. It's the only way to be sure," Shane said.

I raised an eyebrow. I knew I had to go back if only to get my bat back, but I didn't expect any one else would want to go."

"You're crazy," Chad said.

"During the day wouldn't be so bad," Mike added.

"It'd be harder to sneak around," Shane said. "Someone might see us."

"I lost my bat inside. I need to get it back."

"Count me out for today. I have to be home early," Shane said.

"I need to go home, too," Chad said "Probably sleep the rest of the day."

"I'm going to go get a box of cereal," Mike got up and went down through the hatch.

"I don't think I want to go today anyway," I said, rubbing my chin. "We made a lot of noise getting out of there. Might be too obvious for us to show up there so soon."

"Right. We need to hang low, let the dust settle."

"We'll pass by on our way to church tomorrow. "I'll take a look and see if anything's changed."

"Guys, come here!" Mike's desperate voice hollered from below.

We clambered down to the bottom and noticed Mike staring at the other side of the tree.

"Oh, man, not another bug. You called us down for this?" I moved to see what he looked at stopping so suddenly in my tracks that Shane and Chad ran into me, and then filed to the side so we all looked at the same thing.

There, propped up at the base of the tree on the side facing the road, was my baseball bat—the one I had dropped in the Round House.

"Did…?" With mouths open, Shane and Chad shook their heads as they joined me staring at the bat.

"Did you?" Mike asked.

"No. I never went back after I dropped it. You guys had to pick me up off the floor, remember."

"Then how did it get here?"

"Are you sure it's yours?" Shane asked.

I stepped forward and grabbed the bat slowly rotating it until I came to the notches I'd scratched into it.

"Your home run record," Shane said.

"Confirmed," I said. "Remember when we kept looking back like something was following us?"

Shane nodded.

"We've entered a departure from reality."

I walked to the top of the driveway, Shane followed. The two of us stared down the road. Empty. Had the bat shown up in the few minutes we'd been in the tree house or was it there all night? It was a question we could not answer.

"I better go get my stuff ready," Shane said. "If I get home early, my parents might let me spend the night again next week."

"I better get going too," Chad said.

Mike and I walked to the house and helped Shane and Chad gather their stuff. They were soon on their way home and I sat watching cartoons until lunchtime. Mike had disappeared. I looked around the front room and kitchen and finally went back to our bedroom where I found him sound asleep in his bed.

"Good idea," I said and passed out on my bed. I don't think I woke up until Sunday morning.

🍃   🍂

We passed the Round House on our way to church Sunday, and it remained deserted. It would be another week before I journeyed back to the house on Saturday. Mike and I rode there together.

"Too bad Shane couldn't come over," Mike said.

"I know. It's still really nice outside. Perfect day to be out riding. Chad was sick?"

"I don't know, I think he might be scared of you wanting to go back to the house."

"And you're not?"

"Not in the daylight."

We slowed our pace as we came close to Mutt's house.

"Come on," I said picking up my normal pace. Mike stayed on the other side of me away from Mutt's house. We made it by without incident.

"Mutt doesn't dare come after you now," Mike stated as we continued down the road our jackets on to protect us from the cold.

"I'm hoping that memory lasts him awhile."

"Shane hasn't been able to come over either. Do you think we scared them? It was creepy. Weren't you scared?"

"I ran as fast as the rest of you," I said.

"So why we going back?"

"For closure. Before we went, we all talked about ghosts and strange things. Now that I've seen if for myself, I need to know more. I want to see if we can find an explanation for what happened. I mean, it couldn't have been the Falter brothers. They would have been bragging about it by now. Besides, they're not smart enough to pull off a stunt like that."

Approaching the house I felt a sense of hesitation and slowed down. Mike followed suit, and we stopped with the house just in our view.

"The for-sale sign is gone," I said. "And now there's one on the neighbors house."

"We could move in and be right next to it. Then we wouldn't have to ride so far," Mike grinned.

"Ha, ha. Let's get closer."

We continued on, staying on the far side of the road as we passed the Round House, then we doubled back and rode by again. There were still no curtains in the windows, and the broken window on the top floor still had plastic taped over it.

"No additional glass is broken from before. But I know I heard glass hit the door."

"Me too," Mike said. "Looks empty."

We stopped riding. The wind had a definite chill to it; the sun not quite as warm it was weeks earlier, a reminder father winter was closing in. "I need to get closer."

I moved to the head of the driveway and looked down the road to see if any cars were coming. Mike didn't follow but stayed on the opposite side of the road. I looked toward him; he didn't budge and simply looked back, slightly shaking his head.

"You stay there," I called back. "I'll be right back." I took off down the driveway getting close enough to see into the garage. "Still no cars."

Suddenly, I felt a prickly sensation on the back of my neck and whirled around. Nothing. I had the unmistakable feeling of being watched.

I looked at Mike who stayed on the opposite side of the road, his cheeks red from the cold, one foot on the ground, the other on the pedal ready to head back. Again the sensation hit me. A cold chill ran under my jacket, my inner voice called out a warning, *danger!*

Without getting off my bike I looked around to the back of the house. Nothing. I followed the sensation up the side of the house to the second floor. THERE! It came from the window in the hallway. That's where I felt something staring down at me.

My eyes squinted to make out what I could be there—a small patch of fog against the window appeared, and then disappeared like someone was breathing against the glass. I remembered the stairwell and the small window at the top where the moonlight had trickled in. Over ten-feet high, I couldn't imagine what might be there. It was impossible for someone to stand there.

"Can we go now?" Mike hollered from the end of the driveway distracting me.

I looked at Mike and then back at the window. The sensation was gone. I turned and made my way back up the driveway and we headed home.

"We're coming back," I said. "Next time, we'll be prepared!"

CHAPTER TEN

UΠEXPLAİΠED

WINTER SET IN THE next week. An October snow fell right before Halloween, and the cold nights and snow put our late-night adventures in a state of hibernation. We talked about going back but we knew we might not get the chance until spring.

With the adventure fresh in our minds, it was the strange occurrence of the baseball bat showing up seemingly on its own that kept us inside when it was dark. For the next month we stopped watching scary movies on Friday night, and we passed on dressing up to go trick or treating for Halloween, voting instead to spend the night watching a nice adventure movie.

I did manage to convince my dad that going down County High Road to church every Sunday was the fastest way to get there, and managed to keep my eye on the Round House. It was during these drive-bys that the story continued to unfold.

From the backseat, my brother and I watched as the neighbor's house sold and someone moved in making me wonder what happened to the old man. More alarming to us was that something was definitely going on at the Round House. Thanksgiving Break was the first chance the four of us got together to talk about the latest events.

Chad and Shane came over the weekend of Thanksgiving. Late Saturday morning, with our heavy winter coats on, we went to the tree house.

"It's cold up here, we need a heater," Mike said.

"You always say that," I said.

"Here," Chad said being the last one up, "try these candles." He handed me two candles and a lighter.

"Okay, but lets be careful," I said pointing to the walls as I spoke; "We are in a place with wooden walls, covering ourselves with dry blankets, in a tree that I'm sure would make good firewood."

I lit the candles tipping them to allow wax to drip off in a puddle and then used the drying puddle as a base to hold the candlesticks in an upright position.

"Wow," Shane said. "I would have never thought of that."

We huddled over the candles sticking out our hands over the small flames.

"This isn't helping much," Chad said. He removed a ski cap from his coat pocket and placed it over his head.

"Now we know who's most likely to be a criminal in our group," Shane said causing us to laugh. "So, Professor, what is it you wanted to tell us?"

"Mike already knows this because we've been passing by the Round House on our way to church. The property has been marked off with an orange construction fence like there's work going on."

"Maybe somebody bought it," Shane said.

"No, well, maybe. But that's not it. The fence went up two weeks ago. But last week is what worried me. The house is on stilts. Like it's going to be moved away."

Shane's eyes widened, Chad breathed a sigh of relief, and Mike just stared into the flame of the candles.

"How can they move the house?" Shane asked.

"I don't know, that's what it looked like to me. It's not like I asked my dad to stop the car."

"Maybe we can try to ride there this afternoon," Shane said.

"It's too cold," Chad said.

"I don't know if we could get close enough. The construction fencing goes all the way around. Someone might see us crossing it during the day."

"We'll have to wait until it warms up then," Shane said.

"That's what I'm trying to tell you," I spoke with such force I blew one of the candles out. Chad frowned and relit it. "I don't think the house is going to there much longer."

The four of us shivered in silence for the next ten minutes.

"I don't know why it matters to go back," Mike said. "You got your bat back."

"To prove what we saw," I said.

"What's it matter," Shane said. "Maybe it's better this way, leaving it a mystery."

Mike unzipped the front of his jacket and pulled out a box of cereal. He slammed his hand down into it and out poured the circular colored shapes trickling down his lap onto the floor of the tree house, a small few made it into his mouth. A look of satisfaction upon his face as he chewed fulfilling his need.

I wanted to laugh, but suddenly found a deeper meaning. I was taking everything too serious. He spied me watching him.

"Whant sum," the words from his stuffed mouth barely audible.

I looked up to the roof of the tree house searching for inspiration. None came. "Sure," I said and he passed the box to me. The rest joined in and we spent the rest of the morning eating cereal and laughing until the candles burned out.

Since we hadn't planned on riding our bikes, Shane didn't bring his and we didn't take a bike ride that afternoon. That Sunday as we rode to church in the back our tan, family station wagon, my fear had come true: The Round House was gone along with the chain link fence that surrounded it. Only the tin shed and the garage remained.

On Monday, my bus got to school late and it wasn't until recess that I talked to Shane after we'd slammed our bologna sandwiches and headed out into the cool air. Only a few kids braved the cold and were outside on the asphalt pad where the tetherballs hung lifeless. Air took form as I breathed out.

"It's gone," I said. "Now we'll never be able to know exactly what happened."

"It was a great adventure," Shane said.

"But who's going to believe it?"

A commotion broke out across the playground as voices rose. No teachers had ventured outside; one occasionally glanced out the triangle of a window. Recognizing one of the raised voices as that of Jay Falter, Shane and I went to see what was happening.

"The house was not haunted," Jay said through his yellow teeth. His undersized lime-green jacket hung about his shoulders making them appear larger than normal. His fingers pointed at a kid with uncombed brown hair, lanky with a tall frame. I didn't recognize the boy.

"That's the new kid," Shane said. I shrugged my shoulders.

"It was too haunted," the kid said.

I leaned in and whispered to Shane, "Kid better watch it. He doesn't know who he's messing with."

"I know because we moved in right next to it. And those workers picked it right up and moved it away."

I looked at Shane and both our eyes widened. *Could it be?* I wondered.

"The Round House?" Shane said out loud catching the attention of the small crowd. He closed his eyes and then peeked.

Too late, I thought, *you blurted it out.*

"That's right," the new kid said. "The Round House. It had those funny windows and the front door."

Jay's face turned red and he stepped forward. I stepped behind Shane and Jay looked at me and hesitated.

"He's right," Shane said. "The house was haunted. I know because I went there."

Several gasps rang out from the group and some of the sixth graders fled inside. Shane had a captive audience as he started to tell our story. A larger audience joined as they noticed the group huddled around. Shane told our story; I assisted and simply nodded occasionally for added clout.

The teacher called out from the doorway once lunch period ended and we trickled inside. The new kid whom now lived next to where the Round House stood came up to me.

"I'm Russ, Russ Mueller. Just moved here from Riverside, California.

I glanced at Shane and rolled my eyes knowing that all we needed was another person from California at our school. We all thought people from California had outlandish ideas.

"Well, Russ, you're lucky they moved that house away," I said. "You would've been in grave danger."

"My grandpa lived by it. We moved into his house."

"Really," I stopped in the doorway. "Is he an old guy, gray hair, wears a cap all the time and chews on a cigar?"

"You knew him?" Russ asked.

"Met him briefly."

"My parents were going to sell his house after he passed away in August, but decided to buy it instead. Said something about moving to Colorado for the clean air."

"What? He passed away in August?" I said knowing the man I described I'd seen in October.

"You can kind of say that," Russ stated. "My mom says he helped the neighbors out by stopping a robbery or something like that. Pushed the robber out the second-story window. She says he was a hero."

"Did anyone else live at your Grandpa's house?"

"No."

"Well," I put my hand on Russ' shoulder, "you're Grandpa was a hero." I didn't want to scare Russ so I didn't tell him about our visit to the Roundhouse or what I thought I saw there.

"Hey," Shane interrupted our conversation, "that's what my parents said when they moved here; they wanted the clean Colorado air. But you know what? It's cold here a lot more than they say it is."

Russ smiled and went into the building.

"That was a brave thing to do," I said. Shane looked out across the empty playground.

"You think you saw a ghost?"

"I wasn't sure what I saw, which is why I didn't tell you guys anything at the treehouse. I spotted an old man push someone out the window. But when nothing hit the ground, I thought it was just my imagination."

"You saw a past event," Shane said.

"I think so. But that's not all that happened there. The doors slamming and lights going off and on. Maybe the ghost of the robber is stuck in limbo because he met a tragic demise. Or maybe the house was already attracting bad luck which is why the robbery happened. Either way, we'll never know. We better get to class." I led the way into the building.

"I guess it's like searching for Bigfoot."

"What?" I looked down the hall and then back at Shane.

"Every time I read a book or see a show about it, there's always just enough evidence that makes you want to keep interested but never any solid proof."

I nodded and walked fast noticing the halls were empty. Shane and I were the last ones to walk into our science class and as we did, I heard someone mention a haunted house. The room went silent as we entered and every face turned to us.

We walked with our heads high and took our seats. We weren't popular athletes, nor had we won the spelling bee or any other major competition, but word got around of our bravery. We thought it a shame that the Round House had been removed, but with the house gone, no one could top our feat. We alone had visited the house.

We never found out where the house was moved, but by the end of December the foundation had been filled in and the fence torn down. No part of the house remained.

In the spring, the garage and small shed were removed, and the plot where the house once stood was cordoned off with a high chain-link fence. Small trees were planted there, making it impossible for a structure to be built in the same location as the

Round House. It remains this way today. I don't know who owns the land, but it's apparent they didn't want another house built there.

Mutt never chased Chad or I again. Whenever we rode by, he came to the edge of the yard and looked on, chest out, eyes forward. If he'd had hands he would have saluted us as fellow warriors who'd bested him.

As for our group, this was the beginning of shared adventures. Our curiosity about the unexplained had been piqued, and our questing had just begun.

In the months to come, Shane and I continued exploring strange mysteries and increased our knowledge about the paranormal through books and videos. We would find a need for our new-found knowledge when we were faced with *The Moaning Walls*. Mike and Chad joined in our adventures, and we decided to call ourselves the Questors, using the tree house as our staging area.

The episode at the Round House kept us searching and questioning. Never again would any of us be quick to judge the possibility that something existed beyond our understanding, beyond our senses.

END OF LINE.

THE
MOANING WALLS

If you love adventure and are not faint of heart, read on.
If you are easily scared, go no further.

To the Quest!

Contents

CHAPTER ONE
A PRECARIOUS SITUATION

I GRIPPED THE FLASHLIGHT so tight my knuckles turned white. The four of us huddled together in the middle of the front room. Present were my brother Mike, eleven years old and the tallest in our group next to me; his best friend, Chad, the smallest of our group and the same age as Mike; and my best friend Shane, the same age as me at thirteen.

It was ten minutes after midnight and the lights of the green, double-wide trailer were off. By all appearances, the occupants were sleeping soundly and all was calm. Only the strange sounds on the roof dared to differ.

"Sounds like footsteps," Shane said.

I nodded. "Mike. You and Chad get ready at the windows. Make sure you watch to see if anyone jumps down." I looked at his shoes and shook my head.

Shane knelt down and tied the shoelaces on his new blue-striped high tops.

"Wait," Chad interrupted before we moved. "What do we do if it turns out to be, you know, something that might hurt us?"

"Good point," I said.

"Even if it's bigger, there are four of us," Shane said. "Mike's a linebacker, he'll knock them down and we'll pile on. Remember our code."

Chad shrugged his shoulders.

"To fight and defend each other," Shane said.

"Right," I said. "No running away like in the movies. If one of us gets in trouble, we help. Now, just like we planned; we go out fast and quiet. Keep it down; we don't need to wake anyone."

"What if we don't see anything, again?" Mike asked.

"Last time we all ran outside. Whatever it was could've jumped down by that time. That's why you and Chad are going to watch from the windows this time as Shane and I go outside, make sure we don't miss anything."

"Let's get to the bottom of this," Shane said pulling a faded Boston Red Sox hat down over his tangled blond hair.

"Got your shoes tied, Shane," I said. "Let's catch this culprit; I'm tired of these footsteps on the roof."

Breaking from our huddle, four boys headed to adventure. I went into the hall between the living room and kitchen. A single, dim, hallway light allowed me to see that twenty feet away, my parents' bedroom door remain closed. "Listen," I whispered to Shane who stood behind me. "Wait until we hear it again, and then go."

We reached the back door and I looked at Shane, who nodded. One hand gripped my flashlight and the other gripped the doorknob. The only sound emanating from the green double-wide trailer on 25th Lane was that of four boys' nervous breathing.

"If somebody is up there, the only thing I can think is that they are jumping down somehow before we get outside," I said. "So we have to be faster this time."

"Wait, there's only one way to make sure," Shane said heading for the front door. "We go out on opposite sides."

I glanced at Shane, who took his position at the front door. In our house, the front and back door lay directly opposite each other along the short end of the rectangle that made the double-wide trailer. I nodded, understanding that Shane would go out one side while I went out the other. "Mike, Chad, you each take one side of the house and look out the window in case we miss anything."

Poised for action, I slowly turned the knob and cracked open the door. I nodded to Shane. I looked to see that Mike and Chad were in position, one at the living room window and one at the kitchen. We waited.

The seconds seemed like hours and I wondered if somehow it knew our plans. *It,* I thought to myself. I'd already given it an identity. Although I pretended as if I didn't suspect anything, the sounds were too intelligent to be the wind or an animal, and it only came when the four of us were together. We had failed on prior occasions to determine a cause. This time, fully dressed, we had waited for the sounds and like the happy ending of a fairy tale, it had come as expected. Now, flashlights in hand, we were ready.

I heard the sounds! ***Someone is walking across the roof,*** my senses shouted at me.

"Now," I said in a soft voice. With lightning reflexes, Shane and I acted. I ran out into the yard and shone my flashlight on the roof of the trailer. I caught glimpses of Shane's flashlight as the beams went skyward and he moved along the other side of the trailer.

I looked to the window and Chad looked at me, shaking his head.

"NOTHING!" There was no one there.

Mike came out to the backyard where I stood.

"Shane?" I asked.

Mike shook his head. "He didn't see anything."

I looked across the yard to the only tree, a crabapple tree, too small for anyone to hide behind. The gate still latched, I looked beyond the yard toward the shed and then beyond that to the acre of frozen land. Nothing.

"We didn't see anything from the windows,' Mike said. "The sounds stopped right when you went outside."

"How could someone get down that fast?"

"You think it's a person?" My brother's voice trembled and he kept a close watch on the roof.

"What else could it be? It's the middle of winter; there are no leaves on the trees that could be rustling. Most of the birds flew south."

"But how would they get up there?"

"Not only that," I said raising my right hand, finger pointing to the trailer. "It's too high for someone to jump without making noise or getting hurt." My tongue ran across a chipped tooth I received while jumping off the roof to the ground in an attempt to mimic our invisible adversary.

"Unless whatever it is, is still up there," Chad said joining the group in the backyard.

The three of us looked at each other and then slowly our gazes went back to the rooftop. In the distance, a cat meowed and a dog howled, distracting us into looking in that direction.

"We can't see anyone standing on the roof from the ground," I said. "And we didn't see anyone jump down. If someone's up there, they'd have to be crouching down against the roof."

"Maybe that's why we always fail to find out what it is. It just hides until we go back to sleep," Mike said.

"Not this time," I said. Determined to find out what caused the footsteps or who was playing tricks on us, I took a deep breath and walked toward the trailer.

"Where are you going?" Mike said.

"I guess there's only one thing left to do," I said forcing my feet in a direction my brain told them not to go. "Hold this," I handed Mike my flashlight. "Go around to the front and tell Shane to keep watching. Chad, stay on this side, just in case."

"By myself?" Chad's voice emerged from a woolly hood he'd pulled over his head. "What if something jumps down while you're up there?"

"That hood will probably scare it. You look like a little Bigfoot baby or something. If that doesn't work, scream," I said.

"Scream?" Chad asked.

"No," I stopped and turned back. "I was just kidding. Run or something. We don't want to wake anyone."

I headed to the side of the trailer where a lightpost stood. The wooden post extended beyond the roof of the house and held a light that hadn't worked as long as I could remember. There were several bolts and pieces of wood attached to the post allowing me, with my long legs, to use it as a ladder. Luckily, all the bedrooms lay at the back of the trailer so I didn't have to worry about waking anyone as I climbed up the post.

Mike disappeared around the corner. I took a deep breath and reached up grabbing the end of a large bolt sticking out of the post and hoisted my foot to the first step. In a moment, I would be able to peer onto the roof of the trailer.

The cool air went across my face and shivers ran up my spine. Suddenly, I stopped short of my next move and considered my options. What was I going to do once I was on the roof? My mission was to identify the culprit, but what if it was a stranger, or worse, something from the world of the supernatural?

What exactly was I going to do? My inner voice asked me.

I looked down to the yard to see Chad standing with the flashlight, his coat hastily thrown on and still unzipped, his eyes peering out from the woolly hood. Everyone waited for me to move onto the roof and all I could do is wish I were somewhere else. I turned my head, listening first with my left ear and then turning my head to listen with my right. Silence.

Without further delay, I hoisted myself up and settled into a crouching position. I could see across to the end: nothing there. I looked from side to side, but could see nothing on the roof that could cause the sounds we'd heard. My mission wasn't over. Mounted at the center of the trailer sat a swamp cooler, covered until summer; it made a great barrier to seeing what was on the other side. I knew I couldn't go back down until I made sure no one was hiding behind it.

"Why me?" I whispered.

A plan came to me. I would surprise whatever was on the other side of that cooler and pretend I wasn't scared. I crept forward, keeping my distance, and attempted to see around the cooler without getting too close. I rounded the corner and looked at the other side of the cooler when Shane's flashlight hit me. The light blinded me!

I waved my arms frantically, sure that I stood easy prey to whatever crouched by the side of the swamp cooler. "Douse the light," I said as quietly as I could.

RETREAT! My senses yelled at me.

Shane laughed and moved his light away.

Encouraged by the fact that I had close backup, I redirected my attention to the cooler. Nothing. Empty. No animals, no people, not even a branch existed that might explain the sounds we'd been hearing.

"Mike, go back inside for a moment and stand in the living room," I called down.

I waited a minute and then strolled around the roof right above where Mike would be. He came back outside.

"That's the same sounds," Mike said.

"Thanks, that's what I wanted to know." Confounded, I made my way back down to the ground and we gathered in the back yard.

"Man, you scared the life out of me," Shane said as he approached. "If I hadn't seen that bushy red hair and freckled face I would've screamed like a girl."

"Really, a girl?

"A sissy girl."

"There's nothing up there."

"Well, what did you expect?"

"You don't think something followed us back," Mike began but was cut short by my dad, who was at the back door, yelling, "What the bleep are you doing outside in the middle of the night. Get in here and go to bed! Louis Paul, you're the oldest, I expect you to set the example.

I cringed, knowing that whenever one of my parents used my first and middle name in a sentence it usually meant I was in trouble. We headed inside and crawled into our sleeping bags.

"We need to meet tomorrow," I said. "Tree house after breakfast." That seemed to calm everyone's nerves, because no one spoke.

Before I went to sleep, Mike's question came to mind. He didn't finish asking. He didn't have to. Four months had passed since our experience at the Round House, a haunted house we'd visited that left an impression on all of us. Shane and I read books on the unexplained and when we got together, our Friday night ritual consisted of watching scary movies and telling ghost stories. The paranormal had become our obsession.

The sounds on the roof started shortly after our visit to the haunted house we named "The Round House." None of us wanted to believe it possible, but we considered something not of this world followed us back and was now taunting us. Like me, Mike felt the presence. It didn't seem to affect Chad or Shane as of yet, and it wasn't threatening. We had no way to prove what was making the sounds on the roof.

🜺   🜺

"You ever notice how it hurts more when your body's cold?" Shane said.

"What?" I opened my eyes, barely aware that it was day until I spotted the soft rays of the sun filtering their way slowly through the rose-colored curtains.

"Sorry," Shane said. "I thought you were awake."

"I am now," I groaned. Rolling over, I propped my head up on one hand with my elbow on the floor so I could see his face. "It's cold this morning."

"I know. That's what I was saying. Ever notice how it's harder to move when you get too cold. Almost like the liquid in your joints is freezing up. What?" Shane said.

I couldn't see my own face but I must have given him the "you're an idiot" look.

"Is this what you think about in the morning?" I asked.

"I think about a lot of things, important things," he scowled.

"Well, maybe that's why people want to sleep in when they get older. You know, parents like to sleep in on a cold morning. Maybe they don't feel good."

"What a waste of time," Shane said. "I'm never going to sleep in. There's too much to do."

"No kidding," I said.

I watched the rays of the sun come through the window, touching the multicolored brown-shaded carpet that was our mattress during the night; the beams stirred fresh expectations of adventure. I listened to the sounds of the house crackling as it too came to life and stared at the white, textured roof above me.

"If it never got cold, we wouldn't know the joys of indoor living, hot cocoa, and a good book," I said.

"Sounds like something my mom would say," Shane said.

"That's exactly what my mom told me." I laughed.

"Did you finish that book you were reading about ghosts, Professor?"

Shane nicknamed me Professor because I was always reading and tended to give out lots of information. "I've read every book I could find about mysterious places, poltergeists, vampires, and any other legend or strange occurrence. All seven that the school library stocks. Lots of beliefs but little evidence. I hoped for more. But that won't stop me."

At the young age of thirteen, I suffered from two conditions that infect teenagers. The first is the feeling of invulnerability and the second is being a know-it-all. Both conditions drive parents crazy but to this day, there is no known cure.

"I found out one important thing."

"What?" Shane asked.

"I learned that adults don't have all the answers and that many mysteries in the world remained unexplained," I wisely stated.

"Oh, that. Then I suppose it is up to us," Shane said, "to solve the unsolvable."

"That it is."

"What's up to us?" Chad asked raising his head, eyes half-closed, out of the sleeping bag.

"Cool hair!" I said.

"You should see yours."

"How come girls worry about that kind of stuff?" Shane asked. "You know, how their hair looks all the time."

"I don't know."

"Because they don't have one of these." Chad pulled his Brooklyn Dodgers cap out of his sleeping bag and fit it on his head.

"You sleep with it?" I asked.

Chad frowned. "It's a classic. So, what's up to us?"

"Nothing, we're just talking."

"Should we wake Mike?" Shane asked.

"If you can wake the dead," I said. "Let him sleep."

"I was thinking about what Ms. Brown said, that no poltergeist had ever hurt anyone."

"She's a good teacher. I wish they all could be interesting like her."

"And pretty too," Shane said.

"What? You think she's pretty?"

"You know, I heard of a ghost town right outside of Pueblo."

I noticed Shane had changed the subject. "Maybe your brother could take us there," Shane said.

"I heard about it too," Chad said.

"But how do we get there?" Mike asked, sitting up and stretching. "All Eric's concerned about now is cars and girls. He doesn't even come in and tell stories with us on Friday nights."

"A ghost town?" I asked. "Who told you that?"

"My brother," Chad said.

"How do we get there?" Mike asked. His red hair stood up on his head as though the mere mention of ghosts scared it that way.

"I don't know," I said. "I heard that ghost towns aren't haunted, just no one lives there anymore."

"It's too far to walk there or even ride our bikes," Shane said.

We all sat up now. I rubbed my head, trying to get my hair to lie down. Our quest for adventure into the paranormal had hit a brick of reality. Unable to solve the mystery of the footsteps on our roof, we failed to find anything close by of interest. This resulted in us spending most of our time telling stories and talking about things we didn't know much about.

"Eric has his license," Mike said. "And he started his job at Ben Franklin so he isn't around as much."

"I know, but you're right, all he seems to worry about these days is borrowing the car and chasing girls. Last time we all sat and told stories together on Friday night was two months ago.

"Girls?" Chad said. "They can't even play football."

"I guess it's going to happen to all of us," Shane said.

"What happens?"

"We'll all like girls. If only there was something else to do."

"It's already happened to you," Chad said. "Oh, Ms. Brown, marry me." His lips feigned a kiss.

"Shut up," Shane said.

"I guess our quest isn't going so well," I said. "For all our efforts in the past months all we've done is explore a couple of abandoned houses, and a couple of scary old barns. The only real mystery is the footsteps we hear when we're together but we can't seem to identify the cause."

"Those bats were cool," Shane said.

I smiled. "I know. I don't understand why people are so scared of them, they're cute." At the time, Shane was my best friend and followed any crazy idea I had. Like me, he also dived into ghost stories and tried to find places to visit.

"I don't like bats," Chad said. "How do you think they came up with the name baseball bats?"

"Geez," Mike stated. "It's already six-thirty. I've got to go feed Herman and Reggie."

"You guys got new pets?" Shane asked.

"No, he's going to feed his bugs," I said.

"Insects!" Mike corrected me.

While my brother hastily put on his shoes and headed out to the shed to feed his insects, the rest of us turned on the television and headed to the kitchen that was adjacent to the living room, and took our places around the table. Each sat on the side or end so we could eat and watch television at the same time.

"How come parents never get up early on Saturday?" Shane asked.

"Mine do when they are doing something fun," Chad said.

"I don't know. I have more trouble getting up during the week than on Saturday," I said.

"Maybe it's because we get too much sleep during the week. You know, because they make us go to bed on time. I mean, we stayed up all night and yet, I'm not even tired."

"You've got a point. Maybe they just want to have some time without us making noise," Shane said. "I think that whole nutrition thing is a hoax, too. We ate popcorn, brownies and anything else we could convince your mom to give us. I don't think I drank any water last night and my stomach kinda hurts, but after a few bowls of cereal, I usually feel fine."

"Same for me. Works every Saturday."

"All week I went to school." Chad's mouth hung open and his lips curled like he'd eaten something bad. "Math, science, grammer, homework. It's hard work being a kid. We deserve to stay up late Friday night and eat junk food even if it makes us sick."

"You said it." Mike came back and sat down with us.

We tuned in to the hypnotic tones of cartoons and watched all the commercials about the latest and greatest fads.

"Hey, look Chad, it's a commercial about some new shoes," Shane said. "You better go get them; you haven't had a new pair in what, two weeks?"

We laughed and Chad frowned.

"Maybe it's the cereal that gives us the energy?" Mike said.

"Sure it is," I said taking the opportunity to practice my storytelling. "It's a known fact that for every action there is a reaction and for every cause there is an effect."

"Uh oh, here we go," Shane said raising his eyebrows. "Go ahead, Professor."

"Quiet, class." I raised my index finger as all eyes focused on it. "Somewhere along the span of lifetimes, a person who became an adult kept some of his childhood knowledge and realized that after struggling to get up Saturday morning to watch his favorite cartoon he needed instant energy." I held up a box of Fruit Circles. "And he invented sugar-coated cereal," I lowered my voice as if doing a commercial, "currently an American staple for children between the ages of six and sixteen." My comments drew laughter.

"Ah, but that's not where it ends." Crunching sounds emerged from my audience as Mike, Chad and Shane began eating and I fed on the opportunity to speak while their mouths were full.

"After the introduction of this overnight success, the industry came up with many ideas and a multitude of colors, shapes, sizes, and flavors to sustain the craze." I gestured to the many boxes across the table. "Animated characters were brought in to market the product to kids. Special mention must go to the person who invented cereal that changes the color of your milk while you are eating. It's cool."

"It is," Chad nodded. The rest agreed.

"But," I waited for everyone to look at me, "Since its introduction, there is only one major promotion noted in the annals of sugared-cereal history that deserves the most honorable of mention."

All eyes were upon me, all chewing stopped. I pushed my chair back across the cream-tiled floor and raised my hand; fist clenched over the brown, laminated wood table, and lowered my voice. "At a time when sales stalled, and certain doom faced the sugary coated pops, and moms everywhere were switching back to oatmeal at the request of health gurus, a man came forward, who in the industry was simply known as 'The One.'"

"Oh, the one," Shane nodded and started chewing again.

"Right," Mike said.

"Shh!" I shook my head and waved my pointy finger. "He presented the single most important change that revived the industry: He answered the single question of 'How do we get children to eat more cereal?' His idea was incredibly simple."

"More sugar?" Chad's eyebrows rose.

Shane and Mike shook their heads and shrugged their shoulders. I waited.

"He told the makers to put a toy surprise in the bottom of the box, which encouraged kids to eat it faster," I looked at Mike, "because they are supposed to eat the cereal before they dig through it."

"What's a guru?" Chad asked.

"What?" Mike said. "There's nothing wrong with getting the toy first. I still eat the cereal."

"Didn't you just get done feeding your bugs?"

"Insects," Mike corrected me. "They're cleaner than us."

Shane, who was eating from the same box as Mike, put his spoon down and looked like he might get sick.

"Right," I said. "As I was saying, he single-handedly started the biggest war waged between siblings since the invention of bubblegum and multiple TV stations as brothers and sisters competed to get to the bottom of the box and find the buried treasure. And so, cereal and its long and upstanding career, were saved."

"Bravo!" Shane said. "You need your head examined, but good story."

"Did you ever notice how tired you are on Sunday?" Mike said as he grabbed the box of cereal I had just opened.

I cringed as he dug his hand deep down into the box of cereal to find the toy surprise at the bottom. The plastic wrapper rattled as he removed it from the treasure chest, and, smiling, displayed his prized jewel: a book of washable tattoos.

I shook my head in disgust and reached for a different brand to fill my bowl.

"What are we going to do about last night?" Chad asked.

"I don't know if there's anything we can do until summer," I said. "Then we can sleep outside and nothing will be able to sneak up on us."

"What if we don't find anything, like last night?" Chad questioned. "I mean, no one was there."

I scratched my head as though the stimulation would jar a response. "Whatever it is hasn't tried to hurt us."

"So, you think it is a ghost?" Chad asked.

"I don't know what it is," I said. "It's strange that the sounds only happen when all four of us are together. And since Shane only comes over about once a month, we'll have to wait another three weeks or more to come up with something. Maybe by then we'll know how to deal with ghosts."

"Right. We're taking a class on it," Shane added.

"Your house is haunted," Chad said, looking to Mike and then to the roof, as though he were waiting for something to appear. A grin crossed his lips and we laughed.

""Nothing's happened here that would make a ghost want to haunt the place," I said. "This was the original land our family settled on, and nothing tragic has happened here."

"Accept me missing that pass the other day," Chad chuckled.

"The Professor is right. If I were a ghost I'd want to haunt a big mansion, not a doublewide trailer," Shane said. "No offense."

"None taken," I said. "I don't think they get to pick where they haunt," I said.

"I'd rather haunt a cemetery," Chad said.

"The footsteps on the roof didn't start until last year after we visited that haunted house," Mike said.

"The Round House," Shane said out loud. We had visited the haunted house that we'd nicknamed "The Round House" in October of the previous year on a dark, wintery night. The events of that night had left us shaken and curious to find out more about the supernatural. The Round House was moved away and we never had a chance to go to it again.

"It's possible that something unseen followed us back here that night," I said. "Or, it could be our imaginations acting up. We shouldn't jump to conclusions when we don't have proof. Whatever reason for the sounds on the roof, it appears to be harmless."

No one spoke. I chewed my cereal as though it were steak. Denial set in. We didn't want to believe something unnatural followed us.

"Cemeteries are already haunted," Shane said. "Because there are dead people there. No mystery to solve. Night's the best time for scaring."

"I'd like to scare Ms. Cole," Chad said. "Maybe she'd move."

"Your English teacher? Ours is cool," Shane said.

"Not possible to have English teacher and cool in the same sentence," Chad said.

"Are you learning anything that class you're taking about ghosts?" Mike asked.

"It's not exactly about ghosts," I said. It's called, "In search of strange phenomena."

"Oh, strange stuff, such as Chad doing his homework," Mike laughed.

Chad stuck his tongue out at him.

"I can't believe they're letting her teach that for open lab," Shane said.

"Hey, it's the eighties. We have a right to know."

"I was scared I wouldn't make it to 1981; now I'm scared I won't make it to 1982 if I keep hanging out with you guys," Chad said.

"Very funny," I said. "Ms. Brown tells us there are two types of hauntings. One type is called residual, where some event has happened that was so terrible it left a mark on the house and it occurs over and over again.

"The thing about this type is that there is no real threat to those witnessing the event, other than maybe being scared. It's kinda like watching a movie. Maybe that's what happened to us last time at the Round House."

"They moved the house away and planted an orchard," Shane said. "I think something must have been wrong."

"Let's not talk about that," Mike said. Everyone nodded.

"The second type of haunting is by a spirit," I said. "Usually one that has some unfinished business; something in this world that is keeping it from being at rest and moving on." This description drew wide-eyed looks from the others.

"If you can find out what it is that is holding this spirit back," Shane added, "you might be able to make it go away."

"How?" Mike asked.

"You have to discover what it wants. Some untold truth or mystery that needs solving," I replied.

"Sometimes it's someone that has been murdered," Shane said. "The only way you can put them to rest is by finding the bones, and bury their remains properly."

"In a cemetery?" Chad asked.

"Shh," I said. "Listen," I heard someone down the hall. "Someone's coming; we can talk more about this kind of stuff later."

My sister, Dee Dee, older than me by two years, walked down the hall toward us.

"When do you have to go home?" I asked Shane.

His eyes darted from left to right, in the same manner as when he was scared, and then looked at me. "Do you think your mom would mind if I stayed another night?"

"What? No chores today?" I asked.

"Not as many in the winter."

"I don't think my mom will mind, but what about yours? You never get to stay two nights in a row."

"She thinks we're working on a science report together. All I have to do is tell her we still need to finish it and she'll probably let me because she wants me to get good grades. Besides," his voice turned to a whisper as Dee Dee entered the kitchen, "I think we need to have a meeting at the tree house." His face took on an adult-like appearance. "I've got something on my mind and I decided I better tell you."

"I have to go home early," Chad said. "My mom's taking me to get some shoes."

"Didn't you just get new shoes a week ago?" I asked.

"Those are jumping shoes. I need running shoes with big treads, you know, for winter conditions. They help me get traction and go faster."

"You should get Shane some new shoes before he trips on those shoe laces," I said.

"Hey," Shane said. "Hi-tops are in, the latest fashion."

"I'll pass for function," I said.

Dee Dee eyed the table cautiously and then sat at the only chair left with her back against the television. Her presence prevented me from questioning Shane further, as I feared she would not keep quiet about our adventures. She looked around the table, frowning, but no one spoke.

"Looks like snow," I said breaking the silence.

"Does look cold outside," Shane said.

"I like the snow," Chad said. "You can go sledding and tubing."

"I hate getting sick. Or when your nose runs, until the boogers get frozen," Mike said.

Dee Dee, her bowl still half-full of cereal, raised her eyebrows, lifted her bowl off the table, stood and proceeded down the hall to her room.

"I guess she doesn't like the cold either," Shane said, making all of us laugh.

After watching three and a half more hours of cartoons, Chad went home and the rest of us put on our flannel shirts, jackets, caps, and gloves and headed outside. Although the front of the trailer faced the main road, it was fenced all the way around to the back which faced the yard and the driveway. For all purposes, we used the back door as our front, and the front door had come with the house, but was rarely used.

Mike led the way through the gate and around the driveway to the tree house as the snowflakes began to trickle around us.

"What luck," Shane said. "Too bad it couldn't snow tomorrow; maybe by Monday we'd get off school."

Eric had started construction of the tree house that stood in the tall oak tree at the base of our driveway. Mike and I finished the fortress and boasted that it was the sturdiest one for miles. Made of plywood and two-by-fours, it stood fifteen feet high from the ground, and had a large, single room with a makeshift staircase to a patio roof. When the weather allowed, we often sat on the roof to look over the surrounding territory. The entrance to the tree house was through a hatch in the floor.

During the winter months, we didn't spend too much time in the tree house. The cracks between boards provided plenty of light but did little to insulate against the cold. We managed to round up some old blankets and pillows to make the place more comfortable but even with these, it was too cold to stay out for long.

"There," I said dusting the snow off the wood sign until the words "Keep Out" were visible. "I guess it's good that Chad's not here." I looked up to the entrance.

"Right. He'd probably slip on his way up and break his leg or something," Shane's hand slipped off of the board we used to climb to the opening. "See, really slippery. Are you ever going to fix this entrance?"

"What's wrong with it?"

"It's too hard."

"It keeps the wimps out. You have to have strong legs, upper body strength, and be flexible to get up here. It's a gym teacher's dream."

Being the last one up, I closed the hatch behind me.

"Man, it's cold in here," Mike said.

"At least we don't have to worry about spiders," I said as I tried to hang a blanket to deflect the wind coming in through the cracks in the wall.

"Hey, there's nothing wrong with spiders. They're just misunderstood. Do you know how many insects there would be around if spiders didn't eat them?"

"You can keep 'em all," Shane said shifting around to find a comfortable seat. "It's kind of dark in here; maybe we should go get a lantern. Maybe that battery-powered one you guys have."

"It doesn't last that long when you keep it on," I said. "I wish we had a heater."

I sat still, having found a spot in the tree house that offered protection from the wind. In a moment the cold found me again and I knew I wouldn't last long. "That storm's moving in fast. Are you guys sure the sun came up this morning?"

"I think it's time to go back inside," Mike said holding a stiff blanket in front of him. "The blankets are frozen."

"Not yet. Shane had something to tell us."

Shane didn't reply. He pulled a blanket over his head. "Hey, you can use your own breath to warm up if you do this."

"Sure, but you can't breathe very long."

Soon, Shane's head emerged from under the thick, brown blanket. "I'm too cold to think. I can't move my hands."

"Hey, guys, if you pull the blanket over your head, your breath will keep you warm," Mike said from under his blanket.

I raised my eyebrows and looked at Mike, who remained under his blanket. "Weren't you paying attention? You'll run out of oxygen. "Which in your case is already a problem. This is ridiculous. We need to go back inside. We need heat."

"No," Shane pleaded.

"Why?"

"I need to tell you something."

"How about a candle?" Mike said. His head emerged from the blanket and he breathed deeply.

"You know where one is?"

"Mom keeps some above the stove."

"Those are for a power outage," I said. "I guess it won't hurt if we take one. We can replace it later when we go to the store."

With that, Mike exited and headed to the house.

"If we get power out here we could have heat and light," Shane said. "It would last a lot longer than a battery, too."

"Can't we talk inside?" I asked.

"No," Shane said. Crossing his arms, he looked away from me. "I don't want anyone outside of our group to know."

"It has something to do with the paranormal?" I asked.

Shane nodded. My brain went into overdrive.

"There's an outlet outside by the lightpost," I said. "We can get an extension cord out of the shed."

"Let's go," Shane stood up and headed down the tree.

I hesitated. I knew my dad would not be pleased that we were using an extension cord strung out across the driveway, but my best friend was in trouble. I climbed down to the base of the tree.

"Wow, it's really snowing." Shane pointed to the grass where the large flakes had blanketed the short, brown stems. "We could run the cord alongside the house to hide it. The snow will help."

"What about getting across the driveway? If cars run over it, it could get caught."

"Then we dig a shallow trench to bury it across the driveway. If we do it soon enough, the snow will cover the fresh dig and no one will notice it at all."

Mike returned with a long, white dinner candle.

"Did you get matches?"

Mike grinned from under his green, woolly cap and pulled out a pack of matches. "Dad shouldn't miss these."

We scrambled back up to our fortress, proud that we had fire. I lit the candle, allowing some of the wax to drip down on the floor, and used this wax as a holder.

"Great idea," Shane said. We all closed in around the glorious flame.

"I guess that's why everyone used to have fireplaces instead of just candles," Shane commented.

"I can't even feel a difference unless I'm directly over it, and then only that part's warm," Mike said."

"Still too cold for me," Shane said."

I heard a car start and looked through a crack in the wall. My dad was in his car, warming it up before he headed off to work at the mall. Once he was gone, the coast was clear.

"Plan B." I turned away from the wall and looked toward Shane. "Mike, go inside and sit at the table by the kitchen window. Sit with your back facing the yard and act normal. If Mom comes in the kitchen, turn around and look outside or raise your hands behind you like you're stretching." I demonstrated the move. "That'll be the signal that someone's coming."

"What are you guys going to do?" My brother asked.

"We're going to get power! This way we can have heat and light. I have a feeling we are going to be using the treehouse a lot now that we have a new quest."

As my brother headed indoors, Shane and I headed for the shed. Our driveway came off 25th Lane on a steep incline and ran fifty yards before it looped around a centerpiece. The closest side of the loop faced the house and the other faced a one-acre field. On the opposite side of the loop was a tall toolshed.

The toolshed could be viewed from the kitchen and we needed to be cautious. I knew my mom wouldn't mind if she saw us going into the shed, as long as she didn't see us hauling tools out.

"Make sure you don't break anything and watch out for my brother's bug collection," I said to Shane as we entered the shed.

"We should meet in here," Shane said closing the door behind him. "It's warmer."

"Sure, but it would be easy for someone to sneak up on us or be listening outside, plus there's nowhere to sit."

"You're right. And we can defend the tree house better." Against whom, I didn't know, but at the time this seemed like an important feature.

"Besides, this is my dad's toolshed. He comes in here when he's working outside. The tree house is our place. We don't have to worry about anyone changing it or making us clean up."

"But it is warmer in here," Shane said leaning up against a shelf.

"Watch out!" I pointed to a row of bottles where several spiders, one cockroach, and multiple other bugs of species I couldn't name lived out the remainder of their lives. "My brother's bug collection."

"Gross. Your brother is weird," Shane said, and went over to get a closer look at the bugs.

"I don't know," I stepped up beside him. "Some of them are kind of cool. He's been teaching that cockroach how to go through mazes. As long as he doesn't bring them in the house, I don't mind."

"I guess you're right," Shane said as I moved to the wall where the extension cords were stored.

"About what?"

"This place is too grown up. Reminds me of work and all the chores I have to do. The tree house is always fun, like when the wind is blowing and we get up on the roof and pretend like we're sailing on a ship."

"Like we're out on the ocean," I finished his thought.

Shane shivered. "Do you have that extension cord?"

"Take your pick," I answered. "My dad hates gasoline engines. Everything we have is electric."

"Why?"

"I don't know. Says something about the oil companies are crooks and they're robbing us."

"Wow. I never knew there was an electric lawnmower," Shane leaned against the orange handle and propped it up to see under it. "That seems dangerous, to have an electric cord alongside the chopping blade and all."

"Yep, one of these days." I ran my hand across my throat in a slashing motion and pointed to three taped-up cords on the wall. "Victims of the blade."

"You're lucky to be alive," Shane said patting me on the back.

"These are just the ones that I nicked," I pointed to some cords with multiple wraps of electrical tape. "The ones I cut clean through went in the trash." I looked around for a shovel. "My dad won't miss one. Just don't grab that orange one," I said. "It will show up too easy."

"This one will do," Shane said, hoisting it across his shoulder.

I grabbed a pick and shovel to dig the trench and we headed to the door. I looked to the house before leaving the shed. I spotted Mike in the kitchen window. He waved me clear and I headed back up the driveway, while Shane headed toward the light post to plug the cord into the outlet.

I laid the pick against the tree and, with shovel in hand, planned my next move. Looking left, then right, I raised the shovel with both hands, took aim, and slammed it against the frozen tundra. "Uggh!" A guttural sound emerged from within me as my hands clutched the vibrating handle. Tremors ran all the way to my brain and I lost vision as my eyeballs quaked.

I quickly looked around. Shane was still preoccupied with hiding the cord along the side of the house and had his back turned. I spared myself the humiliation of anyone else seeing my act.

Altering my technique, I took small chips out of the ground and slowly began to make progress. After ten minutes, my hands were feeling the pain and my progress was far short of what we needed.

Shane walked up beside me as I removed my jacket and gloves and massaged my sore hands. He shook his head, grabbed the pick and took a big swing.

"NO!" I shouted too late.

As the pick contacted the ground, I could physically see the vibration travel through Shane's hands all the way to his head which he shook trying to regain his vision.

"Ground's too frozen for that," I said.

"Thanks for telling me," Shane said grasping his hands. "You better let me do this and put your jacket back on before you get a cold." Shane grabbed the old, wooden-handled tool in both hands, and with smaller swings, began chipping away at the ground.

I followed along Shane's strikes with the shovel and removed the loose dirt, relieved that we'd found a faster way to get the project done. After a few strikes, my confidence faded when a different sound emerged: "Crack!" The pick handle had snapped under the pressure as the head connected with the ground.

Holding the broken handle, Shane looked up and me and shrugged his shoulders. "Got another one?"

We solemnly walked over to the edge of the driveway and put the broken pick at the bottom of the trashcan, being sure to conceal it beneath some recently dumped garbage.

"It was a good tool in its time," I said as we turned and headed back to the shed.

Against the far wall was my father's new pick. So new it hadn't been used.

"That one will do," Shane said grasping it with both hands.

"You don't think the ground is too hard that we'll break this one too?"

"No, that pick was old. This one looks new, sturdy," Shane said.

"My dad just bought it at the end of fall from the clearance rack."

"See, he must have known that old one was wearing out. He probably won't remember it by the time summer comes. He'll think he threw it away."

"Grab it. Let's go." We headed back to the tree house, making the mistake of not checking with Mike.

We were already out of the shed when I spotted my brother sitting at the table. He turned his head and looked over his shoulders at us. Suddenly, I realized his hands were raised.

"The signal!" I grabbed Shane by the shoulder and we dove to the ground behind my mom's car.

"DUCK," I said as I hit the ground.

Shane looked at me and frowned. "Nice warning."

I counted to thirty before I cautiously raised my head. Mike stood at the window looking out at us, shaking his head.

"We're taking too long," I said looking around to make sure it was clear. We stood, brushed ourselves off and proceeded to the side of the house. "Let's take turns. We'll get done faster."

We made great progress digging the trench. Toward the end we tired and our swings became longer and higher as our hands numbed. With the handle in his hands Shane breathed heavily as he neared the end of the trench.

"That should be good enough," I said. The cold air froze my words in a white puff as they exited. The snow still fell heavily and carpeted the ground. "It's getting colder."

Shane looked at me and nodded. "Just one more bit here," he raised the pick high above his head. With his arms shaking and barely supporting the weight, he came down with one last grunt and contacted the ground.

"SNAP!"

Thoughts raced through my head as I looked around trying to see what went wrong. The pick handle was still in Shane's hands but the head flew toward the trunk of the tree.

Frozen in fear, Shane didn't move as the iron head bounced off the tree and deflected back toward him. With lightning reflexes he dove to the side and out of the way which left only one problem; the pick head came directly at me.

Suddenly, life went in slow motion as the threat of death or severe injury became real. My brain reacted on sheer instinct and I jumped. The pick's head landed clear of me, only inches away from my feet. I came down off balance and tumbled to the ground, landing flat on my back; what wind remained in me exited upon impact.

Moments passed and my head throbbed. I felt like I would suffocate. Finally, I breathed in and the frozen air filled my lungs. I coughed.

"What just happened?"

"We got lucky. We'll have to be more careful next time."

Shane helped me to my feet.

"That was close, are you hurt?"

"No. Good thing we're done." I bent down and picked up my Yankees cap, putting it back on my head.

"What do we do now?" Shane asked.

I shrugged my shoulders and bent down to pick up the pieces of the pick and headed to the trashcan. We hid the broken pieces of the pick in the bottom of the trash alongside the older pick.

"Well, we've got at least two months before my dad will be looking to use it. I guess we can try to save money for a new one. Either that or let it end up on my dad's list of inexplicable missing tools. Try not to break the shovel while we bury the cord."

"Let's cover it with some dirt, and then add some snow on top of it," Shane said. "With any luck, the ground will harden by the time the snow melts and with the cars driving over the path, no one will ever notice. I'm not sure what you can do about the grass, once the snow melts."

"No one mows the grass but me. They probably won't notice," I said. "Now all we need to do is find a portable heater." I looked across the yard and spotted Chad coming from the gate that separated our properties. "And here comes the guy that can get us anything."

"We should call him Gadget," Shane said.

"Why?"

"He's always getting us any gadgets we need."

Within minutes of telling him what we needed Chad headed home and returned with a heater. We ran the extension cord up the side of the tree facing away from the driveway and through a hole in the floor. Soon, we were all in the tree house enjoying our success. Huddled around the small electrical device, the light of glowing red bands reflected off four contented faces.

"No one's going to miss this heater, right?" I asked.

Chad looked at me. "It's been in the closet all winter."

"Good. But nobody can leave it on up here, and don't fall asleep with it on."

"Why?" Shane asked.

"You can start a fire," I said.

"Anyone for football?" Mike said.

"It's too cold to play football," Chad said. "Although I got these cool shoes." He wiggled his shoes for all of us to see.

"Okay. Now it's time to talk about our next quest," I said. "Men our age need adventure!"

"Oh," Chad said. "I didn't think we were men yet."

"Does that mean we have to like girls now?" Mike said.

"Not until we can drive." Shane said.

"Why?"

"Because, stupid, you can't ask a girl out if you can't drive. Why do you think they give you your license when you're sixteen? So you can take girls on dates and get a job to pay for it."

"Oh. I'm going to get a Ferrari like Magnum and you'll all be eating my dust."

"I know. We could go to the mall. My mom would probably take us," Chad said.

"No, no, no," I stood kicked the floor and shook my head. "I'm talking about a real adventure." I looked between the spaces and could see snow still falling.

"We could go see that old abandoned house off of North Road," Mike said.

"In this weather?" I said. "We've already been there twice and there's nothing to see but an old brick fireplace. Besides," I went back to the heater and sat down, "Chad's right. It's too cold outside to go anywhere and it's still snowing."

"It took me all morning to get this place warm, I'm staying right here," Shane said moving closer to the heater. He put out his hands and warmed them.

"Maybe we'll just have to wait until it gets warmer and try to ride to that ghost town. Why did we come out here anyway? Let's go back inside."

"Shane wanted to tell us something," I said. "That's why we spent all day getting this heater out here. Right?"

Shane sat staring into the heater, oblivious to the question I had asked.

Chad and Mike shrugged their shoulders. I was about to ask again when Shane started talking.

"I know what our next quest should be. I know someone who lives in a haunted house."

"Why didn't you say so? How far away is it? Can we get there on our bikes?" I asked inching closer.

"How do you know it's haunted?" Mike questioned.

Shane stared into the heater and then looked at the three of us. I was ready for him to deliver his punch line and tell us he was kidding.

"Joke's over. What's going on?" I said.

"It's my house. It's haunted."

CHAPTER TWO

A MYSTERIOUS PLACE

THE EYES THAT LOOKED out from under a faded Red Sox hat and the voice that spoke were serious. There was no humor in Shane's telling of the sounds emanating from his second-floor bedroom. Genuine fear showed through his eyes when he finished.

"Why didn't you say something sooner," I asked Shane.

"It just started. Besides, I didn't want you guys to think I was a chicken. But since we seem to be wanting to find something mysterious to solve well…"

"So your parents never told you about any of this when it was their room?" I asked.

"No. Never heard a thing. They just moved into their new room downstairs a few weeks ago, and then I moved into their old room. That's when the sounds started."

"Just move back to your old room."

"I can't, Stacey moved into my room. I thought it would be cool to have the bigger room. I should've given Stacey the bigger room."

"You've only been in the house for two years; maybe your dad's remodeling stirred something up."

"Holy crap," Chad said. "I'd start finding a new place to live if I were you."

"You got it," Mike said.

"That really bites," Chad said.

"Chad," I held my hand up. "Not helping." I looked around the room and tried to come up with some words that would help Shane.

"I'm sorry, we'll do our best to try to help you," were the words that left my mouth. But what I was thinking was "Cool. An adventure right around the block from where I live."

That's how our next quest began.

"What about the sounds on your roof?" Shane asked.

"Well, we haven't had any luck so far," I said. "The sounds only happen when all four of us are together and from what you're saying, we need to stay at your house which means we won't be over here."

"I visited your house before you moved in."

"What about it?" Shane asked.

"This is what I remember. My mom has these friends, Bud and Jan, who buy old houses and fix them up. The house you live in looks nice now, but it wasn't always that way. When I visited it looked like a giant, old barn. We didn't go past the first floor because there were holes in it that went down into the basement."

"We don't have a basement," Shane said.

"Curious."

"That's it!" Chad exclaimed. "They buried the bodies in the basement and covered it up! That's why it's haunted. All we have to do is dig them up and bury them in a cemetery. I saw it on a show once."

"That might be true," I said.

Chad's eyes widened. "My brother took me out to the basements of the old honor farm, you know, the nut house. They tore the buildings down but the underground tunnels and basement are still there. There are strange noises at night."

"I've never been there," Mike said moving back from the heater and resting against one of the walls.

Chad smiled and nodded, as though satisfied to be the only one to have visited the infamous site.

I looked at my brother. "Sounds like we all have an adventure in front of us. There'll be plenty to talk about later."

"Then, you guys are going to help me?" Shane asked.

"You are one of the Questors and we promised to help each other," I said.

"We did?"

"Yep, it's part of the Questors' code."

Mike and Chad gathered around and we put our hands together.

"Do we have a code yet?" Mike asked.

"Shane was going to come up with one," I said. "Is it finished?"

"Uh, not really," Shane said. "I'm working on it."

"Just go with what you have so far," I said.

"Oh, right." Shane pulled a crumpled piece of paper out of his pocket and smoothed it out. He cleared his throat before he read it.

"We Questors do swear to help one another in all matters through rain, sleet, hail, snow, or fire and to keep all secrets between us and tell no one else unless tortured or threatened with exile."

A look of confusion passed between Mike, Chad, and me at the mention of the word "exile."

Shane stopped and looked up.

"All right, then," I said. "To the quest!"

"Can we sit here and stay warm for a little longer?" Shane asked.

"I hope this doesn't raise the electric bill too much."

"How could it?" Chad said. "It's just a couple of heating coils. Can't take that much to run it. I bet we can leave it on all day and they won't even notice."

Three contented faces sat and watched the bright, orange bands glow, sending out their miraculous warmth. "Ah, technology." My mind wondered. What past event happened on the land Shane's family occupied that would continue to make itself known in the present? I intended to find the answer.

🙖   🙖

Shane did stay a second night and the next week, we decided to learn what we could about haunted houses. I did everything I could to learn about ghosts and hauntings by rereading every book I had on the subject which wasn't much. The public library was too far away for me to ride my bike too, so I only had access to our school library. It wasn't until the middle of the week during lunch that Shane talked to me about his problem.

"We need to get to the library. I can't work with such limited information," I said as I sat down on the white, fold-out table. "We need a ride." I looked around but no one came to mind.

"You're lucky," Shane said looking up at me as I sat down. "Your mom packs you a lunch every day."

"That stuff will shorten your lifespan," I pointed to Shane's mac and cheese. "I think that's the same batch they served last week."

"Why are we sitting way over here by ourselves?"

I looked down the long line of lunch tables stretched out in the gymnasium and noticed Jay Falter staring in our direction. "That's why. Now that we have a new mystery, we need to keep our plans a secret."

"Oh," Shane sat his tray at the table and sat down. "What's the plan?"

"Shh, keep it down," I looked around to see if anyone heard. "Ever since we let the secret out about the Round House, the Falter brothers have been keeping a close watch. They could spoil everything." I lowered my voice. "It's the middle of the week and you figure I've had enough time?"

"Just asking."

"I don't have a plan, yet." I said. "I would like to know more about the whole subject. I feel like anything we do that goes right is probably just an accident." I finished my last bite and stood up to go outside. Shane followed.

"That's not so bad," Shane said. "Some might call it good luck."

"If something goes wrong, it's not like we can redo it."

"Okay, that's bad luck. Not so good. What are we up against, Professor?"

We headed to the exit to the break area, stopping briefly to put on our coats. I looked down the hall to make sure we weren't being followed before we went outside.

"I've read seven books on haunted houses and another one on poltergeists. That's all our school library has on the subject," I said. "Too bad we live out here in the county, the library is too far to walk or ride too."

"We can ask your mom to take us," Shane said.

"But then she'd see the books we were getting. It might make her suspicious."

"I guess. What about that book you had on mysterious places?"

"I read some stories about places in England, but none here." We exited the building and stood on the rectangular asphalt slab in the cool air with our backs against the wall of the building. In front of us were three tether ball poles minus the balls and an empty playground beyond the fence.

"Did you ask your mom anything about her friends who worked on my house?" Shane asked.

"She didn't know anything other than you're the second family that's lived there since it was fixed up. Her friends who fixed the place live in Utah or something like that."

"Bummer. I guess we can't go visit them."

"I should come by today and look things over. Have you noticed any moving furniture or anything like that?

"No. Why?"

"That's a sign of a poltergeist."

"What?"

"A poltergeist."

"Oh, right," Shane said. "Didn't hear you the first time."

"It's a ghost that plays tricks on people," I said. "Unlike other ghosts that may just appear and walk through hallways or something like that, these ghosts actually move things around."

"That might be fun," Shane responded. "I wonder if you could play catch with it. I wish it would snow."

"Like four feet or something, and just shut everything down."

Shane shuffled his feet grinding small rocks on top of the asphalt pad. "So what do we do?"

"I guess all we can do is wait and see what happens next," I said knowing that we didn't have an answer of how to go about dealing with ghosts or haunted houses.

"You *are* coming over tonight?"

"I have to, eventually. See if we can find the source of the sound."

"Then what?"

"I don't know. Obviously, if it's a ghost, then we need to figure out how to evict a ghost."

"I know!" Shane said. A confident look crossed his face, as though he could answer all of our problems. "We can ask Ms. Brown. We just need to be careful not to draw suspicion."

"That's a good idea," I said. Our conversation was cut short as two of our friends came over and invited us to compete in relay races.

"I guess it's time to go show these guys they still can't catch me," Shane said. Easily the quickest off the starting block, Shane often frustrated those who played by using his ability to get ahead quickly. Soon the bell rang and it was back to class.

We headed into the red brick building and marched down the black-and-white checkered hallways to our rooms, just like the kids did in every other middle school.

After our regular English and math class, we headed to our favorite class of the day: open lab. If there were one thing different about Pleasant View Middle School, it was that every kid looked forward to the last class of the day on Wednesday through Friday. On these days, each teacher picked a subject that interested them and students signed up for the one they wanted. It was freedom and liberty for students and teachers alike!

"Open lab," Shane said. "What a great way to end the day."

"You said it. If they'd make every subject this interesting, we'd all learn more."

"Doesn't it seem strange?" Shane said as we walked to class.

"What?"

"Ms. Brown is an English teacher. This fact alone makes it unlikely that she can teach a subject that would hold our interest."

"In Search of Strange Phenomena," I said. "She sure picked an interesting title."

"And the class is full. I wonder why we're the only students chasing ghosts," Shane said.

"Maybe we're not," I said. "You never know."

"Hmm," Shane mumbled. "Remember when you took that reading class and there was only like, four students and you were the only boy?"

I rolled my eyes. "I didn't choose it; I was selected because I was a good reader. I got teased for weeks." We entered the class and took our seats in the room of about twenty desks. "We'll have to wait until the end of the day when everyone leaves," I whispered. "Then we can talk to Ms. Brown."

"I can't believe she lets us pick our own seats," Shane said. "I never heard of a teacher doing that."

"No kidding. I wonder how long it will take us to recover from the alphabetically ordered seating chart?"

"What do you mean?"

"In all of my years as a student, I have never sat by anyone whose last name started with a letter lower than a J. I can only wonder how many friendships, quarrels, or relationships are going to be voided or avoided due to this. If not for gym and band, I wouldn't have gotten to know you because your last name starts with an 'S.'"

"Wow," Shane said. "You think about that kind of stuff?"

"No. Just an observation." I looked around to see who was in class today.

"Ms. Brown is always interesting," Shane said. His eyes fixed on her as she sat at her desk.

"No kidding. If teachers weren't so boring, I'd learn more. I like reading. But you can't learn everything from a book, and you can't have interesting discussions with no one else around."

Standing only five-foot-two, with short brown hair and brown eyes, Ms. Brown wasn't a fearsome teacher by any means. Some of the boys in our class and a few of the girls were already as tall as she was, but her energy and persuasiveness kept us in awe. I imagine it was how she got permission to teach her class.

"Why do you suppose she chose such a weird subject?" Shane asked.

"I suppose it's because she's from California," I said.

"Oh, that explains it. My mom says people from California have outlandish ideas and clothes to match."

"By whatever coincidence she's ended up at our school," I said, "Her interests might help us. But we'll have to wait until after school to ask her."

We listened to her talk about strange creatures and mythical beasts until the end but didn't leave with the rest of the students. We waited in our seats until the others filtered out.

Ms. Brown, who often sat on the front of her desk and talked to the class instead of standing, now sat in her chair filing some papers. She looked up, noticing Shane and I were still in our seats.

"Did you two have a question?"

I looked at Shane and he looked back, shrugging his shoulders.

"We wanted to know about haunted houses?" I said, frowning after the hasty words left my mouth.

"Don't worry," Ms. Brown said, standing. She walked to the front of her desk. "It's normal to be curious." She leaned back on the edge of her desk and faced us. "By avoiding something that is not understood it only makes it more mysterious than it really is. Now, what do you want to know?"

"Do you think there are any here in our town?" Shane blurted out.

"I'm sure there are. Every town has them. Pueblo is the oldest city in Colorado; lots of history here."

Shane's mouth hung open. He slowly turned toward me and then back to the front. Ms. Brown had confirmed that there were haunted houses in Pueblo, but that didn't mean Shane's house was one.

"How does a house become haunted?" I asked.

Ms. Brown looked to the door as if checking to make sure no one was watching before she answered Shane's question.

"We talked a little about this last week. There are lots of reasons a house could be haunted," she began. "Many times a person passed away in the house and their spirit remains behind. Some believe this happens when the death occurs unexpectedly, trapping the person between this world and the next world."

The sound of three hundred students in the hall making their way home became distant and the classroom grew quiet and cold. I noticed my arms, stretched out across my desk, filling with goose bumps under my blue-and-orange shirt. The bumps pointed toward the door.

A thought came to me: *Is it knowledge that helps us find the truth or makes us face the truth?*

"Louis?" Ms. Brown looked at me.

"Sorry," my face turned red. "I got distracted."

Ms. Brown continued her explanation:

"Other times, there may have been a traumatic event and the person who died is unsettled; they have some unfinished business."

"Like an unsolved murder," I said, remembering a story I read.

"Correct," Ms. Brown replied. "Or an untimely death."

Shane's eyes grew wide again and I felt the hair stand up on the back of my neck. A quick look behind me assured me there was no one besides us in the room.

"And then there's another theory that sometimes the past imprints itself on a place and the event keeps repeating itself," Ms. Brown continued. "Most of the time, it is a sad event. In England," Ms. Brown stopped as she noticed another teacher peeking in.

"Are you going to the meeting?"

"I'll be right there," Ms. Brown returned. "Sorry, boys, I have to go."

"What about something that makes sounds?" Shane said, trying to get in one more question.

"Well, that sounds like a poltergeist. We'll talk about them next week," Ms. Brown said as she picked up her books and headed out the door. "On Friday, we need to finish our study of unusual creatures, or Cryptozoology."

Shane's gaze followed Ms. Brown, trying to will her to stay longer. After she left, he turned to me, and then his eyes searched the floor.

"That didn't help, I only have more questions," Shane sighed. His hands gripped a pencil he held out in front of him. "Next week?" He was clearly frustrated. "I need that information now." The pencil he held snapped in two and I watched a piece of it slingshot across the room. He turned and looked at me. "You're still coming over Friday right?"

I looked at Shane and then at the piece of his pencil across the room, gulping. "Of course. I can't think of anything more exciting to do than face imminent *doom* together."

"We can sleep downstairs," Shane said. "Maybe we should wait to get more advice before we try to figure all of this out."

"I don't know," I said. "I think when older people tell you to be patient it's just an excuse for a lack of energy or maybe they don't know the answer. If the world weren't so patient problems would get fixed sooner."

"Maybe we're getting into something that's too big for us," Shane said. "I mean, I know you like the adventure and stuff, but you only hear about the great explorers because they survived to tell the story. How many others set out that didn't make it? We may be opening doors to the unknown."

"That's the intention."

"What worries me is that they could be doors not meant to gone through."

"Wow, for a moment there you sounded just like me. I don't think we have a choice," I said. "This time we didn't go looking for anything strange to happen, it came to us. Ignoring it won't make it go away."

"You're right. I can't let this bother me for the rest of my life. I just don't think we know enough."

"Don't worry, we can ask her some more questions Friday after class," I reassured Shane. "Let's get to the bus. I'll ride home with you and walk home later."

"You sure?"

"I want to take a look around," I said. *I'll pay more attention now that I know the house is haunted,* I thought.

We left class and went to our lockers. I met Shane outside where we boarded the large yellow school bus and our minds went blank in the drone of the engine laboring to stop, and start, and stop, and start.

"You okay," Shane said. "You look like you're about to hurl."

"No. I was just wondering what they pump into the air system in these things. I mean, every time I get on the bus, I zone out. Like a zombie."

"I know what you mean," Shane said and raised his arms and moaned like a zombie.

We both laughed. Then I noticed we were approaching Shane's house. The bus stop was a mere two-hundred yards away from his front door.

"If the weather is nice, we can get Mike and Chad to come by Friday. I'll have to brief them on our plan."

"What plan?" Shane questioned.

"I don't know yet. That's what we have to decide today. Why does your garage look different than the house?" I said, getting off the bus.

"My dad just put it up this summer, remember? It didn't used to be there."

"What was there before?"

"Nothing."

"Hmm, it would have been easier if you would have said a cemetery," I smiled.

The house I looked at was not the old, dilapidated structure I had witnessed years ago. With the garage and two additions to the bottom floor with a fresh coat of paint, the house looked serene and too new to be haunted.

"Hmm," I said, looking behind the house. About a hundred yards from the back door, a series of splintery, leaning structures ran east to west. The wooden buildings consisted of a stable, a barn, and several, small dilapidated storage sheds.

"A house with buildings as old as those sheds has a history," I said trying to sound smart.

"My dad just added these new rooms," Shane pointed to the side of the house."

"Aha! I remember him working on them during Christmas break."

"What about it?" Shane asked.

I looked around and rubbed my chin. "Remember what I was telling you about your dad remodeling stirring something? I think, yes, in one of the stories I read, the haunting started after the people did some remodeling. They disturbed the spirits there who didn't want the house changed. Maybe your dad stirred something up. Something that had been resting."

"Really?" Shane's face went pale.

"I need to go in and call my mom. Make sure she doesn't want me home right away."

"Then we need to check the chickens to see if any of them laid eggs." Shane headed toward the door. "You coming?"

"We need to look at the barns back there," I said.

"Why?"

"The house has been remodeled. They haven't been. There might be some clues out there. Plus, that might be a perfect place for Chad and Mike to hide when they come over Friday."

"They're coming over Friday?"

"That's the plan."

"Oh." Shane led the way inside and to the phone.

I called home, letting my mom know I had ridden the bus home with Shane and that I'd be home soon. After we gathered eggs from the chicken coop and fed the chickens we headed out to the barns.

"Why do you think your parents have never used these old barns?"

"I don't know. My dad thinks they're unsafe. He doesn't like us playing in them."

"Is your dad home?"

"No."

"That one might make a neat clubhouse," I pointed to a single room dwelling that looked to be a newer addition than the other wooded structures. It stood a little forward of the other buildings and had all the walls intact. The front door of this building faced Shane's house.

"There's only two ways to the stables," Shane said and started walking toward the barns. "Through this room that you pointed out or around the back of the stables."

"The room has two doors?" I asked.

"Yes. One faces the house, as you can see. The other one is inside and opens up to the barns. I think some workers probably lived there at one time."

"How come we've never come back here before?"

"Like I said, my dad doesn't like us playing back here. Wait until you see inside, they're kinda creepy." We opened the wooden door and stepped inside.

"This would be a good place for someone to be," I stated closing the door behind me. "All the windows are intact, roofs good. It's weather proof." I looked around the barren room. "You can see the back of the house through this window. A clear view to your bedroom window."

"Wouldn't it be weird if we saw someone looking down on us from my window right now?"

"How do you know someone isn't, and we just can't see them?"

Shane shivered and stepped back from the window. "Who would be out here?"

"Mike and Chad."

Shane nodded. "You're thinking we need someone out here observing, just in case something happens that we don't know about."

"Right," I scanned the room for footprints across the dirty wood floor. "Who knows, someone might be using this very room to play a prank on you by hiding out here at night. Or something external is making the noise that we can't see from inside. It might explain everything if we can see your room from outside."

"This might be the only room that's warm enough."

"Whew," my nose twitched, "what is that smell?"

"Follow me," Shane said.

We headed through the side door into the stables and several enclosed buildings that were attached through a series of winding hallways. The musty smell of hair and damp hay permeated the air.

"It's manure," Shane said. "When we first moved in the last people to live here had a few ponies and never cleaned up after them. My dad and I shoveled it out before school started. I thought we were going to get horses or something to keep back here." His tone changed to one of disappointment. "But we never did."

"Think of it this way: You'd probably have to take care of them every day and it would only add to your chores."

We trod down the narrow aisles. The maze of wooden structures, full of splinters and cracked paint, leaned on one another and looked as though they were ready to fall were I to breathe too harshly on them. The musty smells, dark corners, and constant turning kept my senses occupied and my nose twitching.

"Looks like they just kept adding on," I said. "There's no real plan."

"Even the wood is different types: light, dark, hard, cheap wood building to building. These are the oldest ones here."

We entered a black-wooded hallway that was totally enclosed and wound around to a slanted enclosure, taller on one side then the other. I noticed a change; I felt as if I were lying down and someone sat on top of my chest.

"My legs and arms feel like I just ran a marathon," I said. "Do you sense something?"

Shane stopped and faced me and nodded. "I've never liked this place. Don't know why, but it just feels dark."

Some areas of the buildings were well lit from the sun and other areas were damp, dark, and musty. In these hidden areas I felt a presence, an imprint of the past. "Something happened here." *A foul deed. A wrongful death.*

"I hope you're kidding, but I feel strange too," Shane said.

"I've felt this way when I'm standing over a dead animal," I said.

"That's it," Shane said as he looked around and started heading back the way we came. "I already have a problem with the house; if the barns are haunted too, I'm moving in with you. Besides, your mom makes good snacks."

I stepped lively to catch up and Shane and smiled. "Sorry, let's deal with the house first. I think I've seen enough out here."

"Do you want to go inside and look at my room?"

"Yes. I was just hoping to find something out here that might explain what's happening," I said.

"Out here?" Shane said.

"Remember when we were at the Round House and the doors started slamming and lights going on and off."

Shane nodded.

"It could have been that someone came in to the house when we were upstairs. If we had someone on the outside of the house, we would've have known what was happening."

"How does that help me?" Shane asked.

"Out here in these barns might be evidence that someone is playing a prank on you or we might find a clue about the history of the house because some of these barns are just as old."

Shane stopped as we exited through the room where we'd started. He looked down at his feet and then back toward the new stable. "Out there," Shane pointed down a row of trees.

I looked beyond the new stable to a pile of wood and shingles and a row of trees overrun by weeds and grass that were now brown. "I've never been out there," I said.

"That's because my dad doesn't allow us to go over there."

"Why?" I asked.

Shane looked forward to his house and then headed back to the row of trees. "Let's hurry."

I nearly had to run to keep up with him. He marched past the new stable and straight into the thick, brown weeds and grass stopping at the base of a large, thick Maple tree. Shane reached down and uncovered a stone. He brushed away the dead leaves and revealed the engraving.

"Timmy Wallander, 1940-1946," I read the writing on the small, rectangular stone that was nearly buried in the ground. "Is it real?"

"I guess so," Shane said. "My dad stumbled on it one day and told me to leave it alone and never come around it."

The branches of the sleeping Maple rustled as a chilly breeze blew by causing me to shiver. I reached down and zipped my coat.

"I would say this is our first lead," I looked at Shane. "Is there anything else?"

"Like what?" Shane said.

"Like, you didn't want to tell us about the sounds in your bedroom, and you didn't think to show me this grave until now. You don't think these things could be related?"

"I guess so. But you can't tell anyone about the stone," Shane said.

"We're going to have to tell Mike and Chad," I rubbed my chin as I said this. "All this thinking is making me thirsty. Let's get something to drink," I said.

We walked around the barns and back toward the house. I studied the house as we approached it. Shane's bedroom window faced south, away from the main road. A large yard of brown hibernating grass ran between the house and the barns with a few blackwood trees that ran along the eastern boundary. To the west were the garage, driveway, and chicken coop.

The large four-paned window on the second floor stared down on me. That's where our mystery awaited us. Shane, tormented by the sounds, anxiously sought our help. I eagerly wanted to solve the mystery of the house. I just didn't know the right way to go about it.

"What were you doing in the barns?" A young girl's voice rang out and I turned to see Shane's younger sister, Stacey, as we entered the kitchen.

"Never you mind, stick to your own business," Shane said harshly.

Brown eyes flared from under long brown bangs, which Stacey threw back across her head as she defiantly took a seat at the kitchen table. At ten years old, she was the same age as Chad and my brother Mike, but we never included her in anything we did—because little sisters were designated pests.

"Here." Shane handed me a small cup of juice. "Let's go up to my room where we can have some *privacy*!"

"I'll have to make it a short look. I've got to get going soon," I said and followed him down the hall to look around.

We climbed three flights of stairs to get to Shane's room.

"Like I said, I just moved into this room after Christmas vacation, when my dad finished the downstairs bedroom," Shane said. "Stacey got my old room."

"And your parents never complained about any noises?" I asked. Shane shook his head. "At least you're closer to the bathroom and closer to the stairs." I stopped at the top to look in his room. "Dresser, bed, clothes on the floor. Correction, stinky clothes on the floor." I plugged my nose and feigned a faint. "It's your room, all right."

"At least I have my *own* room. I don't have to share with my brother."

"You got me there. So, when do the sounds happen?"

"They don't happen every night. Just some nights."

"At the same time?"

"What do you mean?"

"At the same time, you know, like always at midnight?"

"No."

"Ever hear it during the day?"

"I'm not up here much during the day."

"I haven't spent the night over here since you moved into this room. Your bed looks bigger."

"It's my parent's old bed. They bought a new one."

"What about your closet. Anything unusual there?"

"The sounds actually come from that direction." Shane pointed to the area of the ceiling that ran to his closet.

"But not directly from the closet." He nodded. "New room, new bed."

"Man, I feel like I'm on one of those police shows my dad watches. Any more questions."

"No, some advice. Be careful."

Shane led me downstairs and out to the driveway.

"I'll be back on Friday with Mike and Chad."

Walking away, I didn't know what we were getting into. Mixed feelings swirled in my head. A sense of reckless courage told me to rush in without fear and help Shane. Another part of me hesitated and instructed caution.

"Maybe I should go back and tell him to just tell his parents what's going on." I stopped walking and turned around. "Of course, they might think he's crazy and lock him up. Or they might find out we're interested in ghosts and make us quit exploring." I decided both outcomes were bad.

"I should stop talking to myself before they lock *me* up."

I took one last look at the house before it was out of my range. "Have a quiet night, Shane."

❧ ❧

Father Time favored our plans, as the week quickly played through to the end. Shane and I found ourselves walking to the last class of the day on Thursday, the short half-hour class with Ms. Brown, and the only class that day where I actually paid attention.

"Man," Shane said, "I'm sure glad today's about over. The week, for that matter."

"Thursdays are easy," I said. "All my teachers stick with the routine of no quizzes or tests. Not on Thursdays. But Friday's always a quiz or test."

"Sometimes I don't know how they expect us to learn everything they keep piling on. Don't they know there's life outside of these walls?"

"I'll let you tell 'em."

"You're still coming over?" Shane asked. "To spend the night?"

"Yep. Mike and Chad will be over, too. Your parents still going out?"

"They should be gone for a few hours. That should be enough time, don't you think?"

"Plenty," I said as we headed into class.

After our last conversation, I hoped Ms. Brown might change her class plan and talk more about ghosts and hauntings, but she stuck to her schedule and talked about strange and mysterious creatures. At the end of the class the other students left, and Shane and I were still in our seats.

We talked about sticking around after class but neither of us knew exactly what we were going to ask her this time. I wasn't sure what Shane felt as he sat there. He didn't ask her anything, but after a few minutes of silence, stood up with his books, and slowly walked out of the room.

Ms. Brown's eyes focused on me. I feigned a smile, knowing that there was no easy way out. Slowly, I stood from my seat midway back in one of the center rows. I searched the floor for some inspiration and avoided direct eye contact.

It wasn't until I got to the front of the class that I felt compelled to look at Ms. Brown, who usually put her things away at this time but seemed to be expecting more questions and sat still watching me.

"Did you enjoy class today?" Ms. Brown asked.

"Yes, of course. I mean, other than the fact that everything you talked about was so far away and I wished there were something closer to go explore."

"Louis?" she said.

Louis? Stop calling me Louis. No one calls me Louis. Not unless I was in trouble. I froze and awaited the horrible news. Had Ms. Brown contacted our parents and told them about our strange questions?

"I have this book I'd like to loan you. I think you might find it interesting," Ms. Brown said.

"What?"

Ms. Brown opened her top right desk drawer and took out a small leather-bound book. "It was given to me by a special friend and it's not an easy one to find, so please be careful with it."

I put out my hand to grasp the book. I turned it over and read the title, which was embossed in gold lettering. *Ghost Hunting: A Reach Into the Realm of the Paranormal*, by Ben Mers.

"I hope you find it useful. I got to meet the author at a book signing and he's the real thing."

"Thank you!" I said, smiling at Ms. Brown. I felt energized with confidence. Finally, I had an ally that I could trust. "I haven't been able to get to the library to find any books on the subject." I started to leave but turned suddenly. "And, you can call me Louie, everyone else does."

I flashed the book in front of Shane outside the school as we waited to load our buses. I wanted to read it and mentally cleared my schedule for the night. Then, I looked over and handed it to Shane.

"Here, you need this more than me," I said.

He pushed it back. "Oh no, Professor, you have more time to read it and you're a faster reader than me. Besides, she gave it to you."

"That's because you left."

"I know, I couldn't figure out how to start the conversation without embarrassing myself."

"I understand, especially when you have a crush on her. Ouch," I rubbed my shoulder where Shane punched me.

"So what did you say to her?" Shane asked.

"I didn't have to say anything," I said. "She started talking to me." I held my head up high. "She probably doesn't get to share much of the subject with the other teachers."

"Too bad we can't just ask her to come over and solve my problem," Shane hung his head.

"What problem?" The distinctive voice of Jay Falter rang out.

I turned to see the beady eyes looking out from under red-matted hair staring at Shane. The dark-freckled cheeks puffed up, as though he were pouting. Although stouter then I, I stood as tall as Jay and this kept him from challenging me. Shane was eight inches shorter and had a small build. He didn't have a chance of intimidating Jay.

"We are just talking about an English test," I said. "You interested in getting together and studying?"

Jay's eyes switched from Shane to me and from ill-tempered to confused. He looked around, as though I had spoken to someone else. "I know you guys are up to something." His bottom lip curled and he walked away.

"We're going to have to do something about him if he keeps it up," Shane said.

"One more night and we're there for you," I reminded him as I patted him on the shoulder and boarded my bus.

Our bus stop was conveniently one house from where I lived. I ran down the driveway and spotted Mike and Chad at the shed. They were checking their bikes. I walked over to the woodpile that lay between the shed and our house and sat on a log watching them. I pulled out the book Ms. Brown had given me.

"We oiled your chain and put air in your tires," Mike said.

"Thanks. Did you tape over the reflectors?"

He nodded. "I hope it doesn't snow tomorrow night."

"I don't think it will; it's been pretty nice so far this week. Everything ready?"

"We need to take Chad's pump. Ours is broken." Mike looked at me as he held up the pump our dad had purchased for us and flicked his finger across a hole in the hose.

"I think the guy that makes bike pumps and the guy who makes inner tubes are part of the same family and they're making their fortune off of us." I shook my head, looking at the pump and then at Chad's bike. "Those look like new tires."

"Solid tubes," Chad said and patted the tire. "So I can never get a flat."

"They should just come that way," Mike said. "With tires that don't go flat. And they should just leave the chain guards off. That's the first thing you have to remove because it rubs all the time."

"And why is it so hard to adjust the back tire so the chains actually stay on?" I added. "The first thing a guy has to do when he gets a new bike is replace the tubes and adjust the tension on the chain."

"You just need new bikes," Chad said, and patted the seat on his bike.

"In case of emergency, we're all piling on your bike."

Chad and Mike laughed at my comment.

"You should ask for one," Chad said.

"Nope." I put the book down on the log and walked over to my bike, painted with a mixture of yellow with orange flames up and down the side. I picked it up and sat down, noticing the polished seat. "Did you use mom's furniture polish?" Mike nodded. I rubbed my hand across the "BMX" sign with the number "38" in black, bold lettering. "This bike and I've had too many adventures together to trade it in."

"It's a cool bike," Chad said.

I sat there for a moment, considering what else we needed. I looked down at the book Ms. Brown had given me. I didn't have time to give the book a thorough reading but I intended to browse the chapters.

"So you're gonna tell mom you're going over to Chad's uncle's tomorrow night, right?" I asked Mike.

"Right. He's going to take my bike home with him tonight."

"Good. I'll meet you guys at the intersection by the little white church at about 3:30."

"You sure we don't need football helmets?" Chad asked.

"No. But you better dress warm."

"Why?"

"You guys are going to stay out in the barns until Shane's parents are gone," I said. "I already have the space picked out. We need to have you out there to make sure nothing is happening on the outside of the house while we are on the inside."

"Maybe we can get some candles," Mike said.

"I'll get some," Chad said, and headed home, with Mike helping him take both bikes.

I rolled my bike into the shed. It had several scratches up and down the frame. I reached down, pulling on the chain guard and bending it back to make sure it didn't rub the chain.

I patted the bike, hoping it would get me safely to my destination. The sound caused Mike's pet tarantula, Herman, to move and I jumped, catching the motion out of the corner of my eye. I looked at Mike's bug collection. He had them stored in old mason jars and a few cast-away Tupperware containers with holes in them.

"You just stay in that jar, Herman," I said leaving the shed. "And don't eat Reggie," The cockroach came to the edge of the jar as I said this.

Thursday night, Mike and I sat on our beds on opposite sides of an imaginary line that separated our room. We broke the boundary often to listen to a set of large radio headphones tuning into the 9:00 countdown on our favorite radio station, hoping the song we voted for would make it to Number One.

"Here," I said, handing the headphones to Mike. "They're all yours tonight."

Mike smiled and took the headphones. "I'll let you know when it gets close to the end if you want to listen."

I waited until he was in bed and had turned the light off—since we were supposed to be going to sleep—and used my flashlight to skim through the pages of the book Ms. Brown loaned me. The author followed a group of scientists dubbed "ghost hunters" and recorded their adventures. The first chapter introduced the members of the group and described how they came to know each other during their college years. I zipped through most of the introductions, trying to get to the action.

"What are you reading?" Mike whispered across the room.

"A book about ghost hunters and parapsychology. It's based on actual events. Is the countdown over already?"

"No, but Queen didn't get Number One because 'Flash' already played. Parapsycho what?"

"I can't believe my song didn't win. I made at least fifty calls to the radio station. It's parapsychology, study of the paranormal. Are you ready for tomorrow?"

Mike didn't respond right away. "Do you think Shane's house is haunted?"

"It appears so. Why, are you scared?"

"Not really. I know you guys are going to figure it out. Just wondered why people in haunted houses don't just move out. I mean, I would just move out. You know. Like the people in that movie mom wouldn't let us watch but we went over to Chad's house and watched it anyway on satellite. Why didn't they just leave?"

"Good question. I guess they should unless they can't afford it."

"Can't Shane just tell his parents about the sounds and tell them to move?"

"I don't think it's that simple. Would you tell mom and dad if it were happening to you?"

"I suppose not. Not unless I wanted to take the chance of going to the nut farm, or as Chad calls it, the honor farm."

"One of our teachers tells us sometimes the ghosts actually need our help."

"You asked one of your teachers?" Mike elevated his voice.

"Shh, keep it down. I don't want to get caught reading this book. Don't worry. We're safe. She's on our side. She's a believer like we are. We didn't tell her anything about Shane's house being haunted."

"Do you think the ghost Shane has needs our help?"

"I think we need to find out what's going on first. We need to investigate," I stated proudly, making what we were doing sound scientifically important. "There are lots of things that could be happening. Heck, it might not be a ghost at all but some animal running around in his walls or something."

"That would be better than a ghost," Mike said. "Maybe it's an insect. Well, not likely in the winter. Unless it's a cockroach. A whole lotta them."

"That scares me more than if it's a ghost," I said. "Sure you're not scared?"

"Are you?"

I put the book down and turned my flashlight off. The room expanded in the darkness; the endless void made plenty of room for large thoughts. "I guess sitting here in the comfort and safety of my own bed it would be easy to say no. Kind of like every time we talk about going off the high dive at swimming, it's no big deal. Then when you get to the top and walk out on the board, and it's bouncing and things don't feel solid, you're okay as long as you don't look down."

"Right, because if you do, it looks so high! And there's always a line behind you that makes it hard to back down."

"I always look down at the end. I can't help it. The water seems so far down I worry that once I jump, I'll go under too far and won't be able to get to the top before I run out of air. Then I remember, I've done it before and it's not so bad. Sometimes, I try to recapture that feeling when I'm trying to do other things that are hard. I tell myself, 'Don't look down, and just jump.' Being prepared is what I intend to be." I turned my flashlight on and held up the book. "I think it's the ghost that should be scared."

I finished my speech and received no applause. I angled my flashlight enough to see that Mike was fast asleep. I went back to reading. I continued looking through the book, particularly interested in a page where the author listed the conditions at a place he visited. He started a log that contained information about the time of the occurrences, the temperature readings, and who was present.

"I need to start a log book," I said. "There's so much to do." I briefly shone my light in Mike's direction: still fast asleep. Tired myself, I bookmarked the section I was on. Before I closed the book, I read one more line: The author suggested the other reason to keep a log was, "In case something goes terribly wrong, it serves as a record that will help in an investigation to find out what happened."

Unsettled by the last statement I read, I stared at the ceiling; tired but unable to rest. Finally, sleep claimed me.

Chapter Three

🌿   🌿

RUSHING IN

I RAN THROUGH THE house, trying to find Shane, but I didn't even remember going to his house. My head was cloudy and my senses dull, like when I take cold medicine. His parents weren't around and I imagined they'd left as planned. We had the house to ourselves.

"Mike and Chad should be out in the barn," I said to myself. Wait, I didn't remember seeing them come over. I didn't know if they were out there!

"*SHANE!*" I called out, but nobody answered.

Confused, I continued looking for Shane in the living room. It was night and the house was dark, with only a small light off in the distance. My heart raced and I turned the corner, only to catch a glimpse of Shane running up the stairs toward his room.

"Shane, wait!" I called out. "It's not time!" He didn't look back at me, but continued up the stairs.

I shook my head trying to clear the sound ringing in my ears. A woman's voice called my name! *Something's wrong!* My stomach churned. I recognized it as the same feeling when the teacher said, "Pop quiz!" and I didn't study. *I'm not ready!*

I began to panic as my legs trembled. I felt weak, tired. The house, colder and quieter than I remembered, grew dark around me except for the light in the stairway. A woman's voice came from there. It knew my name and sounded familiar.

I started up the stairs, but there was something wrong with them because I couldn't climb up. No, it wasn't the stairs; there was something wrong with my legs. My legs were tangled! I couldn't move.

I thrashed wildly. The woman's voice came again, louder this time; "*Wake up!*"

I woke from my sleep entangled in my covers, sweat on my brow. I looked across the room; Mike still slept soundly. My mom's voice called out the final warning for us to get up.

"We're up," I called out. "Mike, wake up."

"I heard," a groggy voice said from my brother's side of the room. "Finally, Friday. Except for the pop quizzes, it should be a good day. I bet you're excited today to finally solve your mystery."

After the dream I had, I wasn't so sure. My mind operated on automatic, going through the morning routine, while another part prepared for the night to come. I managed to get on the bus and made it through to lunch. The warning of the dream remained with me: "Be prepared."

During lunch, Shane and I sat apart from our usual group as I went over the agenda for the night. We sat out on the gym floor that doubled as the school cafeteria on fold-out tables.

"Mac and cheese again," I said. "That doesn't even look like real cheese." I sat down and took out my sack lunch of peanut butter and jelly with chips.

"Maybe that's why I'm so short," Shane said. "The cheese has stunted my growth." He looked at his plate, then took another forkful and shoved it in his mouth. "So, you sure you want to show them to gravestone."

"Why not? If there a little scared, they'll pay better attention," I said. "Right, we still need them to help us."

"You're sure your parents are going out tonight?"

"Yep. My mom reminded me this morning."

"Great. How long will they be gone?"

"Probably until eleven or so." Shane hung his head and grumbled.

"You look like you just flunked a test. What's wrong?"

"My mom said I have to watch Stacey."

"Obviously, that makes it more difficult to achieve our plans."

"She'll rat us out first chance she gets," Shane frowned and shook his head. "Then we'll all get in trouble."

"We're going to have to keep her busy," I said.

"And if she finds out?"

"Then we'll need a bribe. Some advantage. Has she done anything wrong lately that we can use against her, done someone else's homework, cheated on chores, anything?"

Shane shook his head. "I don't pay attention to what she does as along as she leaves me alone."

"We've got to think of something to keep her out of our way." My hand went to my chin and I leaned on my elbow.

"We can let her watch whatever television she wants to watch; that will keep her downstairs," Shane said.

"Good idea. I knew you'd come up with something."

"Did you finish that book yet?" Shane asked.

I looked at him for a moment. He didn't flinch or smile.

"You're kidding. I've only had it two days. Geez."

"I know. I guess I just wanted us to be ready. Are you getting sick?"

My dream came rushing back to me. We weren't ready. "Why?"

"Your face just turned white. I mean, you're already white, but it got whiter, like that time you came to school with the flu."

I shook my head. "We'll just have to be careful and brave," I said, coming up with the best words I could find. "And stick together! No running up the stairs by yourself, no matter what."

Shane stood up to leave the table. I reached out and grabbed his arm. "I'm serious!"

"Okay!" Shane jerked his arm away. "You sure you're not getting sick? You seem kinda grouchy."

"Hmmph," was all I managed to get out.

❧   ☙

After school, I got home and put all my books away and changed my shoes. I headed outdoors. Dressed in black pants, black shirt, and with some black dress socks I took from my dad's drawer, I put on my coat. I walked outside to see Mike and Chad, all dressed in black as well, by the shed getting their bikes ready. I took mine; I lifted it enough to shake it back and forth a few times and then I set it down.

"Why do you do that?" Mike asked.

"What?"

"Every time you get your bike out of the shed, you shake it like that. Why?"

"Just worried that one of your creatures might've gotten out and is making a home in my handlebars or under my seat."

"Oh. I thought maybe it was something important."

"Nice shoes," I said, looking at Chad's new shoes.

"They're guaranteed to have better traction." Chad lifted his right foot and angled the show to show the tread. "See," he ran a finger across the bottom.

I nodded. "Yes, obviously a work of art." I grabbed my bike and headed toward the driveway. Mike and Chad followed. We rode to the intersection as planned and turned left down the road to Shane's house.

"What's in the bag?" I asked, noticing a small bag Chad carried.

"Flashlights mostly and stuff for our stakeout: snacks and such. Oh, and here, I brought these eggs."

"Eggs?" Mike asked.

"Yep," I said. "I brought three of them too."

"Eggs?" Mike asked.

"Shane has to do his chores before he's allowed to do anything else. One of those is to check the chicken coop for eggs. If we already have some, it will make it faster. Come on, we've only got two hours before it gets dark. Let's go."

We rode down the two-lane country road at a steady pace without interruption. County High road had swaths of tight-packed houses, followed by long spans of fields. Lucky for us, the dogs in this direction were few and usually fenced in. We rode to the last intersection before Shane's house and I stopped.

"What's wrong," Mike asked pulling up beside me.

"I forgot the bats," I said looking back the way we'd come.

"Should we go back?"

"I'm not sure we need them." I envisioned broken picture frames and mirrors in Shane's house. "It might do us more harm than good to have them."

From our position at the intersection, we could see Shane's house in the distance. Only one house stood off the road in front of his, and was largely surrounded by an open field, giving us a clear view of the back barns and stable.

"This is where we split up," I said, and pointed. "You two go around the back and sneak into the shed there. I'll come and get you as soon as his parents leave. Give me the eggs."

Chad handed me a large bundle of paper towels with eggs tucked inside.

"We'll ride to the back," Mike said.

"Watch out, there's a barbed wire fence. See if you can get to the back of the barns, but don't go in the stable." I instructed them on the route I wanted them to take, so that they wouldn't see the surprise we had in store for them.

I arrived at Shane's house about a quarter after four and found him outside.

"Hey, I just got done hauling wood in; now I have to go check the chickens," Shane said.

"Here." I unwrapped the eggs Chad and I brought. "We made sure we only brought the brown eggs like you get. It might make it easier."

"Great. I still need to check but I'll only do one side. Shane raced through the chicken coop, looking where the hens sat; he reached down in the hay and found a few more eggs. Then he spread some feed on the floor before we went into his house.

After a brief hello to his parents, Shane and I headed upstairs. As we walked up the staircase, I took out my notebook. We entered his room and Shane closed the door.

"The first step to detection and solving where the strange noises is coming from is to try to find a connection," I said. I took out a pen.

"A connection," Shane said. "Like what Ms. Brown was saying. If we find out what, we might found out why it's happening."

"Exactly," I said holding the pen up in the air. It pointed to the closet and I walked in that direction as I continued my explanation. "There's a reason these sounds are occurring." I stopped in front of the closet door and whirled around. "Find the reason, find the solution." I felt confident I was on to something.

"What are you guys doing?" Stacey asked, bursting into Shane's room unannounced.

"Playing a game that's not for little girls," Shane said, and pointed to the door. "Out."

"How come you get to have someone over?" Stacey stomped her foot.

"I'm the oldest, I get to have more friends over more times," Shane said. "Why don't you go put some makeup on or play with your dolls?"

"I don't like makeup," Stacey said.

"Well, you look like a boy with long hair in those jeans," Shane said.

With a flash of her tongue and scowling eyes, Stacey stomped away.

"Why do girls do that?" I asked, not expecting a response.

"If they don't do that then they shrug their shoulders or pout by stomping one foot down." Shane answered.

"It must be a natural response for girls," I said. "My sister does the same thing, and they don't even know each other. At least she left us alone." I pointed down the hall as the door to Stacey's room slammed shut.

"It won't last. Once my parents are gone, she'll be in our hair all night."

"That's why we're going to let her have the TV tonight," I reminded Shane. "And we can't make it too easy for her to get it; otherwise she'll know we're up to something."

"I just hope she knows it's just for this one time. I'm the oldest and I should get to watch what I want. I wish I had my own TV in my room."

"Right. Like parents are ever going to let us have our own TV sets in our rooms. We'd never need to come out of our rooms except to get food and stuff."

I walked around Shane's room opening the closet doors and looking for anything that might help me explain what he was hearing.

"The sound comes from that wall and kinda goes into the roof there," Shane pointed. I followed the wall up to the roof and across. Then I noticed something. There, in the middle of his room, was the entrance to the attic. I jumped on his bed but couldn't reach the door.

"Don't even think about it." Shane followed my glance. "My mom told me more than once that I'm not allowed to go up there because it's dangerous. Besides, we'd need a ladder to reach it."

"Don't you think it's a good place to start?"

"Yes. But we can't get caught. How we gonna reach up there?"

"Put a chair on the bed."

"The sounds come more from the sides, anyway."

"Have you opened the closets when the sounds start?"

"No way. I just stay in bed with a flashlight and hope the closet doesn't come open."

"Are you sure it's not just a squirrel or some other critter?"

"Not these sounds." Shane said. He moved a small wooden desk chair over to me and I hoisted it onto the bed.

"Ever been up there?"

"Nope. I think my dad went up there when we first moved in but no one's been up there since." Shane shook his head.

"What the matter?"

"I feel like I'll be getting in trouble soon. I'm not supposed to go in the attic."

"Ha. We won't get caught. This chair's not high enough. Get some books and we'll see if we can get the door open. I'll just peek inside."

"I guess it's safe, since it's still light out. Besides, if my mom catches us we're both dead and I won't have to worry anymore."

"Then life will be simple. Here, grab those books and hand them to me. Now, go to the door and make sure no one's coming."

I braced the legs of the chair with the books and stood on the chair, teetering on the bed. I barely kept my balance. I stretched up but realized I didn't have enough height to reach the attic entrance. I sat down on the chair, crossing my arms, frustrated.

"Do you have a ladder?"

"In the garage," Shane said. "But we'll never sneak it up here."

"Give me a few more books." I wrapped Shane's bedspread around the base of the chair for support and piled the books on top of the chair. "There."

Shane leaned against the side of the door. "Don't blame me if you break your neck."

I slowly placed one foot on the edge of the chair, then the other, holding on with both hands to the back of the chair for stability. I lifted my right leg first and planted my foot, knee bent, on top of the stack of books. I attempted to stand and put weight on my right leg. The chair rocked back and forth on the soft mattress. I backed down and then tried again, this time more quickly and getting up high enough. I touched my hand to the handle on the attic door and braced against it to steady the chair.

I looked at Shane who no longer leaned but stood straight, mouth hanging open. I smiled and lost my concentration. My balance shifted and I overcompensated, causing the book pile to come out from under my legs. The chair and books tumbled off the bed as I fell to the mattress extending my right hand in flash;

I caught the leg of the chair before it crashed to the floor, lowering it quietly to the ground.

"Good save," Shane said as he picked up the books.

I righted myself and sat down on the chair.

At that moment, Shane's mom poked her head into the room.

I looked only once, unable to maintain eye contact, afraid that I would turn to dust.

Shane, back to the door, picked up the last book and smiled at me as my eyes went to him and then behind him and back to him. He slowly turned.

"Oh, hi, Mom," Shane's voice quavered. "Sorry if we're making too much noise. I was reorganizing my room and accidentally dropped some books. I need more room to do homework."

Sitting on a chair in the middle of Shane's room I did my best to smile and pretend everything was normal. Shane's mom looked at me and then up at the attic door. I kept my gaze down. *Attic, what attic? I don't know anything about an attic door. I just moved this chair here to sit and think. That's it.*

"Why don't you two go play outside while there's still a little light out?"

It was more of a command than a suggestion and it played right into my plans. I grabbed my notebook as Shane grabbed our coats and we headed outside to the barns.

"That was a close one," Shane said brushing his hand across his forehead.

"I thought she'd bust us for sure. Why did you say 'homework'?"

"What do you mean?"

I stopped walking. "Any time you tell your parents you're eager to do homework they're not going to believe you. You have to say it's a science project. All kids like that stuff."

"Oh, okay." Shane said. "Did you see the look?"

"Yep. She looked right up at that attic door, like she knew we were thinking about going up there."

"Moms have some sixth sense like that. They always know when you're getting into trouble. Let's not try that again until she's gone."

"Agreed," I said.

"It's going to be a while before my parents leave," Shane said.

"Then we have plenty of time to brief Mike and Chad."

We entered the first room and closed the door behind us.

"Hey, guys," I said as Mike and Chad came out from behind the sheds.

"It's about time," Mike said. "It's starting to get cold out here."

"Come on, this way," Shane said as we went to the room where they would stay in. "Be careful around the corner, it can be seen from the house." Shane peeked around the corner. "Okay, you're clear. Go around the front into the door on the other side."

We hurried through the door and into the room Shane and I had made our unofficial clubhouse.

"This is the only room with four walls and two doors. It has some protection from the cold," Shane said. "And you can see the house through that window."

"That's where I want you to keep watch," I said. "We want you to keep an eye on the yard and the outside of the house to look for anything that might explain the sounds Shane is hearing. Including any critters that might be scurrying across the roof."

"Speaking about roofs," Shane said, "has your house been quiet?"

I looked at Mike and he shrugged his shoulders. "We haven't heard any footsteps on the roof since that night you came over. Like I said, it only happens when all four of us are together. Let's focus on your problem. Were there any sounds last night?"

"No. It was quiet," Shane said.

"That's good," Chad said going to the side door. "Maybe it's gone. Nothing to solve."

"No," Shane said. "It doesn't happen every night."

Mike sat down on the wood floor at the center of the small room but Chad's curiosity seemed to get the best of him as he continued to look at the side door.

"Did you ask that teacher anything like you said you were going to?" Chad said as he walked to the back window and looked out.

"We asked her if she thought there were any haunted houses in Pueblo and she said there probably were because every town has haunted houses," Shane said.

Mike seemed content sitting in the room. His eyes, wide as they could be, darted about the room as he listened to the conversation, unaware I was watching him.

"She said we needed to start exploring and find out if there is any evidence of some pneumatic, no, that's not right, traumatic," Shane struggled with the words, "event that happened."

"So we started looking last weekend and we found something," I added, purposely leaving the sentence hanging. Mike looked up and Chad turned from the window.

Chad looked at me and then at the side door.

"That's why we wanted you guys out here. I think you need to know what we're dealing with. We won't blame you if you don't wanna stay."

I nodded to Shane, who went to the side door and opened it.

"It's through here."

Up to this point, Chad seemed ready to bolt through the door, but now that it was open he hesitated.

"What's that smell?" Chad said.

"Manure," Shane said.

I stepped forward. "Follow me."

Chad plugged his nose and followed. I walked quickly through the maze of interconnecting buildings. The rooms we traveled through were scary enough with their damp, musty smells, poor lighting, and dark corners where shadows played. We made it to the back and crossed quickly to the row of trees, hidden from the house by the stable and barn.

"Where are we going?" Mike asked.

"Just keep up," I said.

"But we seem to be going in circles."

"We have to stay hidden from the house," I said. We reached our destination and crouched down.

"My Dad said I could never tell anyone." Shane stated. "Now that we're all in this together, you should know."

Chad's hands reached inside his jacket pockets and something shiny emerged. "Never can be too careful," he said, holding a silver charm out in front of him.

"You still have them," I said.

"I've got twenty-four. One saint for every hour of the day. Want one?" Chad's hand went into his pocket and emerged with five more shiny charms.

"No. I'm okay."

"I'll take one," Shane said.

"Ms. Brown tipped us in the right direction," I began. "She said we needed to look for a reason why someone was not at rest. So, Shane thought of looking out here."

Shane carefully brushed the weeds aside again as Chad and Mike looked at the stone.

"What should we do?" Mike asked. "Call a priest or something?"

"I don't think we want to disturb it," I replied.

"That's bad luck if you do!" Chad added. He removed his hat, put one of his charms under it, and put it back on his head.

"Now we have a clue why the house may be haunted," I said.

"But we don't really know what happened to him," Mike said. "He could've just been sick. Look at the dates. That was so long ago who knows what could've happened."

"Exactly," I said.

Chad and Mike looked at me then followed my eyes as I looked at Shane. "We took the long way around to get back to the room where we'd started, choosing not to walk through the old sheds. We entered and Chad immediately shut the side door. He looked around for a minute.

"What is it?" I asked.

"Do we have anything to keep this door shut?"

Shane went outside and returned with a large log to put against the door.

"Happy?" I asked. Chad nodded. We sat down in a circle and I waited for everyone to be quiet.

"So we have a grave in the field that may or may not be related to the sounds in Shane's room," I said.

"But no connection as to why it would be," Shane said.

"Sounds like our usual position on things," Mike said. We don't really know what we're dealing with."

"We still have some time before my parents leave," Shane said. "Tell us a story."

Three sets of eyes turned to me.

Chapter Four

i WAПT mY BOПES BACK

"My dad told me not to tell this to anyone," I said. "You have to promise to keep it a secret."

The four of us sat in the single room attached to the barns behind his house. Both doors were closed and since the room had no furniture, we sat in the middle of the floor.

I nodded. Mike and Chad looked at me.

"Cross my heart, hope to die, stick a needle in my eye," they said promising.

I shivered and shook. "Sorry, I just got a scary feeling when you said that. You know, like someone or some*thing* is in the room with us. Anyway, the grave out there reminds me of another story I heard about a haunted farm. You wanted a story, so here it goes."

The light from the window began to fade as night approached and the air in the room grew colder.

"A long time ago when a farmer bought his land, he discovered the horrible secret," I began the story. "He looked out at the land and wondered why no one had used it for farming because it looked good for growing things. So he got his tractor and started plowing one day. After about three hours, he noticed his dog, which followed him around, was missing. He found his dog sitting in the back of the field standing over something. He got down from his tractor and went over to see what the dog found and noticed it was a bone. Not just any bone; a human bone!"

The air turned colder. Everyone focused on me.

"How did he know it was a human bone?" Mike asked.

"Because it was a human skull!" I quickly responded.

This quieted my brother for the moment. "He took the skull into his house and puzzled over it. It looked old, ancient. Like the kind you see on those TV shows about mummies. He left it on his dresser when he went to bed."

"Did he have a family?" Mike asked another question.

"No. His family died from a terrible disease," I answered without missing a beat. "So he moved with his dog to get a new start. Later that night his dog, Max, started growling and woke the farmer up. He looked down at the foot of his bed and could see Max sitting, hair standing on end, teeth showing.

"The farmer reached for Max to settle him when he heard the front door open and footsteps coming from downstairs. Someone was in his house!

"Before the farmer could reach for his shotgun, the footsteps stopped at the base of the stairs and an eerie voice came up those stairs and froze him; his muscles locked and he couldn't move. The voice whispered:

"'I want my bones back,'" I whispered in a ghostly voice. I did it so well I got goose bumps.

"'I want my bones back,' the voice said. Then the footsteps started up the steps. Max crawled under the bed. The farmer was frozen with fear. He looked across his room where his shotgun hung on the wall, but something told him it wouldn't do him any good. Then the sounds stopped. The voice and footsteps were gone. He didn't sleep all night but kept his eyes on the bedroom door.

"The next morning when the sunlight came through his window, he looked around his room. Max returned to the foot of his bed and the skull sat on his dresser where he put it. He thought he just had a dream. He decided to keep plowing his field because he needed the money from the crops. Again, Max was out with him and this time, he found a whole pile of bones."

"Why didn't he call the police?" Mike innocently asked.

"He couldn't," I replied. "He thought about it, but he needed the money from the crops and the police would have kept him from using the field during the investigation. Besides, he figured if anyone had missed the people, they would be looking for them. So he took the bones inside.

"This time, he left them down at the bottom of the stairs. Before he went to bed, he made sure he locked his front door and put his shotgun by the side of his bed.

"Once again, the farmer woke because Max was growling. He heard his front door creak as it opened. He knew he'd locked it!"

I spotted Chad looking at the side door. He kept shifting his eyes from Shane to the door and back to me. By this time, he had a half-dozen of his charms in his hands.

"He heard footsteps going across the floor to the base of the stairs," I continued. "He hoped the footsteps would stop there because he had left the bones downstairs. He tried to reach out and grab his shotgun but his arms were frozen in fear when suddenly, the voice came. 'I want my bones back...I want my bones back,' the ghostly voice called out. The footsteps started coming up the stairs and the farmer looked for an escape when he suddenly noticed," I heard the others inhale deeply in shock as I informed them of the farmer's mistake. *"He had left the skull on his dresser!"*

Chad shifted his position; his eyes scanned the room, causing Mike to look as well. I considered stopping the story as I didn't want to scare everyone so much that they didn't want to deal with the task at hand. I continued anyway.

"The footsteps began up the stairs and the voice grew louder, 'I want my bones back....I want my bones back!' Then the sounds stopped just outside his bedroom door." I paused, taking time to let everyone breathe.

"This time, the farmer knew it wasn't a dream. The next day," I heard everyone breathe a sigh of relief that the farmer survived, "he called a friend over and told him what was happening. His friend told him to call the police but the farmer told him why he couldn't.

"So the two of them went out and explored the field until they found the bones of three bodies. The farmer thought if they buried the bodies then the sounds would stop because they would be at rest. He told his friend that the ghostly voice didn't start until he plowed the field and disturbed the bones. So he put the bones in gunnysacks and buried them in the unused stable.

"That night as the farmer went to bed; Max would not come inside, but stayed outside in the doghouse. He tried to convince Max to come in, but he wouldn't. The farmer thought he would be safe now that he buried the bodies. This time, he put the Holy Bible by his bed because he knew his gun would do him no good.

"At midnight, the same time as he heard the sounds before, the farmer woke with a start and sat up in bed. He looked down to find Max and then remembered his dog was outside. He listened, but there were no sounds." Three sighs emerged at Shane's statement but were short lived as he continued: "Before he could get comfortable he noticed something...he *still* had the skull on his dresser!"

Mike and Chad stirred from their sitting positions. Their hands went from in front of them to their sides, ready to push themselves up if they needed to leave in a hurry. I was sure they were going to run at any moment.

"The farmer realized there must have been a fourth body that he hadn't found. The front door flung open with a crash. The ghost was mad at the farmer and the footsteps were louder than before as they pounded across the floor to the base of the stairs. They started coming up the stairs. Then the voice started: 'I want my bones back...I want my bones back.' It got closer and louder, 'I want my bones back...*I want my bones back!*"

Before I could say the next sentence, the door came open behind us.

"*Holy crap!*" Shane yelled out.

We were on our feet in a microsecond and headed for the side door, sure the ghost from the story had come to get us, but we couldn't move the log out of the way in time. "Chad!" I yelled out in frustration. Because of him, we were all going to die. With no choice, we turned to face our attacker!

A girl entered the room. It was Shane's sister.

"Stacey!" Shane stomped across the room. "What do you want?"

"Mom told me she wanted you two to come in for dinner. What are they doing here?" Stacey pointed to Mike and Chad.

"They were just leaving," I said, walking up to her. "And if you don't tell your mom they were here, we'll let you watch anything you want on TV tonight."

Stacey's eyes lit up and she smiled and nodded. She whipped around, her braided ponytail barely missing my nose as she headed toward the house.

"Why did you tell her she could watch whatever she wanted?" Shane asked his hands outstretched. "We could have gotten more."

"Hey, I panicked under pressure. It'll keep her out of our way. Let's go eat before your mom starts wondering why we're out here."

"Bring us back something to eat," Chad said.

Shane smiled and looked back. "We'll bring you some bread and water."

Shane and I ate dinner with Stacey, as his parents got ready to go out. She smiled through the entire meal.

"You and Dad don't have to worry about a thing tonight," Shane said. "Just go out and have a good time." He smiled and received a smile back from each of his parents.

Stacey smiled too but I didn't. Instead, I worried about the fact that Mike and Chad were in the barns, about the fact that Stacey knew they were there, and about the fact that I was spending the night in a haunted house. It was a lot of facts that I knew could go wrong.

"Absolutely no more friends over tonight, understand?" Shane's mom said.

I choked on my next bite.

"Make sure you chew your food. Are you all right?" Shane's mom asked, stepping into the kitchen.

I nodded. Tears came from my eye as I coughed.

"Take a drink, that'll wash it down."

It didn't take long for Shane's parents to announce they were leaving. We were ready. Shane's dad left to warm up the car and his mom walked outside. "Make sure you watch after your sister," Shane's mom called back.

We're in the clear, I thought to myself. It wasn't until his mom yelled back one more thing that I became worried: "And stay out of the attic. It's dangerous up there."

Shane and I looked at each other. No verbal communication was needed. Shane's mom might as well have told us to not be boys, to not be curious, and to wash our hands before dinner. Her statement did nothing more than confirm our belief that we needed to go there.

"I'll do the dishes," Shane said.

"I'm going to take some food out to Mike and Chad," I said. I put on my coat and headed outside to the barns.

The yard between the back door and the barns was mainly grass, with a few trees to the east side and one to the west. As I approached the barns and the first room, I spotted Chad peeking through the window.

"Are you guys ready?" I said as they walked out. A single outside light shining from the back of the house lit the yard enough that we could see each other.

"What do you want us to do?" Mike asked.

"Stay out here and watch the outside of the house. Stay in that room, so if someone is playing a prank they don't know you're out here. Watch through the window. If you keep the doors closed, it might be warmer. Just keep watch."

"For what?" Mike asked.

"An animal. A tree branch rubbing against the house. The Falter brothers sneaking over here and causing trouble. I think they live just south of here."

"Those guys? They're in trouble if I catch them," Mike said. "I'll show them my new sandwich move, the linebacker special." He put his hands together. "Me on one side, the ground on the other, and the Falters in the middle."

"I'm not saying it's them," I said. "Maybe an owl is roosting on the house at night and making the sounds that Shane hears."

"An owl?" Mike said.

I shook my head. "That's what we're here to find out." Part of me wanted to remain outside with them instead of going back to the house. "Watch the driveway and make sure his parents don't come home earlier than expected."

"Is Stacey still here?" Chad asked.

"She's watching TV. If she comes outside, hide. She doesn't know you're still out here. I'll signal you from Shane's bedroom when we start exploring." I turned to leave.

"What's the signal?" Mike asked.

"I'll flash the bedroom light on and off twice."

"What should we do if we see something or if his parents come home?"

"Throw a rock on the roof. Be careful not to hit any windows." I looked at the old barns in the background. "I don't know what's creepier tonight. The house or these old barns."

Chad walked under the tree and picked up a large stick, swung it like a bat. "Just in case." With a nod of satisfaction, he headed back to the room.

"What if something goes wrong?" Mike asked.

"I guess if we come out screaming you'll know," I said, chuckling.

"So, we don't have much of a plan?"

"Sure we do. You guys are out here watching to make sure it's nothing out here. We are going to find out the source inside. What could possibly go wrong?" I asked, putting my hands in the air.

"Any more questions?" After a moment of silence, I turned to go back to the house.

"Remember," Mike said, "we've got to be home before ten or else we'll get in trouble.

"Don't worry. Shane's mom and dad won't be back until eleven. We'll be done way before that." I walked toward the house. Before I went inside, I looked back.

Mike hovered outside of the door to the room instead of going inside, and through the window, I could see Chad playing with his flashlight. I felt worried, because they could be seen if anyone were to drive in the driveway. I headed back to them.

"What are you guys doing? Hide in there." I pointed to the room. "And tell Chad to keep his light down so it can't be seen from the window.

"That was a good story," Mike stated.

"It was good," I agreed. "I need to write it down."

"Do you need us here?" Mike asked.

"What do you mean? You don't want to be here?"

"No, it's not that. I just don't want you to make up stuff because you think we need to be included."

"I think it's the reverse. I need you here the most. You're the only voice of caution out of all of us. You keep me from rushing in. Besides, you're the linebacker of the group. I may need you to tackle someone or something like that."

Mike chuckled. "Okay. I guess it's more exciting than staying home. "

"Hey, Mike," Chad called from inside the room. "I found some cool candles in my dad's car. I think they're for camping and stuff. Let's light one and tell ghost stories."

"Don't forget why we're here," I told my brother. "Keep an eye on the house."

"I will. I don't want to have to come back and do all of this again," Mike said, rubbing his hands up and down his arms. "It's getting colder. Go in that house and make whatever is bothering Shane know if it messes with one of us, it's messing with all of us."

I left Mike and Chad in the room and walked back to the house. I looked back once; Mike turned on the flashlight and waved so I could see him through the window.

Low clouds hid the stars and the moon would not be up until later. I approached the house and stopped to look up at Shane's bedroom window. It was there, in his room, that our quest would end tonight. It was there that Shane heard the sounds. A rustling of branches caught my attention as the wind's hand brushed against them.

I looked up at Shane's bedroom window. "What worries me is I think it already knows we're here." We had no means of dealing with a supernatural force. No weapons, no strategy, and our only escape plan was to run. As I reached for the door handle, I noticed my hand shaking. I glanced back to the barns. I took a deep breath and opened the door to go inside, when suddenly, there was a flash!

I looked up! I scanned to the left and right of me. I could see flickers of light but couldn't tell where they came from.

Reflections! Flashes of light! *It's behind me!*

I ducked my head and spun around to confront whatever it was. The flashes came from the windows of the room where Mike and Chad were.

"Oh, no; Mike, Chad!"

Instinct took over and I ran back to the barns, giving no heed to caution. I leaped and sprinted faster, my steps longer; as I flew above the ground, my mind whirled. *I was right about the barns being bad. Is it too late? I should be there by now!*

Almost at the door, I slid to a halt when the door opened. I dodged to the left when a bright flash zipped by me. I felt the heat as it passed by my shoulder and dove to the ground, rolling away to avoid what might be next. Nothing came. I looked behind me and spotted the stick sizzling on the ground. I picked myself up and looked in the room. Mike and Chad stomped out the small fire on the floor. The panic was over.

Mike and Chad exited the room and in the bright light of the flare Chad had mistakenly set off, we stood there, catching our breath.

I ran over and kicked dirt on the flare with little success as the ground was still frozen. Mike and Chad came to help. With a combination of dirt and stomping we finally got the flare to fizzle out.

"This is not a cool candle, it's a road flare," I shook my head. "We don't need the whole neighborhood finding out we're here. Chad, do you have any more of those?"

He went back into the room and reappeared with a small backpack. He pulled out two dinner candles and another road flare.

"I thought they'd keep us warm."

"Give me that," I took the flare and gave him a sour look. "No one is supposed to know you're here. *Be quiet!*" I headed back to the house and made it through the back door.

I found Shane and Stacey sitting in the living room watching television. "Well, what do you want to watch tonight?" I asked Shane, immediately drawing a look from Stacey as her head spun around and eyes flared.

"Hey, you guys said I could watch whatever I wanted!"

"That was before," Shane said. "Mom and Dad are gone now."

"That's not fair!" Stacey exclaimed.

"If you leave us alone and stay in here, we'll let you watch what you want to watch the rest of the night," Shane said. Stacey nodded.

Shane and I stepped into the hallway. I glanced at the clock.

"I'm glad you noticed the time," Shane said. "You were gone so long, I thought you'd left. Why do you still have your coat on, is something wrong?"

"No," I took off my coat. "I didn't even notice it was still on."

Shane twitched his nose. "Do you smell something, like, something burning?"

"No," I hid my coat and the extra road flare behind me. "We should get started."

"Hmm, probably just from my parents smoking. Let's see," Shane said. "I estimate we have three hours before we have to worry about my parents."

"Let's get started." I didn't have the heart to tell him about the mishap in the barn and threw my coat into the living room, where it landed on a green recliner.

"Where are you going?" Shane asked.

"I need my notebook. Let's start down here and search for anything unusual."

"Are you sure this is what we should be doing?" Shane asked. "I mean, aren't we wasting time not going upstairs?"

"We need to explore all possibilities. Anything unusual that sticks out or is out of place. Something maybe you haven't noticed before."

"Didn't you say you thought this place had a basement?" Shane asked. "When those friends of your mom's were remodeling?"

"There were holes in the floor that I looked into and they went down for a long way. I thought there would be a basement. I wasn't really paying attention."

"Well, there's no way to get there. Not that I could find, anyway. I guess we'll go upstairs, then," Shane said.

"Just a minute," I jotted some notes down. "You just moved into the room after your dad finished the downstairs bedroom?"

"That's right."

"You think your parents heard the sounds and that's why they wanted to move? Maybe they thought they were going crazy."

"I don't know," Shane said. "You've never spent the night since I moved into my new room; maybe after tonight you'll know more."

"What time do the sounds usually start?" I asked.

"Not till after nine or so, I guess. I mean...I'm downstairs until then anyway."

"So, they could start earlier but you're down here," I tried to piece the puzzle together. "Okay, keep your eyes open. If anything looks out of place or different, let me know. You left the lights on in your room, right?" We headed for the stairway.

"Of course," Shane said. He peeked into the living room. "Stacey is glued to the tube."

With the lights on, it was easy to head up the stairs; we didn't delay, but went straight to Shane's room. At the doorway, I reached in and flashed the light switch to let Mike and Chad know we were entering the room. On the second flash, the lightbulb popped.

Simultaneously stepping back from the entrance to Shane's room, he and I looked at each other.

"Hah…What is the chance of that?" my voice cracked as the words hung in the air.

"I guess if the whole house had gone black, I'd be worried," Shane said. As though we had read each other's minds about the next thing that would happen, we immediately headed back downstairs for our flashlights.

"Just in case," I said, holding up my flashlight. I pushed the side button and flicked it on and off to test it.

"Right, just in case. Here, I got a new bulb. And let's take this." Shane had a three-step stool under his arm.

We headed back upstairs with the step stool and lightbulb. Once at the door, I beamed my flashlight into Shane's room and he stepped in. Going to his desk, he pulled back the chair and slid it under the light fixture.

"It's too high," he stated, as he stood on the step stool; he was still too short to reach the socket.

"You're too short," I said, handing him the flashlight and taking his place on the stool.

"*Whack!*" A loud *thump* sounded on the roof. It was the signal from Chad.

The thump caused me to flinch, and I dropped the new lightbulb. I looked on in horror as the glass bulb contacted the floor and shattered.

Dodging the breaking glass, Shane whirled, causing the flashlight to blind me. I lost my balance, fell off the stool, and crashed flat on the floor.

"Quick," I said, getting up off the floor and rubbing my back. "That's the signal. Someone's coming. We need to get downstairs."

At the base of the stairs, Shane peeked in on Stacey. His face looked distressed when he turned around and shrugged his shoulders. "She's gone." We headed down the hall to the kitchen, hoping she was there. As we rounded the corner to the kitchen, we were taken by surprise.

"How did you get in?"

"Stacey let us in," Mike said. He and Chad sat at the table around a bag of chips and glasses of juice Stacey had just finished pouring.

"Oh, great! Am I in trouble," Shane exclaimed, sitting down. He put his head down on the table and folded his hands over the top.

"Why are you in trouble?" Stacey said. "I won't tell on you guys."

"Is someone here?" I asked looking out the kitchen window to the driveway.

Shane stood and went to the window. "No. The coast is clear." He continued looking out the window.

I sat down in the last chair available and Shane leaned back against the sink facing us.

"Listen," I began, looking at Mike and Chad. "This is important. How long have you guys been in here?"

"We came in after we saw the lightbulb pop. We figured you guys wouldn't go back until you changed the bulb."

"So you didn't throw a rock on the roof?"

"What rock?" Chad said.

Shane and I looked at each other. I cocked my head and slowly looked up toward the roof.

"We heard a rock against the roof right before we came down," Shane said.

"Well, it wasn't us," Chad said.

The look that passed between Shane and I was the same an actor gets at the end of a murder mystery when they realize the killer is among them.

"Something's up there!" Shane said.

Mike and Chad stopped eating. Everyone listened and all eyes slowly went to the ceiling.

Stacey looked around, confused, her ignorance the only defense against the wave of fear that overtook the rest of us. The phantom upstairs had made the first move!

"*Brrriingg! Brrrrriingg!*" We jumped simultaneously as the phone sounded. Since I was closest to the phone, I picked up the receiver and handed it to Stacey, who stood and stretched the cord across the table.

"You hear anything else up there?" Mike's voice quavered.

"We heard," Shane started, but I motioned for him to stop and pointed to Stacey, putting my finger to my lips.

"Okay. Goodbye," she said, hanging up the phone and looking at us. "You guys don't need to keep secrets. I've heard the sounds too, and they scare me. Is that why you're here?"

I looked at the group. Wheels of reasoning spun in my head but couldn't get traction. Stacey was the same age as Mike and Chad, and she was Shane's sister. If there was something threatening the house, it was after her, too.

"Look, it's all over school that you guys visited that haunted house, the Round House, last year. Although, your popularity is going down if you don't do something else soon."

"We don't want to be popular," I said.

"I do," Chad said.

I shook my head, but decided we needed to let Stacey know what was going on.

"Yes. We're here to help your brother. We need you to keep it quiet."

Stacey nodded. Mike and Chad chewed quietly and Shane stared at the ceiling.

"Okay, then," I said. "We need to get this right. But you two," I pointed to Mike and Chad, "have to be outside so we make sure it's not something outside that's causing the sounds.

"The wind's coming up and it's getting cold out there," Mike stated.

"I'm not going out there if something's throwing rocks at the roof," Chad said. He folded his arms and sat back in his chair.

"Look," I said. "We don't know what we heard. It may have been a branch or something with the wind blowing. We don't know what made the sound because, *you guys are in here!*"

"Sorry," Chad said. "Let's go."

"Watch from the window and keep the door closed," Shane stated, "and light a candle to keep warm."

"*No!*" I stood waving my hands. "*No more* stuff that can start a *fire!* Button up your coats and do jumping jacks if you need to keep warm. You're not going to be out there that long. Use your flashlights sparingly. We'll be quick this time and you guys can get on your way."

"Fire?" Shane looked confused. "What about a fire?"

"I think you guys better get going," Stacey stated.

"We're trying to get organized!" Shane put his hands on his hips and shook his head. He leaned back against the counter and folded his arms.

"No. I mean, I don't think you have time," Stacey said. "That was mom and dad on the phone and they're on their way home now."

"What'll we do?" Shane asked.

"No choice," I said. "We have to stop now before we get caught."

"You're still staying the night?"

"Yep, but we need to get Mike and Chad out of here, come on, guys."

We headed out with Mike and Chad to get their bikes. Shane and I helped them move down the driveway to the main road.

"You need to get across the first intersection so my parents won't see you on the side of the road," Shane said as Mike and Chad headed off.

"Be careful!" I shouted after them. "With any luck, the road won't have much traffic at this time of night. I hope they get home okay."

"I'm more worried about us," Shane said.

When Mike and Chad were out of sight, Shane and I headed down the driveway to the back door. Before we went in, we searched the backyard with our flashlights.

"It sounded like a thump on the roof," I said. "What could have caused that?"

"Do you smell fireworks or something?" Shane asked before we stepped inside.

I looked around and shrugged my shoulders.

"It's like something's burning? Out there by the barns?"

"Nope. I don't smell a thing," I replied quickly, hoping no one would ever catch on to Chad's mistake. "Let's get inside before your parents get home."

"Are we sleeping in my room?" Shane asked.

"Of course, that's where the sounds are coming from. If we get lucky, maybe they'll happen tonight."

Shane went to the hall closet and grabbed the sleeping bags and laid them out in the living room. "Just in case."

"Should we go fix your lightbulb?" I asked.

"Let's hurry."

We went upstairs and I hoisted Shane up on my shoulders so he could replace the bulb.

"It's in," he said as he jumped down. "I'll go turn it on."

Just as Shane hit the floor, a thud sounded on the roof above his room and we both stood perfectly still waiting for another sound.

"Look out there. Something's on the roof of the stable," Shane said pointing out his window.

We stepped to the window and looked to the stable. I wiped my eyes and shook my head and looked again. A fuzzy blue silhouette stood on top of the new stable to the east of the old barns. I struggled to focus on the shape.

"Is that someone out there with a flashlight?" Shane said.

"Let's go," I said and we both ran down the stairs and out the back door. As we exited, I looked up but the figure was no longer on the top of the barn. We ran to the opening between the barns and looked back into the field beyond. What I saw caused me to step dead in my tracks. Shane stopped directly beside me.

In front of us and in the direction of the grave, a glowing blue-tinted figure went across and stood at the base of the tree.

"If that's a person, it doesn't have feet," Shane said and pointed.

I looked and it appeared that whatever the light was, it hovered above the ground.

The appearance of lights behind us caused us to turn around and Shane's parents drove in the driveway. When we looked back toward the field, the blue form was gone.

"We better run before my parents see us out here," Shane said.

We sprinted to the back door making it inside before Shane's parents rounded the corner to the house. Standing at the base of the stairwell I tried to catch my breath.

"Was that what I think it was?" Shane said. "It looked like a lady in a dress. You know, those long, formal gowns."

"Let's not jump to conclusions." I said. "It could have been a flashlight or the reflection of headlights. We need to go back out there and investigate when we have time."

Shane looked down the hall to the back door as his parents stepped inside. "I think it will be better to do it in the morning."

"I agree."

"Come on, let's go watch some television."

By the time Shane's parents came through the kitchen and down the hall, Shane, Stacey, and I were sitting in front of the television as though we'd been there all night. Seeing us there, Shane's father came over and lit the wood-burning stove to keep us warm. I heard him walk back across the room and the sound of the bedroom door closing.

The flickering lights of late night entertainment soon had us hypnotized and the next thing I remember is waking up half inside the sleeping bag still on the living room floor. The TV was off; the stove glowed with a red hue, radiating heat across the room.

I couldn't help but think about all the mistakes we had made. Our first chance, and we didn't help Shane at all. I rubbed my hip, which was sore from my fall off the stool. I sat up and looked around, not knowing what had caused me to wake up but I felt tense as though an alarm had went off and I was supposed to be doing something

Shane and Stacey were both too far away to have hit me. I heard a small crackle of wood from the stove. The wind howled against the window and then subsided.

Looking to my left, I could see by the light of the stove that Shane lay face up, his eyes open. Then I heard what had awakened me: What sounded like a soft voice was traveling down the stairway. I held my breath and kept still, focusing all of my energy on listening. There it was again! Not a loud sound like someone talking; it didn't sound like a human sound at all, but a l-o-n-g, inhuman moan!

"Let's just stay down here tonight," Shane whispered.

Tired and feeling like I'd had enough excitement for the night, I laid back down. *What have you gotten yourself into*, my inner voice said as I stared into the darkness.

The next day, Shane and I made sure his dad wasn't looking and snuck out toward the grave.

"No footprints," Shane said as he looked down around the path where we'd seen the blue specter.

"Maybe we were just imagining things," I said. "You know, kind of like when we stay up and watch too many sci-fi movies and then you dream about them all night."

Shane stood and looked around and remained quiet. He shuffled his feet on the path and kicked some dirt. "Well, my dad's off all day. It's too risky to do much investigating."

"We can fix up our clubhouse," I said. "I'd start by sweeping up the floor and then getting covers for the windows."

We spent the day in the small room adjacent to the barns cleaning it and coming up with secret codes and passwords until it was time for me to go home.

"What's our next move," Shane asked me as I readied my bike for the ride home.

"I'm not sure," I said. "I need to put all that's happened down in some notes. You know, like studying for a test, and see if anything makes sense."

"I wonder what will happen first," Shane said. "If we'll solve the problem of the footsteps on your roof or the sounds coming out of my closet and attic."

"The footsteps on the roof only happen when all four of us are together," I said. "You don't suppose?" I left the question hanging but it occurred to me that whatever force taunted us at our house was the same force that taunted Shane at his house and followed him whenever he came over to spend the night. I shivered as the thought crossed my mind.

"I'll get back to you as soon as I think of something," I said. "Let me know if that blue light shows up again."

CHAPTER FIVE

MONUMENTAL KNOWLEDGE

"WATCH YOUR FINGERS," MY dad called out. The magnificent structure barely fit through the door! Huge, heavy, old, and scarred, no one understood why I wanted the "piece of junk," as Eric put it. To me, the desk was a treasure beyond imagination. A monument to the pursuit of knowledge.

My dad had driven to my grandma's house right after church and used his brother's truck to pick it up. It was the best kind of gift; I didn't have to wait for my birthday or Christmas.

I knew little about wood; only that some wood was light and others were heavy. Usually, heavy wood that was a darker color meant more expensive. The dark, burgundy color and straining and grunting we made as we set the desk down into place let me know it was the heavy kind of desk and built to last. A solid wooden chair accompanied the desk.

"You call your grandma and thank her," my dad said. "I've got to take this truck back to Uncle Carl." He left the room.

Mike, in awe of the huge structure, didn't complain when the desk stretched over our imaginary boundary. I looked at him and back at the part of the desk that stretched to his side of the room.

"It's okay," he said.

I smiled. The smell of lemon furniture polish filled the room as I went over every surface, every inch of it, including the chair. "My first big desk!" My mouth hurt from grinning. My brain swelled with ideas and I imagined the great thoughts that would pour forth just from sitting behind the masterpiece.

"It's big," Mike said looking at it. "Why did you want this big one?"

"All great thinkers have big desks," I said confidently. I put my books and notebooks in the drawers. "We need space to plan," I gestured across the large, spacious top. I pulled out my notebook and the book Ms. Brown lent me. I took out a pencil and began to write.

"Failure." Not total failure, I reminded myself, but our mission to help Shane ended badly.

"Are we going to go back to Shane's this weekend?" Mike asked.

"No," I shook my head. "His parents don't go out that often. And they never let him have a friend over multiple weekends in a row. So, we'll have to wait another week or two."

"Maybe it'll be warmer next time."

"Obviously, after the way our first night went, we needed a better plan. We can't afford to have another night like that. Shane will have to hang in there."

I picked up the book Ms. Brown gave me and flipped through it. I knew I could finish it within a week. That would help us. "Then we can ask better questions."

"What?" Mike asked.

"Nothing. Just thinking out loud."

Mike sat on his bed, still mesmerized by the desk.

"Someday when you're ready, you can use it, too," I said. "You might even inherit it from me, just like I did from Gema." I used the less formal name we called our grandmother.

"Thanks, I guess. What are you reading in that book?"

"Look," I pointed to the page, "it says here we need to keep a log of events in a journal." I wrote down the tip in my notebook.

"Will it help?"

I turned and faced my brother. "Think about this; we don't know what happened that night at Shane's house. I mean, what caused the lightbulb to burn out at that precise moment? What caused the sound on the roof that made us think you and Chad signaled us and led us downstairs?"

Mike's eyes glazed over. I needed to explain it a different way.

"When I start writing this stuff down, it's like putting out the pieces of a jigsaw puzzle. You lay all of them out first and then try to find ones that fit together. Maybe something will come together when I review my notes."

"So, that helps?"

"It can't hurt. Just like your football coach shows you films so you can improve your playing, a log might help us learn from mistakes."

"How?"

"For one thing, it's obvious we need better equipment: flashlights and a better way to communicate between the barns and the house. We need to start looking for patterns and coming up with some leads, like a real investigation with clues and stuff. A journal will help that."

"You heard the sounds?"

"Plain and clear. The only thing I can figure is that Shane left his door open because we slept downstairs. His parents sleep with their bedroom door closed, so maybe they never hear it."

"Then it really exists," Mike stared at the carpet. I went back to reading. "You're going to want us to go back and help you, me and Chad."

I put the book down. "Yes. There's something there that we need to figure out. But we're not going back this time until we prepare."

Mike stood and headed toward the door.

"Where you going?" I said.

"I'm training Reggie how to run a maze. Scientists do it with rats, so I figure, why not cockroaches? They've been around since the dinosaurs, so they've got to be smart." He stopped and turned around. "You done with this?"

I nodded. He grabbed the bottle of furniture polish and the rag and headed outside.

"A maze?" I said aloud. Then a door opened wide in my mind and a fresh breeze of ideas came in: We need training!

I began writing down ideas. Two pencils later, I called Shane.

"An obstacle course?" Shane said from the other end of the line.

"Yes. It's the only way I think we can get prepared. I mean, you practice for football, band, and baseball, study for tests. Why not train and study for this?"

"Okay. What do I do until then?"

"I think we need to ask Ms. Brown for help. Maybe she knows something that could help us. Until then, get a Bible and some crosses. Garlic might be good, too."

"Garlic?" Shane asked. "I thought that was for vampires."

"Who knows? Maybe it works for ghosts to. I've seen it in the movies. You should ask your parents for a cat. Supposedly they can sense spirits."

"No chance, my mom likes poodles. I'll see about the garlic."

"That should keep you safe until we come up with something better."

"Thanks. I'll see you tomorrow at school."

I hung up the phone and looked outside. Chad stood against the shed and I thought it would be a good time to ask for his help. It was late afternoon and in a few days March would roll in. It hadn't snowed since we put the heater in the tree house but the temperature was still chilly, so I grabbed my coat and headed outside.

"Hey! Where's Mike?"

"In there," Chad pointed to the shed.

"What are you doing out here?"

"He got mad at me because I kept cracking jokes about the exterminator," Chad said.

"Yep. I know. He wouldn't talk to me for a week after Christmas."

"What did you get him?" Chad asked.

"A can of bug spray."

Chad laughed.

"I thought it was funny too," I said. "Did he get Reggie to do the maze?"

"Strangest thing. I didn't know they could do that. Your brother would probably be famous, but I don't think his bugs will last that long."

"I don't know." I leaned up against the shed. "He told me that cockroach could live up to twenty years. And the tarantula, I mean, Herman, can live up to thirty. Kind of makes you feel bad when you kill one."

"Wow, thirty years? That's longer than some people live," Chad said.

"Do you think we can use your basement for a project?"

"As long as it doesn't involve tarantulas."

"We need someplace bigger than the tree house, and somewhere we won't be disturbed."

"Shane's right," Chad said.

"What?"

"Your ears change color when you have a risky idea. I'm not going to get in trouble?"

"Don't worry," I said and put my arm around Chad's shoulder and led him down the driveway. "Besides, you owe me."

"What?"

"You're the one who gave my brother that tarantula." I put my hand around the back of his neck and squeezed.

Chad stopped walking. His eyes grew wide and he looked at me. "Sorry."

I released my grip. "That thing got out and went into Dee Dee's room. We almost got busted saving him. What I have in mind won't hurt anyone. We just need to come up with some ideas on how to get better at, well, not being scared."

"Not being scared?"

I did my best to lay out my plan to Chad as the day passed and we headed into the next week.

The week passed quickly; with our teachers trying to catch up to their lesson plans before spring break, we had plenty of assignments to keep us busy. Chad and I met in the tree house during the week to continue talking about my plan to get us prepared to deal with a haunted house.

On Thursday afternoon, Shane and I stayed after class to ask Ms. Brown some questions.

"You don't have to raise your hand, class is over, Shane?" Ms. Brown had taken her usual place, leaning back against her desk.

"I read that while ghosts move stuff and make scary sounds, they don't hurt anyone," Shane said.

"That's correct for the most part," Ms. Brown said. "But there have been cases where a haunting resulted in death, whether it was from fright or other reasons. In one case, it appears the ghost actually caused the victim's tongue to swell and he ended up choking to death."

Shane turned pale as a new bedsheet and I lowered my gaze, searching the floor for answers that were not there. Ms. Brown hadn't calmed our fears, but raised them.

I considered never stepping foot in Shane's house again. The risk seemed too high, if it meant my death. Shane would have to move, and that's all there was too it.

Driven by my heightened sense for adventure, I blurted out my sentence:

"What would you do to protect yourself if you knew a house was haunted?" I said. "I mean, how would you protect yourself from the spirits?"

Ms. Brown looked at me. She walked over and closed the door to the classroom, slowly turning her head around, her hands folded together before her. "Have either of you ever been to a haunted house?" she asked.

The look that passed between Shane and me needed little interpretation.

"I see," Ms. Brown said. "Anyone who witnessed a true paranormal experience has the look the three of us share: It is not happy or sad, it is simply a look that conveys confusion; the confusion of brushing up against the unexplainable and being afraid to tell anyone else because there is no way they could believe you unless they were there."

My shoulders relaxed and in that moment, I realized Ms. Brown had tangled with something she'd yet to tell us about. I knew she was an ally.

"Many things that are attributed to ghosts or paranormal phenomena have perfectly good explanations and I would warn anyone to be careful before drawing any conclusions," Ms. Brown said, and then turned and walked back to her desk. She started putting her notes away.

"How would you go about investigating a house if you thought it might be haunted? You know, to prove whether it was or wasn't?" Shane said.

Ms. Brown looked at Shane and then me. *Nope, we're not budging.* Ms. Brown sat down on the front of her desk facing us, like she did when she taught class.

"I would first begin by logging everything in a journal. That way, you could try to rationalize events and try to form a conclusion. Look at everything scientifically."

I nodded remembering the same advice from the author of the book she'd loaned me.

"You wouldn't want to claim you have a ghost," Ms Brown said. "Only to find out it's a member of your family sleepwalking or an animal making noises. Look for any logical explanations before you reach for something that is out of the ordinary. Write down the time, date and even the weather conditions of any strange occurrence."

I thought about the notes I'd been taking.

"Louis," Ms. Brown continued. I cringed at the use of my formal name. "That book I loaned you has some of that information in it.

The author uses some of the techniques I'm talking about during his investigations."

"Right. But he uses a lot of equipment I don't understand or have," I said.

Ms. Brown looked at me with her large, brown, curious eyes. I imagined she might join our crusade were she not an adult. Worried that we were telling her too much, I looked away.

"I sure hope you boys aren't up to something that might get you into trouble." Ms. Brown looked at Shane and then back to me.

Shane and I exchanged glances. He looked down at the floor and I looked back at Ms. Brown with the most innocent face I could summon.

"No trouble," I said, laughing nervously. "We just wish there was some adventure around here like you talk about in your class." I decided it was time to leave and stood. Shane followed me to the door and Ms. Brown continued putting her things away.

"You do believe in ghosts, though?" Shane asked, looking back at Ms. Brown from the doorway.

"Yes," she replied. "But I think they are rare and those that do exist probably don't like us much."

"Why?" Shane asked.

"Because we are still living."

Her answer brought dead silence. We left the room slowly, marching to our lockers down empty hallways as the school cleared out for the day. My mind swirled.

"Kind of reminds you of tubing," Shane said.

"What?" I shook my head, not sure that I heard him.

"Tubing. You know. It's really exciting riding down the hill at breakneck speed. Everyone's smiling and yelling. Then the tube goes too far off course and you're heading for a tree."

"Then you realize the danger is real," I finished his thought.

"Exactly. But it's too late to do much. You can try to get out, but the moment carries you forward regardless."

"I remember watching a movie in which strange sounds emanated from a bathtub at the same time every night because it was at that time a tragic event occurred."

"The sounds at my house occur at night," Shane said. "Do you think some tragic event happened there like in the movie?"

"It's a possibility, but don't jump ahead. Ms. Brown said we should take a scientific approach. I mean, how do you know the sounds don't happen during the day and you don't hear them because it's too noisy or you aren't up there during the day?"

"Hmm," was all Shane said.

As we walked down the hall to our lockers, I felt satisfied that I had gained some knowledge. Ms. Brown was right: We needed to take a scientific approach to our problem and figure out what was happening.

"Do you think she's on to us?" Shane asked as we headed down the hall.

"Honestly, I think if she could she would join us. But it's too big a risk."

"For her or for us?"

"Both, I think. Maybe later when we trust her more, we can tell her everything," I said.

"How long do you think this will take?" Shane asked, still looking pale and worried.

"Don't worry. We'll have this solved by the end of spring break," I said. "That is, unless we get caught."

"We need to be careful," Shane said. "Let's not ask Ms. Brown any questions for a while. Play it safe." Shane nodded and I nodded.

I decided to ride with Shane on his bus so we could talk longer, but Shane hardly spoke on the bus ride. I didn't know what to say to him.

"Hasn't snowed for a while," Shane said.

"I can't wait until the weather changes, and then I can walk home again instead of riding this bus."

"I guess I'll start walking too," Shane said. I followed his eyes as they looked to the back of the bus, where Jay Falter, a direct descendant of Neanderthal man, sat by himself. "As long as you're on the bus, he leaves me alone."

Jay looked up and Shane and I looked away. Direct eye contact would only encourage a confrontation. *A problem for another time,* I thought to myself.

I got off the bus at the closest stop to my house and walked the rest of the way. I threw my book bag in my room, changed my shoes, and headed outside. The snow had completely melted from the driveway so I checked the extension cord to make sure it remained hidden. Then I headed to the tree house.

I climbed the tall oak tree and entered the tree house. "Hmm, where did you come from?" I noticed a small lamp sitting inside the hatch. I turned on the heater, warming my hands before I began to organize my notes. I switched the cord to the lamp so I could see better.

Shane's House
Ghost of some kind
Past haunting
Poltergeist. No furniture moving or other object moving.
History of house—don't know all—Holes in floor covered and no basement anymore.
Murder or death!!! Indian burial ground. Graveyard!!
Sounds in bedroom? Attic: What's in the there?
Equipment needs: flashlights, batteries. No change in pockets. Wear dark clothes. No sunglasses.
Group Name: Need to come up with something.

"Hey!" Mike's head peeked in the hatch. "I knew you'd be up here. Why do you like it up here so much?"

"I wanted to get away from my noisy little brother," I smiled. "I need a place to think where I can use my imagination. It's hard to do that in the house sometimes. Something about the fresh, crisp air brings out my best thinking."

"Eric's got his loud music on again," Mike said rolling his eyes. "Between that and Dad's chores and homework, I'd live outside forever if I could. We'd have no chores like doing laundry or dishes, and we could always explore and have adventures."

"You're so right." I put my notes down, unplugged the lamp, and plugged in the heater.

"Where'd you get the lamp?"

"Chad must have brought it over. I'll have to thank him. It kind of puts out heat, too."

I moved over so Mike could sit in front of the heater. "I think people who live in cities are crazy to give up all this space, clean air, and the ability to actually hear Mother Nature."

"Maybe that's why they don't pay attention to the Earth as much."

We sat there in silence, knowing that this place we made was ours. A place where we could speak our mind and where any subject was open for discussion, regardless of the topic. A place where we planned our adventures and did what we wanted without adults saying "no."

"I'm glad we finished building it," Mike said, looking out a crack in one of the walls.

I stood up and put my hands along the roof. "I think we created a new geometric shape because we aren't exactly square or rectangular. At least the roof doesn't leak."

"Here comes Chad," Mike said. "He's carrying something."

"You guys up there?" Chad's voice rang out. "Help me with this."

We hauled up three lawn chairs Chad brought with him.

"My parents bought new ones so I thought…" Chad raised his eyebrows.

We unfolded the faded, worn chairs. I picked an orange-and-yellow-striped chair and sank down in it, listening to the fabric stretch around my rear as it nearly touched the ground. The chair held. Chad frowned.

"These are great!" I said, leaning back in my new seat. Chad's eyes lit up.

"Sorry, I couldn't get a fourth one," Chad said.

"That's okay," I said. "This log I hauled up still works good if we need another seat when Shane is over. And hey, thanks for the lamp."

"So did he tell you?" Chad said. He looked at me and then at Mike.

I shook my head and looked at my brother, who flushed.

"What am I supposed to say to her?" Mike said.

"I don't know. My dad says you just got to do everything they want and that's what makes them like you."

"'What are you guys talking about?" I asked.

Mike sat back in the lawn chair and folded his arms, grinding his teeth. "It's cold out. Now that we have a lamp in here, we should put some more boards up on the walls to keep out the wind," he said.

"Don't change the subject," Chad said.

"If we put up any more, we won't have any way to see who's coming," I said. "But we could probably improve a few sections after we solve Shane's problem. It's a good spring project."

"Hmmph," Mike muttered.

"What's going on?"

"Mike's in love," Chad giggled.

"I am not!" Mike said. He moved his chair closer to the heater, scowled at us, and tilted his body away.

Chad adjusted his seat as the three of us tried to get used to our new accommodations. I ended up in my usual spot against the east wall.

"Oh, is that all," I said trying not to make too much of the situation. Any normal day, I wouldn't hesitate to poke fun at his crisis, but I could tell my brother was sensitive to this topic and I needed his support for our next mission, so I tried to offer the best advice I had. "So, Chad, your dad said what?"

"He said all you have to do to make a woman happy is just do everything she says because it gets you what you want."

"But I heard if you treat them too good they think you're a nice guy and a pushover," Mike said.

"I thought we weren't even supposed to like girls," Chad said as though he just remembered an important item and looked at me. "Not till we can drive."

"No," I stated. "You can like girls. Just don't let them know you like them; I mean, you can't let on that you like them too much or else they think you're a pushover. Just act cool.

"How do you do that?"

I scratched my head. "I don't really know. I'm too busy to worry about that."

Chad scratched his head and yawned and Mike adjusted his seat.

"What are we talking about?" I raised my hands and shook my head. "We have more important things going on." I leaned forward in my chair and put my hands out to warm them.

"We should try to go tubing before it's too late," Chad said.

"We've got to go to the church," I said.

"Mom makes us go every Sunday," Mike said.

"Not that way," I said. "I've been thinking about how we can help Shane. He needs a way to protect himself until we have time to come to go over there again. We have to go to the church when no one is there and get some holy water."

"Holy water? What happened to going tubing?"

"We need it to protect ourselves and Shane."

"Protect us against what?" Mike asked.

"Something baseball bats and football helmets won't help with," I said. "Shane and I saw something else that night after you guys left. But, it could have just been our imaginations. We need to be careful."

Silence overtook the tree house, interrupted only by the creaking of our chairs as we shifted about, trying to get comfortable. The wind whistled through the cracks. Sitting in perhaps the only space in the tree house out of the wind, I felt a cool chill overtake me; it started at the base of my neck and ran down both arms. I stood up with a suddenness that startled Mike and Chad out of their seats. I stretched my arms in front of me to see if I could shake the chill.

"This is sounding too serious," Chad said.

"I know," I said. "We have to help Shane. And we don't know what we're up against. It could be as friendly as the friendly ghost or as horrible as the exorcist!" All smiles disappeared and three sets of feet shuffled across the tree house floor making patterns. Eventually, we settled back into our new seats.

During the next ten minutes, we sat listening to the drone of the heater as it provided us some warmth from the cool wind that rocked the branches above us. The tree swayed back and forth in a hypnotic motion. Staring into the red, glowing coils I thought about my plan.

"Shane has a Bible, a cross, and garlic. The only thing that might protect him more is holy water."

"Does garlic work on ghosts?" Mike asked.

"I don't know," I said. "But we really don't know what we're dealing with and it can't hurt."

"I saw it in a movie once," Chad said. "To keep someone in their grave, you have to sprinkle holy water across the place where they are buried."

"I don't know anything about that," I said. "I just know we have to do something."

"So, our baseball bats and helmets are no good to us now?"

"I guess there's the possibility that someone is playing a prank, so we can keep them close, but I don't think that's the case. I think something is trying to tell Shane something and we just need to figure out why. It could be serious, or it could be nothing at all."

"I vote for nothing," Mike said. "It's easy to find and easy to do."

"Very funny." I smiled. "This time, we aren't trying to visit a house just to brag about it. This time it's real."

"Then we have to be more careful," Mike said.

"Anyone wants out, now's the time," I said. I looked at Chad, but he quickly turned his face to the floor. Mike looked at me and nodded.

"Ohhh," Chad groaned. "Holy water, huh? What do we carry it in?"

※   ※

"Then we need to get the holy water fast," Shane said in a shaky voice.

It was after school on Friday and as Shane and I waited for the bus. Shane looked at his watch.

"The bus is late on a Friday; this is inexcusable. And it's a nice day, too."

"The holy water can protect you in case there's an unnatural presence. It's definitely not a monster such as a vampire or zombie," I said. "The evidence points to a supernatural being and holy water is something you can keep in your room without calling attention to yourself. It'll look like regular water; just don't drink it."

"Why. Is it dangerous?"

"No. If you drink it, you won't have any to use when you need it."

"Right," Shane agreed. "My mom made me get rid of the garlic. I told her it was for a science experiment but she said it smelled too bad."

"What about the cross and Bible?"

"I only take them out at night. That way my folks won't get suspicious."

"It's kind of cold outside but at least the wind isn't blowing. We could probably go today after school since it's starting to stay light longer. If we go early enough, I'll bring it by." I started walking.

"What, you're not waiting for the bus?" Shane asked.

"No. I can get home faster if I start now and cut through the fields," I said. "Besides, the walking will give me some time to think."

"I'll meet you in the barns, okay? That way we can talk before my mom knows you're over. Just call me if you go so I know when to start watching for you."

Chapter Six

THE HOLY WATER FUNERAL FIASCO

"Hurry. Call Chad!" I said as I darted into my room to change my clothes and shoes and get my backpack. Mike stared into the space in front of him, but didn't move. I figured my impatient tone caught him off guard.

"Look," I said, trying to remain calm, "we need to go to the church now and get the holy water. If you don't want to go, that's fine, but I need Chad's canteen so Shane's parents won't get suspicious."

"Canteen?"

"Yes. To keep the holy water in."

"Oh." Mike jumped up and headed out of the room. I grabbed my backpack, threw my Yankees ball cap on my head, and headed down the hall.

"He's on his way," Mike said, handing me the phone. "Did something happen?"

"Why?"

"Why all the rush and hurry?"

I peeked around the corner into the living room to make sure no one was around before turning back to Mike. "Obviously, we failed in our first try to help Shane. Since then, I've been worried. I know rushing right back into things could only cause us to mess up again." I laced my shoe. "Now, I think we've finally found a way to protect him until we can get over there again."

"Oh, we better get going."

"You better change out of your school shoes," I said.

We both had two pair of shoes: one for play, and one for church and school. Mixing them up could spell disaster.

Mike rushed down the hall so fast he stumbled. By the time he returned, I contacted Shane to let him know we would bring the holy water by his house later that evening.

As I hung up the phone, I looked at the calendar posted above the phone. Spring break was only two weeks away. It would give us a chance to go over Shane's house on what would normally be a school night since we'd be off. The only problem was Chad.

"You're going where?" I asked as we headed out to the shed and got our bikes for the journey to the church.

"Disneyland," Chad said, grinning as he sat on his bike.

"Haven't you already been there?" Mike wondered, pinching the tire on his bike to check the air. "Like a gazillion times?"

Chad didn't answer, but just kept smiling from ear to ear.

"Just go then. Have fun on all those fake rides and stuff while we stay here and have real adventure," Mike jumped on his bike and started riding.

"How will we pull this off with just three of us?" I said. "It won't be safe to leave Mike in the barns all by himself. No one is supposed to be alone!"

"Why?" Chad asked.

"Never mind. We'll have to talk about that later. Right now we need to get to the church and to Shane's house by 5:30, and then back in time for dinner."

With our hats and jackets on, we roared down the road to the church. I caught up to Mike first and pulled beside him.

"Are you mad at Chad or something?"

"I'm just tired of hearing all the stuff he gets to do that we never get to do," Mike said.

"I know," I said. "He has satellite TV and we don't. He gets new shoes every two months and we get them once a year. And now he gets to go to Disneyland while we chase ghosts."

"Is this supposed to be helping?" Mike asked.

"No. I just want you to think about the fact that Chad is our friend and could probably do a lot more stuff or pick other friends, but he's chosen us."

"So."

"He's got good taste," I smiled at Mike. He smiled back as Chad caught up to us.

"You got the canteen?" I called over to Chad as we turned at the first intersection. He patted the backpack attached to the handlebars.

"Why aren't we going to that church?" Chad asked and pointed to the little white church on the corner. We called it the little white church because it was a small old church painted solid white. Even the doors were white.

"For some reason they don't have holy water there," I said. "At least when we did Bible school there I didn't see any."

"Why not?" Chad questioned. "It's a church."

"I don't know. I don't know why they don't have holy water and I don't know why we don't go there instead of the one farther away from where we live."

"Maybe you got to have special permission from the Pope or something."

"Mom said they are a different denomination," Mike said.

"What does math have to do with it?" Chad asked.

"I don't know," I stated. "Some have communion and some don't. I guess it has to do with what you believe.

"Communion?" Chad said. "What do they talk about?"

"You've never went to church?" Mike asked.

"Nope," Chad said.

"All I know is that we need holy water, so keep pedaling," I said and started pedaling faster

"I saw a movie once where holy water was used against vampires," Chad said. He pulled up beside me. "It caused them to burn."

"I don't know if the Bibles will work. Shane doesn't go to church and he already has one. I think the holy water is blessed and it can be used on anything that's bad," I said. "That's why we're going to get it."

The back road we took to the church had little traffic and we traveled beside each other at a fast pace.

"Hey, look," Mike said. "Greenhorn still has a lot of snow on the peak. It sure looks pretty."

"The whole mountain range looks pretty," I said. "But I'm glad we live out here in the flat part of Colorado. The closer you get to the mountains, the more snow and cold you get."

"Good thing we're still close enough to go camping and fishing."

"I expect we'll be up there a lot this summer."

"What'll we do when we get to the church?" Chad asked.

"There's a tray of holy water right inside the doors," I said. "The doors are never locked so it should be easy to get."

"Not stealing, is it?"

"No. Why would they keep it in the back of an unlocked church if they didn't want people to have it?"

"Do you suppose other people like us need it?"

"Hmm," I said. "I never thought of that. Maybe that's why it's back there. We should stake out the church some day and see. We might be able to find someone who deals with ghosts."

"There's no church on Friday right?" Chad asked.

"There is for some religions," Mike said.

"I don't think our church has it on Friday. At least, not during the evening. Even if they do, we can go tomorrow," I said.

Our conversation was interrupted as we approached the driveway of the elementary school. Five screaming kids raced out of the driveway on bikes and were on a collision course with us. At the pace we were riding, we didn't have time to stop. Chad went to his left, Mike to his right. I did the best I could to steer through the melee of bikes that passed us.

The five boys went by in a flurry of panic. Their faces, white with terror, indicated they weren't stopping for anyone. I slammed my brakes and braced for an impact but we cleared the group with everyone upright. My hands gripped the handlebars so tight my knuckles popped. I could smell burning rubber as Mike and Chad came to a stop.

"You can open your eyes now," I said.

"That was a close one!" Chad said. "What's wrong with those guys!"

"I don't know," I said looking down the school's driveway. "I don't see anything. You'd think a tornado was chasing them."

Only one of the boys managed to look back at us and get some words out: "Watch out! Black Dog!" he yelled.

Screech!

"Look out!" I called out to the boys and pointed to the oncoming traffic. In a state of hysteria, the group failed to stop at the intersection, causing an oncoming car to slam on its brakes.

"Those guys are going to get themselves killed," Chad said. He looked forward. "The black terror strikes again."

The three of us looked to the double-lane road in front of us and started riding again. There was no traffic as far as we could see and the wind died down. To our right, we passed the elementary school that Mike and Chad attended.

"Mike," I said, "get to the far right. You're the only one in danger here."

Chad positioned himself in the middle and Mike rode to our right side, keeping his distance from the house adjacent to the school, a house that had a reputation of having the meanest dog in the neighborhood, usually left unchained. I looked over to Chad and he smiled back at me.

"Mutt," he said. "The black terror, the dark death, the supremo of meano, the road reaper..."

"Okay, we get the point," I said. "He must be glad spring is here. Now he can get his exercise."

"Amateurs." Chad looked back at the group of boys who were now far down the road. "I bet every school kid hates dogs after going here. I wonder how he got his name."

"I don't think his real name is Mutt," I said. "We just call him that because we can't figure out what kind of dog he is."

"I bet he's part wolf."

"He looks like an ordinary dog until he snarls."

"He's a flesh eater!" Mike said. "You used to be scared of him too."

I nodded. "Yeah, we understand each other," I wiped the sweat from my forehead. "I wish Pueblo County had a leash law."

"They only have them kind of laws in big cities," Chad said.

"You know, I have to give him credit," I said.

"What?" Mike and Chad said in unison.

"I guarantee that we can all run and ride faster because of him. You can say he's challenged us to be better people," I laughed. "By making us live up to our potential. Besides, I've never seen him bite a kid."

"I've seen him flatten a couple of bike tires and even chase a few cars," Chad said. "How crazy is that?"

With Mike riding on the far side of the house where Mutt lived, we slowly crossed the zone others feared. Once we could see around the small wooden fence that bordered one side of Mutt's house, we spotted Mutt. He stood on the front lawn with his tongue hanging out, panting; black, fierce, and ready to charge.

I looked directly into those black eyes, and Chad kept steady pace with me. We'd bested Mutt once and hoped he remembered. Without so much as a growl, Mutt sat back on his hind legs, closed his mouth, and stopped panting as he watched us pass. I believe if he'd been able, he would have saluted us as fellow warriors who'd met on the field of battle and respected each other.

"Let's hope he never forgets the firecrackers," Chad said. "I'm all out until this summer."

"Let's hope he's not smart enough to know we don't have any on us," I said.

We continued down the road until we rounded the last corner, turned north, and headed to the church.

"You know, you guys didn't have to come," I said.

"Like we have anything more exciting to do," Mike said.

"Hey, we should go ride through the cemetery while we're over here," Chad said.

I grinned and nodded, detouring to the entrance of the cemetery.

"I thought you said we were in a hurry," Mike protested.

"Then we'll have to ride fast," I yelled back.

We rode through the arched gate, full of ivory-colored symbols of birds and angels, and down the windy paths of plots dotted with monuments of stone that rose above the ground to remember those who no longer were above ground. In late spring or summer, the grass would be a plush green and flowers would dot the landscape. Today, the leafless trees and dull, brown backdrop made the old graveyard look creepy.

"Wow, look at that!" Chad said.

A marble pillar reached up to the sky over one of the sites. We stopped and strained our necks to see the top of the huge monument.

"I hope no one spends that kind of money on me when I'm dead," I said. "It's kind of pointless."

"Looks like that thing has a big point on it," Mike said. "Pointing right up to heaven."

"We need to come here and spend the night," Chad said. "That would make us tougher."

"I prefer it in the day, when it's safe," I said.

"You wanted something to test our courage and get us ready for haunted houses; what could be better than staying the night in a graveyard?"

"Good point. The oldest graves are in the back. Let's go."

We rode down narrow, one-way roads to the furthest reaches from the entrance taking turns pulling out in front and then slowing down to watch the others pass.

"Wow!" Chad exclaimed as we stopped along the road. "Look at that one. 1886. My grandpa wasn't even born then."

"Maybe the person whose haunting Shane's house is buried here," Mike said.

"The way Ms. Brown talked, if it is a ghost, then we might have to find the bones. See, that's why the ghost is haunting the house: It's restless for some reason. Might have died suddenly or been murdered. If that's the case, the bones need to be buried in hollow ground or something like that."

Mike and Chad's eyes grew wide as I made this statement.

"Probably at midnight in the graveyard. Right?" Chad said.

"I wouldn't want to be here at night," Mike said. His right foot stayed on his pedal, ready to ride.

"Why, I hear this is a popular place and people are just *dying* to get in," Chad giggled.

"I heard the music is okay, but they dance a little stiff," I said, laughing with him.

"And no matter what time you start the party," Chad blurted between laughs, "everyone's late!" His punch line started Mike laughing.

"I don't care how popular the place is, I wouldn't be caught dead here," Mike said, joining our joking jamboree. The three of us laughed until our sides hurt.

The wind shifted and the sun went behind a cloud, causing a heavy chill to overtake us. Our sobriety returned.

"I think I laughed too hard," Chad said. "I feel a little sick."

"Me too," Mike said.

"These graves are so old, no one comes back here anymore," I said looking around at the headstones. The wind picked up again as I looked down the next row. Suddenly, I hear a crack of wood above me.

"Watch out!" Mike hollered and pointed.

I dove to the ground barely missing a branch that fell from the tree above me. As I started to hoist myself up, I realized I was face to face with a gravestone and jumped up brushing myself off.

"You were just laying on top of that person's grave," Chad said. "That's bad luck. You better apologize to Mrs. Wallander."

"What?" I looked down at the gravestone. "Shannon Wallander, 1916-1946."

"Does that mean something to you?" Mike asked as he walked across to where I stood and looked down at the name.

"At Shane's house, the name on the grave was 'Timmy Wallander," I said.

"That's just freaky,' Chad said.

"Yes," I said. "What's the chance that we'd ride right to a plot where someone was buried that had that name.

"Do you think they could be related?" Mike asked.

I didn't have time to respond as I was jolted from my thoughts by a voice from behind me.

"*Hey!* You kids got a reason fer being here?"

Chad backed up and fell over a tombstone and I spun my head around so hard I hurt my neck. Stunned, I turned to see an old man looking at us from a battered light-green pickup truck. In the back of the truck were rakes, shovels, and a mower.

I focused on the face that spoke to us. Underneath a faded brown hat, not a cap, strands of gray hair came out. Lines of age sculpted the weathered face. A calloused hand moved to reinsert a fat unlit cigar between dry lips. The cigar shifted back and forth and up and down as he chewed on it. It stopped only when he spoke.

"Well?"

"Just visiting family," Chad said as he scrambled to get back on his feet. Mike and I moved toward our bikes.

The cigar shifted back and forth as the eyes stared beyond us to the graves.

"I don't think you boys want to be back in this area. These spirits back here are mighty restless."

The weight of his words grounded our lighthearted mood.

I looked at him again, and it occurred to me that maybe I'd seen him in church, but I couldn't remember. By the tools he carried, I assumed him to be the groundskeeper. His face, wrinkled and sunken, and what was left of his gray hair made him look old.

"Seems to me you boys have enough spirits to deal with already without disturbing more."

Chad looked at me. I looked at Mike, who was looking at me and then back to Chad. As though we'd spoken clearly about our next move, the three of us took off in the opposite direction that the old man's truck pointed.

Years of racing around our gravel driveway and setting up obstacle courses paid off as we tore across hills of grass around tombstones and toward the entrance. I looked back to make sure we weren't being followed, but couldn't see the truck anywhere on the road.

"He couldn't have moved that fast!" I said.

We rounded the corner and a row of trees cut off our view of the back. I picked the straightest route possible to the exit. Chad and Mike followed dangerously close. We cut through one gathering family and I yelled back an apology.

"Keep up the pace!" I yelled out, still scanning for the green truck.

Finally, we made it to the straightaway and the exit was in clear view. Once outside of the gates and down the road, I stopped to catch my breath.

"What was that all about?" I said gasping for breath.

"How did he know?" Mike said looking back, his face red. "Did you know the guy?"

"No. Why?"

"It seemed like you recognized him and he looked at you when he spoke."

"He looked familiar, but I don't know who he is."

"Maybe a friend of dad's or something," Mike said.

I raised an eyebrow, lifted my cap, and scratched my scalp.

"That was creepy," Shane said

"Enough delays," I put my lid on. "To the church."

St. Joseph's Church was only a block from the cemetery. We attended church on Sundays because our parents did. Sometimes we went on holidays, even if they didn't fall on Sunday. We had no clue how anyone decided what days to go. Bible classes were on Wednesdays for parts of the year but not usually during the summer. Friday was not a church day for us, and so I was surprised when we approached the parking lot and found it full.

"Look at all the cars," Chad said. "Something must be going on."

We watched as people in black suits and dresses went into the church. "That kind of gives it away," I said, pointing to the hearse. I frowned and led the group around to the side where we would be out of view from the main doorway.

"What now?" Mike asked. His face distressed.

"We're definitely not dressed to blend in. Once the ceremony is in session, we can sneak in. The holy water is at the back of the church. There are no seats there and maybe no one will notice."

I dismounted and moved my bike close to Chad. "Hold this in the upright position so I can jump right on if needed."

"Where's your kickstand?" Chad asked.

"I took it off. It only gets in the way and adds a lot of weight. I go faster without it."

"Oh," Chad looked down at his kickstand.

"Mike, we're going in. Shane needs our help," I said. "It's up to us."

Mike remained on his bike.

"Look, the water's in the back, and the church is so big, everyone should be looking to the front. No one will even notice us. We're already here. Chad can stay and keep the bikes safe."

Chad took the canteen out of his backpack and handed it to Mike as he held his head down, then dismounted his bike.

Unknowingly, we'd prepared ourselves for this mission. The many times we crept up on each other to play pranks, and the countless hours we spent playing hide and seek and sneaking around gave us invaluable skills.

"We should probably leave these at the front in case we need to leave in a hurry."

We escorted our bikes across the front of the large church and positioned them, one on each side of Chad so he could hold them up.

"We'll be right back." I motioned Mike to follow.

We cautiously made our way through the large, wooden double doors and tiptoed into the back of the church. From here, I could see the ceremony underway. We were twenty feet or more away from the back row of pews; only the first several rows, which were fifty feet or more away from us, were full. Everyone's attention was directed to the front of the church.

"This is where it all comes together," I whispered.

Mike lowered one eyebrow and curled his lips.

"Let's go, and be quiet." We made our way down the side of the church, edging close to the wall.

"There," I whispered. The holy water we were seeking sat in a small metal tray at the end of either aisle. We went to the one on the left first.

Mike held the canteen while I carefully picked up the tray and tilted it, draining the water into the mouth of the canteen without spilling a drop. Amazed at the mastery by which we were pulling off our feat, I carefully placed the dish back in its holder and we quietly made our way to the other side.

I raised the second tray to the mouth of the canteen and began to pour. Images of ninja movies flashed through my head as I continued pouring the water without spilling a drop. Only strict skill and discipline could make the pour so perfect. Mike held the canteen with such care, I was sure he was destined to be a brain surgeon. I pulled the tray up just short of emptying it, sparing some for those who might want to dip their hand in the tray.

I nodded to Mike and he put the cap on the canteen and tightened it. I turned my head and looked to the front of the church. Good! Everyone was still focused on the ceremony and we remained invisible.

I carefully lifted the tray up to put it in the holder making sure not to make any noise. Suddenly it became quiet. Too quiet!

Out of the corner of my eye, I could see that Mike faced the front of the church. His mouth slightly open, I knew something was terribly wrong.

The priest performing the eulogy noticed us in the back of the church. In doing so he looked at us and stopped speaking. This in turn caused everyone else in the church to follow his stare and soon the entire group focused on us.

I could tell by his height it was Father Huse. I pulled my hat down tighter and hoped I was far enough away that he wouldn't recognize me.

Just need it for a school project. It looked dirty. My dog needed something to drink. I was thirsty. My mind worked fast for an excuse. Luckily, my hands remained steady enough to place the container back in its holder. There was no saving face. I looked to see that Mike's feet had smartly carried him to the door and he exited the building.

The longer I stood there with people staring at me, the greater chance I had of being recognized by someone who might know my parents. I did the only thing that came to mind and dunked my hand in the tray, knelt down, and made the sign of the cross. "Amen," I whispered. Then I stood, turned, and hurried out the door.

Mike opened the door as I zipped through, grabbing the canteen. Chad didn't need an explanation as he spotted us heading toward him. He had our bikes up and at the ready, holding them by the seats in either hand beside him. I shoved the canteen in Chad's pack and zipped it. Mike and I jumped on the seats and the rubber hit the road as we made our getaway at top speed. We didn't slow down until we were at the first intersection that led back home.

"I haven't ridden that fast since last October," Chad said as we came to a halt. "That was exciting. What happened, anyway?"

"You don't want to know," I said, too tired to go into details. "If anyone asks you any questions about me being at church today tell them I was over at Shane's and that Mike was with you all day."

Chad looked confused.

"Trust me, you don't want them to find out we were at the church."

"That was wild," Mike said. "As long as we don't get caught. Did you ever notice how things are more fun when you are doing something that borders on being in trouble?"

"Yep. Kind of makes you wonder why adults give up being adventuresome," I said. "Probably takes too much energy."

"Guess that's why they need to eat kid cereal again, to give them energy."

"Let's go."

We headed back at a fast pace. Approaching the turn to our house, I stopped. Chad removed the pack from his bike and strapped it to my handlebars.

"I'm going to go drop this off for Shane," I said. "I might be late for dinner, so see if you can delay Mom somehow," I told Mike.

"We don't have to be home right away," Mike said. Chad nodded. "We can ride with you most of the way."

"Sounds good, but you guys keep up," I said as we rode together. Still shaken from the church fiasco, I enjoyed the company. "Now we have something to keep Shane safe until spring break. We can do some planning and real investigating," I said.

Mike and Chad grinned, looking at each other.

"I saw that," I said. "If you guys have something better to do, don't let me keep you."

"No," Chad said. "I got a gazillion satellite channels at home, and being with you is more exciting than any movie."

As the three of us headed to Shane's house, I thought back to the words I had spoken. *"Real investigating."* What was I talking about? It was then I realized that two of the best friends in the world were riding beside me. Mike trusted me. Even if it meant that he'd have to face things, he didn't like, such as ghosts, dark places, and scary stories.

Chad could have done anything he wanted to, but chose to stick with us. Maybe our adventures were better than the normal kid life of playing games and watching television, going to school and learning about far-off places and people no longer living. We were on a quest, a safari through the world of the supernatural, and I was the tour guide.

We came to a stop at the last intersection about a quarter mile from Shane's house.

"You want us to wait for you?" Mike asked.

"Sure, if you want. I'll probably go inside but I'll make it quick. I want to take a look at his room one more time. If I take too long, start heading back and I'll catch up."

I pulled out the canteen and handed Chad his pack. "I'll carry it from here." I looked at Mike, who stared at the canteen. It was a hard-won prize.

"I can still remember the looks on their faces," Mike said, "when they spotted you taking the holy water."

"I won't forget that anytime soon," I said. My pointy finger shot toward Mike. "Don't ever talk about it, to anyone." He smiled, and nodded.

"I can't believe it. It seams unreal, like something in a movie."

"See, like I said, it's always an adventure," Chad grinned.

"At least we're not boring." I took the canteen, wrapped it in a handkerchief, put it inside my jacket. "See you guys in a few minutes."

I rode straight to Shane's driveway. As I reached the front of it, I dismounted and walked my bike the rest of the way. In the background, I heard the sound of hammers; a new housing development was being built on the land that bordered Shane's house.

"My dad says it's a sign of the times," Shane said, startling me as he approached. He pointed toward the housing development. "He says pretty soon there will be nothing but houses out here where there used to be farms."

"Then we'll be like those kids on the movies that have to play ball in the street, I guess," I said.

"That's gonna bite. We'll be living so close to the neighbors they'll be poking their noses into our business wondering what we're up too," Shane said.

"Let's get inside."

Shane led me to the one room in the barns we had unofficially made our clubhouse. "Look, someone's been out here playing with fire." He pointed to the floor.

I didn't have the heart to tell him about the flare Chad had lit the night of our first visit.

"Hmm," I rubbed the black ashes around. "Maybe it was like that before and we're just noticing now."

"You don't think it has anything to do with what's happening in the house?" Shane innocently asked.

"No, not a thing," I said, knowing the truth.

"Probably my sister out here, playing with matches or something."

"You think it'd be okay for me to go up to your room for a minute and look around?"

"Sure. I finished my chores and my mom's still talking about how many eggs we got the other night."

"I guess I'll have to remember to bring some more over another time."

"Better not. Then she'll think our chickens are able to have more and expect me to find them," Shane said. We headed indoors.

"We're just going up to my room for a while," Shane called out to his mom as we entered the house. The canteen remained concealed in my jacket. I tried not to draw too much attention to myself.

"We could ask if you could stay the night," Shane said.

"I think we're already pressing our luck with how many times I've been over. Besides, I got something for you." His eyes lit up. "A hard-earned treasure guaranteed to keep you safe." I patted my jacket. "I told you I'd bring it."

"Thanks." His shoulders dropped and his voice relaxed.

"Sorry I can't do more," I said. "With the stuff we're learning in Ms. Brown's class and from what she's telling us, I think we're just about ready to deal with ghosts and strange happenings a little better."

"Aren't you glad I'm here for you to experiment on?" Shane said.

"Actually, I am." I grinned. "There's something else I have to tell you. On our way to the church we took a ride through the cemetery. I won't go into details, but we spotted a grave that had the name 'Shannon Wallander' on it. The year she died was the same year as Timmy out there."

"Timmy's mom?" Shane said.

"It's worth looking into," I said.

Entering Shane's room, I took out the treasure we had journeyed to get: Shane's eyes lit up at the canteen full of holy water in my hand. We sat on the edge of the bed close to the doorway and I handed him salvation.

"I can't believe you did it!" Shane's hand started shaking as he held the canteen.

Before I could say anything, he opened it and poured some out in his hand.

"*No!*" I grabbed the canteen and gave him a scolding look as I put the lid back on. "Treat this like gold," I said.

"It doesn't look that different to me. Can't you just get some more at church if we need it?"

I felt faint as I shook my head, trying to clear the flashback of our mishap. "Not as easy as I planned and I'm sure my day of atonement will come."

Shane raised an eyebrow. "I thought it would at least glow or something."

"That's just in the movies."

We sat there looking at the water as it trickled down his hand along his arm. I felt a chill up my spine and wondered if the presence in his room was listening to our conversation. The silence unsettled me and I looked around the room.

"What should I do with it?"

"I don't know; sprinkle some on your bed every night before you go to sleep or something."

"I dare any ghouls to mess with us now," Shane boldly declared.

"That's right," I added, looking around the room and hoping the presence in the house had heard and knew we meant business.

"I wish we could go back to the old times with swords and stuff. I wouldn't be afraid of any monsters." Shane wielded an invisible sword in the air.

"I'd be there, too." I pulled back on a pretend bow and let the arrow fly, striking the enemy dead on. For a moment we lost ourselves in a world of monsters and demons attacking as we fended them off.

"Over there!"

I spun around, heading off an ambush as the monsters tried to sneak up behind us. They didn't stand a chance as we defeated multiple attackers with ease.

Suddenly, there was a tear in the fabric of imagination and we were under attack! A real figure moved silently through the door behind us!

With our backs turned I caught a glimpse of white and blue. The monsters in our vision had come to life and something real had moved into the room.

Bravery and courage fled as our survival instincts took over; we jumped to the other side of the bed and away from the door in a single bound. Our imaginary weapons useless, there was no time to make a stand. We were under attack by…Shane's mom?

With her lips tightly clasped together, Shane's mom looked at us through the pile of clean laundry she carried. Her eyes scanned the room. The canteen of holy water lay on the bed; luckily the cap was on.

Nothing out of place, just a harmless canteen on the bed. I did my best to look innocent.

"Please put this away neatly," she said to Shane, setting the laundry down on his bed. She turned to leave, looking back momentarily. No words were spoken, but we both understood her instructions.

"That was close!" I said.

"You noticed the look?"

"Right. The 'You better not be messing up' look. My mom does that too. I hate that."

"Yep. Makes you want to spill your guts even if you're not sure what you've done wrong." Shane moved to his door and shut it. "This way we won't be surprised again. What's wrong?"

"I'm worried."

"About what? I don't think she suspects anything."

"That's not what I mean." I sat down on the bed. "We were real tough a minute ago and as soon as something surprised us, well..."

"I'm a firm believer that a fast retreat can save your life," Shane laughed.

I didn't return the laugh. "We need to get tougher."

"Now that I think about it," Shane said, "in all the movies it seems that panic causes people to freeze. You know, like when the killer is attacking and two people could probably take him on but one person just stands there and screams. Or runs away. That's how they make the movie longer because there's no escaping."

"You're right," I said. "We can't get to the bottom of things if all we do is run away."

"So, what do we do?"

"There's only one thing to do and I've been thinking about it for some time. We have to train to be tougher. Chad and I are working on a plan."

"That makes me feel better." Shane rolled his eyes.

I looked sideways at him, not sure if I should laugh. "I better get going." I picked the canteen up and handed it to Shane. "Remember, treat it like gold."

Riding down the road from Shane's house I knew Chad and I needed to finish our idea of creating a training camp. "By next weekend," I said to myself. Then something attracted my attention down the road.

"What?" I noticed Mike and Chad were stopped up ahead. "Oh no, the Falters."

My height advantage kept me out of trouble with the Falters and they tended not to pick on Mike because he was on the football team. Like most bullies, they picked on anyone smaller than them. Mike and I watched out for Chad and Shane when the Falters were together. As I approached I overheard my brother talking to Jay, who was older. The brothers were on foot but stood in front of Mike's bike blocking the road.

"If you think you're so tough, let me see you hold this guy," Mike pulled Herman out of his pocket. The tarantula crawled out onto his hand. Mike moved closer, causing Herman to raise his front legs. Jay started backing away.

"Hey, man, keep that thing away from me," Jay's voice quavered. "Those things are poisonous."

"They can kill a man if you don't know how to handle them," Mike confidently said. He stepped closer to the Falters, who exchanged glances and then broke into a run passing by me without so much as a hello.

"Glad to see we're all getting along," I said making my presence known.

Chad and Mike looked back. Laughing.

"You had Herman with you this whole time? Are you crazy?" I said.

"Those guys drive me crazy. I'd like to put them in their place," Mike said.

"Looked to me like you did," I smiled.

"You know what I mean."

"Then we'd all get in trouble. Where did you run into them?"

"They were out here waiting for us. They live in that new housing development behind Shane's house." he pointed. "They saw us riding down the road and came down to see us. Jay said he was going to go to the next haunted house before we could."

"So, they're watching what we do."

"Exactly. I just wish we could fix them good."

"There might be a way."

"What do you mean?"

"All we need is a dark night, a hanger, a sheet, and a zip line. I'll tell you more later."

Mike took a small, round, plastic container out of his coat pocket and gently placed Herman inside and put him back in his coat pocket.

I cringed. "Won't he suffocate?" I asked.

"No. It's got little holes in it so he can breathe. It kind of fools him into hibernating so he'll stay put."

"Where you going to carry him in the summer when you have no coat pockets?" I said but got no response. "Come on, we need to get home for dinner and then I need to tell you my plan."

"Plan?" Chad asked.

"Yep, we need to get tougher."

CHAPTER SEVEN

†RAI∏ OUR BRAI∏S

"SOME OF YOU MAY not survive!" I let the words hang in the air, eyes low; I gave no hint of compassion. "I think we've been lucky so far. But make no mistake, if we are not ready, someone could die." I finished my statement looking straight into the six eyes that followed me.

We assembled around the table in Chad's kitchen, eating chocolate-chip cookies. "I better have some more of these if I'm going to die soon," Shane said as he grabbed two more cookies.

"Make that two more for me," Mike said.

"Your parents don't mind?" Shane asked.

"My dad's at work until late," Chad said. "And my mom will be watching her shows for the next few hours."

"Exactly what is it we're gonna do?" Shane asked.

"You remember when I was talking about being prepared," I said. "You know, after what happened at your house?"

Shane nodded.

"What happened?" Chad asked.

"Never mind," I said not wanting to relive the memory of Shane's mom scaring us. "Chad and I have spent the week getting his basement ready for our training camp. Follow me."

We put our dishes and cups in the sink and headed downstairs. Chad's basement was a full-size finished basement. It had three bedrooms, the largest of which had its own bathroom, and a living room furnished with an old leather couch, two lazy chairs, and a white bean bag.

"It's dark down here," Shane said.

"Just stay out of that room," Chad pointed. "It has my brother's stuff in it. The other rooms we can go in."

"I can't really see; my eyes haven't adjusted yet," Mike said.

"Just stay out of the room that has the door closed," Chad said.

"Okay. That's easy," Shane said.

I took a seat on the couch Shane sat beside me while Mike and Chad sat on the bean bag.

"You remember when your mom surprised us, right?" I said.

Shane nodded. "This is the answer." I circled the room, with the beam of my flashlight bouncing off scary figures and pictures. "Chad had a bunch of old Halloween costumes and masks, so we used them to make those guys," I pointed to the life-size figures we'd rigged to stand up against the wall.

"We're going to train to not get scared?" Mike asked.

"Unless anyone has a better idea," I said.

"What do we need to do?" Mike asked.

"Sit down," I sat down on the thick, brown carpet. "I hold the light; I'm the only one that can speak." I put the flashlight slightly under my chin so it lit my face. "I think we need to be ready for whatever scares us. So, starting with Shane, I want everyone to tell the group what they're afraid of."

Shane's eyes looked to the stairs as he hesitated so I added, "And everyone has to promise right now in the name of the Questors that you won't tell anyone else what happens here tonight."

"We promise not to tell," the group stated in unison. I handed Shane the flashlight.

"Okay." Shane said. "My fear is...clowns." He stopped and looked at each of us, waiting for a response. "They freak me out with the makeup and big boots and all."

I wanted to be serious and as the leader, I knew it was my responsibility to be serious but I couldn't help it. Images of clowns came to mind and I just had to laugh. As I fell into a state of hysteria, Mike and Chad followed like a row of dominos. We laughed so hard we shed tears.

"I'm sorry," I finally managed to tell Shane. "Is there anything else?"

"No." Shane held his lips tight. He held out the flashlight for the next taker. Chad grabbed it.

"My biggest problem is bugs," Chad said. "I hate the way they just kind of wander around, bumping into you and biting you. I mean, hey, I don't go out of my way to kill 'em, but as soon as one lands on me, it's toast."

"Yuck," Shane said. "I agree. And they can crawl on you when you sleeping. You know, if you have your mouth open when you're sleeping."

"*Ooh!*" I cringed.

"What about your ears and nose?" Shane said.

"They like warm places," Mike said.

"Gross, I'm getting sick, stop," Chad said.

Shane put his hand behind Chad's neck and tickled it, causing Chad to jump up. "A bug's got you!" he said and laughed.

Chad retaliated by hitting him in the shoulder. The flashlight fell to the floor. Mike picked it up.

"If you don't like bugs," I said, "you sure picked the wrong best friend."

Mike didn't laugh but turned the flashlight off, putting us in total darkness. The room went silent.

"My greatest fear is the dark," Mike said turning the light on and holding it to his face. He looked at me. "You already knew that."

"Me, too," Chad said.

"I can't stand it when you can't see," Shane added. "You never know when something can show up in the dark or what it is."

"Right."

"Yep, scary."

"Looks like we found a common thing that bothers us all," I said. "That's why we're here. We need to draw on all our experiences from every horror movie we've ever seen, every book and comic book we've read, and use that to prepare ourselves for things that can scare us. That way if we're in real danger, we won't freeze up."

I stood, causing everyone else to do the same.

"It's already dark down here," Mike said. "That's one of the main things."

"Chad and I put towels on the windows," I said.

"What's with the floor?" Shane stumbled around.

"We put blankets and pillows on the floor to make it hard to walk so that we could practice our balance," I responded.

"Good idea," Shane said. "Let's create a haunted house down here and have some fun, I mean, prepare like you said."

"Most of it's already done, thanks to Chad."

"Good going, Gadget," Shane said.

With strings hanging down to simulate spiderwebs and towels covering the windows to make it dark, we started the course.

"I'll see if there are any scary movies on the satellite. Maybe you can stay long enough to watch one," Chad said.

"Shane, you go through the course first because it's your house that's haunted. Go upstairs, and we'll call you when we're ready," I said.

"One blink means to stay where you are and two blinks means the coast is clear," Chad said.

"What are you guys doing with the flashlights?" Mike asked.

"Working out a code to communicate. Only..." I watched Chad blink the light two times.

"What?" Mike said.

"When we use the flashlights in the dark they give our position away," I said. "I mean, if someone sees a light blinking from the barns, they'll probably call the cops."

"Then we need something else," Mike said. "Anyone got a jar?"

"What, why?" I wondered.

Chad ran into one of the rooms and got a jar for Mike. Mike went under the staircase and came back.

"Here, there are two harmless crickets in the jar. If you want to be brave, I dare you to put your arm in there," Mike challenged us.

"Where did you get crickets?" I asked in shock.

Mike didn't answer. Chad and I looked at each other. He shrugged his shoulders and stepped up to the jar. We took turns as Mike placed them on our arms so that we could get used to having them crawl on us without screaming.

"That was gross. Let's get ready for Shane. I'll lead him around the room; you guys jump out and yell after we pass through the fake spiderwebs."

"You got the Silly Putty, right?" I said.

Chad pulled out two eggs of Silly Putty and we strung some up between the ceiling fan and the doorway to the bedroom farthest from the door.

"Looks good," I said. "Everybody ready?"

"I'm going to lie down in this pile of pillows," Chad said. "When you walk by, I'll reach out and grab his leg."

I turned out the lights and waited a few minutes for my eyes to adjust before climbing the stairs. "We're ready," I said.

Shane started down the stairs slowly. "It's really dark down here."

"Is it!" I shone the flashlight in his face.

"Whooo," Mike let out a ghostly howl.

I shone the flashlight on his face again.

"Stop that."

"It's all part of the experience. If I shine the light in your eyes, they can't adjust to the dark and it makes it scarier."

Shane stumbled over the pillows on the floor as we approached the far bedroom where Mike hid. I ducked under the fake spiderwebs and Shane walked right into them.

"Yuck," Shane said. "Silly Putty?"

"How did you know?"

"I tasted it once, you know, just to find out. It looked kinda like gum."

I watched as his hands tried to clear the Silly Putty from his face. Chad moved from under the pillows and grabbed his leg.

Shane kicked his leg to get free of Chad's grasp. Chad rolled away from the kick, right into my legs, and I fell. I turned the flashlight on as I went down. The light rolled from my hand and zigzagged around the room as it fell. Mike jumped out of the bedroom yelling, "Booo!"

Shane turned to run back upstairs and fell over the pillows. Mike turned the lights on to find the three of us, Shane, Chad, and me, on the floor. We looked at each other, and then started laughing.

"That was good," Shane said. "A little too easy. Maybe we shouldn't have a guide. It makes it scarier when you're in the dark alone and you don't know what could happen. I don't think shining the flashlight in my face was realistic. I would let my eyes adjust before going into a dark room."

"No guide?" I said. "Okay. Then the goal will be to get to that back room and find the flashlight and make it back to the stairs."

"Uh, one more thing," Shane said. "I was chewing gum when I came down here and—"

"—found it," Mike said, raising his shoe. "Yuck."

After a brief delay in which Chad ran out to his dad's toolbox to get a putty knife so Mike could scrape the gum off his shoe, we agreed there would be no more gum chewing during the obstacle course.

"It's Chad's turn to go upstairs," I said. "Remember, your goal is to get to the flashlight."

"Just make sure no one goes in my brother's room," Chad said.

"Gather around," I said. Shane and Mike walked over. "This is Chad's house so he knows where things are. Or he thinks he does. We need to move all the furniture in this room."

We began by moving the couch close to the stairs and aligning the chairs to make a path that would keep Chad on a direct course with the bedroom.

"Mike, stand over here," I pointed. "Flash the light in his face right before he enters the back room. That way he won't be able to see. Shane, when he comes down, you stay at the base of the stairs and make creepy sounds. He'll know you're there so he'll want to go this way. Hand me that helmet."

"Where are you going?" Shane asked as he handed me the Denver football helmet.

"I'm going to make a dummy on the bed. We'll put the flashlight in the shower stall so he can see the light. When he goes in, he'll think it's me lying on the bed. Since he heard you two out here, he'll think he's accounted for all of us. I'm going to hide in the shower stall and when he reaches for the light I'll grab him."

"You're cruel."

"Give me those raisins," Mike said.

"Why," I handed him the box.

"Chad said he was afraid of bugs. When he comes close to me, I'll throw these at him. They're black and squishy. He might think they're bugs."

"Gross," Shane said.

"Let's get into position," I said. "We're ready," I called up the stairs, turned out the lights and headed toward the back room. I heard the footsteps come down the stairs. Mike started by spraying water at him.

"Ooh, that's cold," Chad wiped his face and stepped forward.

I threw what was left of the Silly Putty over him to make it seem like he was going through a spiderweb. He brushed himself off top to bottom as we'd practiced.

"Good," I whispered to myself and moved back, staying in front of Chad.

After stumbling several times on the blankets and pillows on the floor, he started walking to the back room. Mike blinded him several times with a bright flashlight as Shane ran past him holding up a blanket, pretending to be a ghost. Chad stopped walking and Mike doused him with the raisins.

"What?" He shook and jiggled, causing Mike and me to snicker. "Raisins?"

"Whoooo," Shane called out in an eerie voice, "Hee, hee, hee," he cackled. Chad looked in Shane's direction, which gave me a chance to sneak around him and make it into the bedroom. There I waited inside the shower stall. The flashlight lay on the floor with the beam pointed toward the wall.

I could see through the bathroom door to the bed. On the bed in front of me was the fake dummy I had created by taking clothes from one of the closets and stuffing it with pillows and towels. I topped it off with the football helmet for a head. *When Chad reaches for the flashlight, he's gonna get a surprise.*

I peeked out through the shower curtain and spotted Chad near the bed. He stopped and in the dim light, I watched him discover the figure on the bed. He stepped away from the bed, his back toward the bathroom, and walked backwards.

Good, my plan is working. Chad kept his eyes toward the bed, waiting for the figure to jump up. He bumped up against the shower stall and I spotted his hand reaching for the flashlight. As soon as he got close, I grabbed his arm.

"*Boo!*" I yelled and Mike and Shane jumped into the bedroom and joined in the hollering. Chad was startled but held his ground.

"How did you get there?" Chad took the flashlight and shone it on my face.

"You passed," I said. I walked out of bathroom and turned on the lights. Blinking as our eyes adjusted to the lights, we looked at each other, hoping that our day's work had not been in vain.

"That was fun," Chad said. "You had me with the guy on the bed. I thought it was you."

"I figured that would get you," I said. "It's too bad you didn't have any clown masks or anything, but don't worry." I winked at Shane, "I don't think we're going to run into many clowns with what we're doing."

"Go ahead and laugh. I bet there's a lot of horror movies with clowns in them." Shane looked at his watch. "Hey, I've got to go."

"Hold on, I'm coming with you," I said.

We left Chad and Mike to clean up as I walked with Shane to the edge of the driveway. "I should probably go back and help clean up," I said.

"What are you afraid of?" Shane asked.

"What?"

"I noticed you didn't say it when we were going around the room. Are you supposed to have no fear or something like that?"

"I don't know. I just didn't want to say anything around my brother. If he sees I'm not afraid, well, you know, maybe some of that will rub off on him. You know, like when you're watching a scary movie and you're okay with it. But if you sit by someone who is jumpy and scared..."

"You start jumping every time they do?" Shane said. "So, as long as you're not scared, he'll come along."

"That's how it is." I knew Shane could relate, because his younger sister was the same age as Mike.

"I don't think I'd worry about your brother being brave," Shane said.

"Why."

"Would you pick up a tarantula?"

"Guess not."

Shane got on his bike. He leaned back and looked up and down the road.

"No one's here now. So what are you afraid of?"

I sighed. "My fear is that you guys will find out I'm scared of all of that stuff you guys are scared of. Well, maybe not the clowns. I was there that night at your house. When I heard those sounds, I didn't want to go upstairs. I didn't want to stay at your house anymore," I confessed.

Shane sat on his bike. He looked down the road in front of him

"Don't worry," I said boldly. "No ghosts better mess with us!" I stuck my chest out as if I were a bodybuilder. "We'll get this settled next week and the worst part is…" I hesitated until Shane looked back at me. "The worst part is when it's all over, we'll have to go back to being bored." This brought on a smile as he rode away.

CHAPTER EIGHT

A LIGHT GOES ON IN THE ATTIC

"*SLAM!*" I WOKE WITH a start. I looked over and my brother was gone. I jumped out of bed, suddenly overtaken by a feeling that I had overslept and could miss the bus!

"*Slam!*" The sound came again, reassuring me I was safe. I opened the door and looked at my mom, making sure I made eye contact. "*I'm awake!!!!*" I wanted to scream, but didn't. Mom only vacuumed this early on Sunday morning.

I headed into the kitchen, grabbed a bowl, and sat down at the table, surprised to see Mike there before me. I knew I shouldn't talk to him this early but I did.

"Do you think Mom does that on purpose?" I asked. I couldn't see Mike behind the wall of cereal boxes he had surrounded himself with, but I knew he was there. "I think she hits the door on purpose to get us up on time for church. Either that, or she's just mad she has to vacuum."

Mike didn't respond.

"If she wanted help, she should ask," I reasoned with myself. "Are you listening?" I received no reaction from behind the cereal boxes, so I moved one to pour myself some cereal, which exposed the zombie to light. With a quick movement that a karate master would be proud of, my brother quickly repositioned the boxes to remain unseen.

"What are you worried about?" I asked. "We all have bad hair in the morning."

"Hmmph!"

I knew better than to press my brother, who wasn't a morning person. With nothing to keep me company but the sound of my own cereal as I crunched it down, I lost myself in thought about the book Ms. Brown loaned me and the notebook where I'd been keeping my notes.

The only assurance that my brother remained at the table came from his arm reaching out from his concealment and taking back the box of cereal I used. I shook my head as I left the table, put my dish in the sink, and headed back to my room to review my notes.

"Ahhh," I felt at ease sitting down at my big desk and stretched my hands out over the expanse. I spread my notes out and had plenty of room. I began to write.

Shane's House
1. Sounds in attic
2. Always at night
3. Shane and Stacey hear sounds but parents don't
4. Sound of wailing, moaning, calling....in walls and above in the attic.
Poltergeist, past event/spirit? Good or BAD!
Shane's Room
1 .Mom won't let us go in attic.
2. Where's the basement? Are the barns a factor?
3. Need a log: time, date, weather, temperature, who experiences what and where. Anything scientific.
4. Need a tape recorder.
5. Light outside, blue. Could be a flashlight or car light.

Then I noticed it! Springing forth from the paper as if in **BOLD CAPS**, it got my attention. I ran to the phone and dialed Shane's number.

"Can you talk?" I asked as Shane answered the phone.

"Wait a minute." I heard the television in the background from the other end of the line and then it disappeared. "I moved into the kitchen so no one can hear me. Go ahead."

"I've been reviewing my notes. From what I've read in the book and from what we've learned in class, I think what we are dealing with is a past experience that has left an imprint on the house."

"Really?" Shane said. His voice brimmed with excitement.

"From what you've told me and the notes I've been taking, the sounds only happen upstairs and are only noticed at night."

"Like I said, I'm not sure if they ever happen during the day because I'm not up there much during the day.

"If it were some type of ghost, I would think it would move around instead of staying in one place. It probably was a kid or someone your age, because you and your sister are the only ones that hear the sounds. So it's trying to connect with you."

"The kid buried outside. Am I in any danger?"

"I think if something were out to get you, it would be too late."

"Thanks a lot!"

"If it's a poltergeist, furniture would move or something like that. It seems fairly harmless and just making noise at this time."

"I think you're right."

"I'm guessing that's what it is. But I could be totally wrong."

Shane paused before his reply. "What do you mean?"

"It could be something that wants you gone and is trying to warn you or annoy you enough to get you to leave. If we start meddling, we could make it mad. And then it might do something more than just make sounds."

"No," Shane said. "Go back to the other story about how I'm not in any danger."

"Sorry. Just being honest."

"So what do we do? Keeping in mind I'm too young to die."

"Have you seen the light outside anymore?" I asked.

"No."

"I think we need to go into the attic."

"*WHAT?!*" Shane's voice rose to a new level and I momentarily held the phone away from my ear. "You know how many times I've been warned not to go in the attic?"

"The noises happen upstairs. It's the only place we haven't been," I paused. "It only makes sense that whatever is happening has to be coming from the attic. There's got to be something up there."

"Maybe that's why my mom won't let us go up there. Do you think she knows?"

"I don't think they'd have let you move into that room if they knew about the sounds. It must have started after your parents moved downstairs."

"So, we need to investigate the attic."

"We do."

"I don't know. We can't go up there when they're home," Shane said with a long sigh. "We need to get to the bottom of this."

"I'm with you on that one. We need time in your house without being disturbed."

"My parents want to go visit my aunt this weekend. They're going to be leaving Thursday after work and staying Friday and Saturday night. I suppose, since it's spring break, I can ask them to let me stay at your house and hope they don't check with your mom."

"Hey, why don't you tell your dad you'd even come by and check on the chickens and the house? That way they won't be worried. It might help convince them."

"Good idea. Don't you feel a little guilty about this?"

"We're thirteen years old. Practically adults. I think if we were out being destructive or doing something we're not supposed to do, I would feel bad. But we're solving a mystery."

"I guess when you put it that way, it doesn't sound so bad. I'll offer to do some extra chores, too. You might have to help me, though."

"So the stage is set and the show must go on," I said.

"Let's just hope the play isn't a tragedy," Shane said. "I'll ask at dinner and call you as soon as I find out."

⚜   ⚜

"I felt like my heart would beat out of my chest. It's the biggest lie I've ever told," Shane said from the other end of the line. "I just hope I don't get good at it because my mom said people that do bad things bring bad things on them."

"You must've had a fast dinner; we just talked less than an hour ago." He didn't respond. "Look, sounds like something parents say just to see if they can get you to worry. We're not being destructive or stealing anything," I reasoned. "Your parents are going out of town for the weekend and you told them you would be staying over my house working on a science project. Technically, we are working on a science project and you are going to stay one night at my house. Besides, I bet they would be proud of you for solving your own problems like this."

"I guess you got it all figured out, Professor. Only one problem," Shane paused. "Stacey overheard me asking if I can stay at a friend's house and she asked if she could, too."

"Why is that a problem?"

"I'm just worried that she's going to get in the way somehow. Ever since that night you guys were here, she keeps asking me questions about what we're doing."

"Do you think she knows we're planning something?"

"I can't talk anymore because she's coming down the hall."

"Don't upset her; that could be bad."

"Bye." The phone went dead.

"Catch," Mike said, throwing the football as he walked down the hall. "Let's go outside. It's spring break!" Mike exited the house and I followed.

We played catch for hours and ran every pass play we could think of. Between this and riding our bikes around the yard, time passed quickly.

On Tuesday afternoon, Shane rode his bike over to visit. Mike and I were on our bikes and we spotted him coming down the road.

"Race you to the top," I said, and headed to the top of the driveway. Unprepared to race, Mike stayed where he was and looked on.

"I can only stay for a few hours," Shane said as he pulled up. "But I have to be back for dinner."

"Here come Chad and Mike. Let's go up to the tree house."

After brief statements about how spring break was going so far, we talked about our weekend plan to go to Shane's house.

"I'm not staying outside by myself," Mike said. "Not in the creepy barns."

"You sure you can't stay?" I asked Chad as he tilted back too far on the lawn chair and crashed to the floor. I shook my head. "No wonder you break bones."

"Hey, I'm not passing up a trip to Disneyland," he stated defiantly. He picked up his chair and in the process, something fell out of his jacket pocket. "I forget." He said picking up the rectangular device. "I figured out what you guys need. You need these." Chad held up two battery-powered walkie-talkies.

"Wow!" I said. "You did it. What a great idea."

"Great!" Mike exclaimed. "Where did you get these?"

"They're my brother's, so don't break them."

"I guess I shouldn't ask if you have permission," I said. "I know my little brother never asks permission."

Mike frowned.

"He never uses them," Chad said. "Probably won't even notice they're gone. But take care of them anyway, just in case."

"I know," Mike said. "Just when you want to play with something, it becomes their favorite toy." He flashed his eyes my way.

"Their?" I said. "Well, if the younger generation would take better care of things, there wouldn't be a problem!" The three of us laughed.

"The batteries are good, so you don't need to buy any, and they've got Morse code." Chad demonstrated the use of the side button by clicking it several times while I held the other walkie-talkie. I could hear the sounds clearly.

We hung out for several hours in the tree house before Chad and Shane had to go home.

Perched on his bike, Shane looked back from the driveway as I stood at the base of the tree house. "So, we're on for Thursday right."

"Yep. That way we have time Friday night if something else goes wrong and we have to do it again."

"Even without Chad?"

"I'd like him to come, but we can't delay any longer. Unless you want to wait?"

"No," Shane responded quickly. "Get it over with fast."

"If Mike doesn't want to stay outside, the three of us will have to stay inside. We'll just have to take a good walk around the yard before it gets dark."

"Obviously, we have a better plan this time," Shane said taking a word out of my dictionary.

I grinned and nodded.

"What could possibly go wrong?" Shane grinned and took off down the road.

Shane's question worried me as I dwelt on our previous night of failure for the rest of the evening until bedtime. I thought I had a better plan, but without Chad's help and with the risk of Stacey close by, we had more to worry about this time. I grabbed my head.

"What's wrong?" Mike asked.

It was time for bed and I sat at my desk while he lay in bed.

"I don't know. Just worried about our plan. I took more time to plan, and we have better equipment and I have more knowledge from the book I'm reading."

"Great," Mike said. "What could possibly go wrong?"

I grabbed my head again. "Ohh, don't say that. Not my own words against me."

"Well, goodnight."

I turned off the light and lay on top of my covers. I worried about how we were going to watch the outside of the house. I looked over to my brother's side of the room. The light from his flashlight reflected off the ceiling and cast a small glow across the room. I could tell he wasn't asleep when the beam started moving in circles.

"Remember when you asked me if I really needed you along?"

The flashlight stopped moving. "Yes."

"I need some way to get to the bottom of this. I need your help."

"Why are you so into this stuff, ghosts and weird things?"

"I don't know. It fascinates me."

"Well, it scares me."

"Kind of like your bugs."

"Insects," Mike snapped. "What do they have to do with anything?"

"They fascinate you, but some of them freak me out."

"Oh. Me, too, sometimes. That's why I give them ridiculous names. It's kind of hard to be afraid of a tarantula named Herman or a cockroach named Reggie."

I laughed. "I guess you're right. Maybe we should give Shane's monster a funny name."

"I don't think that's going to help," Mike said. The beam of his flashlight began spinning circles against the ceiling again.

"You don't have any of your bugs, sorry, insects, inside right now, do you?" I asked.

"No."

"That was a good idea using Herman to scare the Falter brothers. Maybe he can come with you when we go to Shane's house and then you won't be in the barns by yourself."

"I suppose so," Mike said.

"And we got the walkie-talkies."

"Great. You can hear my dying words, or screams."

"We'll figure out something. But I want you to go because you want to go. Tell me if you don't want to go. It's like that football coach of yours says: Keep your head in the game. If you don't really want to be with us, you could jeopardize the whole mission."

"Wow, that sounded really serious," Mike said. "Last time we went to a haunted house, it would have helped to have someone outside."

"It might have helped explain what was happening. Instead, we never did figure it out."

"You don't have to keep trying to convince me. I'm going." Mike turned off his flashlight.

I turned off my flashlight and tried to sleep. I couldn't. Anticipation crashed like waves upon me as I lay in bed throwing me into a storm of excitement. With Shane's parents gone, we would finally be alone to solve the mystery of his house. With my flashlight still in hand, and my left shoe close by just in case my brother had a bug in the room, the waves calmed and rocked me too sleep.

※　※

The sun, barely showing through the window, brought forth a new day. A day of doubt. I sat at my new desk, still in my pajamas, elbows down, head between my hands.

"Shane's house doesn't fit the description of a haunted house. Not as I imagine it."

"Ahh, spring break. I like being able to sleep in." Mike made no movement to indicate he would get out of his bed.

"That's all you did yesterday: Sleep."

"What day is it, anyway?"

"Thursday."

"Oh, it's time, then."

"I just have a weird feeling about the whole thing."

"Maybe it's initiation."

"What?"

"You know, that thing where you know something before it's going to happen."

"You mean intuition?"

"Whatever. I mean, there is some danger involved. That's what makes us all want to follow your plan. It's the most exciting thing to do."

"My instinct is telling me to be ready to run, while my conscience is telling me to help Shane."

"What about taking a dog or cat or something?"

"What are you talking about? Are you sure you're awake?"

"I heard they can sense when something's wrong."

"Right. *I'm* the one who told you that. But where are we going to get a dog or a cat?"

"Oh, I forgot," Mike said. "Why don't we find one?"

"It's just another thing to worry about. Besides, when I think about it, something can always go wrong. Just like every time Chad climbs up the tree house and I think, man, he's going to break his arm or something. Or when we're playing football and I throw a bad pass and one of you guys intercepts it."

"You throw a lot of those."

"I do not. But what I mean is, if I didn't throw the ball because I worried it would be intercepted, I would never know because I'd never take the chance to throw it. You know?"

"Then you'd never win." Mike propped his head up on his hand, his elbow on the bed as he looked at me. "No matter how many times we run a play in practice, there's always that chance something will go wrong. It's how fast you adapt that matters."

"Reaction time is key."

"Exactly what I was thinking." Mike jumped off his bed and headed for the door. "I need to react to my stomach telling me it's time to eat breakfast."

I looked down at my notes one more time before I decided to get dressed. "Today's the day," I said to myself. Then it occurred to me that I hadn't investigated every angle. I immediately went to my parent's room. Neither of them were there so I knew I could have some privacy using the phone. I took the phonebook that they kept under the old-style corded phone and starting thumbing through it.

"What are you doing?" Mike asked. He came into the bedroom. "I thought you'd come and eat breakfast.

I sat on my parent's bed with the phone book out in front of me without looking up at him. "It occurred to me in town full of Italians, Irish and Spanish people that I might be able to find less than one 'Wallander' in the phone book," I said.

"A relative?" Mike asked.

"Someone who might shed some light on what happened."

"Wow," Mike said as he plopped down on the bed beside me. "You're starting to get some real detective skills like," he stumped.

"Like Sherlock Holmes," I grinned.

"I was thinking like more like Carl Kolchak. You know, the Nightstalker," Mike said.

"Oh," I replied still happy with the comparison. "Too bad they only made one season of that show. I wish I had enough money to keep the shows I like on TV."

"That would be cool," Mike said.

"Bingo! Only two listings under that name," I said. I picked up the phone and dialed the first number. "This address is clear across town. " I let the phone ring five times and then hung up. "No answer."

"Aren't you going to try the other one?" Mike asked.

I pointed to the address which was a thirty-minute bike ride away from our house. "We got some time to spare before we go to Shane's house. If I make the call, the suspense is over quick. If I ride over there, I can enjoy the suspense the entire trip. You up for a ride?"

We put our shoes and jackets on, noting the weather was warmer and we didn't need coats, and headed down the road at top speed down Twenty-fifth lane. Thoughts of what questions I'd ask if we did find someone there raced through my head. The address we headed to lay on the opposite side of the highway from where we lived but still not that far away.

The houses were thicker on this side of the highway as there was less farmland standing between the highway and a hill that dropped off and ended at the Arkansas River. The lack of wind made riding conditions ideal and we soon approached a red, brick house surrounded by a short chain-link fence.

"Is that the house?" Mike asked.

I took off my Yankees cap and ran my fingers through my hair to cool it down. "It's getting warmer outside. How come you never wear a cap?"

"I don't want to ruin my hair," Mike said. "Besides, if I did, it would be of a football team, not baseball."

"That's the house," I pointed.

A late model, white Oldsmobile was parked in the driveway beside the house that lacked a garage. A small strip of grass and several pots lined the sidewalk that ended at three cement steps that led to the doorway. Mike remained on his bike as I went through the gate and up the stairs. I crossed my fingers and took a deep breath as I knocked. Seconds passed like hours and my thoughts swirled in my head. What chance did I have that someone actually lived close by that knew anything about the people living in the house Shane's family occupied

I knocked one more time and started to leave when the door began to open. I turned around and found myself facing a short, silver-haired lady who looked at me with the surprise of someone not expecting visitors.

"Can I help you?" the gentle voice asked.

I wasn't sure how to start. I looked back at Mike who'd noticed I'd made contact and looked on. I turned to the lady at the door. "Pardon me, Ma'am, I didn't mean to bother you, but I wondered if you were by any chance related to Shannon Wallander?"

The aged eyes looked beyond me to a road in the past as memories long since catalogued were called to the front. Her eyes slowly returned to me.

"You've seen her?" the question caught me off guard. I paused, looked back at Mike and nodded. He got off his bike and started heading my way.

❧ ❧

"I'm not sure what we saw," I looked back to the silver-haired lady and said. "A friend of mine lives in the house and some strange things have been happening. Do you have a minute to talk to us?"

We graciously accepted an invitation to sit down and enjoy some oatmeal raisin cookies with our host who introduced herself as Lucille Wallander.

"She was my sister-in-law," the silver-haired lady responded. "But much more than that to me. We got along just fine and she was so sweet. She and her husband, my brother Paul, moved from back east. He wanted to farm. When the war started, he went away leaving her with more than she could handle. I moved out here to help her and we were getting along. Then Timmy died."

I looked in Mike's direction at the mention of Timmy's name. She had confirmed that we were dealing with the right names. "He was killed by the horse in the stalls, a tragic accident. She didn't last long after that. I wrote Paul to come home but the mail took so long back then and we didn't really know where he was. It happened so quickly that she became withdrawn. She was away from all she'd known back east. Her husband off at war. It was a lot to bear.

"Timmy was buried out by the old tree. She'd go out there and sit by his grave for hours and hours. Hot nights. Cold nights, it didn't matter to her. One night, we just found her, out by Timmy's grave. The life gone out of her. I stayed around long enough to see to her things"

"What happened to her husband?" Mike asked. "Mr. Wallander?"

"He never came back from the war," Lucille said. "I've often thought that maybe he did get the letters telling of his son's death, and of Shannon. And that after the war, he just settled down in Europe. But I never heard from him. Then she started showing up. Never in the house, but out there, by Timmy's grave. It was more than I could take so I sold the house." She sat back in her chair and folded her hands across her lap.

Mike enjoyed another cookie while I fiddled with my first and thought of what else to ask. I looked around the house and noticed many quilts and blankets that were hand sewn. At the base of Lucille's chair was a bucket full of yarn, thread, and needles.

"When you answered the door," my next question came to mind, "you asked me if I'd seen her?"

"Yes," Lucille responded. "You're not the first to come to my door. Shannon walks the field at night looking for Timmy. That's one of the reasons I couldn't stay in that house."

"But you said she never came in the house?"

"That's right."

I held a cookie in my hand while Mike chomped down on his. Done with my questions, I sat in silence thinking about the tragedy that had taken place at Shane's house. We had our answer to why the house was haunted and why the small barns felt so foul; it was where Timmy had his accident.

I stood up from my chair causing Mike to stand. "Thank you for talking to us," I said but noticed Lucille had drifted off to sleep. I reached back to the blanket on the couch behind me, stepped over to her chair and put the blanket over her legs and we exited the house.

"You going to eat that?" Mike asked.

I looked down and noticed I still held a cookie. "No. I don't like oatmeal raisin. "

"Why? You like cookies and you like raisins?" Mike said.

"I just think that if someone is going to put something in a cookie, it should be chocolate chips, not raisins. Here," I handed him the cookie. He smiled. "We need to get going."

My hopes for an uneventful ride back were shattered as we crossed the highway and spotted the Falter brothers riding down our lane heading toward us.

"Let's speed up and get on the other side of the road," Mike said. "Maybe they'll just ride by. What are you doing?"

I started slowing down as the Falter's did the same. Somewhere in my brain a plan formed of how we could take care of the brothers and get them out of our business.

"Hey," Jay said as he approached and jumped down off his bike letting it hit the ground. "Where did you guys go that you were on the other side of the highway?" His lime-green jacket hung about his shoulders. I silently wondered if it was the only jacket he owned.

"I bet you guys aren't supposed to cross the highway," Jim said peeking from a protected position behind his brother.

"You know," I began, "you guys might be just what we're looking for." The two brothers exchanged confused looks. "You've heard about us around school, that we visit haunted houses right?"

"What are you talking about," Jay said. His lower lip pulled under his upper jaw as he took a neutral stance and put his hands on his hips.

"You guys live right behind Shane's house right?" I said. They both nodded. "Meet us in the back field behind his barns at eight-o-clock tonight."

"That is unless you're too scared," Mike added.

After an awkward moment of silence from the Falter brothers they agreed to meet us and Mike and I were on our way back home.

"I hope you know what you're doing," Mike said as we pulled in the driveway.

I looked at him and smiled. "We're going to need some string, a hangar, and a sheet."

CHAPTER NINE

A DARK AND STORMY NIGHT

"IT WAS A DARK and stormy night. Long past the last remnant of daylight, in the middle of winter when the night is at its longest point. Trapped in the cold, in the dark, two young boys searched for their flashlights, knowing at any time the beast would be upon them."

"Reggie is not a beast," Mike replied his head peeking out from under his hood. "It's still light outside for a few more hours and it's the middle of March and not that cold. Quit talking in that creepy, deep voice."

Standing in the shed amongst all the gardening tools we prepared our bikes for the journey to Shane's house.

"Did you teach him to do that maze?"

"Yes. He's smarter than a rat."

"You sure you want to take him?" I asked, looking outside. "There's a line of clouds coming this way and they look dark." I looked back at him. "It could get rough tonight."

"This little guy's got armor plating."

Reggie crawled out onto Mike's middle finger and sat along the entire length of it.

"Wow, and it's shiny." My nose twitched and I breathed in. "Does it smell like furniture polish in here to you?"

With Reggie in his pocket, my brother wheeled his bike out and I followed. "It was a dark and stormy night," I said in a deep voice as we walked to the top of the driveway.

"Why do you keep saying that?"

"I don't know. I think it's because my English teacher made us write a story once. And when she gave us an example how to start the story, she used that line and we all got it stuck in our heads. Then she told us we couldn't use that line to start our story."

"That's a shame, it's a good line."

"I know. Now, every time I think of a story to write, that line keeps popping into my head."

"You wrote a ghost story for the homework?" Mike asked.

"Of course."

"You used that line?"

"Of course. But then when she read it, she made me change it."

"I hate when teachers do that: give you an example but you can't use it."

"I don't think anyone minds doing homework, but last time she made us write a poem and then she displayed them in front of the entire class!"

"Ouch! I don't think teachers understand what they do to us with those assignments. Hanging them up in front of everyone. It's embarrassing."

We shook our heads in agreement as we reached the top of the driveway and looked down the road.

"Wind's getting worse."

"Yep," I said. "We better get going now in case it storms. You got your flashlight, bat, shoulder pads?"

Mike nodded. He turned and looked west at the row of clouds coming over the mountains. "It was a dark and stormy night." He smiled as he said this, mounting his bike and heading down the road.

I got on my bike and followed him. "The two adventurers rode headstrong to their quest and possibly," I pulled up beside him and looked over, "possibly to their doom!" I opened my eyes as wide as I could as I said the last part. Mike shook his head.

Four feet pedaled fiercely down a windy road to Shane's house. With traffic nearly nonexistent, Mike kept close beside me.

"What are we going to do if we can't stay in the house tonight?"

"What do you mean?" I said.

"If it gets too scary and we need to get out of the house. We're all supposed to be somewhere else. We can't go home. Where will we sleep?"

"Good point," I said. "But I don't think we have to worry. Shane said the sounds never happen downstairs. We can sleep down there if we need to. We did last time."

Both of us picked up speed as we passed a house with dogs out in the yard.

"Maybe it's because his parents were home. Maybe if it's just us, whatever it is will come downstairs."

Suddenly, my front wheel went under me and I tumbled forward to the ground. *Tuck and roll,* I screamed out to myself. My hands hit first and I pushed off enough to roll on my back saving my face. I skidded a few feet before stopping.

"What happened?" Mike's panicked voice rang out as he skidded to a halt. "Are you okay?' He was down off his bike, helping me up.

"I'm all right," I brushed myself off. "My shoulder's scraped a little bit." I walked back to see what was on the road expecting to find a pothole. I didn't see anything.

"I guess we'll have to sleep out in the barns," I said.

"What?"

"You asked where we were going to sleep if the noise came downstairs."

"You mean the creepy barns?"

"You're not trying to back out on me, are you?"

"NO!" my brother said raising his tone. "Just pointing it out. Besides, then we'll all be stuck out there together and I'll have company."

"Well, my plan's not foolproof." I picked up by bike and inspected it for damage noticing a small scrape across the sign that ran across the handlebars. "Don't worry, we'll figure something out." I got back on my bike and we started riding.

"At least we don't have to worry about any neighbors being too close," Mike said pointing to the field adjacent to Shane's house.

"That's just on this side and behind," I said. "The new housing development on the other side is getting closer as they build more houses. Pretty soon, there won't be any space left. We'll have to watch for cars pulling into the driveway. That's why we need someone outside."

"Does Shane's dad own all that land?" Mike asked pointing to the area behind and to the west of Shane's house.

"I think so. Shane said his dad wanted to have a farm and it didn't work out. He had to go work in town."

"I wonder how many bones they dig up when they dig the foundations," Mike said. "Who knows how many settlers or Indians were buried all over the place. They'll have to relocate poor Timmy's grave."

Mike's statement about relocating Timmy's grave got me thinking. I remembered our visit to the cemetery and seeing Shannon's grave with only her name on it. It occurred to me that the real tragedy of the family is how they were all separated. Even in death.

Let's park the bikes behind the garage so no one can see them."

Stashing our bikes behind the garage we headed to the back door. Shane, pale as a lightbulb against his all-black shirt and pants, answered before I had a chance to knock.

"Are you okay?" I asked.

"Fine," Shane replied. "I told my dad I would finish my chores, clean up, and then ride straight over to your house. They already left for my aunt's house. I'm just glad to see you guys got here before dark."

"Is something going on?" I asked as Mike and I stashed our bikes in the garage. We entered the house and went into the kitchen.

"I haven't been upstairs. I was worried where I was going to sleep if you guys didn't show up."

I smiled and looked at Mike. "You're not the only one worried about where we're going to sleep tonight. I hope you guys aren't tired. We have a lot of stuff to do before we talk about sleep. You're not going to believe where we went today?"

I recounted the story of our visit to Lucille Wallander's house and the information we found out.

"What does any of that have to do with the sounds in the attic?" Shane asked?

"Could be related," I said.

"But," Shane paused, "when I see her outside by the barns, the sounds in the wall and attic still happen."

"Then it may be unrelated to what's going on in your room," I said. "Obviously that's what we're here to find out."

Mike and I emptied our bags on the kitchen table.

"Here's some more of Chad's medallions if anyone feels the need," I pointed. "He left some behind just in case. The squirt guns are for the holy water."

"Flashlights, walkie-talkies, Twinkies. You guys thought of everything. Let's have a toast." Shane removed a jug of punch from the refrigerator and put it on the counter.

He opened the cupboard and began removing three small glasses, hesitated, looked at me, smiled, and reached for the larger glasses. We were on our own tonight.

"I guess this is it." Shane handed each of us a tall glass filled to the rim. He took a seat at the small, rectangular kitchen table. No one drank as we sat there in silence, looking at the empty chair where Chad would normally sit. Shane stood, filled one more glass, and put it in the empty space. "We'll miss him."

"He's going to be sorry he missed this."

"I can't believe our parents didn't call each other," Shane said.

"Well, you remember when we first started hanging out together they called all the time," I said.

"So, they must trust us now," Shane said.

"Right. Let's hope we are bending that trust for a good cause and don't mess up," I said. Each of us took our turn staring into the emptiness of silence thinking of what we were doing.

"This is it!" I said, bringing myself and the group back to the present. "This is the moment we've spent the last month planning for. The experience that can change our lives forever."

"Or end them," Shane said. "Sorry. Chad wasn't here to make a wisecrack, so I did it for him."

"To the quest," I said holding up my glass.

Visions of warriors toasting before a battle appeared in my head and I could tell by the smile on Shane's face that he was experiencing the same feeling of awe.

"Who wants one of Chad's medallions?" Mike asked.

"We'll put them in our safe area," I pointed to the living room.

"Safe area?"

"I'll explain in a minute. Let's make sure these work." I handed Shane one of the walkie-talkies.

"Cool," Shane said as he took hold of it.

"We need to check the range. Mike, take one and go out to the barns where you stayed last time and we'll make sure they have the range we need."

"Okay," Mike said and headed to the door. "Be right back."

"Let's go over our plan." I pulled out the map from my jacket pocket as Mike headed for the door.

"You have a map?"

I pointed to the rudimentary drawing. "You and I will make the living room our safe zone. We are going to need some candles in case the lights go out in the storm."

A beeping sound emitted from the walkie-talkie on the table. Shane picked it up and shook his head. "I think it's broke."

"It's supposed to do that. It's Morse code." I took the walkie-talkie from him and raised the volume.

"Go ahead, Red Baron," I said making up a code name on the spot.

"I'm in position," Mike said.

"Can you see the bedroom?" I asked.

"I can. The curtains are open and there's no one there."

"I left the curtains open so that Mike could have a clear view from outside," Shane said.

"Golden Eagle," Mike's voice crackled. "You have a bogie inbound."

Shane and I laughed. "He's good," Shane said. Then we heard a knock at the front door.

"Oh, crap," accept that's not what Shane said as he jumped out of his chair and headed to the front door. I trailed along.

"Who is it?" I asked in a whisper as he pulled a stepstool to the door and looked through the peephole.

"It's one of my mom's friends."

"Do you think she knows your parents are supposed to be gone?"

"No. Otherwise she wouldn't be stopping by. Plus, she's using the front door. If she were a close friend, she'd come to the back." Shane opened the door enough to speak to her while I moved to the side and peeked through the curtain.

"Oh, hi, Mrs. Jones. My mother's not home right now."

Brilliant! I thought. Shane started by telling her what she might already know. If Mrs. Jones knew his mother was out of town, Shane would be able to tell by her response.

"Oh," Mrs. Jones replied looking back to her car.

I peered through the window and could see there was someone else in the car. "Will she be back soon?"

I put the curtain back in place and looked at Shane. He stood there with the door barely open, blocking the entrance enough so that she couldn't come in. So far, he'd been doing well but he seemed stuck. *Say something!*

"She's visiting my aunt," Shane finally blurted out as though he read my mind. "I don't know how late she'll be. But I'll tell her you stopped by."

The next few seconds ticked by slowly. I didn't know what to do to help. *Leave, lady! Go! I would show you to the door but you're already there.*

"Brrrinngg!" The phone rang and startled me enough that I knocked a picture off a small side table onto the floor. I tiptoed as quickly as I could to the phone, picked it up, and quietly laid it back down, hoping I was hanging up on a telemarketer.

"Is everything all right in there?" I heard Mrs. Jones ask Shane, and spotted her trying to peek in the door. She pushed on the door a little and put Shane back on his heels, but he stood his ground and didn't let her inside.

"Shane, get the phone, it's for you," I said in the deepest voice I could muster, "then clean up your room like I told you."

"I gotta go," Shane said. "I'll tell my mom you stopped by; she'll probably call you tonight."

My heart didn't stop racing until Shane closed the door. I peeked through the curtain to make sure the car backed out of the driveway. I looked to see Shane still standing at the door. He turned and locked it, and then looked at me and frowned.

"Man, what are you trying to do, get me busted?"

I laughed and picked the small picture up off the floor and put it back on the table.

"That was close," Mike said from behind us. Shane and I jumped, startled by his voice. We gave him dirty looks. "What?" Mike shrugged his shoulders. "I came in to see if everything's okay."

"Make sure that door's locked." I pointed and Shane turned the lock. Then he made sure the front curtains were closed. The three of us walked through the house, locking all the windows.

"There. Now no one can get in. Let's go back to the kitchen. You got anything to snack on?"

Shane hunted for something to eat while Mike and I sat at the table.

"That was a close one," Mike said.

"Luckily she doesn't see my mom much. If she says anything, I'll just try to make it sound like it was a while back that she stopped by and I forgot to mention it. Maybe she won't even say anything."

"Right. Your parents do go out and leave you and Stacey home once in a while."

"Just not for the whole night."

Shane put a bag of chips and some store-bought cookies on the table. He bit down slowly, chewing quietly. "It's really happening, isn't it," he said. "We're in the house alone, no parents around to help us, and it's getting dark outside." He hesitated, face flushed, hands shaking. "And whatever's in this house is here with us," he added and his eyes went to the ceiling.

We sat there eating slowly, chewing, thinking, and listening. I looked out the window. Black. Darkness fell, taking with it any remnant of the light and the safety it provided.

"Where's the holy water?" I asked.

Shane went into the living room and then came back with the canteen that held the holy water. I took three small squirt guns from the table and held them while Shane carefully filled each one.

"Don't use it all," I ordered. "Leave the rest in the living room. Come on."

We moved to the living room, which had two entrances, one from the dining room and one from the front door. The entrance by the front door was also directly across from the stairs. I set up our safe area there.

"Here," I said and made a circle with four throw pillows and Chad's medallions. I sprinkled a little bit of holy water on each pillow and we put a cross and a Bible toward the side of the circle that faced the staircase. "This is our safe area. If anything goes wrong, we meet back here. We should be protected here."

BAM! Shane hit me in the back of the head with one of the pillows, and I turned around to see him smiling. "Sorry, it slipped."

I waited a minute until he turned away and then I grabbed a pillow and smacked him hard on the back.

"Sorry, I thought I saw a bee on your back." Chaos broke out as a pillow fight ensued. Mike joined in and for a moment, we had fun, forgetting the real reason we'd convened. It wasn't until Mike used one of the squirt guns that it stopped.

"No!" I said as he squirted Shane. "What are you doing? Don't waste the holy water. It was too hard to get."

"You sound too much like a parent sometimes." Mike rolled his eyes. The melee ended. We put the pillows back in a circle and walked to the kitchen. "I guess it's time to get these on," Mike said. He and I started putting on our shoulder pads. I pulled my shirt down over the pads and helped Mike with his.

"Shane, tie your shoes, tight," I said looking at the laces flopping around his ankles. "If we need to run, I don't want to have to pick you up because you tripped over your shoelaces."

Suddenly, there was a noise at the back door! Shane jumped from his chair and started toward the door. Looking on in horror, I realized it was too late to do anything. The handle turned and the door opened. *I thought he locked it!*

"*STACEY?* What are you doing here?!" Shane exclaimed. He threw his hands into the air and walked back to the kitchen table with his sister in tow.

"I knew you guys were up to something," Stacey said, her tone defiant, her lips clasped tight, her eyes flaring with excitement. "I want in."

I knew Stacey wouldn't back down.

"Why don't you just invite the whole neighborhood?" Shane stomped to the counter, leaned back on it, and folded his arms.

"Did you tell anyone else?" I immediately asked.

"Of course not. I'm smarter than you think," Stacey shot back. "Shelly's parents didn't know mom and dad were out of town. I simply told them I felt sick and needed to come home. They tried to call and someone picked up the phone and hung up on them so they knew someone was here. Plus all the light were on when they dropped me off."

I grinned and shrugged my shoulders. "Sorry, but no one was supposed to be here anyway."

"Luckily, you guys were here; they saw that the lights were on and didn't even check," Stacey said.

"Okay," I said. "It's already bad enough that we could be messing with a force of unknown origin; we don't need to add the wrath of our parents if they find out."

"That's if we survive," Mike said. "Hey, that sounded like something Chad would say.

"I think Mom would understand that we were helping a friend," I said, "and that this is all in the interest of science. We'd still get in trouble, but maybe not so much."

"*We'd* be grounded for life," Shane said pointing a finger back and forth between Stacey and him. Stacey nodded.

I walked over and closed the back door that Stacey had left open and walked back to the table. Shane glared across the room at his sister.

"If Mom finds out," Shane started, "she'll never let us go anywhere again."

"Look," I said, "Stacey is in this just as much as you."

Shane raised his eyebrows. "You're taking her side?"

"There are no sides. She's heard the sounds, too. Besides, with Chad gone it gives us another person to help. She can go outside with Mike. Solves our problem of making sure someone is watching the outside and that Mike isn't by himself"

Mike nodded.

Shane's arms remained crossed. His eyes stared at the floor in front of him.

"She's not going to tell on us!" I said. "She's supposed to be over her friend's house so if your parents find out she would get in trouble too, right?" I finished my argument and looked at Stacey, who was about to speak but I put my fingers to my lips and shook my head.

Stacey and I waited for Shane to respond. Mike sat in silence, first looking around the room and then finding a comfortable spot on the floor to stare at so that he didn't have to make eye contact with the rest of us. It was a defining moment for our group; we were about to let an outsider participate in our quest.

"She's a girl."

"I'm your sister. Besides that, I have running shoes on and can run as fast as you."

"Can not!"

"Can too!"

Mike and I exchanged glances and I hung my head and raised my hand.

"Hold it," I said. "We don't have time for this. She is your sister. And she does have a stake in this. Maybe what we need is some rules. Stacey," I looked at her, "if we let you help us this time, it doesn't mean you are automatically included in our group, you know, like next time we do stuff."

Stacey nodded. "But just this once?"

"I guess you're right," Shane said. "It's okay if she helps us."

"I knew you guys were up to something!" Stacey said.

She seemed pleased with her powers of intuition. I considered it a good sign that she'd been paying attention enough to decipher what we were planning. "She might have some investigative skills we could put to use."

Shane raised an eyebrow. Then he looked at Stacey. "We're going to find the ghost in this house. I hope you can handle that."

Stacey and I sat down at the table and Mike looked up, eyes darting from Shane to Stacey.

"Why are there four glasses of juice?" Stacey asked but no one answered.

"You have to take the oath," Shane said. "It's the only way. Raise your right hand."

Stacey did as instructed and repeated Shane's words. "I promise not to tell anyone outside of this group anything. I will be loyal, honest and help the poor, sick and hungry. I will always be faithful to the quest and help my fellow Questors in sickness and in health; through richer or poorer, until death do us part. And if I fail to live up to my duty, may I die under pain of torture."

Our mouths hung open. Mike and I looked at each other and then at Shane.

He shrugged his shoulders and looked at his sister. "I'm still working on it, so it may change later."

"Why do you guys like this stuff so much?" Stacey asked. "I mean, most boys are into sports or television shows or shooting BB guns."

All eyes turned to me. I looked at Shane, he shrugged his shoulders, and Mike cleared his throat.

"I guess it's because everything else has been done. I mean, the world has been discovered. There's no place left to go or explore. Except space and that's kind of out of our reach for now. Dealing with the paranormal might be the last great adventure and it takes courage."

"Wow!" Shane said. "I thought we were just bored because we live out in the county and there's nothing else to do." Everyone laughed but me.

"Okay, let's go over a few things first." I pulled out the map from my pocket. "Shane, you still need to tie your shoes." I pointed to the slack shoestrings hanging about his ankles.

"Now, if anyone gets scared or something goes wrong, meet in the living room." I looked at the way everyone was dressed, but couldn't see Stacey's shoes under the table. "Are your shoes tied?"

She smiled and put one foot up on the table so that we could all see that she was prepared. "Of course. I don't have those stupid high tops."

"Hey, they're the latest fashion," Shane said.

I raised my hand again to stop the sibling rivalry. "Stacey, take any change or keys out of your pockets and make sure your jacket fits you tightly enough so that it doesn't swish."

"Doesn't what?" Mike asked.

"Swish," I said, standing up and demonstrating by moving my hands back and forth across my jeans. "Each of us has a partner. Don't leave your partner no matter what. And don't leave your flashlight lying anywhere. Keep it with you at all times. Now, what time is it?"

"About seven-thirty," Shane said.

"Then there's no time to waste," I said. "We have some visitors coming over and this is what we need to do."

※　※

Just like every class they attended at school, Jay and Jim were late. It gave me time to mentally prepare. The two came from the back through the field just as I instructed and were arguing. I overheard part of what they were saying:

"If dad finds out we'll get a whooping worse than last time," Jim said.

"Then you just better shut up about it and be quiet when we get back home."

I blinked my flashlight so they could see me and stood still why they came up to me.

"Why are you all dressed in black?" Jay asked.

"So no one else can see me back here," I said. "You guys bring flashlights?

"Uh," Jay shrugged his shoulders, "we must have forgotten to bring them."

I noticed he wore the same lime-green jacket while Jim had on an oversized brown coat that looked uncomfortable as he fidgeted.

"Well, you ready?" I asked.

"This better be worth it or I'm going to tell everyone at school you're a fraud."

I looked at the two brothers. Both of them had holes in the knees of their jeans and the blue plaid shirt that stuck out from under Jay's jacket fit so tight around his neck that it looked like it restricted his breathing.

"You said there was a grave back here," Jay said.

"Yes," I knelt down as though I was worried someone was going to see me which caused Jay and Jim to kneel down. I looked around into the night and then back at the brothers. "The spirit of the person buried there haunts this very field." I looked around again and this time Jay and Jim looked where I did.

"Why would someone bury someone in a field?" Jim asked.

"Because they ain't got no money for a funeral stupid," Jay answered.

"Or because no one wanted anyone else to know," I said gaining the attention of the two brothers. "If you murder someone, it's a crime. Follow me."

I led the falter brothers through the field of dormant grass and weeds to the small stables behind the dilapidated barns where Mike and Shane had our prop ready. I turned the flashlight on the burial mound of dirt that was surrounded by rocks.

"Wow," Jay said. "A real grave.

I nodded my head in approval of the work Mike and Shane had done. From inside the barns, Mike and Shane waited for my signal.

"Like I said," I began, "if someone was murdered, you wouldn't want anyone to know about it. Shane said he sees the ghost out here all of the time. People that meet an untimely demise don't rest well; they walk the earth not sure if they're dead or alive."

"Where is Shane?" Jay asked looking around.

It was too dark to see very far without a flashlight. I kept my light on and close enough to Jay and Jim so that their eyes could not adjust to the darkness around them.

"Shane won't come out here at night," I said. "He says he hears screams and sees the ghost moving in the barns."

Nothing happened. Jay shifted his weight from foot to foot and started looking toward the barn. I looked at Jim and then at the barns hoping he would follow my gaze.

"The ghost moves in the barns," I said in a louder voice. Suddenly, a white figure appeared on of the windows and glided across it. Our eyes followed the solid wall at the same speed the figure moved and just as expected it appeared at the next opening; the door of the small stall.

"That thing has no feet," Jay said stepping back in the opposite direction from the barns.

"It's seen us!" I said and flashed my light into both Jay and Jim's eyes and then toward the direction of the barn. The tall grass starting moving as though something was coming toward us. This motion combined with the white form reappearing in the window was too much for the brothers to handle.

"I'm getting out of here!" Jim yelled and turned and ran.

"You're crazy to mess with ghosts," Jay said and ran away. "Get out of my way."

I watched what I could as the two boys ran away into the field.

"That was a good prank."

"The voice beside me startled me but I realized Shane had come out of the barns.

"Yep. The sheet on the hangar suspended on the string really made it look like a figure floating across the air. But how did you guys make the grass move like that?"

I turned to where Shane was standing but he'd left. I went to the small stable. "They're gone, you guys can come out now." Mike and Stacey came out laughing.

"That didn't take long," Mike said. "We didn't even have to do any creepy voices and Stacey didn't have to scream."

"Where's Shane?"

"He's still in the clubhouse," Mike pointed.

"Then who was out here?" I asked.

"We were in the barns," Mike said. "Hey, I hope you're not trying to scare us now."

"No," I said looking around as far as I could see in the dark. "Let's get Shane and get to work."

We walked to the clubhouse where, just as Mike said, we found Shane. I considered for a minute that the person I'd spoken to outside a minute ago hadn't been Shane.

"What is it?" Shane asked as he rolled up the string used to sail our fake ghost."

"Nothing. It's just…you've been here the whole time?"

"Who do you think kept the line tight so the ghost didn't fall," Shane said.

I shook my head to clear it. "Mike, you and Stacey need to stay outside and warn us if anything is going on out there."

"Like what?"

"If anyone shows up or if you see anything strange outside on the roof or by the window. You know, like a small animal or something that might be causing the noise. Then call me on the walkie-talkie. Everybody ready?"

Three nods were returned and I heard Stacey and Mike talking as Shane and I headed to the door.

"You afraid of bugs?" Mike asked.

"No, why?"

"There's someone I want you to meet. His name's Reggie and he's very smart."

I closed the door as Shane and I entered the house. I took one step inside and looked across the kitchen down the hall. *Now's the time to run, open the door and run!*

"What's wrong?" Shane asked. "You look like you're about to hurl."

"Nope. I'm fine. Just worried about those two. Mike brought his cockroach and I hope Stacey doesn't freak out when she sees it." I didn't want Shane to know I was scared, so I walked across the kitchen floor. "Let's go." I summoned my courage. "Straight to the heart."

This time there would be no delays in going straight to the attic and Shane and I headed to the base of the stairwell.

"The wind's really blowing," Shane said.

"Those clouds brought a storm with them. Don't know if it's going to rain or snow or just be windy."

"Why didn't we investigate the attic when it was still light outside?"

"I don't know. Same reason all the spooky stuff in movies happens at night. I suppose it's one of those things that we'll never understand. If we had tried to go up earlier, something would have delayed us."

"Right. Like my neighbors stopping by or Stacey showing up unexpectedly?" Shane said. "Just like the first time we tried to solve this and the lightbulb broke. Seems like everything that happens is out of our control. Like the more we plan, the more things go wrong."

"That's all the more reason to be prepared and determined," I said. "Ready?" I paused, hoping Shane would lead the way. It was his house and he knew it better than I did. At least, that's the logic I used to convince myself he should lead.

"We go at the same time," Shane said. I sighed.

"Okay. On three. One, two…"

I never got to three. A chill ran across my arms as I heard a sound coming from upstairs. It wasn't the wind blowing against the house or a car driving by, and I knew there was nobody in the house other than the two of us. It sounded like a low voice humming. No, it sounded like a low-pitched *moaning!*

CHAPTER TEN

A FABULOUS BUG, I MEAN INSECT

I COULDN'T MOVE!

Shane stood there looking up the stairwell, which was lit by a single bulb where it cornered to go up. On a normal day, the stairway was a simple climb, a few steps, an easy task. Tonight, it was Mount Everest.

I waited for him to break and run but I realized this was the sound he'd been dealing with for some time. Now, he had someone to share the experience. For him, it was probably a relief.

"You hear it?" he asked.

"Yes. And we should leave right now and you can just move in with us. We'll send for your stuff later." I reached deep inside and tried to find my inner voice to see if it was warning me of danger. No response. "Probably left, I didn't listen to it anyway."

"What?"

"Nothing. Just talking to myself."

Shane held a flashlight in one hand and the squirt gun full of holy water in the other. I held a flashlight and bat in one hand and the walkie-talkie in the other. We left the other baseball bat against the railing by the foot of the stairs. I placed the squirt gun of holy water in the back of my pants as I'd seen my favorite private investigator do on one of my favorite television shows, so I could have both it and the bat, not knowing which one I would need.

"King's Knights to Bishop One," I said into the receiver.

"Bishop One," Mike responded, barely audible.

"We're going up." Gritting my teeth and summoning my courage, I counted. "One, two, three." Shane and I, side by side, took the first step. Then we stopped.

"Why are people afraid of the dark?" Shane asked. "I mean, we're all afraid of the dark. Why?"

"I think fear of the dark is common in many people. I mean, we make a lot of effort to avoid the dark. Most people I know leave a light on even when they go to bed."

"You sleep with your flashlight, don't you?"

"Yep. But not because I'm afraid of the dark. I do it because I'm afraid of my brother's bug collection."

Shane laughed. "I think if aliens landed here they would think we are all crazy with all the lights and candles and stuff."

"I'd say it's not without reason; many bad things can happen in the dark."

"That's why it's good to always have a flashlight."

"This conversation is great, but are we going up the stairs or what?"

"I guess so. I just needed to work up some more courage, is all, and talking helps keep my mind occupied so it's not paying attention to what my feet are doing."

"On three. One, two, three."

As Shane and I took our next step up the stairs, our feet simultaneously contacted the step. As though we had tripped a switch, the house went dark. It only took me a split second to turn the flashlight on and send the beam directly up the stairs in front of us.

"Great reflexes," Shane said.

"Did it help your courage?"

"I don't think my legs can move, or else I would be running down the stairs."

The grip I held on the flashlight turned my knuckles red. I led with the baseball bat out in front of me to protect myself, should something come down the stairs. The pounding in my ears I recognized as my own heart rate increasing.

"*Wow!*" We jumped as Mike's voice came across the walkie-talkie. "The whole neighborhood just went dark. You guys okay?"

"We're all right," I responded, turning the volume down. "That makes me feel better."

"That the power is out?"

"No. If it's every house, then a power line is down. Means we're okay. If it had been your house alone, I'd probably be on my way home. Look at it this way, with the darkness we'll have more obstacles to overcome. We can put all our training to use."

"Just like we planned," Shane chuckled. "Like I said, always smart to keep a good flashlight around."

"Mike," I said abandoning our code names. "I'm going to have to put the walkie-talkie in my pocket and turn the volume down. If you see something, use the side button. When I hear the beep, I'll know to pick up."

I put the walkie-talkie in my back pocket so that I could have the flashlight in my left hand and keep the bat ready in my right hand.

"The attic isn't lit, anyway," I pointed out calmly and began climbing the stairs slowly.

As the two of us rounded the first bend, I could see the next set of stairs. Once we were at the end of this set, we would be able to look upstairs to the bedrooms. The moaning sounds continued and I tried to put them out of my mind and concentrate on going up the stairs. Shane kept right beside me and held his squirt gun ready.

A sudden feeling of déjà vu struck me.

"Kinda remind you of something we've done before?" Shane said. "If I remember right, that didn't turn out so well."

"Uh huh. Let's hope this turns out better," I said knowing that Shane referred to our trip up the stairs at the Roundhouse.

"Right. I can't run away if something happens like it did at the Round House, I have to live here."

My nerves were giving out, and the hand holding the flashlight started to shake. I needed to summon some courage. Shane's light bounced up and down, his hand nervous as mine. I looked over my shoulder to make sure nothing was behind us.

"You okay?" I asked. Shane's wide eyes looked at me and then back to his room.

"If there's anyone or anything in this house, leave now!" I said in the deepest voice I could muster.

Shane didn't react to my words. I was so surprised I had the courage to speak out, I did it again. "I said, if there's anyone or anything in this house, you are to leave *now*. This is Shane's house!" We were at the top. The beam of my flashlight grew steady, as did my hand, and I overcame my fear—for the moment, at least.

We stood in silence and waited. Shane guided his flashlight down the hall to the left, away from his room, and we both looked down the hall. "Clear."

I nodded. With my newfound courage, I picked up the walkie-talkie and with confidence stated, "Red Baron, we're going in." As the words left my mouth, I wasn't sure my brain wanted to do what my mouth was talking about. Neurons fired and a message went forward, commanding my feet to move into Shane's room. Anyone who was listening closely would have heard the second message sent: "Be ready to turn and run at any moment."

"Let's go in," I said. "You shine your light on that side and I'll take this side."

We entered Shane's room simultaneously and panned our flashlights around the room to make sure there weren't any surprises. From my position just inside the doorway, I could clearly hear the moaning sounds from either side of the room. It came from the closets and above the room in the attic.

"Not loud, but consistent," I said. I focused my light on the doorway to the attic. "Keep your flashlight on the attic. Anything moves, squirt it with the holy water."

Shane grabbed the chair from under his desk and put it on top of his bed. Then he grabbed a blanket and wrapped it around the chair. He then used some weights around the legs. "For balance," he said.

"You've been planning this?"

"Since last time." He took some books and stacked them on top of the chair. This gave him enough height to reach the attic door.

Holding his squirt gun in his mouth, Shane climbed up on the bed, and reached back. I handed him the bat and took out my reliable squirt gun and readied it for action. Using the bat, Shane pushed on the door. The trapdoor swung up and back, crashing with a loud *thud* that echoed eerily across the room.

Unconsciously, I took a step backward, planting my feet to keep the rest of my body from running. I listened and waited, but nothing jumped out of the attic. "Can you get in?" I asked.

Shane stepped to the corner of his bed and handed me the bat. "Hold your flashlight this way," he said guiding my hand so that the light was shining through the doorway.

We both turned to look in the dark opening. The light flickered off dust particles stirred by the door opening. Shane took his squirt gun and blasted away, letting streams of holy water go in through the doorway.

I stood holding the light and let him do whatever he felt was necessary to provide for our safe passage.

"Now, keep me covered," Shane said.

"You want to go first?" I said incredulously.

"It's my house," Shane replied defiantly. "Uh, just don't get under me in case I have to come back out in a hurry. And, once I'm up there, move the chair so I don't land on it."

In order for Shane to get up into the attic, he would have to use both hands to hoist himself, making it impossible for him to hold onto anything at the same time. He tossed his flashlight, still on, just inside the opening.

My shoulders tensed. I watched anxiously, expecting something to grab the light but it didn't. I leaned across the bed and held the chair steady as Shane stood on it and jumped, grabbing the side of the attic opening. With one motion, he pulled himself up.

I quickly removed the weights and chair from the bed and readied my squirt gun. Minutes passed like hours. I could tell Shane had picked up the flashlight as the beam moved about. What happened next made me panic. Suddenly, the light beam moved wildly and then dropped. I heard sounds of a struggle and then spitting.

"SHANE!"

I dropped the bat and stuffed the flashlight in my front pocket and the squirt gun in my back pocket. I grabbed the chair, threw it back on top of the bed, and climbed up. Keeping my balance as best I could, I launched myself off the chair in one desperate moment, reaching for the opening.

"Ugh!" I cried out, barely grasping the sides with both hands as the chair rolled off the bed and crashed to the floor. My left hand fell free as I lost my grip and I hovered with one hand. The walkie-talkie and squirt gun fell from my pants. I swung my arm, reaching for something to grab and caught the side of the doorway.

With my heart pumping and adrenaline rushing, I found the strength to hoist myself up. *Something's grabbing me!*

"Here, take my hand," Shane said. He helped me up and I sat down on the floor of the attic, rubbing my right arm.

Shane stood over me, brushing off his clothes.

"What happened?" I asked, taking my flashlight out of my pocket, not pleased that it was the only piece of equipment I had left. With one flick of a switch, it was on.

"I walked into a spiderweb. Did you hurt your arm?"

I felt foolish. "No. What's up here?"

Shane sent the beam of his flashlight to search the room. The dust particles glittered as the light flickered from one corner to the next. "Just some old chairs and boxes. Nothing unusual."

"Good."

An eerie silence overtook us and then I heard a sound start slowly and begin to grow. We turned our attention to the side of the attic where the sound was coming from. *SOMETHING MOVED!* I jumped to my feet!

"It's in here!" Shane yelled.

Scrambling to the opening of the attic, we tried to get through at the same time. I tumbled down and hit the bed first, rolling to the side barely clearing as Shane dropped.

The flashlight bounced off the bed to the floor. I got off the bed and scrambled to pick it up, but ran into Shane's bookcase, which crashed to the floor.

Shane was also down and he jumped off the bed. I ran through the doorway to the top of the stairwell but heard a loud crash behind me.

"*OW!* "

Turning around, I pointed my flashlight to the spot where I could see Shane on the floor. He had tripped over his bookcase. Grabbing his knees, he groaned as he got up.

C'mon, move! I thought, not wanting to go back into the room to help Shane out. I did anyway, moving the flashlight to my left hand, and picking him up. We raced down the stairs, although I wasn't sure where we were going.

"The squirt guns, the bat?" Shane yelled out.

"Never mind."

"*Ahh!*"

"Look out!"

"*Ahh!*" Three separate voices screamed out as we reached the bottom of the steps and crashed into two figures as they rounded the corner. Shane and I toppled our attackers, and all of us were on the floor.

I struggled to get one of the two flashlights that were rolling around, the beams going wild. I spotted a hand reaching for the same flashlight I was going for and smashed my hand down on it, causing the attacker to pull away. I heard a familiar grunt as I rolled away with the flashlight in hand and stood up.

Suddenly, the house lit up. The power was back.

"Mike?" I looked at the stunned face of my brother as he held his hand to block the beam of the flashlight. His other hand curled to his chest.

"That hurt."

"Sorry, I didn't know it was you two. What are you doing in here?"

"We heard all kinds of sounds over the walkie-talkie, and when we got closer to the house we heard some loud noises like furniture being thrown around. So we came in. You guys *okay?*"

"I'm not sure." I walked to the bottom of the stairs and grabbed Shane's bat, turning around to make sure nothing was coming down.

"You lost your bat again?" Mike asked.

I shook my head. "It's up there."

All eyes turned to the stairs. Seeing the look on my face, Mike and Stacey moved behind me. "Everyone goes to the living room to the safe area," I said.

"This is nice," Stacey smirked as she crossed over the throw pillows. Shane rolled his eyes and sat down facing the stairway.

"It's our safe zone, stupid. You have no idea what we're dealing with."

Stacey stuck her tongue out.

"Hey, I know you two are brother and sister but we're all in this together," I said. "Keep an eye on those stairs. Let's figure this out."

From our position in the living room, we could see through to the stairwell. I positioned myself so I could see the entrance. Mike and Shane did the same. Stacey sat with her back against the stairs.

"At least the lights are on," Shane said.

"So what happened?" Mike asked.

I didn't know how to respond.

"It's up there!" Shane said. "In the attic."

Everyone looked toward the stairs. Stacey shifted her position so her back no longer faced the stairs.

"What is it?" Stacey asked.

Shane looked at me and I shook my head. "I don't know," he said. "I just know we're never going to find out if we keep running away."

I looked at him as I reflected on our frightening experience. "Did you see anything?"

"Not really," Shane replied. "Once you came up, things kind of went too fast. Something moved at the side of the room, I ran."

"I caught a glimpse of it too, but I couldn't tell what it was."

"It sounded like a lot of commotion," Mike said. "On the walkie-talkie, anyway."

"I dropped the walkie-talkie and we knocked some stuff over. Maybe something fell against it and pinned the transmitter button. You probably heard that."

"Where is it now?"

"It's still up there!" I looked at the ceiling and all eyes followed my stare.

Immediately Mike reached into his pocket and took something out. "Oops, wrong pocket," he said, and handed a plastic butter container to Stacey, reaching into his other pocket. He took out his walkie-talkie. "If something's up there, maybe we can hear it with this."

I shivered as Stacey opened the butter container and Reggie crawled out onto her finger, his antennae probing around. "Turn it up." We moved close to the speaker and listened.

"I don't hear anything."

"Just the wind," Shane said.

"It's getting really windy out there," Stacey said. "That's the other reason we came in. I don't like being in the barns when it's windy. They creak and make sounds worse then the house."

"I hate the wind," Shane commented.

"Shh! Quiet."

We waited and listened, but nothing unusual came from the walkie-talkie.

"Just the wind," Shane said.

"What did you say?" I asked.

"Just the wind," Shane answered. "Same thing we've been talking about."

I snapped my fingers. "Obviously!" I ran into the kitchen and looked outside the window toward the barns but did not spot the ghostly form of Shannon that I was looking for. I returned to the living room with my notes. "Look here." I pointed to the page. That's one thing we missed!"

"What?"

"Stay with me on this. Do the sounds only occur when it's stormy out?"

"I don't know. I never thought about it. I guess that's when I notice it because the storm keeps me awake."

"Obviously," I said.

"Would you stop saying that," Shane said. "You think what happened to Timmy happened during a storm and so every time it's stormy outside, the ghosts come out?"

"No. I think we need to look for another reason for the sounds. Stacey, you said the wind was causing the barns to creak?"

"Yes."

"That started me thinking," I said.

"What are you talking about?" Shane said. "It's up there. You think something is in the barns, too?"

"Yes. I think the barns are creepier than the house, but that's not my point. Look, you're the one who's got to live here. The sounds are happening right now. We need to go back upstairs and find out where they are coming from."

"Then what?" Shane asked.

"We need to face it! Whatever it is." My words hung in the air and everyone looked at them a long time before speaking.

"Who's Timmy," Stacey asked.

"We don't have time to explain that now," I said.

In the silence, I tried to visualize what we experienced in the attic. With the flashlight zigzagging around in our panic, it was difficult to remember if I'd seen anything at all. Then it struck me! Like a slow motion picture, I zoomed in on a scene from my memory.

"Let's go," I said standing up with the flashlight. Both my squirt gun and baseball bat had remained upstairs. The second bat was there on the floor in front of me where I had left it, but I didn't think I would need it.

"Wait for me!" Shane said.

With the squirt gun full of holy water lying on the floor of Shane's room and without the second bat that remained in the living room, I steadfastly headed up to Shane's room. I turned around when no one followed. "Are you coming?"

"He's lost it," Shane said.

"He gets that way when he thinks he's right," Mike said.

"Wait, we forgot the canteen," Shane hurried back to the front room and came back with the canteen. He nodded to me.

With no fear of the lights going off this time, I headed upstairs, and when I hit the squeaky stair, I didn't hesitate at all but pressed on, with Stacey and Mike following closely. Once in Shane's bedroom, I turned on the bedroom light and held my flashlight up to the attic door, which had remained open.

"Wow," Stacey commented looking around at the room, "What happened in here? I knew you were messy, brother, but this is bad. Better hope Mom and Dad don't come home early."

Navigating around the chair that had fallen over on the floor and the books and papers strewn about, I made it to the bed.

"Mike, you're going to have to help me up there," I said as we stepped up on the bed. Placing the flashlight through my belt, I used my brother's back as a stepping stool. As he stood, I grabbed hold of the side of the entrance and hoisted myself into the attic.

"I made it. I'm okay." I looked down to see Shane looking up at me. "Now everyone be quiet."

I pulled my flashlight from my belt and with one click; I managed to dispel the myths in the darkness. Shadowy corners out of sight played tricks on my imagination, but I stood firm.

Scanning the sides, I reached the spot I was looking for: Something moved there! Defensively, I stepped back toward the opening, keeping the light in front of me. The moaning sound we'd been hearing came from the direction I faced.

"What do you see?" Shane asked from below.

"I don't know. But I found the sound. I just can't tell what's making it."

"Be careful. Do you want the bat?"

"No. It's not coming toward me. I think it's stuck."

I approached the side of the attic where the sounds came from; getting closer to the movement, I could see something snake-like. I froze, examining it before moving.

"What's going on up there? Are you okay?" I heard Shane's voice call out.

"A hose?" I followed it along the side of the wall to where it went through the roof. The other side of it went down into the floor. I pulled slightly and it detached from the floor, exposing an eight-inch round hole.

"Hey, I'm going to stomp on the floor. Try to find out what I'm standing over," I called down to the bedroom.

"It's coming from in there," I heard Mike call out and heard footsteps travel across the wooden floor below me. The closet door opened. "Okay, I'm almost under you," Mike's voice came up through the floor. "There's a wall in front of me."

I knelt down and inspected the ducting where it went through, spotting some tears. "Can you hear me?" I called down to Mike.

"Yes. Your voice is coming out a hole in the wall."

I heard his response come back through the floor. "Ductwork?"

"Wait a minute," Mike said. "Keep your light on the hole, I've got an idea. Stacey, where's Reggie?"

I kept my flashlight on the hole. In a few minutes I heard scratching sounds and to my surprise, I spotted antennae emerging from the crack in the duct.

"Hi, Reggie." I reached out my finger as I'd seen my brother do so many times and let the Madagascar hissing cockroach crawl onto it. "I'm glad Mike brought you and not Herman." I stood up and looked around. "No ghost up here, Reggie. I don't know if I'm happy or sad."

I told Shane to get a screwdriver and something to plug a hole with and within a few minutes he returned to his room and came up into the attic with me.

As I handed Reggie down to my brother, Shane handed me a screwdriver and I proceeded to remove the clamp around the ducting that led to the roof. We stuffed an old shirt in the hole leading to his closet.

"There," I called down. Then I went to the other side of the attic and removed the hose that was in a similar position and used some insulation to close it off.

"Hey," I heard Shane exclaim in surprise. "The sounds stopped."

Indeed, they had.

CHAPTER ELEVEN

AΠ UΠΤAΠGLED MATTER

"I DON'T BELIEVE IT!" Shane kicked dust across the attic floor.

I couldn't help but laugh. He placed his arms on the side of his hips, face scowling.

"You know how many times I didn't get any sleep, too afraid that something was out to get me?" His statement only caused me to laugh more.

The scowl changed to a smile as he shook his head and we burst out laughing. "Great ghost hunters we are." The two of us stood in the attic recounting the night's events.

"There must be a hole in the roof on the other end of this," I said. "When the wind hit it just right, it howled just like when you blow into the top of a bottle. Probably some old vent line that got changed in the remodeling."

"What are you guys doing?" Stacey called from below.

"We're scaring ghosts!" Shane yelled out. "We're real tough!"

"Nothing got broken," I said. "We haven't been caught, we solved the mystery, and no one's been hurt."

"We haven't solved everything," Shane said. "But so far we haven't found anything that exciting."

"I wouldn't say that," I said. "Getting here was quite the adventure. In addition, our skills improved. And, I overcame my fear of touching Reggie."

"What?"

"Never mind. Let's take a good look around while we're up here."

Shane and I used our flashlights and looked around the attic mostly finding dusty boards and old ducting. Then Shane lifted something with care that he brushed off.

"Look here," Shane said. "It's an old, black and white picture."

I walked over and looked down at a medium sized picture of a small boy and a beautiful young woman framed in silver. The two people in it were smiling. "Shannon and Timmy Wallander I presume."

"Maybe those sounds weren't as unrelated as we thought," Shane said. "But what does it mean?"

"I don't know," I said. "Let's get down from here and quit while were ahead."

"Good idea."

I jumped down, landing on the bed and moving clear. Shane didn't follow right away. I watched the flashlight flicker back and forth and then finally, he jumped down.

"I had to check and make sure nothing else up there was out of place," Shane said.

"So that's it?" Stacey said through her long curls of brown hair. "No ghost? Just a stupid exhaust line?"

"I guess so," Shane said. "That's what was making the noise."

"At least we didn't waste the whole night," Mike said. "We can still tell ghost stories or see if there's anything on television."

"How about a game of truth or dare?" Stacey said and we all headed out of Shane's room and down the stairs.

"Wait a minute," Shane called out. "I've go to clean up this mess."

"Hey," I grinned while Mike and Stacey ignored us and went down the stairs, "we just solved all your problems; don't you think we deserve a break?"

"I guess it can wait until tomorrow, but I'm staying over your house tomorrow night," Shane said as Stacey and Mike headed down the stairs.

I went out into the hallway but noticed Shane didn't follow. I stepped back into his room. He had turned out the light but was staring out his window. I followed his stare to the stables where I spotted the light, blue ghostly form. This time, the form did not move but seemed to be looking toward the house. We both moved closer to the window.

Shane held the picture, looked down at it and looked outside. "A few weeks ago if I had looked outside and spotted something like that I would've had to change my underwear, why doesn't it bother me now?"

"I think we know she's not a threat," I said.

"She just misses her son," Shane said.

The blue form went across the top of the stable and faded away.

"There's one more thing we have to do," I said.

"What? I hope we're not going out there."

"I have an idea," I said. "But it'll have to wait until tomorrow."

We stayed over Shane's house and the next morning we helped him clean the house so his parents wouldn't be suspicious. Although I didn't tell Shane my plan, I convinced him that we needed to wait to solve the rest of the mystery and Shane spent Friday and Saturday night over our house. Stacey went back to her friend's. We took Shane home after church Sunday morning as his parents had come home.

As soon as I got home I changed clothes and told my mom I was going bike riding. I asked Mike if he was up for some adventure, but he decided he'd had enough for a while.

I headed down the road at a fast pace, carrying with me a special gift. Within thirty-minutes I was at my destination and arrived just in time as Lucille Wallander pulled up in her car. She stepped out in her Sunday clothes.

"Hello," she said to me. "I just got back from church. I suppose you have more questions? Please come inside."

I didn't want to be delayed by going inside so I got straight to the point and headed her off before she could reach the steps. "Ms. Wallander," I stated as I took the picture out of my backpack, "I have a gift for you."

She took the silver frame from me and gripped it on both sides and stared down at it for a long time. Her eyes became misty as she held back the tears. I knew by the reaction the picture was one of Shannon and Timmy Wallander.

"Shannon still searches for Timmy," I said. "But I think I know a way to let her soul rest but I need your help."

After a few words and asking her not to tell Shane's dad, I rode off and headed to Shane's house. I found Shane out in the chicken coop cleaning the floor.

"What are you doing here?" Shane asked just as the late model, white Oldsmobile entered the driveway behind me. "Who is that?"

"That's Ms. Wallander," I said. "She's promised to keep everything a secret so act like you don't know anything."

We watched from the yard as Shane's dad exited the house and spoke to Ms. Wallander in the driveway. He looked back to the barns and they slowly walked back toward Timmy's grave with her.

"Come on," Shane said throwing down his rake. We went around the garage and headed around to the barns where Shane's dad couldn't see us. We got as close as we dared without being noticed.

"I guess it's the right thing to do," I heard the deep voice of Shane's dad as they stood over Timmy's grave.

"What's going on?" Shane whispered.

"I took the picture to her just like we'd planned," I said. "Then I asked her to come and talk to your dad about moving Timmy to the cemetery. I think it's time he and his mom are together."

Shane smiled. "You think that will put her soul to rest?" I nodded. "Good thinking Professor."

After watching Ms. Wallander leave, I left Shane to his chores and headed home. As I pulled into the driveway, I spotted Mike and Chad walking toward the treehouse so I stopped my bike and parked it at the base of the tree.

"He wants to know what happened," Mike said as he and Chad walked up to me.

"I thought you'd be all ready to tell us about your trip to Disneyland," I smiled and headed up to the treehouse.

"Come on, guys!" Chad pleaded and climbed up.

As I made it to the entrance I looked back noticing Chad had another cast on his arm and Mike and I had to help him climb through the entrance.

"I guess we just can't let you out of our sight, can we?" I joked, pointing at his cast.

"I guess I have brittle bones; I'm going to have to take special pills. At least it's not in a sling so I can still use it fairly well," Chad said.

"Sorry to hear," I said. "I have to take an allergy pill every day so I know what it's like."

"What happened at Shane's house?" Chad didn't sit down. "Come on, tell me!"

I slowly sat back in the old lawn chair like a grandfather getting ready to tell a story about the good ol' days. I thought about making up a lie and telling a whopper, but I didn't. I simply stated the facts.

"An old duct system?" Chad raised his eyebrows. "That was it? That was the ghost? What about the grave?"

I told Mike and Chad how I went to Ms. Lucille Wallander and asked her to have Timmy moved to the cemetery next to his mom and how she went to Shane's dad.

"That's all," I summed up my story. "The air made noise during the days when it was windy outside, just like blowing into the top of a bottle. There was too much other noise to notice. So, the only time Shane heard it was at night when it was quiet. And only on nights when the wind was blowing."

Fearing they wouldn't believe my story, I decided to leave out the part about seeing the blue light that Shane and I thought was the ghost of Shannon Wallander.

"Well, if that's all it was, you guys must have had a boring night," Chad said.

I looked at Mike and we shook our heads at his comment.

"Any ghost would have taken it easy on us after what we put ourselves through," I said. "I guess we learned not to jump to conclusions."

"I wonder where we are going to find our next adventure." Mike said.

"I hope it's a real haunted house this time," Chad said.

"I thought you guys didn't like doing this stuff."

"It's not like it's boring," Mike said. "Besides, what else are we going to do?"

"Right, it's just, well, we thought you liked it," Chad said.

"I see. Well, until we find something else, it's back to the same boring routine."

"Boring? Are you calling us boring?" Chad raised his arms up and started darting back and forth like a boxer.

"Look, don't make me get out of this chair. I don't want to hit a guy in a cast."

"I guess we won't be playing football today," Mike said, looking at Chad's arm.

Chad shook his head and looked down. We sat in the treehouse the rest of the day enjoying the last moments of our break.

꿈 ꗦ

Monday rolled around and I found myself getting off the bus at school. Spring break seemed a distant memory. I daydreamed my way to the front door, nearly toppling Shane, who met me outside.

"Hard coming back after vacation, isn't it?" Shane said.

"Yep. What happened after I left?"

Shane and I walked around the corner away from the watchful eye of our teachers and keeping our business to ourselves.

Shane relayed the story of the cops and a crew of men showing up that exhumed Timmy's coffin and took it away gravestone and all.

"My dad had to answer some questions but didn't seem mad at all," Shane said. "Last night I watched toward the barns, no ghostly light appeared."

"So, did your parents get suspicious of anything?" I asked.

"No. In fact, they complimented Stacey and me on how clean the house looked when they got home."

"Hmm. That's good."

"Was this the adventure you were seeking?" Shane asked.

"Mike and Chad didn't see all of the stuff we did. I didn't tell them about the real ghost."

"They're still skeptics," Shane said.

"I'm just glad we helped you out."

"Me too. C'mon, Professor. I know you'll find something exciting for us to do." Shane elbowed me in the ribs. We laughed. "After all, you're the adventurer here."

I stood there for a long time looking at the clouds and watching the sun. "It's the most beautiful during the sunrise and sunset. But it's the in-between time that lasts the longest."

"What?" Shane asked.

"I guess we still have the footsteps on the roof at my house," I said. "We'll have to see if they happened again if you come over."

"After what we found in my attic, I'm less likely to blame the sounds on something paranormal," Shane said.

"Right!"

"And the way you found out information about the house and a relative in all," Shane nodded. "You're starting to be like a real detective and all"

"I know, I know," I said. "Just like the Nightstalker."

"I was thinking more along the lines of Sherlock. Uh, by the way, there is something else I might as well tell you."

"What?"

"Well, you know how Stacey found out what we were doing?"

"Did she tell on us?"

"No. No, that's not it. She shut up about it. It's just that, well, she wants to be part of our group."

"I guess she's proven herself. Did you see the way she held Reggie without flinching?"

"What? I was hoping to tell her you wouldn't let her join. You don't mind?"

"Not so much. It's probably going to be a while before something comes up. By that time, she'll probably lose interest."

"That's if we find something else."

"Something's out there, all right," I told Shane as I stared down the road watching the last bus pull away. "Something unknown. We've brushed up against it."

"That's the spirit!" Shane said as the bell rang.

"You gonna stand out here all day?"

I shook my head no and we turned the corner and headed toward the doors.

"Shane?" I stopped. "There is one thing we gotta do with our motto or oath or whatever we call it."

"I know, I know. It needs work."

"No, that's not it." I put my hand on Shane's shoulder bringing him to a halt. He looked at me. "Don't get frustrated. I know it's a hard task and you've done as well as any of us could. In fact, I'm not making fun of anything you did. It's just..."

"Just what?" he questioned as we started toward the school again.

"You need to add something in there so that we don't forget what it means to have an adventure. That's it's okay to be free-spirited and, as Ms. Brown says, 'outspoken.' But not if you are hurting others or in it only for your own gain. I think that's why we hate the Falters so much. It would be fun if they just wanted to hang out, but they're so destructive. And they always want to make fun of people or pick on them."

"I know what you mean," Shane said.

"That's not all. Many times during our quest, I was more worried about me than you. I wanted to be involved in something big."

"I think I know what you mean. And it's all right. I had a lot of fun. It's pretty silly when you think about it."

"Yep. But you were scared."

"Me? I'd be scared if I were you."

"What do you mean?"

"Your brother!" Shane stated as the teacher waved us in. "That roach was as long as my arm. He's probably got some big tarantula hidden away that's gonna get out one night and crawl all over you." Shane ran his hand up and down his chest as though it were a big spider. I hit him on the shoulder and he acted as if it hurt.

"You didn't know? He does have a tarantula and his name is Herman."

Shane's face turned white and his jaw dropped.

"I laughed as Shane and I walked toward the front doors of Pleasant View Middle School. Little did we know that our next adventure was right around the corner: As summer approached, we would be going camping and while my dad fished, which didn't interest us much at the time because it involved sitting still, we would be hiking. It was during one of our hikes when we would find our next adventure with *The Ghost of Greenhorn Mountain*.

END OF LINE.